CW01020790

THE STRANG

Judith Barrow grew up in a small village on the edge of the Pennines, but has lived in Pembrokeshire for over forty years. She is the author of several novels and has had poetry and short fiction published. Judith has degrees in literature and creative writing, makes regular appearances at literary festivals, and presents talks on research and creative writing. She is a creative writing tutor and holds workshops on all genres. Her novel *The Memory* was shortlisted for Wales Book of the Year 2021.

judithbarrowblog.com
Connect with her on Facebook:
www.facebook.com/judith.barrow.3
https://www.instagram.com/judithbarrow2912/
https://www.pinterest.co.uk/judithbarrow/

Also by Judith Barrow from Honno:
Pattern of Shadows
Changing Patterns
Living in the Shadows
A Hundred Tiny Threads
The Memory
The Heart Stone
Sisters

THE STRANGER IN MY HOUSE

Judith Barrow

HONNO MODERN FICTION

First published in Great Britain in 2024 by Honno Press
D41, Hugh Owen Building, Aberystwyth University, Ceredigion, SY23 3DY

1 2 3 4 5 6 7 8 9 10

Copyright © Judith Barrow 2024

The right of Judith Barrow to be identified as the Author of the Work has been
asserted in accordance with the Copyright, Designs and Patents Act 1988.

All rights reserved.

No part of the book may be reproduced, stored in a retrieval system, or
transmitted in any form, or by any means, electronic, mechanical, photocopying,
recording or otherwise without the prior permission of the copyright owner.

A catalogue record for this book is available from the British Library.

Published with the financial support of the Books Council of Wales.

ISBN 9781916821224 (paperback)
ISBN 9781916821231 (ebook)

Cover design – Lynzie Fitzpatrick
Typeset by Elaine Sharples
Printed by 4edge Ltd

For David

Prologue

I can remember my mother ... just. I remember the sound of gentle, soft-spoken words. She was lovely. I know that because I have seen photographs, of her, of us as a family, and I have my memories. I wasn't even aware I was loved. I had no name for the feeling wrapped around me, that made me feel safe, important. We were happy. I'm sure of that.

When she was gone, we were bereft. That I do remember. And I realise now how vulnerable my father was. His grief left him defenceless. Evil is not always found in the dark – sometimes it stands in full view in front of us, daring us to see it.

This is our story...

Part One

Chapter 1

1967

'This is Lynne.' Graham puts his arm around her, pulls her gently to him and smiles. The twins don't smile back, though they can tell he wants them to. 'Come on, you two, where are your manners?'

Charlie glances at Chloe. He wants to go back to playing outside on their swings, he keeps looking out of the patio doors. The light-grey swirl of thin cloud hiding the sun might mean rain. They won't be allowed out.

Neither of them is ready for their dad's next words.

'She's going to be your new mummy. And she has a boy and a girl, Saul, he's thirteen and Evie, who's fifteen. They'll be your big sister and brother. We'll be one big family.' He waits. 'Well? Say something.'

Charlie looks down at the swirly brown pattern on the carpet. His head feels dizzy. His sister is clasping his fingers tight. He can feel she's trembling. He's Chloe's big brother; they might both be eight but he's ten minutes older, so he is her big brother. He wants to say they are already a family but can't think of the right words. He returns the squeeze, then moves his head to one side, and studies Lynne in the long mirror above the fireplace.

She's watching him in the glass, smiling with her mouth, but her eyes look wrong. She isn't smiling like his mum used to.

He pushes away the first image to come into his head: his mum's pale, strained face when she was ill. He closes his eyes and replaces that memory with one that comforts him: his laughing mum, whose scrunched-up eyes matched her huge grin when she tickled him. When she waved to them as they went into school. When she hugged them at the school gate at the end of the day.

'Say hello.' Charlie hears the hard edge to his dad's voice.

'Hello,' Chloe says. When her brother doesn't speak, she nudges him and says again, 'Hello, Lynne.'

Charlie pulls back his shoulders, looks at his father. He knows how to play this smiling game while terror claws at his stomach, makes him feel he'll be sick. He learned it in the last months of their mum's illness. 'Hello, Lynne.' He straightens his lips into a smile that matches hers.

'That's better.' Graham laughs.

Lynne tilts her head.

Charlie knows she knows what he's doing. He knows she knows he remembers her. She's challenging him, like he's seen older boys do in the school playground.

'Charlie.' She's looking at him contemplatively. 'I hope we can be friends.'

'Hope so too.'

But Charlie knows that will never happen.

Chapter 2

Graham settles into his wicker chair and lets his head drop back, looking up through the glass conservatory roof at the promise of sun behind the clouds. He straightens his legs, crosses his ankles, takes a gulp of his Guinness, and sighs in contentment. He's not sure he should be this happy, but he feels relaxed for the first time in years. Almost three years, in fact.

He can think of Anna now without the overpowering sense of loss. He can think of his children without the fear of not being enough for them. The guilt, even though he hadn't caused the cancer that had taken his wife, cell by cell, day by day. Because now he's found someone who will love Charlie and Chloe as much as he does. He's found Lynne.

Lynne came into their lives at the bleakest time and saved the three of them. He will show her how grateful he is for her love, for her care. He will cherish her, make her life perfect.

From what she's told him she hasn't had an easy ride: a violent ex-husband, a house on a run-down estate, a full-time job as district nurse, struggling financially to keep her head above water, and with two teenagers to look after. Yet still, despite all that, she's such a caring person. And she loves him.

He takes another gulp of Guinness. 'We are so lucky, Oscar,' he murmurs to the red setter, sitting by him, panting in his silky ruby-red coat, his snout quivering. 'Everything's going to be fine.' Graham cups the side of the dog's head, stroking the long ears, and holding him against his thigh. 'Lynne will sort us all out.'

Chapter 3

'You do know who she is, don't you?' Charlie sits on the swing, kicks at the grass with the toe of his trainers.

'Who?'

'Lynne.'

'What d'you mean?'

'She's that nurse we saw that day,' Charlie says irritably. 'The one who made Mum cry. That day. *That* day. You know...'

'I think I do,' Chloe offers, but she doesn't.

'The nurse! The one with the no eyes smile.'

'I ... don't...' She wishes she could remember, could agree that the lady they'd just met is who Charlie says she is, but she can't. She's closed down so much of the memories of those last few weeks of Mum's life: the stuffy bedroom, that awful smell, their mum, shrunken, lying so flat under the covers, her yellowed skin, how she restlessly folded and unfolded her hands.

'The nurse who looked after Mum. Or was s'posed to. That night after school. When Mum was home from hospital ... before she...' He stops. Chloe sees him swallow. 'That ... that ... Lynne ... she's the one that Dad always talked about – said how good she was with Mum. But we heard her shouting at Mum. You must remember, Chlo. She told us off.'

All at once Chloe can see that day. An invisible hand squeezes her heart and makes her breathless. Maybe she deliberately forgot because it was so horrid. The shouted words come back to her...

'For God's sake, I haven't got all day!' A woman's voice.

Charlie bumped into Chloe when she stopped on the stairs.

'Who's that?' she whispered.

'I don't know, but they're in Mummy's room.' He pushed past her, leapt up the rest of the stairs and crashed through the door.

Someone was leaning over the bed. Their mum was propped up on her pillows, her face turned away, water dripping off her cheek.

The person leaning over her, a lady in blue uniform, spun round. 'What the...?' She had an empty glass in her hand. 'Get out!'

'What's happening?' Chloe's voice trembled. 'Mummy?' She peered over her brother's shoulder. 'What's wrong?'

'Nothing, nothing,' the nurse said. 'A bit of an accident, that's all.' She refilled the glass from the water jug, took a tablet between her finger and thumb, and dropped it onto their mother's outstretched palm. 'Let's try again, shall we? Make sure we don't spill the water this time.' Mum had swallowed it, and the nurse nodded. 'Good. About time. I do have other patients to see today, you know.'

She turned to Chloe and Charlie and glowered. 'And you two, get out. Get down those stairs. Now!'

Chloe remembers standing between the nurse and her brother, remembers the distress. They'd wanted to do something, but had no idea what, and Mum hadn't said anything, so they'd just turned and ran.

'It's her?'

'Yeah.'

'What can we do?' Chloe holds tightly to the swing's metal chain.

'Dunno. I could tell she was waiting to see if we remembered and I think she knew I had. She might think I'm too scared to say anything. But I'm not.'

'You can't tell Dad.'

Chloe has never seen her brother this angry, his jaw hardened, his forehead bunched into lines. It frightens her. Sometimes he does things without thinking.

'Why not? Why shouldn't I?'

'Didn't you see the way he looked? He's happy. He's been sad for ages. Ever since Mum...' She has to make him understand. 'I don't want him to be sad again, Charlie. Do you?'

'No. But...'

He stops talking, stares towards the conservatory. She wonders why and then hears Lynne's laughter mingling with their dad's deeper chuckle. It should be nice that they're happy – but Chloe doesn't like hearing it.

Charlie mutters, 'She's nasty...'

'She might have changed?'

'She hasn't. I can tell.' Charlie straightens his back to make himself taller. He turns to his sister and must have seen the look on her face because he says, 'Don't be frightened.'

'I'm not. It just bothers me you'll do – say something...'

'I won't, Chlo. Promise. But I don't like it.'

And now Chloe doesn't either.

Dear Sandie Shaw,

I'm eight and I live with my Dad and brother, Charlie. Ive seen you loads on telly and I love your song, Always Somethin There to Remind Me. I play it and dance when I'm on my own – only on my own because I think it wud upset Dad if he herd it. It was Mummy's favouritist song. Dad used to play it for her in her bedroom on his record player. I love you don't wear shoes lots of times, I don't as well. My mummy used to tell me to write about things that woried me because that's what she does. Used to do. So I will. Mummy's in Heaven now. And Dads found a new lady, called Lynne. Shes the nurse who looked after Mummy. Charlie says she did something nasty to Mummy, that's why shes in Heaven. But Dad looks happy now he's friends with the nurse. I don't know how I'm supposed to be. It makes me feel all funny inside. Like all worried. Riting it down makes me feel a bit better I'm pretnding you'll read this.

Love, Chloe x

Chapter 4

Graham stops on the forecourt of the salesroom, studies the line of shining cars precisely placed outside on the tarmac, the latest model on the revolving stand inside the large showroom window. Yolanda, the young receptionist, sitting behind the desk near the door, waves to him. He raises a questioning thumb; she responds in a similar way. All okay. She's new, but apparently keen to learn the trade from the floor manager, Gary. A good find, thanks to Lynne; the daughter of one of her patients. He waves again, satisfied, and drives his car around the back of the building.

The garage workshop is already filled with cars in various stages of being dismantled. The noise – clatter and banging, shouts, revving engines – is almost deafening when Graham presses his Cortina's window button and the glass slides down with a low whine. He breathes in the exhaust fumes, the stench of oil and grease. It's something he loves. The tang of his success, his own business, something that he and his best friend, Phil, have built up over fifteen years, since he bought the garage and salesroom from his father-in-law.

He sits for a few minutes to mull over the last two days. It had all gone pretty well. The twins have taken to Lynne, as far as he can tell. Reserved, admittedly, but that's how they've been since Anna died. To be expected, he reassures himself. They've been through so much, witnessed too much. But Lynne will win them round. She was wonderful with them at the weekend. So thoughtful.

He thinks back to the first time he met her. When he had to open the door to a world he'd been trying to keep away from his home. Medicines and drugs and doctors and nurses. They were told nothing could be done, and if Anna wanted to be with her family for the end, everything could be set in place. It was what she wanted. And, because it was what she wanted, it was also what Graham wanted, even though he was terrified.

So he'd hesitated before opening the door to the district nurse. But then the relief – the kind smile, the reassuring words, the soothing way Lynne took over and made their lives easier by her professionalism and care.

After it was all over, as the days jumbled together, Lynne continued to support Graham. She called in on her way home after her evening rounds; at first stopping for a few moments on the black-and-white-tiled steps in the porch, then, as the weeks went by, coming into the kitchen for a cup of tea and a chat.

As the months passed, he found himself looking forward to her visits. Once or twice, they met up for a coffee in the supermarket café after their separate weekly shops, the shopping trolleys nestled side by side. Hers laden with organic food, wholewheat bread, fruit, and vegetables, his with ready meals, frozen vegetables, pizzas, and white sliced bread. She teased Graham gently, then acknowledged it must be difficult for him, feeding two youngsters with all their fads and his long working hours.

He's late this morning, but it doesn't matter; the hours he's put in since Anna went, trying to bury himself in work, more than compensate for the odd half an hour.

At the back of the workshop, he can see the light in the small office spotlighting Margaret, Phil's wife. They've been good friends to him, he'll never forget that. Holding the phone with her shoulder, she sees him and beckons. He's needed. He opens the car door and gets out. He looks up at the bright April sky, enjoys the faint warmth of the spring air, and allows himself a moment of happiness. It's a good day.

Chapter 5

'How soon do you want us to move in, sweetheart? Now we've told the kids. Sooner rather than later?' Lynne asks, stroking Graham's ear with the back of her fingers. It's soothing, especially after such a busy day at the garage.

'There's no rush, is there, love? You're here most of the time anyway. We're okay as we are for now, aren't we?'

'We are. I know. And I know the kids and I are here a lot any way. It's just I thought you wanted us to move in with you permanently as soon as possible. Saul was asking me this morning.' She pauses, as though waiting for him to say something, then adds, 'Perhaps you shouldn't have introduced me to the twins as their new mummy?' She kisses the tip of his ear. 'But never mind, we can go at your pace, it's your decision.'

'I know.' A headache hovers, heavy, on his temple. He doesn't want to hurt her, but she's right – he shouldn't have said what he did. He should have just told Chloe and Charlie that he and Lynne were seeing one another. 'It's my fault, I should have realised all the kids need time to get used to the idea. I got carried away. I'm sorry.'

'No worries. Saul's quite excited. Still, no need to worry about him. But I'll need to tell the surgery my new address ... when it happens...'

'I must admit I'll be glad to see you off that estate.' Graham's dithering. 'I hadn't realised how bad it is.'

'Oh, don't worry, I'm used to it. You just learn to keep your head down. Though, sometimes I do worry about Saul, you know, getting into bad company. Anyway...' She kisses the top of Graham's head. 'Tea?'

'Please.' He turns to see her face. 'And I'm sure we can sort it out soon.' He gives her an apologetic smile. 'But I haven't told Mum about us yet. She's not got over Dad dying last year...'

'That's understandable, Graham. They must have been together a long time.'

'They were.' He pats her hand. 'And she was very fond of Anna.'

'Ah. Of course.'

'I don't want her upset.'

'Won't she be happy for you? Seeing you happy again?'

'I know she will, but we haven't known one another that long. She might not understand.'

'It is almost two years, Graham.'

'But not like this...'

'No, I know, sweetheart.' Lynne goes into the kitchen. She raises her voice over filling the kettle. 'But I got to know you before, didn't I? I learned a lot about you in my talks with Anna. She became a dear friend as well as a patient. I know how much she loved you. And now I know the twins, and I think they like me. And you've met my two. You like them, don't you?'

'Yes, of course.' Graham follows her into the kitchen, puts his arms around her waist from behind. 'How about I go to Mum's at the weekend? Let her know about us?'

'Couldn't I come?' She turns.

'Best I go on my own, love. Next time, eh?' he adds, seeing the shadow of disappointment in her eyes.

'It's just that I'd love to meet your mother. See what sort of mother produced such a wonderful man.' She puts her arms around his neck.

'The same sort of mum that made you such a wonderful woman, I guess.' He isn't expecting the quick tears. 'I'm sorry, love, what did I say?'

'Nothing. I'm being silly. I think our mothers were probably complete opposites.'

Her smile looks forced. He's upset her somehow. Briskly, she turns away and says, 'I brought some scones I made. Let me butter them and get this tea poured.' He can tell she wants to change the subject.

He would have preferred to talk to his mum alone, but he can't leave things like this. Perhaps it will be a good thing if they get to know one another as soon as possible. His mother won't be able to resist Lynne, once she sees how good Lynne is to him.

'Tell you what,' he says. 'How about we do just that? We go to see her together? It will probably cheer her up.'

'Really?' Lynne claps her hands together. 'Really?' She hugs him.

'Really.' He holds her close. 'And then we can sort out you all moving in. Why not?'

Dear Sandie Shaw, I think Charlie's wrong. Lynne, is reelly, reelly nice to me. Peraps she was tired that day she shouted at us. And I try hard but sometimes I can't reelly remember what she was saying to Mummy ... shouting? And now Dad sings to himself all the time. He still plays your song, Mummy's favouritist – you know that one that's called Always Something There to Remind Me *– and he sings to it, like he did before Mummy went to Heaven. It's just that sometimes I feel odd when I hear Lynne's voice. Sometimes I think its Mummy but then I remember. It makes me sad. I miss Mummy. Love, Chloe x*

Chapter 6

'Charlie?' Chloe hovers by his bedroom door. She's wondering what he will say when she tells him Lynne's taking her shopping.

When Lynne had appeared at her bedroom door the night before, the light from the landing silhouetted her, making it difficult for Chloe to see her face. She'd whispered, asked Chloe if she wanted a 'girls' outing. 'Without the boys,' she'd said. So not Charlie.

Chloe had asked if she could decide in the morning, but Lynne's voice changed. So she'd quickly said yes, to stop her getting cross and telling Dad she was ungrateful. And she wasn't – she really did want new shoes.

But now, when Charlie says, 'What?' Chloe hesitates. He's sitting cross-legged on the floor and doesn't look up from the Lego he's building, his face screwed up in concentration. Oscar is lying on the rug. He stands, stretches, pads over to Chloe. She rubs the dog's ears, watching Charlie.

'Lynne wants me to go shopping with her.' She bites the skin at the side of her thumbnail. 'She says I need new shoes. I didn't think you'd want to come. I did ask but she'd already told Dad we were going to have a girls' outing.'

His mouth shifts into a sneer.

'You don't mind, do you?'

'Course not.' His voice is loud. Casually offhand. 'I wouldn't want to go shopping anyway. Can't think of anything worse. Specially not with *her.*'

Chloe waits a moment. 'I think she's trying to be nice,

17

Charlie. And I do want some new shoes. I've only got my school ones now.'

'Whatever. You go.' He doesn't say anything else.

Before she closes his bedroom door, she glances back. He's pulled Oscar close to his side, his face burrowed in the dog's fur.

Chapter 7

Charlie is lying on the settee with Oscar sprawled beside him, the television blaring out.

'Everything okay?' Graham perches on the arm of the settee.

'Yep.'

'Chloe's off shopping with Lynne, then. You didn't want to go?'

'Wasn't asked.' Eyes fixed on the television screen, Charlie runs his fingers through the dog's silky coat. 'Wouldn't have gone anyway.'

'Too girly?' Graham chuckles.

Charlie shrugs. He isn't going to let his dad know how hurt he is by Chloe's disloyalty. He hates the anger stabbing into his love for his sister. It makes him miserable. He's been holding it in all day.

'I guess shopping just isn't a man thing, eh?' Graham's voice is soft, as if he is embarrassed. 'How about you come with me to the garage next time shopping's mentioned? Just like we used to do. Just you and me? You like Phil, don't you? And all the lads there. Happen they'll show you a thing or two with engines.'

Charlie sits up. 'Or you could?'

'Yes. I'd like that. After all, it'll be your business one day – you and Chloe's.'

'Tomorrow? We could do it tomorrow?'

'The garage isn't open on Sundays, son. You know that.'

'We could still go. You could still take me. Show me things. The new cars and stuff.'

'I'm sorry, Charlie, I can't tomorrow. I have a lunch meeting in town with Phil and a rep from Vauxhall who's coming from Liverpool...'

'You're working on Sunday?'

'It's the only time this chap's in the area. We're thinking of changing the dealership from Ford to Vauxhall; it'll be a better deal for the business. Any other time.'

'Don't matter.'

Charlie must have dug his fingers too hard into Oscar's back because the dog looks at him and whines. 'Sorry, boy.' Charlie strokes the fur flat.

'Next weekend. I promise.'

'Don't matter.' He lifts both shoulders and sniffs, before burying his face against the dog's head.

'You do like Lynne, don't you, son?'

Charlie bites his top lip. What should he say? He doesn't want to upset his dad but should he be honest? Mummy always said to tell the truth. Should he tell Dad about *that* day, how he knows *she* isn't who she pretends to be? That she makes him uncomfortable. Uneasy. If he does say he doesn't want her in their house what would happen?

'Charlie?'

Charlie doesn't answer. It doesn't feel like his home anymore.

He thought Chloe felt the same but now he's not sure. He's on his own.

His dad lied to them. He'd been friends with *her* for ages before he told them. He'd heard them talking about it. He knows he shouldn't listen at doors; Mummy wouldn't have liked him doing that, but it's the only way he can find out what's happening. What's going to happen. If he hadn't, he wouldn't have discovered that Dad is a liar. Does he even miss Mummy?

'What are you thinking, love?'

Charlie lifts his shoulders again, not trusting himself to speak, scared the words will come out all wrong. He closes his eyes. His eyelids prickle with tears.

Graham puts his hand on Oscar's head. The dog's tail thumps slowly on the seat of the settee.

Charlie grips his dad's hand, takes it off the dog's head, puts his own there. He waits. The air is filled with breathing; his, his dad's, the dog's panting. All at once the room dims, rain splatters suddenly on the window.

'They'll get wet through in this,' Graham says. 'But they should be home soon, anyway. Shops close at six.' He stands, slaps his hands together. 'Want something to drink? Ribena? Lemonade?'

'No.' A pause. 'No, thanks.'

'I'm going to have a cuppa anyway. Fancy a Kit Kat, then?'

Charlie shakes his head. He turns up the television even more. Oscar jumps off the settee, pads silently out of the lounge.

'Probably sensible, too close to teatime. The girls are supposed to be bringing fish and chips home.'

The girls! Charlie winces. It makes them sound – like friends. Like they're together. Shutting him out.

Graham raises his voice. 'Right. Okay, then. I'll go and put the plates to warm.'

Charlie waits until his dad leaves the room before turning down the sound of the television. He's lost interest in what was on anyway. Lying on his stomach he stares at the window. Rain is now streaming down the glass. He's glad; Chloe and *her* will get very wet. He pushes down the instinctive guilt for being spiteful. Tells himself he doesn't care.

In the kitchen, Graham is also watching the rain through the window, hoping that Lynne and Chloe are in the car, already on their way home. It's pouring down now.

He's worried about Charlie, but at least Chloe likes Lynne. That should help. He's under no illusion, he knows how much influence Charlie has on his sister. But maybe it'll work the other way around with this. Chloe has a good head on her shoulders. Maybe she will persuade her brother to accept – even love – Lynne. In time. He can only hope.

Because, come what may, she's here to stay, he's determined about that. He's found love for only the second time in his life and he knows Anna would want him to be happy.

Dear Sandie Shaw, Lynne took me shopping today and got me new shoes for school and a dress. It's blue, with white daisies all over. It was nice going shoping with her. Not as nice as when Mummy and me used to go shopping together. Mummy used to make me laugh when she tryed all those hats on in C&As. It was funny. Lynne doesn't laugh. At least she only laughs with Dad. And she knows Charlie doesn't like her. She told me. I didnt know what to say, it made me feel a bit odd. Like she was waiting for me to say something. Like be on her side, like the girls do in school sometimes when thers been a fall out. And tonight I heard Charlie crying. I don't like Charlie crying. It makes me feel all sad. I wish I knew how to make Charlie happy. Love Chloe. X

Chapter 8

'I think Daddy would be pleased if we tried to like Lynne, Charlie.' Chloe thinks it's better if she says 'we', not 'you'. 'She told me she knows you don't.'

'Good.'

'I think she looked a bit hurt.'

She hadn't. Chloe had felt like Lynne was trying to be extra nice when she said it, as though she wanted Chloe to be on her side. It had given Chloe an uneasy feeling in her stomach. So she'd said Charlie was a bit shy, which isn't true but she couldn't think what else to say. As soon as she did, Chloe saw Lynne toss her head and give a sort of shrug, like she didn't care.

'So what?' Charlie turns the page of his *Spider-Man* comic book and studies one of the pictures. 'I hate her.'

He says it so casually it makes the skin on Chloe's arms prickle. 'Mummy always said we shouldn't say that. Don't let Dad hear you say it.'

'Don't care. I do.'

He won't look at Chloe. She sits next to him, strokes Oscar who puts his head on her knee.

'It isn't as though she's done anything really, really horrid. Not since...'

'Since she shouted at Mummy?' He slams the book closed, glares at Chloe. 'And was nasty to us? We should have told Dad then. If we had, she wouldn't be here now.' He rubs the back of his hand under his nose.

Chloe's scared he's going to cry. If he does, so will she. 'I don't know...'

'You don't *know* if she's pretending to be nice now? With her no-eyes smile?'

Chloe bites on her thumb nail. 'How would we know if she's pretending, Charlie?'

'Somehow. I just know she's pretending. She doesn't like us, I can tell. Well, me anyway...' Charlie is glaring at her.

'I don't understand.' Chloe's confused and upset. When she'd come into her brother's room she was certain she was doing the right thing, trying to persuade him to like Lynne.

But it's as if he knows something she doesn't.

'You went off with her.' He's shouting. 'Shopping!'

Oscar jumps up and barks. Chloe pulls him to her to quieten him. 'I would have liked it if you'd come with us.'

'I don't want to go anywhere with her. *Ever.* I hate her. And so should you.'

There's an awkward pause.

'I'm sorry.' Chloe holds herself very still. She's always so sure about her brother, knows how he looks out for her. The same as she looks out for him. But now she feels she's let him down.

'S'okay.' Charlie lowers his voice. 'I know it's not your fault. But I hate her. And I don't like the lad. That Saul.'

'I know.' Chloe can agree about that, so she says it quickly. 'I don't either. Evie's all right though? Isn't she?'

'I don't know.' He shrugs. 'She's not around much.'

'She talks to me when she's here … sometimes.'

'Does she?' His eyebrows raised.

'Just to ask how we are. You know, things like that.'

'Oh.' Charlie's shoulders twitch. 'Well, anyhow, I still don't want them here all the time. I liked it when it was just us. How it was before.'

'Before Mummy went to Heaven?'

Tears slide down Charlie's face, drip from his jaw.

'Mummy might be looking down from Heaven and wants us to try for Dad's sake?'

'No. Mummy knows *she* didn't make her better, because *she* wanted Dad. And nothing *she* says or does will make me think different.'

Chloe sobs. 'Don't, Charlie. Please?'

He holds out his hand. She goes to him, puts her head on his shoulder.

'Sorry, Sis. I'll shurrup now.'

Dear Sandie Shaw, I'm glad Charlie said he hates Saul, because I don't like him either. I wish you could tell me what to do, cos he frightens me. He's nasty. Says nasty things to us. Calls us names like stupid and soft arse, which is really rude. I tell Charlie we should tell Dad but he wont, he says Dad wont believe us, but I think he would, don't you? Evie is nice though. Do you think I should tell her about Saul? She understands when I talk about Mummy. She hugs me and says I can tell her anything and she'll try to make me feel better. I'll ask her to talk to Charlie as well. Love Chloe x

Chapter 9

His mother is pruning her roses in the tiny front garden of her terraced cottage when Graham parks the car at the gate.

'Goodness, this is a surprise. Everything all right at home?' She gives him a fleeting hug while glancing at Lynne, a slight frown creasing her forehead.

'Everything's fine, Mum. In fact, everything is great. This is...'

For some reason she doesn't wait for him to finish. 'Well, do come in, then.' She's being overly polite. Inviting them into her home as if they're strangers. They follow her.

'Mum, you might remember Lynne?'

'I do. Anna's nurse. I think we met briefly?'

'Yes, we did.'

'Not that I really remember you, sorry. It was such a dreadful time for Graham and the children.'

They sit on the floral-patterned squashed armchairs in the front room. The claustrophobic small room is making Graham anxious. He never used to think this house was small. He'd loved it as a child. Looking around, he realises nothing has changed from when he lived here: the maroon and black diamond Wilton carpet, a bit threadbare now, the old-fashioned oak sideboard, the beige-tiled fireplace with the black fire screen hiding the grate.

The atmosphere is strained, with long pauses between stilted words. It's obvious his mother is determined not to ask why he's suddenly turned up. Or why Lynne is with him. She sits, waiting, one eyebrow lifted.

They should have discussed what he would say in the car. Or he should have rung his mum, warned her.

'Mum, I ... we ... wanted to tell you...'

'Yes?'

'Actually, Mum, Lynne is my fiancé.' It feels awkward saying that at his age. He sees his mother's face, her hurt, the bewildered double-take. He glances at Lynne, who's sitting very still, looking down at her hands. 'We've been seeing one another for a while.' Lynne is not moving, except for one thumb rubbing over the back of her fingers. He holds out his hand to her. She takes it.

'We love one another, Mum. Lynne and I are going ... Lynne is going to move in with us ... with her children.'

'You have children, er, Lynne?'

It's the first time she's addressed Lynne since they sat down.

'Yes, two. A boy and a girl. Saul is thirteen. Evie who's fifteen.' Her face stays impassive.

'Well.' Graham clears his throat, smiles from one woman to the other. 'What do you think, Mum?'

'I'm not sure what you want me to say, Graham. This is ... this is rather a surprise.'

He should have realised what a shock this would be. Lynne's lips are trembling. His mother is near to tears.

'I want you to be happy for me, Mum. For us.' He stands and leans over to hug her.

'I am, love. I'm sorry.' Her smile includes Lynne. 'I was just surprised, my dear.'

'Don't worry, Mrs Collins. I understand perfectly.'

Is Lynne's returning smile a little forced? Graham can't quite decide, but it's understandable. It's been a difficult visit so far. But his mother seems all right with everything now.

'Well, that went okay, didn't it?' Graham peers over his shoulder, steering the car away from the kerb. He waves to his mother.

'She doesn't like me.' Lynne looks out of the window on her side.

'Nonsense. It was just a bit of a shock for her. I did say I should come on my own, didn't I? But she came around.'

'I don't know.' Lynne's voice is wistful.

'It's fine.' Graham pats her knee. 'It's all going to be fine, believe me, love. In fact it's all going to be great.'

Chapter 10

They've agreed on the date for the wedding. No point in a long engagement. Lynne's right.

And Graham's impatient for his new life, a fresh start. He looks around the lounge. Lynne's right about this room as well. Even though it's large, the big mahogany sideboard, the dark carpet and the bookcases, crammed with old books that

27

belonged to Anna's father, do make it a little gloomy, despite the light coming from the patio doors. When Lynne's living here permanently she can make all the changes she needs to, so she feels at home.

He wants to spend the rest of his life with her, and the sooner she's away from that dreadful estate, the better. The more he's seen of that place, the more he wonders how she's managed there. He often reflects how brave she's been, escaping from her ex-husband, letting him take everything. Getting out from what sounded to be a toxic marriage.

She'll win Charlie over. Being married will change things: more stability for the twins. He'll get to know Evie and Saul properly as time goes on. Graham hopes so anyway.

Despite her demanding job, Lynne has everything in hand after just a month. She says she knows how busy the garage is, how tired he gets. All she's asked for is a list of who he wants to invite: one or two of his colleagues at the Rotary Club, a couple of his fellow governors from the twins' school, friends from the bowling and cricket clubs, Phil and Margaret, the lads from the garage, a couple of his cousins. And, of course, his mother.

Graham phones his mum every day. He's told her about the wedding arrangements and Lynne's insistence that she must stay with them before and after the ceremony. He hopes she and Lynne will have the same friendly relationship that she had with Anna.

He's toyed with the idea of asking Charlie to be his best man, but he's been so difficult to talk to lately. It's irritating to see his son sulking. Still, he's looking forward to seeing Chloe's face when she finds out she'll be a bridesmaid. She'll love that. Whether Evie will want any part of it is debatable. She and Lynne have their own problems, and he hasn't a clue what's happened there. Lynne says he shouldn't bother his head about it.

And Saul... Graham is still trying to work out how to get closer to her son. He knows she wishes he would, but it's difficult. It's probably the age he's at, but the lad doesn't even make eye contact. No use asking him to be best man.

Still, it will all be a lovely day. His Lynne will make sure of that.

Dear Sandie Shaw, Daddy asked me if I mind he's marrying Lynne. I said no. I didn't tell him that Charlie hates her. I heard him playing your song again on Mummy's old record player yesterday. He bought it for her on her birthday. The one before she went to Heaven. Sometimes I wish Mummy was I'm glad Daddy is happy again. Love, Chloe x

Chapter 11

'Dad says I'll be a bridesmaid.' Chloe can't help being excited. She beams at Sue Fitz, their next-door neighbour. 'I want a blue dress. Blue's my most favourite, favouritist colour in the whole world.' She twirls around so fast her skirt flares out and shows her matching blue knickers. 'This blue.' She flops down onto the carpet, dizzy, and laughs.

Mrs Fitz moves to the edge of her chair. Chloe notices her catch her top lip between her teeth. 'Are you sure, love?'

Chloe feels a small seed of worry grow inside her. She ignores it.

'I like blue.' She spreads her skirt around her, stroking the material. 'Like this. A bit.' She smiles widely, not bothering to hide the gap between her middle teeth, which she's become conscious of lately. 'Blue, with puffy sleeves. Julie, my friend in school was a bridesmaid for her auntie. She had puffy...'

She falters when she hears Mrs Fitz sigh.

'They haven't told them,' she mutters, and crouches next to Chloe.

Chloe's used to Mrs Fitz mumbling to herself. She does it a lot. Dad says not to mind, it's because she's an old lady. She's trying not to listen now, though she's not sure why. There's something about Mrs Fitz's expression that worries her.

'Listen, dear, I'm not sure that's what your daddy should have said – or rather, what he meant.' She moves closer to Chloe, takes her hand. 'You're not going to the wedding, you'll be here with me, you and your brother. Not at the wedding, see?' Chloe sees the veins on the woman's cheeks getting redder. 'We'll have fun, we'll probably go to the park. Hmm?' She nods a few times, little nods.

'No!' Chloe shakes her head, hard. 'You're wrong.' The worry is growing, however much she tries to ignore it. 'You're wrong, Mrs Fitz. We can't go with you, cos I'll be being a bridesmaid.' She watches the woman's mouth quiver as though she wants to say something else, so she has to stop her. Chloe pushes the woman's hand away and stands. 'I'd like to go home now, please. Oscar, our dog, has been on his own for ages.'

'In a bit, love. Your daddy will still be at work and your mummy...'

'Lynne!'

'Lynne, that's right, Lynne is still out on her rounds. She's still out looking after the poorly people in their houses.' Her chin moves up and down as though she's chewing something.

'She's a nurse. She's kind to poorly people.' Chloe repeats what her father has told her so many times. But that's not what she wants to think about right now. The rush of panic is making her whole body shake. 'You're wrong, Mrs Fitz. I'm sorry, you'll have to go to the park on your own. I'll be being a bridesmaid,' she says, stubbornly. 'I want Charlie.'

'Of course. He's in the garden. Let's go and see what he's doing.' Sue Fitz struggles to her feet. By the time she's upright, Chloe is by the back door, pulling on the handle.

'Charlie?' Tightness in her throat makes her voice squeak. 'Charlie?'

He's facing her on the path, holding his red-and-white plastic football. He drops it. 'Here. Pass!' He kicks it towards her. 'Pass it back.'

She ignores him. The ball bounces on the doorstep and rolls into the kitchen, stopping in front of Sue. Who also ignores it.

Charlie walks to Chloe. 'What's up? Why are you crying?'

'Mrs Fitz says I'm not going to be a bridesmaid. But she's wrong, isn't she?' Chloe lifts her skirt and wipes her face on the material. 'Tell her. Tell her Dad said. Tell her I am going to be a bridesmaid.'

Chapter 12

'No, I'm not going back in her house.' Chloe turns on the step to look back into their neighbour's kitchen. The back door is still open. She pulls it shut. 'Mrs Fitz tells lies. Dad said I'll be a bridesmaid and she's being mean. And when Dad comes home, I'm going to tell him.' Chloe twists a strand of her hair round and round her forefinger. 'She's lying.'

'She's not.' Charlie knows he should have told his sister what he heard before, but he'd been hoping their dad would say something first. He won't look at Chloe. 'Won't do any good.'

He kicks the football against the wall, catching it with the inside edge of his shoe as it rebounds. He runs, moving the ball from one foot to the other. 'And Summerbee passes to Bell, the defence can't stop him...'

'Stop it! Charlie!' Chloe runs after him.

'And it's a goal! Man City wins!' He falls to the ground, breathing heavily.

'Tell me.' She stands over him. 'What do you know?'

He raises himself on one elbow. 'It's not Dad, it's *her*. *She* won't let you be a bridesmaid.'

'Mrs Fitz?'

'No, don't be daft. *Her*. Lynne.'

'Why?' Chloe's lip trembles.

Charlie stands up, taps the ball with his foot, makes it bounce a little. 'Cos.'

He inhales and breathes out slowly. 'Let's go there.' He points to the rockery at the far end of the garden. He kicks the ball so hard it flies off at a tangent and disappears into one of the shrubs. He leaves it there. He tugs at her arm.

'Not till you say why.'

'Don't be stupid.' He's dragging her along.

The huge sob that's been stuck inside her comes out as a loud wail.

'Shurrup.' But he knows she'll be worse when he tells her what he heard. 'Chloe? Please.'

Reaching the rockery, he lets go of her arm and sits on one of the flatter stones, pointing to one of the others.

'No.' She remains standing, her chin quivering.

Her distress makes his stomach hurt. He blows out a long gust of breath, looks back at the house. Mrs Fitz is watching them from the window. She's smiling but it's just a twist of her mouth, and she's frowning. She holds up two glasses. He lifts his hand to acknowledge her.

'Mrs Fitz's got some Vimto for us.'

'Don't care.'

'I told you, it's not her fault. We shan't be going to the stupid wedding, and I'm glad. It's stupid. We don't need ... we don't ... it's stupid. So shurrup. Yeah?'

'I just want to be a bridesmaid. Dad promised, he said I could.' She clenches her fists. 'It's not fair.' She stops talking. 'Don't cry, Charlie. Please.'

'I'm not skriking.' He stands up, pulls the cuff of his jumper over his hand and wipes at his face with his sleeve. 'I should have told you. It's not Mrs Fitz, it's *her*. *She* said you can't be a bridesmaid. *She* said we've had him all to ourselves since ... since Mummy ... since Mummy...' He stops.

Chloe stares at him. 'What does she mean?'

'I don't know. 'Cept she doesn't want us to be at the wedding.'

Two nights ago, he'd sat on the last tread of the stairs, his arms around Oscar, watching through the slightly open lounge door, listening to what his dad and *she* were saying. He'd needed to be there, so he'd be prepared for what happened next.

'Please, Graham. Just listen to me.' Charlie saw Lynne put her arms around his dad's neck.

'I am listening, sweetheart, but we can't.'

'Please. I had a horrid first wedding. I couldn't even wear a nice dress. I was six months gone with Evie...'

What did that mean? Charlie scowled. *And did she just want to be married so she could wear a nice dress?*

'So I want this wedding to be a lovely day that I can remember.'

'It will be, sweetheart, I'll make sure. But I don't understand why...'

'I want it to be just me and you.'

'And I don't. We can't have a wedding with just us there. I don't want that. You're being unreasonable, Lynne. You've already asked me who I want to invite.'

'You're not understanding me, Graham. I haven't said you can't have your friends. I mean it'll be just adults.'

Not us? Not me and Chloe?

'Not have our kids there? Oh no, love, that wouldn't be right. I know you said Evie doesn't want to be a bridesmaid, but Chloe...'

'Chloe won't want to be there without Charlie.' She was leaning back from his dad, gazing at him. 'And you know what he's like at the moment. He's not accepted me yet and I don't think we should make him be at the wedding.'

'I'm sure he'll want to be with us.'

I don't, but I haven't said anything about not wanting to be at the stupid wedding. And Chloe is excited about it.

'He won't. Trust me, Graham.' She was cuddling up to him again. 'I've seen how changes in families can upset sensitive children in my job and I don't want us to do anything that will make things worse for him.'

'It wouldn't be right.'

'It'll be better if he's not there, Graham.'

I hate her.

'For his own sake. And Chloe won't want to be there without him. Evie won't care – she's already told me she won't come.'

'Has she?' His dad sounded hurt. 'Why?'

'She's always been awkward. Difficult.' Lynne gave a loud sigh. 'I guess this is just another way of hurting me.'

'Oh, I'm sorry, love.'

'Don't worry. I'm used to it.' She kissed him. 'So, you see, it'll be fairer if the children stay at Sue's next door.'

'Don't you want Sue at the wedding? I thought she was your friend?'

'She is. In a way. I knew her before she moved here. And, as my friend ... our friend ... she's said she will look after Chloe and Charlie.'

What?

'You've already asked her?'

Charlie leant forward to get a better look at his dad. He was frowning.

'I've already told Chloe she can be a bridesmaid.'

'Oh, Graham!'

'She was so excited.'

'Well...' She kissed him more noisily.

Charlie shuddered.

'How about you tell her and Charlie that we'll take them somewhere when we come back from our honeymoon?'

'Honeymoon?'

'Of course. I thought we could go to London for a few days. I've booked us into a hotel on Seven Sisters Road. And a couple of shows.'

'The kids?'

'Sue will have them then as well, she doesn't mind. Evie and Saul are old enough to stay here.'

'Lynne! Honestly, sweetheart, all this is something we should have discussed first, you know.'

'I'm sorry.' She spoke in a tiny voice. 'I only wanted to take the pressure off you – with you being so busy at work.'

'And that's sweet of you. Still...'

'I thought I was doing the right thing.'

She's doing that pretend crying she does a lot. Blowing her nose, wiping at her eyes.

'I've spent my whole life trying to please, not saying how I felt, doing what I thought others wanted for fear of upsetting someone. Of making situations worse.'

'Oh, love.'

His dad was hugging her.

'I've worried about everyone else and not myself.' She was resting her chin on his shoulder, looking towards the door.

Charlie quickly sat back. Had she seen him? She was talking louder now. 'Think about it, it will be making our own lovely memories.'

'I know. I do understand, sweetheart. Listen, how about Charlie and Chloe go to stay with my mother after the wedding? It'll be a treat for the twins to be with their Granny, and my mother will love having them. Everything will be fine. Leave it with me, I'll talk to Chloe and Charlie.'

'Thank you.'

'So adults only.'

'Except for Saul,' she said quickly. 'I'll need Saul there to give me away. Just Saul.'

Charlie put both arms around Oscar and hugged him, his heart racing beneath his ribs, listening for what his dad would say about Saul going to the wedding. But Dad said nothing.

Charlie stayed as still as he could; if he moved, he'd be sick.

He and Chloe sit in silence. Every now and then sobs shudder through her. It wasn't true that they'd had all their dad's attention after Mummy died; he was hardly home for months. They were either with Granny or Auntie Margaret from his garage. It was as though they didn't belong anywhere. To anyone.

Was it happening again?

Sandie Shaw, Everythings all unfair. Chloe x

Chapter 13

'And you thought it would be all right, did you, Graham?' His mother's standing in front of him, her arms folded. She presses her lips together waiting for an answer. When he doesn't speak she walks over to the window of her living room, gazes out onto her front garden. 'Promising Chloe she can be a bridesmaid, and then telling her she won't even be at the wedding? Nor Charlie. That was acceptable, was it?' Her voice becomes harsh. 'Anna would be horrified by what you're doing, you do know that, don't you?'

Graham runs his tongue over his teeth trying to stay calm. 'It's what we've decided, Mum. It is *our* wedding after all.'

'And your father. He'd be disgusted by what you're doing.'

Graham instinctively glances at the 1950s HMV radiogram his dad was so proud of. The sound of a brass band, his father's favourite music, filtering into Graham's head. He has a moment of doubt about the decision he and Lynne have made but ignores it. 'I'm sorry if you don't like it, Mum.'

She's crying.

He pushes himself off the armchair his father always sat in, crosses the room to her. 'Aw, Mum.' He puts his arm around her shoulder. 'Please...' She folds against him, her body shuddering. 'Please don't get so upset.'

'How could you do this to them, Graham?' She pulls away from him, takes a handkerchief from up her sleeve. Scrubs at her eyes.

'It's for the best, Mum. You don't know the half of what's going on. Charlie's really playing up. Making our lives a misery.'

'And that's the reason?'

Graham flinches. For a moment he wishes he'd let Lynne come with him. She'd have been able to explain properly why it was for the best. 'It'll just be adults.' He won't mention Saul. 'Just a small wedding.'

'Well, it will be even smaller now.' His mother goes to his father's chair and plumps up the cushion. Looking away from him she says quietly, 'I won't be there either. And I'm telling you now, son, you need to think long and hard before you go ahead with this marriage.'

Chapter 14

'You love Granny, you know you do. And since Grandad went to Heaven to be with Mummy, Granny's been a bit lonely.' Graham hesitates, knows he shouldn't use his father's death to persuade his children. He studies their mutinous faces. 'She'll be really glad for you to keep her company.'

'I know, but she could come as well. We'd all be there … with you.' Charlie's looking at his sister. Chloe has closed her eyes, tears rolling silently down her cheeks. 'And why isn't Granny going to be there?'

'It would be too much for her. It would be hard, not having Grandad with her.' The lies don't come easy, but how can he tell the truth?

A quietness comes between the three of them. The mention of his father has made his children sad. He hadn't meant to do that.

'Grandad would be proud of you if he saw you looking after Granny,' he says gently, torn between knowing that would be true and despising himself for his deception. He'd always prided himself on being honest with his children. Even through those last days with Anna, he hadn't pretended to them that she would get better.

Graham hears Lynne on the landing, opening the airing cupboard door and putting linen away.

'And you did say you didn't want to be at the wedding, Charlie.'

'So, cos I said that, you're stopping Chloe being there as well?'

'No. Not at all. It'll just be grown ups.'

'Saul's not a grown up. It's not fair. You told Chloe she could be a bridesmaid.'

'Yes, I'm sorry I said that. I shouldn't have. I didn't think.' He makes himself speak with more authority. 'Saul needs to be there; he'll be part of the ceremony.'

'Chloe could be that. I don't care whether I'm there or not, but Chloe…' He looks from her to Graham. 'One of us for you, one of *hers*, Saul, for *her*?'

Graham grimaces. He feels sick. 'It's only for a few days. I'll pick you up when we get back.'

'No, don't bother; we'll stay with Granny,' Charlie interrupts him. The words flood out, crash into one another, to get them out as fast as he can before Graham can stop him speaking. 'We will. We won't ever come home again. We'll stay with Granny – for always.'

'Now then, that's enough of that talk, young man.' Graham's

floundering. He's trying to persuade himself that what he's doing isn't wrong. But he knows it is. He decides he'll tell Lynne that he wants Charlie and Chloe to be at the wedding.

'Look, I'll tell you what, I'll have a word...'

The door opens and Lynne peers around it before coming into the room. 'Everything all right in here?'

'No. I'm afraid not,' Graham says. 'The children are upset, so I'm just wondering if...'

'Oh dear, I am sorry, Chloe, Charlie.' Lynne sits on the end of the bed. 'It's just a boring old wedding, you know. And Evie won't be there either, she's decided to stay with her friend.'

'But Saul *will* be there.' Charlie glares at her.

'I know. But I haven't got anyone else to give me away.' She turns to Chloe. 'You know what that means, don't you, love?' She chuckles. 'Yes, I know it sound silly, but it is a part of a wedding, isn't it?'

'Suppose,' Chloe mutters.

Graham can't help feeling relieved. Lynne's managed to make it right, at least with his daughter.

'And a couple of special days with your grandmother, plus a few days off school as a bonus. Please try to understand.' She looks from one to the other. When neither of them says anything, she says, 'Thank you.' She gives Graham a small smile but her eyes glisten as though she's on the verge of crying. He reaches for her hand. Squeezes it.

'Thank you, both,' he says, standing. 'I'm proud of you, for being so grown up about this. Granny will love having you with her. I'll take you there after school on Friday and I bet you have a great week.'

Dear Sandie Shaw, Charlie was right, it is Lynne's fault. I wish she'd go away for ever. I wish I could majic her away. We'd look after daddy. We could find him a nice bride to marry. Chloe x

Chapter 15

'She wanted a low-key wedding, but it was lovely, and she organised it all in just over three months. Wonderful day.' Sue Fitz shifts her phone to her other ear, 'But she's so popular, you know, so kind, and so many friends wanted to share her happy day... No, not many, I don't think I talked to anyone who was *his* friend. Mind you, I wouldn't have known them anyway; I haven't seen many people coming to their house in all the eighteen months I've lived here. But, of course, I knew Lynne from before; from when I lived in Bridge Street. She was the district nurse; saw to Mother for years.'

Charlie's bored. He'd wanted to watch his favourite cartoon, but Chloe won the game that Mrs Fitz made up, the 'guess which hand the remote is in behind her back' stupid game. And Chloe had chosen this stupid girls' programme. He starts listening to Mrs Fitz on the phone to her friend. He sees her look over her shoulder to where he and Chloe are sitting cross-legged in front of the television. She pushes one shoe off, frowns, reaches down to rub her bunion through her stocking.

She has ugly feet.

'I don't see much of Graham, so I don't really know him that much. He owns that car showroom and garage on the corner of Barnsley Road and Corn Lane. And he must have a bob or two because Lynne says he's told her to keep her salary for herself, and he's giving her a monthly allowance on top...

'What? Well, I don't mind looking after his children; it's Lynne who asks, not him. And she gives me a fiver for doing it. How could I say no – you know what an angel she is, she'd do anything for anyone. And she told me about this house coming on the market. I wouldn't have known except for her. I was so pleased to get it. Thanks to Mother leaving me the money. I wouldn't have afforded it otherwise. You'll have to come and see it sometime.' A pause.

'Yes, they're good. Well, the girl is ... mostly. She played up a bit when she couldn't be a bridesmaid, but I think Lynne was right about that. The girl would have wanted to be the centre of attention as usual, and Lynne didn't want it spoiled. It was her day after all.'

Charlie takes in a sharp breath, glances at Chloe, but she obviously hasn't heard because she's laughing, glued to her television programme. He hears Mrs Fitz say, 'The lad's a bit of a handful but I've got his measure, so we get along. He plays Lynne up no end. She really tries with him, but she knew he'd cause trouble at the wedding, she admitted that to me. She said Graham was worried about that as well, so both children went to stay with their grandmother. Better that way. At least she had Saul to support her. Yes, he gave her away, looked ever so smart too... No, I didn't see Evie, come to think on it. She must have been there. Like I said, there were that many people there.'

Mrs Fitz is making Charlie so angry his clenched teeth are hurting his face. She doesn't know what it's like. He knows. He knows that Lynne doesn't like him, that since she came to live in their house she doesn't want them there. Him more than Chloe. He can tell by the odd looks she gives him when Daddy isn't there; her head cocked to one side, eyes nearly closed.

'Yes, Lynne's two are teenagers, old enough to keep an eye on these, but she says Charlie...' She lowers her voice to a hoarse whisper, but he can still hear. 'The boy, he plays up. He's apparently a little devil with Saul – kicks and punches Saul when he's asked to do anything.'

Charlie half turns, indignant. He's tried to keep out of Saul's way all week since they came home from Granny's. He's as nasty as Lynne is.

Mrs Fitz doesn't see him. She's now leaning right back in the armchair, the wings on the side hiding her head. He gets up.

'Going outside with my football,' he says.

'Okay.' Chloe doesn't take her eye from her programme. 'Be out with you after this.'

'Put your coat on,' Mrs Fitz says. 'It looks as if it might rain.' She exhales loudly when he heads for the back door without taking his coat. He hears her say, 'See? Takes not a blind bit of notice.' As though whoever she's on the phone to can see what he's doing.

He's never kicked Saul. He's too scared of him. But he'd like to. He's heard Saul call his dad horrid names. He's heard Lynne laugh as though it's funny. It's not. Charlie hates both of them.

44

Chapter 16

'There's only cake for pudding, I haven't had time to make anything else. Pass your plates.' Lynne piles them up, stops when she takes Charlie's plate. 'Oh, you haven't eaten your sprouts.'

'I don't like them.' Charlie looks up at her.

'They're good for you.'

He pushes the plate away. 'They make me feel sick.'

'Not the way I cook them. Try them.'

'He's never liked them, Lynne, right from being a little lad,' Graham says quickly, to avoid any tension. 'He loves broccoli, though.'

'Saul's never been able to eat that.' Lynne shrugs.

'It's gross,' Saul pulls a face. 'Proper yukky.'

'Well, I like broccoli,' Evie says. 'I wondered why we never had it. Thanks Saul.' She places her knife and fork in precision on her plate. 'I've finished. I don't want cake. May I leave the table? I have homework.'

'And an attitude, young lady. Yes, do please go. Graham, please.' Lynne gestures towards the kitchen.

As Evie leaves the dining room, Graham picks up Charlie's plate and follows her to the kitchen.

'That's really upset me.' Lynne taps the plate. 'Everything I cook, he hates.'

'You mustn't take it so personally, sweetheart. He's always been a picky eater. And he ate everything else.'

'Ah, well, I guess I'll just have to get used to it. Now I think about it, your trolleys at the supermarket were all full of junk food.'

He laughs. 'I know. But that was partly my own fault. It was the only thing I knew how to cook.'

'How to heat up, you mean.' She kisses the end of his nose. 'Come on,' she says, picking up the cake, 'let's see if he at least likes my baking.'

'Oh, he will, don't worry about that.' He holds open the door for her.

'Now,' she says, smiling, 'who's for a slice of Victoria sponge?'

Chapter 17

'But we had sprouts last night.' Chloe looks with dismay at the plate of fish fingers, chips and sprouts, and then at Charlie.

'I bought a bag of them from the farm shop. They need using. I'm sorry if it doesn't suit everyone, but I don't like waste. And you can stop looking at me in that way, young man.' Lynne turns to look at Charlie, her hands on her hips. 'There is nothing wrong with them. As I said yesterday, they are good for you.'

'It's only five o'clock. We don't normally eat so early,' Chloe says. 'Can't we wait until Dad comes home?' It makes her angry, knowing Lynne is just being mean to her brother.

'I have things to do this evening. And your father will be late home.'

'But it's Friday. He's never late home on Fridays,' Chloe protests. 'And anyway, it's always our chippy night on Fridays. He won't know we'll have eaten. He'll bring our sausage and chips.'

'Not tonight. Your father's working. So I made fish fingers and chips tonight. Especially for you.'

'And sprouts,' Chloe says, pointing at the plate.

'Yes, and sprouts.'

'When Charlie doesn't like sprouts. And he told you last night he doesn't.'

'They make me feel sick.' Charlie scowls. 'These ones, anyway.'

'You are not wasting good food, my lad. Not in my house you're not.'

Not your house. Chloe can't stop the thought. *Mummy and Dad's house. Not yours.*

'There are children starving in this world that would be grateful to eat anything.'

Lynne spits the words out. A droplet lands on Charlie's finger. Chloe sees Charlie put down his fork and wipe the back of his hand on the tablecloth.

What will she do if he doesn't eat the sprouts? Chloe sees Charlie push one with his fork, squash it. Her stomach moves uneasily. She isn't sure if it's fear of Lynne and the way she's standing over her brother, or the green smelly mush splodged on the plate in front of him. Bits of it are stuck on the end of his fork.

What will she do?

Charlie is staring stubbornly at his plate. Just the sprouts are left.

'It's been ten minutes now. But I can wait as long as you. You'll sit there until you finish every scrap of food on that plate.'

Chloe's breathing quickens. She clamps her hands between her knees under the table.

Saul sniggers. He's been eating the sprouts as slowly as he can, watching Charlie all the time. He pierces a last sprout on his fork and shoves it into his mouth. 'Mm, yum-yum.' He grins across the table at them.

'Shut it.' Evie glares at her brother. 'Leave him alone.'

Saul ignores her. 'Leave the table, Ma?'

'Course you can, love.'

Saul pushes his chair back, flicks the side of Evie's face with his finger and thumb, dodges out of the way when she tries to hit him. Jeers at her. 'Hah!' He leaves his plate on the table.

Lynne picks it up and takes it to the sink.

Chloe puts her hand on Charlie's arm and whispers, 'I'll eat them, Charlie.'

'You won't!' Lynne whips round, switching her anger to Chloe. '*You* can leave the table.'

Even though her insides have turned to sloshing water, Chloe stays where she is, defying her stepmother in the only way she dares, by obstinate silence.

'Mum!' Evie rolls her eyes. 'Just leave it, can't you?'

'Mind your own business, madam.'

Pushing past her mother, Evie takes her plate to the sink and drops it into the water. As she leaves the kitchen, she mouths, 'Sorry,' to Charlie and Chloe.

Charlie grabs the five sprouts on his plate and squashing them between his fingers, shoves them into the pocket of his school P.E. shorts.

'I've finished,' he says, loudly. 'Please may I leave the table?'

'You've eaten them?' Lynne dries her hands, looking at him. 'You ate them for him,' she says to Chloe.

'No. Honest.'

'She didn't.'

48

Lynne sniffs. 'Hmm. Well, in that case...' She gestures towards the sink. 'Put your plates in the water.'

As soon as Charlie stands, he feels the trickle of liquid running down the outside of his thigh. He moves to stand behind his chair but Lynne has seen.

'I knew it.'

Charlie ducks, but she's too quick. She grabs his arm, catching his skin between her finger and thumb. It hurts.

'Let me go. I hate you.'

Charlie knows she's pinching him on purpose. Without thinking what he's doing, he bites her hand.

She gasps. 'You little...' Lynne lets go of him, rubbing hard at the red imprint of his teeth. 'Just you wait until your father gets home.'

Charlie doesn't wait. He pulls the sodden vegetable mess out of his pocket, throws it at her, and runs along the hallway and out of the front door.

'Get back here. Now!'

Flinging the door open Charlie runs along the drive and onto the avenue. His skin is tingling all over. He knows what he's just done will get him into big bother.

He sprints until his chest burns and his legs give way under him. His knees scrape the pavement as he falls.

He looks around. At this time in the evening the avenue is deserted, the front doors are closed. He's tempted to stay lying where he is. But he shouldn't have left Chloe. He shudders. It doesn't matter how long he waits. She won't forget. He's in bad trouble.

He stands. Might as well get it over with.

Dear Sandie Shaw, Nothings right. I hate her. I want Daddy to tell her to go away.

Chapter 18

'So, where are you three off to this Saturday morning?' Sue Fitz calls to them from across the gardens, a trowel in her hand.

'Clothes shopping.' Lynne manages a martyred smile, her hands on Charlie and Chloe's backs, ushering them towards her car. 'You wouldn't believe how fast they're growing. Costing me a fortune.'

'It isn't,' Chloe whispers to Charlie. 'I saw Daddy give her lots of money.'

Lynne bends down so her face is next to his. 'And Charlie needs new school P.E. shorts. We had a little accident yesterday, didn't we?'

'Oh dear.' Sue Fitz moves closer, but her voice is still loud. 'Aren't you a bit old for accidents, Charlie?'

He scowls, looks towards Ingram Avenue at the end of the drive, to see if anyone is passing. If anyone can hear her.

Lynne laughs, a trilling high laugh. 'No, Sue, not that sort of accident – well, not this time anyway.'

'It's not his fault,' Chloe protests. 'You tried to make him...'

Charlie gives her a dig in the ribs. 'Shush!'

Lynne pushes them into the back seat of her green Vauxhall Viva. 'Must get on, Sue, before the shops get too busy.'

'Yes, yes, it'll be murder in town later. Always is on a Saturday.' Mrs Fitz peers over the hedge at Charlie and Chloe.

'Well, aren't you two lucky to have such a generous step-mum, eh?' She waits, as if for an answer. When neither of them speaks she straightens up. 'Hmm, yes, well, I see what you mean, Lynne.' She shakes her head. 'You can only do your best, love.'

Lynne runs her fingers over her eyes. Takes out a tissue, gives her nose a delicate wipe.

'Oh, don't get upset. I'll see you later for a glass of red?'

Lynne waves before closing the car door. 'See you later. Right, you two, put your seat belts on.'

Chloe notices her voice change.

'You didn't need to tell Mrs Fitz about Charlie,' she says, twisting her hair between her thumb and forefinger until it pulls. 'You shouldn't have done that.'

'If Charlie hadn't done anything wrong, I wouldn't have to say anything, Chloe.' Lynne switches the engine on. 'Nor would I need to spend my day off shopping for clothes he's ruined on purpose.'

Charlie clicks his seat belt and slumps. Lynne turns. There's a large plaster on the back of her hand. She points at him.

'And don't think I'm going to spend a fortune on new P.E. shorts for you to ruin, my lad. I'll choose the first suitable ones I see.' She faces the front, adjusts her mirror so she can glare at him, tugs at the gears and, with a screech of wheels, they're off.

She raises her voice above the engine. 'I have better things to do with my time than mooch around looking for clothes for you. I have a hairdresser's appointment at eleven. Your father's taking me out tonight.' She looks both ways before pulling onto the avenue. 'And don't think I've forgotten what happened yesterday, Charlie Collins. I'm going to tell him exactly what you did.'

Chapter 19

'It doesn't seem to matter what I say, Graham. Or do. Charlie doesn't like me.' Lynne's voice cracks. 'And how he reacts, Chloe follows him, she does the same.' She looks quickly at him, then down at the table at her hands. 'And now this...' She shows him – the mark is faint, but still visible. 'He bit me.'

Graham is horrified. It's the last thing he could imagine his son doing. He glances around the restaurant. Why has she chosen to tell him this here? It's a few moments before he clears his throat and murmurs, 'No! Why? Why would he do that?'

'It's the truth, Graham.'

'It's just not like him. I know my son, Lynne.'

She lowers her head so he can't see her reaction. He thinks he sees a slight tightening of her mouth. But he could be wrong.

'You don't believe me?'

'I didn't say that.'

'It's what you meant.' She gulps, as though swallowing down a sob.

'No.' He stretches his hand across the table. 'Just tell me again?'

'I don't want to cause any trouble, Graham. Let's just forget it? Have a nice evening. I only wanted you to know I'm trying so hard, but it feels impossible sometimes. I feel so alone with this when you're not home...'

52

'I know. I understand.' He strokes her hand. 'We've been rushed off our feet getting the new dealership up and running. And the garage is crammed with so many MOTs. But I'll try to get home sooner. I promise.'

He feels the tension lift. She looks at him, gives him a watery smile.

'Promise?' She picks up her glass of wine and takes a sip.

'Promise.' He'll say anything to make this evening a good one. With Margaret's help he's bought a gold locket and chain to hold a photo of them on their wedding day. He's been anticipating the moment of giving it to Lynne all day. But now it's been spoiled by what his son has done. He's upset. 'And I promise to have a strong word with Charlie. Get him to apologise for what he did. It's unforgivable, and I'll tell him so. And, by the way, may I say how gorgeous you look in your new dress.'

'You think so?'

'Sensational. Red is so your colour.'

He's rewarded with another trembling smile. 'I liked the style so much I bought another in black. I blew my allowance and most of this month's salary on them. But I do have the Inner Wheel dinner in a fortnight and then the summer ball soon afterwards, and I couldn't possibly wear the same gown to both occasions. I didn't want to let you down with your standing in the community.'

'I'm sure the wives of my fellow Rotarians are all envious of you whatever you wear, love. You always look lovely.' Relieved that the trouble with his son has been put to one side for now, he smiles at the waiter as two dishes of prawn cocktail are placed in front of them.

'Thank you.'

Graham hopes the food will ease away the strained mood. This high-class Manchester restaurant was recommended by one of his friends at the Rotary. It's expensive but he wants to show his wife how much he loves her.

'This looks appetising, doesn't it?'

'It's so difficult,' Lynne says, barely acknowledging him, the waiter, or the food. 'I'm never sure what I should do...'

'I know.' Graham says. 'I do appreciate everything you're doing for us all, love. Leave it with me. Now, let's just enjoy the night. Is your starter all right?'

Lynne ignores him. She empties her glass in one gulp and waits until he refills it. 'I am trying. I so wanted to be their mother.' She takes another long sip. looking at him over the rim of the glass.

He's shocked. He pauses, trying to form the right sentence in his head as he picks up the small spoon and fork. 'I don't think that's what they want, Lynne. They don't want you to be their mother so soon. I think they just want you to be there for them. It'll take time for them to trust you...'

She pulls back her chin. 'Trust me?' She puts her wine glass down on the table with a thump. It splashes.

He's startled, aware that the couple at the next table is looking sharply at them, whispering.

'Perhaps that was the wrong way to put it. Sorry. I meant ... it's hardly three years since their ... since Anna died.'

'But you wanted me – us – to move in with you,' She pushes her prawn cocktail to one side, leans forward, hisses the words. 'It was your idea for us to be married.'

'I know, but...' Graham notices more people are surreptitiously watching them. It's all going wrong. A wave of hot humiliation rises to his throat. 'Lynne...' He gestures with his head, tries to make her see they can be heard.

She takes no notice. 'But now, after just weeks you think it was a mistake?'

He heaves a sigh. 'No. No, of course not. I don't mean that. I mean ... I think you – me – we just have to keep trying with them. Look, let's not argue, love. Try your starter, eh?'

'No! It works both ways, you know. You say you appreciate what I'm doing, Graham, but are you trying with my kids?'

'What?' She's turned it round on him. He doesn't know what to say.

'You need to make sure Saul and Evie feel like part of this family as well. Especially Saul. He hides it well, but he's a sensitive lad. I don't think you've spoken two words to him in this last week.'

'I have, love, honest. But he's not easy. He hardly talks to me either.'

Her face sets, a cold glint in her eyes.

'He's almost fourteen, a teenager. That's what they're like. I just wish you'd make as much effort with him as I do with your two.'

He stops even attempting to eat, puts his cutlery on the side plate and takes a large slurp of his wine. 'I'll try, Lynne.' Though he's not sure how. Saul is such a truculent lad. Graham frantically casts around for ideas. She's watching, waiting for him to say something. There's only one thing. 'I used to go fishing. Perhaps he'd like to come with me sometime?'

'I doubt that. I think that must be the biggest waste of time there is. Standing around, waiting for something to happen.' Her glass is empty. Before Graham can pour more wine for her, she takes the bottle and empties it.

'We need more wine.'

'I'll order another.' Graham gestures to the waiter, indicating the bottle. The man nods. 'And it's not, you know. Fishing gives you a right buzz when you catch something.'

'Like a cold?' Her smile is almost a smirk.

Graham feels an unfamiliar flutter of defensiveness run through him. But he doesn't allow it to show. He's learned how quickly his wife's moods can change and he doesn't want tonight spoiled. So he forces a low chuckle.

She doesn't speak again until the waiter arrives with another bottle and pours wine into her glass. 'Thanks.' She doesn't look at him until she realises he's still standing by the table. 'Yes?'

The waiter looks at the almost untouched prawn cocktails. 'Was there something wrong with the food, sir?'

'No.' Lynne answers for Graham. 'I've lost my appetite. Could we have the bill please.' She drains her glass, pours more, drinks that. When she stands, she's unsteady. 'Ready?' she says to Graham, swaying slightly.

'You can pay at reception on your way out, sir,' the man says.

Graham stands, embarrassed, allows a flicker of annoyance to rise. 'You're showing yourself up, Lynne.'

She staggers her way around the tables and, without collecting her coat from the reception, leaves.

Chapter 20

The aroma of frying bacon is drifting into the bedroom when Graham wakes.

After a sleepless night he's exhausted. At least it's Sunday and he doesn't need to go to work. But he's dreading the inevitable aggrieved atmosphere.

He sits up. It's definitely bacon. Swinging his legs over the edge of the bed he rubs the back of his head, pulls up his shoulders, trying to relieve the tension. When Lynne comes into the bedroom carrying a mug of coffee he's bewildered.

'Morning, sleepy head.' She bends down to kiss him. 'Breakfast in ten minutes.'

She sits alongside him, leans her head on his shoulder. 'I'm so sorry it all went wrong last night, sweetheart. That business with Charlie. upset me so much. It's one thing after another with him. You were so late getting home on Friday; I didn't want to worry you with it all then. And you worked again all day yesterday so there was no chance to tell you about it until we were at the restaurant.'

Another layer of guilt builds up inside Graham. It's his fault; he should have noticed how distressed she was, he should have asked why Charlie and Chloe were so subdued. And he didn't get around to giving her the locket.

'I'm sorry as well, love. I should have seen you were unhappy.'

She pats his leg, jumps up. 'All forgotten now.' She studies him, head to one side. 'But you will have a word with him, won't you?'

'A strong word, love, don't you worry about that.'

'Good.' Her smile is satisfied. 'Thank you.'

Graham tries to judge her mood. He doesn't know whether to feel happy or apprehensive. 'I'll do it now. Get it over with.'

'No.' Lynne frowns. 'Leave it until after breakfast. It's just us. Evie's had a sleepover at her friends – again. And Saul's still in bed.'

'The twins?'

She sniffs. 'In bed. I suppose. Come on.' She holds out her hand. 'Come down in your dressing gown. Then maybe, after breakfast, I can make it up to you.'

Glad that all seems to be okay again, Graham takes her hand. But, at the back of his mind he's worried. He needs to make sure that Charlie knows how wrong he's been, how both of his children have to behave better than they have so far.

Chapter 21

'So – what have you to say for yourselves?'

Charlie and Chloe shuffle closer together on Charlie's bed. Oscar, lying alongside them, lifts his head, gives a couple of slow wags of his tail. Chloe pulls the dog towards her; his soft coat gives her comfort. She'd heard her father and Lynne talking earlier in their bedroom and has been waiting for this moment since. She's ready to defend Charlie.

Lynne's in the next room, opening and closing drawers, moving around. Chloe knows she's listening and wonders what Dad would say if she got up and made sure the door was closed properly.

Charlie doesn't speak. But, when he looks at her, Chloe sees the defiance in his eyes. And she knows he's not going to back down, admit it was wrong.

'I just want to know what happened. Why you ... why you did what you did.'

'I bit her,' Charlie says. 'I had to.'

Chloe catches her breath. It's as though he doesn't care.

Their father sits on the bed, rests his arms on his thighs, holds out his hands. 'I'm ashamed of you, son.'

This isn't fair. Chloe kneels up. 'It wasn't his fault, Dad.' *He has to know the truth. He has to know how nasty Lynne is.* She holds onto his arm. 'He—'

'Let your brother tell me, love.'

'But...'

'Chloe!' He frowns at her.

She sinks back onto the bed, pulls Oscar close again.

She's not sure that Charlie will say what really happened; he looks so angry. And she knows she's right as soon as she sees him keeps his head down, pluck hard at the bed clothes and mutter, 'You won't believe me.'

Even when their dad says, 'I will, if you tell me the truth, Charlie.' Chloe sees that her brother won't speak. But he's struggling not to cry.

I'll say, I'll tell Dad what she did. Chloe puts her arm around Charlie. 'It wasn't Charlie's fault, Dad. It was *her.* She grabbed hold of Charlie and pinched him.'

'Chloe. What did I say?'

'Well, it's true...' Her voice rises with the indignation that's overwhelming her.

59

'Enough, all right?' Graham holds up his hand to stop her. 'I need to hear what Charlie has to say for himself.'

'Charlie?' Chloe gives him a shake. 'Tell Dad what happened. Please.'

The pause is a long one. When he eventually speaks his voice is low.

'Like Chloe says.' Charlie plucks harder at the covers. 'She knows I hate sprouts and she tried to make me eat them then she grabbed hold of me.'

'Lynne says she was taking your plate off you. You'd refused to eat the sprouts and she'd given up. And then you bit her.'

'She's lying, Dad.' Chloe moves from alongside her brother to him. 'It wasn't like that.'

This time he lets her talk. 'What was it like then?'

'She made him sit for ages because he wouldn't eat his sprouts.' She glances at Charlie. 'Then he hid them in the pocket of his shorts.' She waits for a reaction from their dad. When there was none, she said, 'So she grabbed his arm and pinched him.'

'It hurt. *She* did it on purpose.' Charlie looks daggers towards the door.

Chloe sees the disbelief on their father's face.

'I just can't believe she'd hurt you on purpose...'

'I knew you wouldn't listen. I knew you wouldn't believe me.' Charlie scrambles off the bed and stands facing his father, scowling.

'Dad!' Chloe joins her brother, puts her arms around him. 'You're not being fair.' She's shaking really hard.

'Shush, Cloe.' He's frowning. 'I'll talk to Lynne again. But you have to say you're very sorry, and it won't happen again, Charlie.'

'No.' There's anger and defiance in the word.

'Please.'

'No.'

'Apologize, or you're grounded after school until I say otherwise.'

'But I have football practice tomorrow. I'm on the first team, I can't miss.'

'Well, I'm sorry about that, but it's your own fault. No apology, no football practice. In fact nothing after school until I say otherwise.'

'Dad!' Chloe's horrified at the unfairness. Her heart's pounding. She waits for him to say he doesn't mean it; it's just something he's said in anger. But he continues.

'And you can stay in your room until I say you can come downstairs.'

'I don't want to go downstairs anyway.'

'I don't either.' Chloe keeps her voice quiet but determined.

They don't look towards him when he opens the door but Chloe catches a glimpse of Lynne waiting for their father on the landing. She must have heard, because Chloe sees her give him a kiss on his cheek. Hears her saying, 'Thank you, sweetheart.'

'I'm sorry, Charlie, it's not fair,' she whispers.

'I hate both of them,' he says. Turning towards the now closed door, he shouts, 'I hate you!'

Chapter 22

Graham moves across the bed to hug Lynne.

'What the hell do you think you're doing?' She pushes him away. 'Get away from me.'

'What's the matter?'

'As if you don't know.'

'I don't.' Graham runs his hands over his face. 'Honest, Lynne, I don't.'

Lynne switches on her bedside light. Glares at him. 'After this morning? You must be joking.'

Not this again. 'You've been all right with me all day. What's the matter now?'

'You haven't a bloody clue, have you?'

'No, I haven't. For God's sake, Lynne. I know the twins have been sulking upstairs, but I've left them to it.' He'd worried about them until he saw Evie in the kitchen making sandwiches for them when Lynne was outside talking to the neighbour. He'd poured two glasses of orange juice and added some chocolate biscuits on the tray, nodding his thanks to his stepdaughter. Had Lynne seen what they were doing? 'I thought we were okay. What is it?'

Her tone is cold. 'It's you, you soft arse – you and the namby-pamby way you dealt with that thug of a son of yours. And your precious daughter.'

The jibe hurts. There's a hard knot stuck at the back of Graham's throat that makes his voice husky. 'I did as you asked. You said thank you to me. You gave me a kiss, for God's sake. So why are you being like this?'

'Because I've had time to think, and I realised you did what you always do, baby them. Spoil them. He didn't apologize. You didn't make him apologize to me, Graham.'

'Other than drag him down the stairs afterwards, how could I? Even then I wouldn't have been able to make him.' He should stop, he knows he will only make things worse. 'Their version of events was different. They said it didn't happen like you told me. I'm sorry. I don't know what...'

'To believe? Go on, say it.'

Graham makes himself as still as possible. Waits. If he doesn't speak, maybe she won't.

But Lynne raises herself on one elbow, pushes her face into his. Her breath wine-stale. 'So, of course, it doesn't matter what he does, Graham, you will always take his – their side against me.'

'I don't. I didn't. But why should they lie?'

'Because that's what they do, for God's sake. When are you going to get that through your thick skull?'

'But he is being punished for biting your hand. And I also told him how ashamed I was of him, of them both.'

'Punished! By not being able to go to some stupid football practice. The lad deserved a good slap.'

Graham is horrified. 'I've never hit my kids, Lynne. I never would. Anna and I agreed...'

'Ah, the saintly Anna. Never did anything wrong. Perfect mother, perfect wife. Well, let me tell you, I know *you* were not the perfect husband. You should have heard half of the things she told me about you.' There's resentment in each aggressive word.

63

Graham sinks back against his pillow. Why would she say that about Anna? They'd had a good marriage. They'd loved one another. And Anna would never have bad-mouthed him to anyone – ever – anymore than he would have done about her. So why would Lynne say such nasty things?

Dear Sandie Shaw,

Dad wasn't like Dad today. I feel all sad inside. I don't like it here anymore. There's nobody on our side. Well theres Evie but she can't do anything. I see how Lynne looks at her, like she doesn't like her. And Evie goes out of the house a lot. I don't blame her cos Lynnes always nasty to Evie. I don't understand, shes nice to Saul and hes the most horrible boy I know. I wish one of the nighttime monsters would come and take Lynne and Saul away.

Chapter 23

'Does everything have to be a battle with you, Charlie Collins? Leave that light off.' Lynne has her hands on her hips. 'Can't you just give me a break for once? I told you earlier, I've had a bad headache all evening. I don't need this.'

'Chloe doesn't like the dark.' He stands on the landing, his hand hovering over the switch. Lynne doesn't understand. Or she's being mean. 'Dad lets us have the light on.'

'Well, I think this is just another thing for you to challenge me on.'

'What?' He doesn't understand what she means.

'Leave that light off, please. It's a waste of money.'

What's light got to do with money 'But Dad always lets us have the light on. And our bedroom doors open. Ask him.'

'But he's not here, is he? He's at a meeting.'

'Then leave it on for now?' He's trying so hard not to shout. 'Ask him when he's home?'

'No. And I won't be asking him when he gets home, either.'

Charlie sits down on the top stair. 'S'okay, Chloe, I'm here, I'll wait for Dad.'

'You'll do no such thing. You'll get into bed right this minute.'

'No.'

'If I have to come up these stairs...' Lynne grasps the banister. Charlie stands, ready to run, but stays where he is.

'Please?' He flicks the switch, closes his eyes against the dazzle, which lasts a few seconds.

The landing goes dark again. 'No.'

'Charlie.' Chloe shouts from her bed. 'Leave it. I'm all right, honest. Don't get into trouble.'

'S'okay.' He presses the switch again.

Lynne turns it off. 'I'm warning you...'

Charlie's palms are clammy, he knows he's beaten. Under the hall light he sees her face, brittle with anger. He's seen that look a lot over the last few weeks. When one of them does something, says something. Chloe says Lynne frightens her now. Charlie tries not to admit that. The fear sometimes blocks out the hatred he has for their stepmother. And Saul.

'Well, can you leave that one on, then? Down there? In the hall?'

'What have I just said? We're not made of money.'

Charlie feels his shoulders twitch. *One last try*.

'Dad always let us keep the light on when it was just me, Chloe and him.' The breath quivers in his throat. 'Mummy always let us, as well.'

'Well, *Mummy* isn't here either, is she?'

I wish you weren't. 'I wish you...'

She grabs the banister and climbs the stairs, one deliberate step at a time, not taking her eyes off him.

Charlie waits until she's within three treads of him before turning and running back into his room. Oscar looks up at him from the floor at the other side of the bed where Charlie had told him to stay. He sits up when Lynne gets to the landing, a low growl in his throat.

'Shush, boy.' The dog lies down again. Charlie pulls the covers around him, his fingers tight on the edge of the sheet, one hand holding Oscar's collar. She's going to come into his room. He senses her closeness, hears the floorboard on the landing creak. And then she speaks.

'If I hear you get out of that bed again...'

He listens to her noisy breathing. When he hears her going back downstairs, he counts the fourteen treads before daring to call out.

'S'okay Chloe, I'm here.' He doesn't hear her answer.

But he hears *hers*.

'One word, one more peep out of you, my lad, and I'll be up there, and you'll wish you hadn't been born.'

Charlie listens to the harsh cackle of laughter that erupts in the lounge. Saul. And Charlie knows he's not safe in his own home.

Chapter 24

Lynne stands by the sink, her back to the window, blocking out the dull light of the morning. Arms crossed. Watching.

At the back door, Oscar's whining. Every now and then he jumps up at the door.

'Can he come in?' Chloe half-rises from her chair.

'No. Not while you're eating.'

The only noise in the kitchen is the clatter of spoons on dishes, knives scraping toast, Saul's slurping of his tea. Charlie squeezes Chloe's hand under the table. She's pale, her eyes a bit pink, so he knows she's still upset. Daddy hadn't asked what was wrong before he left. He'd only dropped a kiss on the top of his and Chloe's head and said he needed to work on the garage accounts.

Chloe hasn't eaten any of her cereal. The cornflakes float around in the milk, all soggy.

'Okay?' he mutters.

'No.' Chloe shakes her head. 'Can't.'

'We don't waste food, do we.' Lynne turns, her hands on her hips.

Charlie takes a last spoonful of his breakfast, swops his dish for his sister's and gobbles the cereal as fast as he can.

Lynne's dress rustles as she crosses the kitchen. He gulps down the cornflakes and drops his spoon into the dish with a clatter.

'Finished!' He can't keep the triumph out of his voice, he feels like he did when he won that egg and spoon race in the school athletics. When he looks across the table, he's surprised to see Evie staring back at him. She's grinning. Lynne's hand reaches past him to pick up the dishes, one bowl catches him on the ear and he yelps at the pain.

Evie winces. Saul sniggers, tips his chair back on two legs, noisily swallows the last of his tea before slamming the chair forwards and banging the mug on the table.

Lynne doesn't react. 'Come on then, out you go, I haven't got all day to clear up after you lot.' Charlie notices she only touches his stepbrother. She pats his arm as he slouches past her. 'Have a good day in school.'

Charlie sees Saul shrug her hand off, before he turns to sneer at him. He's glad Saul doesn't go to their school. But they'll go to his in a couple of years. The thought brings a nauseous tilt in his stomach.

'See you later,' Evie says to them.

Charlie doesn't look at her, but he sees Chloe glance up, sees the small, grateful smile.

'I like her. Evie.' Chloe pulls her hood forward to stop the rain wetting her hair. 'She's nice.'

'S'pose. Better than him, anyroad.'

'Anyone's better than Saul. Even Barry Norris.'

A chuckle fizzes up in Charlie's throat. Mean Barry Norris – the class bully. Norris leaves them alone because there are two of them and they look out for one another. 'Yeah.' He nudges Chloe. 'You're right.'

'Hey!' She miss-steps into a puddle on the pavement, does a little skip, laughing. Shoves him back. 'Dafty!'

He laughs, hunches against the drizzle seeping through the neck of his anorak.

A double-decker bus swishes past sending up a wave of spray. Rain-smeared windows filled with pale faces pass in a blur. Chloe squeals, dodges behind the thick trunk of a sycamore planted in a square of soil in the pavement. Charlie laughs. She sticks her tongue out at him, and giggles.

'Charlie?' She runs to keep up with him.

'Yeah?'

'We could ask Dad?' She's walking almost sideways, taking small hopping steps. Charlie can't remember her ever just walking. Dad sometimes calls her Skippy, after a telly programme he used to watch.

'About leaving the light on?'

'Yeah.'

'Okay. S'pose we can try.'

They walk past the newsagents, hurry past the greengrocer who also sells fish. Chloe wrinkles her nose at the smell, Charlie holds his nostrils, screws up his mouth to make her laugh. He's glad she's looking a bit better than she did at breakfast.

Nearer the school they catch up with other pupils, separate into their different groups of friends.

'See you later,' Chloe shouts, swept along with the cluster of giggling girls.

'Yeah.' Charlie hitches his bags higher on his shoulder, is slapped on his back by one of his mates.

'Hiya. Footy practice after school.'

'Hiya. No, can't tonight.' Charlie doesn't say why. To be truthful he is ashamed of biting Lynne, but equally determined not to apologize. He's hoping his dad will relent. Or forget the punishment. He watches his sister's blonde hair in the middle of the crowd funnelling through the main doors of the school. Safe – for now. That's what really matters.

Chapter 25

'Is that seat dry enough to sit on?'

Charlie's slumped on the garden seat, his hands in his school trouser pockets.

'S'okay.'

Graham touches the wood; the earlier rain has dried. 'How's your day at school gone then, son?'

'Was all right, s'pose.' Charlie shrugs. 'Missed practice though.'

'I know. But you know what you need to do about that, don't you?' His son doesn't show he's even heard 'You have to apologize.' The thought of Charlie biting Lynne makes him feel so sick he can't even say it.

He knows Anna would insist on knowing the exact circumstances, that she wouldn't have judged until she knew both sides. Unlike him. He'd taken Lynne's word without question. It makes him feel ashamed, so he softens his voice.

'I thought we could have a word before tea.' Graham clears his throat. 'Lynne says you were rude to her last night. Again. What's going on, Charlie? What's the matter?' Graham's not fooled by the nonchalant pose. He can see his son's rapid blinking, the lower lip caught between his teeth. 'Charlie.'

'She doesn't like us.' He won't look at Graham.

'I'm sure that's not true.'

'Tis. She's mean.'

Graham lets the aggressive tone pass. He keeps his voice calm. 'How is she mean, son?' He bends forward, his forearms resting on his thighs, attempting to see under his son's fringe as it flops over his eyes.

Charlie shrugs. 'Last night, she wouldn't listen.'

'About the landing light?'

'Yeah.'

'She's still cross about what you did to her. Can't you just say sorry about that, son?'

Charlie shakes his head.

Graham sighs. 'Do you want to tell me what happened last night?'

'No!' he huffs a dismissive sound. '*She's* already told you, hasn't she?'

'Now then, Charlie.' *Why is it always like this, these days?*
'Now you *are* being rude.'

Graham stops when he sees the tears sliding down his son's face. He moves closer, drawing Charlie towards him. 'I know it's hard, love. I do know all these changes have been hard.'

Charlie bursts into noisy sobs, burrows his face into his father's chest. Graham waits, every now and then giving Charlie a slight squeeze. 'I know, I know.' He's way out of his depth. Anna knew how to say the right things at times like this; how to make them feel better when they were upset.

Charlie mutters something, his voice muffled against Graham's jumper. He pulls back, looks at his son, who only pushes his face further against him.

Graham strokes his son's head. Charlie, like Chloe, has

inherited his mother's thick blonde hair. It makes him sad that they both will only see that from photographs.

'What, son? What did you say?'

Charlie raises his voice. 'I miss Mummy. Chloe and me, we miss her.'

Graham's eyes smart.

'I know,' he says again, slowly. 'So do I.'

Behind them the kitchen window closes with a crash. Graham doesn't turn around to look.

Chapter 26

'Who was on the phone?' Lynne stands at the top of the stairs.

Graham looks up at her. He can't quite make out her attitude: confrontational or merely curious.

She's still in her dressing gown. He'd forgotten it was her day off. She's been cool with him since she heard him talking with Charlie in the garden. Three days ago. He knows they should have talked to Charlie together, sorted out his problems between them. But for a grown woman to sulk for three days is ridiculous. Something in their marriage is being eroded and he's not sure what to do about it.

'Mum's neighbour,' he says. 'Mum's had a fall. Twisted her ankle. Didn't you hear the phone?'

'No.' She walks slowly down the stairs, fingers tapping on the banister.

'It rang for quite a while, you know. I didn't answer it at first because I thought it would be for you, with it not being Mum's week for calling me.' Since the wedding his mother only calls on alternate weeks. He knows she's still angry with him. It's upsetting she doesn't understand he needs to move on.

But his new life isn't working out quite like he thought it would.

He rubs the back of his neck, waits to see if Lynne adds anything. When she doesn't, he says, 'She's asked if I'll go to see Mum. Make sure she's all right.'

'And will you?'

'You don't mind, do you?'

'Why should I?' She angles her head to one side. Stares at him.

You shouldn't.

'Things so quiet at the garage, are they now? Unlike last week when you needed to be there all the time to get your accounts up to date? The accounts you have yet to share with me – your wife.'

'What?' It's never occurred to Graham that he has to tell her anything about the business accounts. 'The accounts? Why would you want to know about the garage's accounts, love?'

'Because I'm your wife.'

'I'm sure you'd find them boring.'

'I'm entitled to know.'

'Not really – and I'd rather we talked about what I should do. After what's happened to Mum.'

Lynne shakes her head as though she's shaking off his words. 'Yet that woman ... the wife of your precious friend...'

'Margaret? Good God, Lynne, she works there.'

'So?'

'So it's her job to know. It's not anything...'

'To do with me? Is that what you were going to say?'

The anger has been rising slowly in Graham over the last few minutes. First the sulking, now this ridiculous obsession about the accounts. He tries again.

'About Mum....'

'Oh, shut up about your stupid mother.'

He can't help himself. He loses his temper.

'Enough! You could cause bother in an empty house, Lynne. I want to talk about my mother. She needs me—'

The violence of the slap across his face stops his words. He gasps, tastes blood as her engagement ring cuts into his lip and it bursts open.

'Who the hell do you think you are?' Lynne's hands are clenched by her sides 'Well, I'll tell you who you're not. You're not my father, so don't start thinking you can control me. And I'm not my weak, snivelling mother. So don't think you can ever speak to me like that – ever again.'

She spins on her heel and walks to the kitchen.

Graham's lip is throbbing and, when he touches it, it's hot and swollen.

He's been sitting on the stairs for the best part of half an hour, waiting to see what his wife will do next. Or say. But there are only the quiet muffled sounds of her moving around in the kitchen.

'Lynne, I don't want to quarrel,' he says eventually. 'I'm sorry if I upset you. I didn't know what your father was like. You've never told me. And I'm not like that, you know that, love.'

The cut opens up the second he speaks and starts to bleed.

74

He dabs at it with his handkerchief. 'But I have to go to Mum. You must see that...'

She doesn't answer.

He tries again.

'You could come with me?' He waits before adding, 'if you'd like to? I'm sure she would appreciate that.'

Still there's silence.

'No, sorry. Silly idea,' he says, louder. 'I know you can't just up and leave all your patients at a moment's notice. Well, how about I get there and back in a day? Just to see she's all right, like? Make sure someone is keeping an eye on her.'

He hears soft footsteps.

When she appears at the door, her face is twisted in fury, her arm raised, a cup in her hand. A flash of alarm zigzags through him. She turns and throws it at the back door.

Chapter 27

'I'll be back as quick as I can.' Graham's trembling as he wraps the last of the newspaper over the broken shards of the cup. He hadn't been prepared for the hatred in Lynne's face when she'd appeared with it in her hand. 'So that's okay?' he says, hears the apprehension in his voice. Silence. 'Lynne?'

He sees her hands are gripping the sink, the knuckles pale through the skin. He's less and less sure how Lynne will react to things these days. But this time she's being totally unreasonable. He drops the parcel of broken cup into the kitchen bin. 'Look, if it was your mother...'

'Which you know I haven't got. Nor any brothers or sisters.' She flings her arm in a huge circle. 'This ... this is all I've got, Graham, and it's all going wrong.' She's blinking frantically as if to hold back tears.

He crosses the kitchen to hold her. She's right, she has no one else but him and the kids. He forgets that. 'I know, I know. I'm sorry.' She lets herself be hugged, but when he adds, 'We'll talk when I get back,' she pushes him away. 'I'll just see how things are with Mum, make sure it is just a sprained ankle, and things are set up so she can manage.'

He really wants to say he's going to bring his mother back with him. That's what he would have done without a moment's thought in the past. But he knows that's not possible now. He doubts either woman would want that.

'Right then, I've packed an overnight bag so I'll be off.'

Lynne's on one of the kitchen chairs, flicking through the pages of a magazine.

'Oh, by the way, if you don't mind, with me not here tonight I think it best if you left the landing light on for Chloe.' He adds quickly, 'Yes, I know she's not a baby, but the dark has always been the one thing she's nervous about.' A voice inside him tells him to stop talking. But he can't – he promised Charlie. 'So, leave the light on when they first go to bed. Please? Lynne?'

'I'm not talking about this.' She continues to turn the pages of the magazine.

'I just—'

She moves quickly. Stands up. Knocking his shoulder with her own, she pushes past him out of the kitchen. He stumbles backwards, catching hold of a chair to stop himself falling. It rocks on its legs. He steadies it, trying to steady himself at the same time.

'So, leave the landing light on. All right?'

The words dry up in his throat when she doesn't answer. But he's kept his promise to Charlie and he's sure she will leave the landing light on. Course she will. She wouldn't be that spiteful. Surely?

Chapter 28

Chloe lets her father give her a goodbye hug even though she doesn't want him to go. She knows she's being selfish; Granny needs him. *But we need him as well.* The rebellious thought hovers.

'I'll be back as soon as I can, yeah? I'll just make sure Granny's all right, and then I'll be home. I'll give her your love. Have a good day in school and just try to be good for...' He looks towards the house. 'Eh?'

'I promise.'

Graham pats Oscar who's standing alongside her. 'Charlie? Just try, eh?'

'Okay,' Charlie mutters.

They watch him get into his blue Vauxhall Cresta. When he smiles and sticks his thumb up, Chloe manages a half-hearted attempt to do the same. Charlie doesn't move.

Their dad sets off along the drive, flashing the hazard lights in the way he always does.

'I wish we could have gone to stay with Auntie Margaret,' Charlie says. 'Mark keeps asking when I'm going to go over after school.'

'Well, you can't. You can't go anywhere 'til you've said sorry. Not even to Auntie Margaret's.' Chloe stands on tiptoes to try to see the car on Ingram Avenue but can't because of the height of the long beech hedge which lines the length of the garden.

When she turns back to the house, she sees the misery on her brother's face. She takes hold of his hand, something he won't normally let her do these days. But this time he clutches her fingers tightly.

'I'm scared, Chlo.'

'Of *her*?'

'*Him*, mostly. Saul.'

'And me. I don't want to be here without Dad,' she says. 'But Evie says we can go into her room after school, if we like. Even before she comes home. She says Saul wouldn't dare go in there. She said she'd clout him one, if he ever does.'

They share a nervous laugh.

'We just need to stay together all the time we're here.'

They look towards the house. There's a figure standing behind the glass of the front door. Very still. A shiver runs along Chloe's spine. She glances at Charlie. He doesn't appear to have noticed. She gives his hand a small shake.

'Granny needs Dad. And we need to get ready for school.'

'I wish we could go and live with Granny.' Charlie shrugs.

'And me. But we can't. So come on…'

They march towards the house. The figure moves away as they get nearer.

'It'll be all right, Charlie. I promise. We just need to stick together.'

'Yeah.' He strides over the step into the hall. His shoulders jerk upwards around his ears. 'I know.'

Chapter 29

'Right place for you, little shit. Say it. Say it's the right place for you.'

Charlie hears the words, the squeals of laughter, through the gushing water pouring over his head. He holds his breath, terrified it will get into his nose, his mouth. He's going to choke. But he still recognises the voice. Saul. Saul shouldn't be here; he shouldn't be in his and Chloe's school with all his friends. How have they got in without any of the teachers seeing them?

His neck hurts where someone is gripping it, fingers digging into his skin, keeping him crouched over the lavatory bowl.

'Flush it again.'

More laughter.

Charlie balls his hands into fists.

'Let me go,' he manages. 'I'll tell Dad...'

'Dad!!' High-pitched taunts. '*Tell Daddy*!'

The vicious pushing increases, forcing him to his knees. The edge of the porcelain, hard against his chest, makes him gasp in pain.

'Take that back.' Each word comes with a shove from Saul. 'Take that back. One word to that useless old bugger and you're dead, you little shit.' A knee in his spine then. 'Got it?'

'Yes! Yes!'

'One more for good luck.' Some other boy's voice.

The lavatory is flushed again. Charlie has forgotten to hold his breath. He's swallowing the water. He's going to drown.

All at once the pressure lifts. He's coughing, choking. There's movement all around him. A series of thumps across the back of his head. He flinches. Waits. What next?

Warmth on his neck. Liquid runs around to his shoulders, down his shirt front. Pee. One of them has peed on him.

Then he's alone with the swish of the cloakroom door and the sound of running footsteps growing fainter. Somewhere a man shouts. 'Hey. You boys. What are you doing in this school?'

The Head. Charlie hopes desperately Mr Harrison doesn't come into the cloakroom. He crumples to the wet grimy floor, his foot stuck under the sharp edge of the door. He blinks against the sudden smarting of tears. He won't cry. And he won't always be this age, this size. Clenching his teeth, he makes himself a promise. One day ... one day, he will make his stepbrother pay.

Chapter 30

'Hey, you two.' Evie appears at the living room door. 'Everything okay?'

Chloe takes in a deep breath, ready to say what Saul did.

Charlie digs his elbow into her side. He keeps his eyes on the television. 'All okay.'

'What are you watching?'

'Blue Peter.'

'Ah, used to be my fav programme when I was your age. Anyway, don't say I don't give you anything.' Evie holds out a paper bag and whispers, 'Our secret, all right?'

Chloe reaches over, takes hold of the bag and peers inside. 'A torch!'

'It's just in case...'

'You heard?'

'Yep. And I'm sorry my mother's being so mean.'

Chloe looks at Charlie, then at the lounge door.

'It's okay, she's in the back garden talking to next door.'

Chloe stands up and hugs Evie. 'Thank you.'

'No telling, mind. Especially not to Saul. No trouble from him?'

'No.' Charlie gives Chloe a warning frown.

But she's determined Evie should know what Saul did to her brother. 'Tell Evie about today, Charlie. Tell her what Saul has done. If you don't, I will.'

When he doesn't answer she quickly tells Evie.

Evie shakes her head. 'You need to tell your dad when he comes back from seeing your granny,' she says quietly. 'My brother can't get away with that.'

'Dad won't do anything,' Charlie snaps. 'He won't believe me.'

'He will if you show him your jumper. Show Evie,' Chloe has great faith that her stepsister will be able to help.

'No. Shut up, Chlo.' Shame burns Charlie's face.

'It's not right. Saul's a bully.'

'Chloe's right.' Evie crosses her arms. 'I could tell your dad, if you like? If he knows that I believe you...'

'No! It would only cause more trouble. And it won't stop Saul.'

'I won't say anything if you don't want me to. But if you change your mind... I'm sorry you're having such a bad time.' Evie shakes her head. 'I bet you wish we'd never moved in.' Neither answer. 'Anyway...' She pats Chloe's hand. 'You know where I am if there is anything you think I can do. I am so sorry.' She nods towards the torch in Chloe's hand. 'You could always clock him one with that.'

When neither of them returns her smile, she shakes her head again. 'Just remember, I'm on your side.'

For the first time in weeks Chloe feels a glimmer of comfort. But when she glances at Charlie, she also knows he doesn't.

Chapter 31

Chloe moves her head on the pillow to look at Charlie. Their noses almost touch. She can smell the spearminty toothpaste on his breath. 'We *should* tell Dad what Saul did today.' It makes her angry when she thinks about it. 'He can't get away with doing something so horrid.'

'I said no. It'll make things worse. I'm okay.'

In the gloom Chloe sees something, an expression, flit across his face, too quick for her to guess what he's thinking. Touching his shoulder, she whispers the only thing she can think to say.

'You don't smell as bad as when you came home.'

'Thanks! Thanks a lot.'

'Sorry. Just meant...'

'I know.'

She hears him gulp, wipes her fingers over his face. Feels the wet tears.

'It's okay, Charlie.'

'I'm all right.' His voice rough.

'What did you do with your shirt?'

'Shoved it under the tap in the bath and put it at the bottom of the wash basket. She won't find it until she washes next Monday.'

'But tomorrow? What will you wear for school?'

'Got my old shirt.'

'It's too small for you.'

'I'll wear it under a jumper. Stop going on about it, Chlo.'

A car passes outside. They watch the line of the headlights cross the ceiling. Chloe hears laughter and voices from the television downstairs, hears *her* laughter, loud and shrill. It feels as if there are strangers in her house.

Dear Sandie Shaw,

Why can't Dad see how horrid Lynne is. Shes made him different somehow. Im not sure hes happy anymore. Evie gave us a torch today for the dark in the night. I like Evie. She's kind.

Chapter 32

The morning sun warms Graham's face as he walks around the garden. It casts a long shadow underneath the lilac tree. He gently tickles Oscar's ears and is rewarded with a warm, wet lick on his hand.

'All right, boy,' he murmurs, gazing past the long back garden to the large, red-bricked house. It was built by his father-in-law. It has been his and Anna's home since they were first married. He's loved living here for the last fifteen years. It's a family home. *Was.* He breathes out hard, ignores the intrusive thought that slides disloyally, involuntarily into his mind. Something's gone wrong and he doesn't know what to do about it.

He watches the swifts darting in and out of the mock-Tudor cladding on the steeply pitched gable ends. They're early this year.

Nothing he said could make things right between him and his mother. She's so angry with him, and annoyed her friend had rung him. The guilt comes back; he should have insisted the twins and his mother came to the wedding. *What the hell is wrong with me?*

He should have tried harder to persuade his mother to come back with him today, so they could look after her. In the past there would have been no question. Anna would have been adamant.

With five bedrooms they could manage easily, if he made what he calls his study at the back of the house into a bedroom. It would stop him worrying about her being alone. Being lonely. He knows his father would have expected him to look after her; to be the son he'd been ... before.

Perhaps it's his fault Lynne and his mother don't get on, but Lynne hasn't helped either.

He rolls his shoulders. Being with his mother has brought back ghosts: his childhood, when he'd always felt loved, safe, happy moments from his first marriage, the joy he and Anna had shared when Charlie and Chloe were born.

The thoughts of the twins abruptly bring him back to the present; he wonders how things went while he wasn't here. Hopes there's been no trouble. They'd already gone to school by the time he arrived home. Guilt and depression consume him.

At least he'd driven home as soon as the carer arrived. That should go some way into putting him in the good books.

He sees his wife pulling back the bedroom curtains, glancing down at him, giving the curtains a sharp tug closed again.

Maybe tonight. Maybe – over a glass of wine tonight – he'll broach the subject of his mother staying with them. If she doesn't decide to visit Sue Fitz, for once.

Chapter 33

Chloe sits back against the side of the bed, holding the pieces of Lego she's been working on. She studies her brother who's kneeling in front of his wardrobe. He's hunched over the Lego garage he's been making all week. He's not the same these days. Every now and then she sees his shoulders move in a sort of half-shrug. His face is tight, no expression.

'I'm glad Dad's home.' Chloe tries a piece of red Lego, decides it doesn't fit, puts it back down on the carpet. 'I wish we'd had more time to talk to him before he had to meet Uncle Phil at the garage.'

'Why?' His hands stop fitting the two pieces he had been clipping together. 'What would you have said to him?'

'Nothing much.' Chloe has the urge to hold him, to tell him everything is going to be okay, but she doesn't, because it won't be okay. Nothing will ever be the same as it used to be. They're not the same family they were before.

Charlie is watching her, his eyebrows drawn together.

'I wasn't going to tell him about Saul, honest.' She shuffles towards him and, knowing he will hate it, hugs him. 'I understand why you don't want to say anything to him about that.'

'Yeah?' He's letting her cuddle him. Perhaps he knows she needs the comfort as much as him.

'Yeah. It would cause a row.' She puts her head on his shoulder. 'I wanted to ask him how Granny is?'

Now he moves, subtly leaning back so she has to sit up; the moment gone.

Chloe understands. She sits back on her haunches. 'You hungry? Want to go down for some supper?'

'I'm not bothered. I think I heard Saul go downstairs a few minutes ago.'

'Right.'

Saul's left his record player on. She heard him earlier, clapping in time to the deep bass. She'd tried to shut him out.

'Is Evie upstairs?' Charlie snaps together two corner pieces of the roof of the Lego garage. He keeps his voice casual, but Chloe knows what he's asking. It means Saul and Lynne will be downstairs together. Charlie won't want to go.

'I think so. There's no sound from her room but I think she said she had to revise.'

'I'm not hungry,' he says. 'We could wait until Dad gets home, have supper with him?'

Lynne has stopped speaking to them when their dad isn't in the same room. She won't even answer questions if they need to know something. Chloe's been watching her – the way she pretends not to hear when one of them speaks to her. She knows Lynne hears – her pale complexion reddens and she flicks her nose with the back of her forefinger.

She's seen Charlie repeat a question over and over again, just to annoy Lynne. Sees the compression of her mouth, the tightening of her hands.

It frightens Chloe.

'Right.' She says now, points to the small plastic petrol pumps. 'Shall I fix them to the forecourt now?'

'If you like.'

'We'll wait 'til Dad gets home, then? To eat?'

'Yeah.'

Chapter 34

When Graham gets back from his meeting with Phil, he's surprised to see Lynne's waiting for him.

After days of not speaking to him she's sitting on the settee. When he sits beside her she grips his hand. She's crying.

'I'm at the end of my tether, Graham. I don't know what else I can do. They were so difficult last night.'

This is different from the biting incident; from other times she's told him that the twins were being awkward. Different from the anger she can barely contain sometimes.

'I'll have another word with them, love,' he says eventually, realising she's waiting for him to say something. 'I'm sure they don't mean to upset you.'

'I suppose not.' She sniffs. 'I know they resent me though, and I don't know what to do. It's so upsetting, Graham.'

'I know. I'll go and talk to them. Are they upstairs?'

'Yes, they won't come down.'

'Don't worry.' Graham is exasperated, he doesn't need this: first, his worry about his mother and her refusal to let him help her, then Phil telling him that money is going missing in the petty cash in the office. Now his kids are playing up again. He won't have it.

'They know right from wrong and I'll sort them out. I know you only want what's best for them, love.'

'I do! I love them. If only they would give me a chance. I was only telling Marlene – you know the receptionist at the surgery – you met her on our wedding day?' He nods, even though he doesn't remember the woman at all. 'Well, I was telling Marlene what great kids they are, how I love them as much as my own two.'

It's not what she says at other times, but he's grateful she says she's trying to make them all into a proper family, despite her erratic moods. He pulls her to him. 'Thanks, love.'

'And Evie and Saul love them as well. Saul especially. He tries hard to be a big brother to Charlie.'

'Does he?'

'Yes.' Lynne looks at Graham, as though expecting him to say something else.

'That's good of him.' He's not sure how true that is, but he's not going to rock the boat tonight.

'Yes, it is.' She straightens up, blows her nose. 'I'm going next door for an hour. Is that all right?'

He's surprised at the change in her. And that's she's even asking; she doesn't normally bother. 'Of course.'

'Top up first though.' She holds out her glass, smiling. 'Sorry about throwing the cup, by the way.'

She says it in such an offhand way, he's not sure how to respond. She's still smiling. So he says, 'Well, at least it wasn't one from the best set.'

She giggles.

But it *was* Anna's favourite cup, wrapped in tissue paper and hidden at the back behind the serving dishes in the corner wall cupboard. He wondered if Lynne had known that. How could she?

He goes to the drinks cabinet, chewing on the inside of his cheek. These days he doesn't know who she's going to be from one minute to the next. Let alone one day to the next.

Chapter 35

'Saul, please, can you keep the noise down?' Graham peers around the bedroom door. 'Saul?'

The boy has his back to Graham. He's bouncing up and down, knees bent, arms flailing, air-playing a guitar, yelling along to the record player. He turns.

'Noise? Oh, man you really haven't a clue. This is music, man, the best. It's the Kinks!'

'Well, whatever it is, please turn it down.'

Grinning, Saul crosses the room to scream in Graham's face. *'You really got me. Oooh, you really got me, yeah. You really got me.'* He bends backwards and forwards, still pretend-strumming.

Graham pushes him back. 'Get away! Idiot.' When he sees Saul stagger dramatically back, he knows he's made a bad mistake. He raises his voice. 'Look, I'm sorry, I didn't mean to push you. But can't you see how thoughtless you're being. It's ten o'clock at night and Charlie and Chloe are trying to get to sleep...'

'And I'm trying to do my homework, you selfish sod.' Evie pushes past Graham and yanks the needle off the record. 'Just stop it, Saul.'

'Piss off, you. If you've scratched it...' He grabs hold of the record and examines it, looking for damage. He scowls at Graham. 'And you.' He shoves him with his shoulder. 'You as well. Go on, piss off out of my room.'

'I'll tell your mother how you've spoken to me. And your sister.'

'I wouldn't waste your breath, Graham.' Evie touches his arm. 'He's really not worth it.' She gestures; raises two fingers at him, before going back to her room. Shouts, 'Idiot!'

Saul clicks the switch on the turntable, the stylus hovers over the record, lowers and the track begins playing.

'Saul! I've warned you.'

'And who do you think Ma'll believe? You or me. Huh?' Saul smirks. 'What you don't seem to realise, old man, is that you're onto a loser every time. Every bloody time, when it comes to who Ma chooses. Because that's what you are ... a loser. Bugger off out of my room.'

Graham leaves. He's shaking, but he can't decide whether it's anger, or trepidation. He knows he'll have it out with Lynne, once and for all. That lad's not going to get away with speaking to him like that. Not in his own house. He won't put up with it. He's had enough.

There's also some problem between Saul and Charlie and Chloe. He's not sure what the little sod is doing to the twins but something's going on. If only he wasn't so tired of all the hassle with Lynne, he'd be able to sort it.

The noise from Saul's room starts up again, but at least it's not as loud. Graham pauses on the stairs, glances at the doors of his children's bedrooms.

His earlier talk with them, when he'd taken them their milk and biscuits, hadn't gone as planned. They'd refused to tell him what had happened while he was away. They were more worried how their Granny was, and once he'd reassured them, they couldn't stop talking about their birthday party next week.

He'd let them divert him; he realises that now. Should he talk to them again? They'd both been in bed for an hour and were probably asleep, despite that lad's bloody noise.

He's dithering at the top of the stairs, hears the back door close. Lynne's home. She'll want to know what he's said to the twins. With heavy steps he goes downstairs.

Chapter 36

Another sleepless night. Lynne was annoyed with him when he'd mumbled his excuse for not chastising the twins. Had gone to bed, turned her back on him.

Breakfast is eaten in silence. He's tried to make conversation, but all he gets are monosyllabic answers, so he gives up. He can be just as awkward.

Charlie and Chloe give him a quick kiss on his cheek before they leave. Evie nods at him. Saul smirks, pushing out his tongue from behind his lower lip. Graham guesses he's given Lynne his version of the night before.

She's banging around the kitchen, clearing away the breakfast things from the table, loading the washing machine. But then she turns to him.

'I am so angry, Graham.'

'Yes, I know. But—'

She doesn't give him a chance to speak.

'You'll never guess what's happened. Apparently, Mrs Mitchell...' She sighs, exasperated when he frowns, not understanding. 'You know, Mrs Mitchell. I've told you often enough about her. From one of the big houses on Backcroft Lane?' She glowers. 'She always said that I was her favourite nurse. I've been going to her for months; we'd become quite close. Suddenly she's been moved to live with her daughter somewhere near London.' She snorts. 'She wouldn't have wanted to go, she always told me what a greedy, money-grabbing woman her daughter was. I knew nothing about it until the surgery told me this morning.' It doesn't justify why she was in a mood last night, but Graham lets that go. 'When I saw she'd been taken off my list...' She closes the washing machine door with a vicious crash.

'You're upset. Were you fond of her? This Mrs Mitchell?' he says when she stops for breath, relieved she's not raging at him.

'No.' She looks at him, exasperation pulling in the corners of her mouth. 'Oh, I knew you wouldn't understand.'

'You're always saying they expect you to do too much,' he says, mildly, 'So this patient, is one less for you to worry about.'

'Sometimes, Graham, you can be so stupid.' She shrugs his arms away as he tries to hold her. 'God, I haven't time for any of that. Move, please, I need to get on.'

'Yes, I suppose I should get on as well.' *Christ, this is hard work.* 'How about I get some steak from the butcher, and I do us a slap-up meal tonight? Just the two of us. I'll ask Phil and Margaret if they'll have the twins over after school. Chloe and Charlie get on well with Mark, their son, with them all being around the same age. How will that suit?'

Lynne's shoulders slump. She turns towards him.

'I'm sorry, Graham. I shouldn't take things out on you. That would be lovely, thank you.'

The kiss is fleeting, but it's enough to reassure him. She's annoyed with the surgery, not him. And he overreacted last night with Saul. So, if the lad hasn't mentioned it to his mother, neither will he.

And then he remembers; he still hasn't reminded her about Charlie and Chloe's birthday party next week.

Dear Sandie Shaw,

I hate Saul as much as Charlie does, he's as nasty as Lynne is. And theres nothing we can do, we cant tell anyone whats happening. Not anybody. Its our birthday in four days. Daddy says we can have a party and invite five friends each. I have to decide which friends and its difficult becos I like everybody in my

93

class. I don't know what dress to wear. I wish I had one like yours – you know the blue shiny one you wore last week on Top of the Pops. I think I might not wear shoes either.

Chapter 37

'What are you going to wear, Charlie?' Bubbles of happiness are popping in Chloe's stomach.

'What? When?'

'Tonight.' Chloe hops from one foot to the other, glancing both ways along the road for Graham's car. 'For our party? I can't decide on my pink dress – you know, the check one, or my blue one. I think the check one is getting too small though. But Susan Lewis says she's wearing her blue one.' She pouts, then grins. Mine's a nicer blue though.' She's decided. 'I'll wear that. Oh, come *on*, Dad!'

'I don't know. I don't care. Gosh, Sis, you do go on about some silly things. Lads don't care about stuff like that. Anyway, like I said last night, nothing's been said about the party for the last two days – we don't know if it's even going to happen.'

'Don't say that.' The bubbles inside her vanish. 'You don't think...?' She shakes her head. 'No, she wouldn't be that mean. I bet she's got some surprises for us and wants to keep them secret.' She glowers at him suspiciously. 'Why? What have you heard?'

'Nothing.'

'Well, shut up, then.'

'I'm only saying. Dad didn't make a fuss like he usually does.

He just gave us our cards and then went to work. Didn't even sing. He's always done that before. And *she* didn't even get up.'

'Evie said happy birthday. My card was lovely from her. Stop it. Don't spoil it.' Chloe decides not to listen to him anymore. 'Where *is* Daddy?' She peers up and down the road, looks around. There are only a few boys waiting outside the school gates now. One or two mums are in the schoolyard chatting, but there are no teachers. She likes the paintings and paper cutouts that decorate the main doors and the tall sash windows. She's proud to see hers in the centre of their classroom window.

'He's here. He's here!' Swinging her satchel, Chloe sets off at a trot along the pavement to meet Graham.

'Don't be daft, just wait until he stops,' Charlie calls. 'Chloe!'

They jostle for the front seat until Graham insists, sharply, that they both sit in the back. He glances at them in the driver's mirror before twisting round in his seat.

'Look I'm really sorry, kids, you can't have a party. Lynne's got a migraine. She can't cope with a lot of noise; it would make it worse.' Graham avoids their eyes. 'Try to understand, eh?'

'Dad!' Chloe wails the word.

'I knew it,' Charlie mutters. 'I knew this would happen.'

'Now, Charlie. Don't start…' Graham turns back. Without another word he releases the handbrake and pulls into the stream of traffic.

All the way home Chloe sucks her lower lip hard to stop herself crying. She's been excited all day; from the instant she woke and remembered it was her and Charlie's birthdays.

When their father stops the car on the drive outside the house, the disappointment washes over her again and again.

95

She doesn't want to get out. She wants to pretend Dad's teasing about no party. But why would he, that wasn't nice. Perhaps he thinks it's funny to do that. She laughs because she's realised something. 'Silly Dad, course we're having a party. Everyone's had their invitations, they'll all be here soon.'

'No, love.' Graham opens the car door, waits while she gets out, rests his hand on her shoulder. 'I'm sorry. I've phoned everyone's parents; they know it's cancelled.'

Chloe's lip trembles, the disappointment huge again.

'Even Mark Baxter?' Charlie says.

'Yes, I told Uncle Phil earlier, at the garage.'

'That means he won't invite me to his party, next week.' Charlie's face is flushed with his indignation. 'You could have let just him come. And just one of Chloe's friends.'

'No, I couldn't. And Uncle Phil understood. He won't let Mark leave you out. We'll do something for your birthdays another time. Anyway, Monday is a bad day to have a party.'

'But it's our birthday today.'

'And you didn't say anything about Mondays before, Dad,' Chloe says, her throat tight with the tears she's trying to stop.

'It's not fair.' Charlie, already out of the car, scowls, digs the toes of his shoe hard into the gravel on the drive. 'Anyway, *she* could stay in bed. We won't go upstairs. We'll play outside. We'll be quiet. It's not fair.'

'Don't be selfish,' Graham snaps. 'That's not possible. I've told you. I've already phoned everyone's parents. Your mum—'

'Lynne. She's Lynne.' Charlie glares at him, arms folded.

'And she can't help being ill. A migraine is very painful.'

'Don't care.'

'That's enough!'

'I wish Granny could have come for our birthday.' Chloe wipes her face with her cardigan sleeve. 'She usually does.'

'I know, love, but she's quite poorly as well.'

'Proper poorly,' Charlie mumbles. He stomps towards the house. 'Not like *her*. *She* just pretends.'

'That's quite enough,' Graham shouts after him

'We haven't seen Granny in ages.' Chloe slips her hand into Graham's.

'I know. It's difficult.'

'*Lynne* doesn't want Granny here.' Charlie's walking backwards, yelling now. 'Like she doesn't want us to have a party. It's crap. It's all crap.'

'Get back here! Now!'

Charlie ignores his father, runs around to the back of the house.

'He's upset, Dad. Don't be cross with him.'

'I'm not, Chloe. Well, I am for his language, but I can understand how he ... you must feel.' He squeezes her fingers. 'Come on, we've got some of that birthday cake to eat, party or no party.'

Chapter 38

'How are you feeling?'

The bedroom is gloomy with the curtains closed, but there is a V-shaped chink of brightness near the rail. Graham crosses on stockinged feet to pull the curtains tighter.

'Head's still throbbing.' Lynne's voice is low. Husky. 'Do you mind asking the children to be a little quieter?'

'Of course, love.'

He stands by the bed, reaches down, tucks the sheet under Lynne's chin.

She moves irritably away from his touch.

'Sorry. I'll leave you in peace. Try to sleep. Are you sure you don't want anything?'

'No. I said. Just ask them to keep the noise down.'

'Okay.' He immediately thinks of Saul. There's no sound from his room so Graham's guessing he's not yet back from school. He can't help anticipating the pleasure in telling him he can't play those awful records this evening. 'I'll go and leave you in peace,' he says again.

'You said!' Lynne drags the covers over her head.

When Graham creeps out onto the landing, Evie is waiting for him.

'I've got a couple of presents for the twins, and I've made some sandwiches and bought some ice cream from the corner shop.' She gestures with her head towards the bedroom. 'One of her headaches?'

'Yes.' He's whispering.

'Thought so.' She doesn't whisper. 'It happens. Often ... at these times.'

Graham has already reached that conclusion but doesn't say anything; he has to show his loyalty to his wife in front of her daughter, even if he's suspicious that Lynne uses migraines as an excuse.

'Perhaps we should...?' He waves towards the stairs.

'Yes,' Evie says. 'Let's try to give Charlie and Chloe a bit of a celebration, even if it's not what was planned.' She opens Chloe's door. 'Come on, you two. Come and open your birthday presents.'

Chapter 39

'It was good in the end, wasn't it? We got presents. Evie gave me this.' Chloe strokes the cover of the pale blue notebook. 'She knows it's my favourite colour, and look, it's got butterflies all over it as well.'

'Funny present? A book with nothing in it.'

'She knows I write things.'

'Things? What about?' Charlie rolls onto his back, squints against the sun, still bright in the early evening sky. He flicks the wheels of the blue racing car along his palm, listening to the buzz it makes.

'Just things I think about. She saw me once and asked me. I told her, I like writing about things that happen. And all I had was that little shopping notebook that was Mummy's, and it was nearly full. She remembered and bought me this.' Chloe holds it close to her chest. 'It's beautiful, I'll use my bestest handwriting in it.' She sees Charlie's puzzled stare and knows he's going to ask her again what she writes about, but she doesn't want to tell him about her letters to Sandie Shaw. So she adds, 'You like the car she bought you?'

'It's okay. It's a bit babyish, but I don't mind. She's nice.' He flips onto his front. 'See, there's a little driver with a red helmet inside. It was funny not to get something from Dad today though?'

Oscar comes and flops by Chloe. 'Hello, boy.' She absently pats him. 'He said we can go to the shops with him and choose a watch each at that shop in town next Saturday.' Chloe's looking forward to them spending some time on their own with their dad. 'I've always wanted a watch. I hope they've got one with a picture of Sleeping Beauty on it; I've always wanted a Sleeping Beauty one.'

'Mummy always bought our presents before our birthday.' Charlie glowers towards the house. The curtains of their dad and *her* bedroom are still drawn but the window is wide open.

Chloe sucks in her lower lip, tries to think of something that will stop Charlie getting cross again.

'What will you spend your five pounds on from Granny?' She asks. 'I thought I'd get some paints.'

'Don't know. S'pose a robot. Timmy Whitehouse has got a smashing one. Don't know what it cost though.'

They watch Saul walking along the drive towards the house. He looks at them.

'What you two gawking at?'

Oscar growls.

'Don't answer,' Charlie says quietly.

Chloe has no intention. She's pleased there's no cake left for their stepbrother. 'I bet he didn't even remember it's our birthday.'

'We wouldn't want him to. I hate him.' When Saul disappears into the house Charlie sits up straight, absently runs the car back and forth across the top of his knee. A sudden nervous jolt pulls his shoulders around his ears.

Chloe can feel the distress in him, knows it comes from seeing Saul.

'Me too.' Chloe has decided it's allowed to hate someone who is really hateful. She has the urge to write that in her new notebook. And she wants to tell Sandie Shaw how disappointed she is about today. She's tried not to let it upset her because she thinks Charlie is angry enough for the two of them and she doesn't want to make it worse.

But it's as though wanting to write it makes her want to say it. 'I would have liked to have had a party though, Charlie.' Glancing towards the open bedroom window she shuffles closer to Charlie. 'I don't know why we couldn't have a party. We had a party even when Mummy was so poorly – remember? She watched us from her bedroom.' Her last words come out on a burst of gulping breath.

'Shush. You don't know where anybody is. Who might hear.' Charlie turns his head to look around. 'You heard what Dad said, she can't cope with a lot of noise. It upsets her when she has a bad headache. I do reckon there's something wrong with her though.'

'Like she's really poorly?' Chloe's jaw slackens.

There's a loud squeak from a latch and another bedroom window opens. The low sun glints on the glass and Chloe sees the blur of a figure. Saul is watching them. Can he hear? The thought makes her feel sick.

'Dunno. Don't think so.'

She hears him swallow hard. Waits. 'What then?' She finally asks.

'Like I've said before, Chloe, I think the thing that's wrong with her ... is that she's just nasty.'

Chapter 40

'Charlie Collins, are you even listening?'

Charlie drags his gaze from the window to the woman standing at the front of the class, barely registering her face taut with exasperation. His stomach feels like it's on that rollercoaster they went on in Blackpool once with Dad.

'What?' His ruler, held tight between his fingers, hurts the insides of his knuckles. He examines the dents the edges of the plastic have left. The redness and stinging are easier to bear than the pain of the fear twisting inside him. The fear that's been inside him for months.

'Do not say "what" in that manner. Show some respect, young man. Say "Pardon, Miss Lampton."'

Charlie stays stubbornly silent. He glances out of the window again. His stepbrother is still by the school gates with a group of other older boys. Panic tightens his breathing.

'Look at me.' The teacher raps her desk with the end of her pen. 'Look. At. Me. What did I just say? What did I ask you to do? Hmm?'

Martin, the boy next to Charlie gives him a nudge. 'Your turn to read.' He pushes his copy of *Wind in the Willows* across the desk to Charlie, points to a line, and speaks out of the corner of his mouth. 'Start at, "The Mole knew well that it is quite against animal etiquette to dwell on possible trouble ahead or even to allude to it..."'

Charlie knows Martin means to be friendly, but he also hears all the muffled sniggers around him. He stands, pushing his chair with the back of his legs and looks again through the window. They've gone. But he doesn't trust Saul; they'll be waiting for him somewhere. His legs shake and he feels dizzy, but he needs to escape, to get out of school before the bell rings.

'I have to go.'

'You'll do no such thing. Sit down.'

'Please!' Charlie's eyes are hot, smarting.

'Sit down!'

'No.' He clenches his fists. Shouts. 'No!'

'How dare you.'

He makes a dash in between the desks but the teacher is too quick for him. She places herself between Charlie and the classroom door, looks over his head.

'Sarah, please read the next passage. And I want you all to be quiet and listen to her.' Holding Charlie's shoulder, she gives him a small shake. 'And you, young man, will come with me to see the Head. For the third time this week. I'm not sure what's going on with you, but I cannot have you behaving like this.'

'Please … I need to go.' Charlie wriggles under her grasp. Her fingers tighten.

'Charlie!' Chloe's voice is shrill with fear. On the other side of the classroom, she half-stands. 'I'll come with you.'

'No! Just go straight home when the bell rings. Straight home.' He doesn't look towards her, his eyes fixed on the teacher. 'But I have to go now.'

'The only place you're going is to the Head.' She leans down to him and whispers. 'You need to learn how to behave.'

There's nothing for it in Charlie's mind. He kicks her ankle. When she gasps, lets go of him to clutch her leg, he runs.

103

'Get back here, Charlie Collins. Get back here. Your parents will hear about this.'

Not parents. Just Dad. And what can he do? Same as always – nothing.

'What's happening out here?' The headteacher steps out of his office, blocking the corridor. Charlie puts his head down and charges forward on shaky legs. He's more scared of Saul than the man in front of him.

'Stop that boy, Mr Harrison. It's Charlie Collins ... again!'

Charlie looks back. Miss Lampton is hobbling after him, her face red. Her hair has escaped from her bun and long strands are falling over her face.

Mr Harrison makes a grab for Charlie, but he ducks, dodges past and skids along the corridor to the emergency door. Shoving on the bar as hard as he can, he pushes. Once, twice, His breath comes in terrified gasps. On the third push the door gives way. He is outside, grateful for the fresh air.

'Thought you might come this way.' A hand grabs the back of his neck, forces him to bend forward. 'Hello, little shit. Fancy seeing you here.'

'Gerroff.' Charlie hopes Mr Harrison will be here any minute. But he's being dragged away from the school, surrounded by Saul and his friends.

'Well that's not very nice, is it, little shit. Come on, move!'

'Let me go, Saul. Please.'

'Not on your life. That's twice you've tried to avoid us this week. We've got something very special waiting for you today.'

Charlie's going under the murky water for the fifth time. Canal weeds tangle around his legs. His heart is racing, the pulse loud in his ears as he chokes and splutters, tries to thrash to the surface.

'I can't … I can't…'

He sinks for the third time. Echoing noises. A voice. He lifts his face, water blocks his nose, stings. The sky moves in wavering lines.

'Grab this!' A thud on his shoulder. 'Grab it!'

Not Saul. A girl. He knows the voice. Frantic he lifts his arms, starts to sink again. But he wraps one hand around a rough stick and clings on, aware that he's sliding though weeds and water to the bank. He clutches the tough grass, is dragged by the neck of his jumper. Then he's face down on the dusty canal path and someone is turning him over onto his side. He's gagging.

'You're all right. It's me. Evie. I'm here. You'll be fine.' She's patting his back.

'I thought … drowning…' He can't stop the great gulping sobs. 'Saul…'

'He's gone. Don't worry. I saw to that. Just wait until I tell—'

'No.' The word is followed by a long gasping cough. 'No … don't. It'll … be worse.'

'Charlie. I know what's going on, love.' She leans over to look into his face. 'You told me before. This can't keep happening You can't—'

'No!' Charlie chokes the word out.

'But…' She waits until he's not coughing. 'It can't go on—'

'I tried once … and Chloe did. *She…*'

'My mother?'

105

'Yeah.' He struggles to sit up. 'Said ... said I was lying. Said if I told Dad, I would be sorry.'

'No!'

'Yeah. No point.' He takes in a spluttering breath, coughs. 'Even if Dad did believe...' He swallows. 'She'll say I'm lying again. Dad won't do anything about it.'

'He doesn't like rows, your dad. She knows that.'

'It would – make everything worse.' His breathing is getting easier. 'Please, Evie.'

'Well, I don't think he should get away with this.' She brushes his wet hair out of his eyes. 'But if that's what you want...'

'Yeah.'

'Come on then, stand up.' She helps him up, takes her cardigan off and wraps it round his shoulders. 'Right.' She takes his hand. 'Let's get you home and dried out.'

He looks around. The canal path is deserted, but the streets won't be.

'We'll take the back path, past the football field – that way. Make sure nobody sees us. Right?' She smiles.

'Right.' He manages a smile but it feels strange. He can't make out how he feels. He leans against his stepsister, lets her lead him along the path, and home.

Dear Sandie Shaw,

Charlie ran away from school. The teachers don't like Charlie now because of what he did to Miss and because he's being naughty in class. But he's only naughty because everything's wrong here, and he's frightend of Saul. How does Saul know Charlie's frightend of water, of drowning? How did he find out? He's horrible. Evie says she'll look after us. But Saul is big and he has a gang. I hate him.

Chapter 41

'You do know that you did a bad thing, don't you, son? Kicking your teacher?'

They're sitting in the car after the most humiliating and upsetting hour Graham can remember. As the Chairman of the board of governors it was doubly humiliating.

'Look, I want to know why. It's just not like you.' Graham pauses. What is his son actually like these days? Or Chloe for that matter? When was the last time he heard either of them laugh? The last time he'd had to tell them to stop chattering at mealtimes and eat their food? The last time they got in the car after school talking over one another in an effort to get his attention?

Charlie hasn't moved. Arms folded; he's staring out of the side window.

Graham is angry; he should have been told about this before today. When he said this to Cliff Harrison the man visibly bristled. He wonders if the headteacher approached anyone else on the board. That would be more embarrassing. To find out that his son has become disruptive in class, that he refuses to join in with any lessons, and answers back when told off by the teacher, is bad enough. That he kicked Miss Lampton is beyond belief. But the evidence was there in the bruise on her leg, and on the school report of the 'incident'. Cliff Harrison even hinted the police might be told, but even that didn't seem to bother Charlie.

Graham shudders when he thinks about the next meeting of the governors. He shakes his head, reminding himself this isn't what he should be worrying about. He should be more concerned about Charlie.

'We can't carry on like this, son. And until you tell me what the matter is, there's nothing I can do to help.'

'There's nothing you can do anyway.' The words were muttered.

'What?'

Charlie twisted in his seat; tears were dripping from his chin. 'I said, there's nothing you will do that will help. Nothing. Just leave me alone.'

'You know I can't do that, love. I have to... I want to understand. I can't bear to see you so unhappy.' Graham rests his hand on Charlie's arm, feels the way he stiffens.

'Don't. Leave me alone.'

Graham stares through the windscreen of the car at the deserted school buildings. All the pupils have long gone. Even the caretaker has finished his chores and left. There are no lights in any of the classrooms. He doesn't know what else to say.

Two people come out of the main doors: Mr Harrison and Miss Lampton.

Embarrassed to be seen still sitting outside the school, Graham ducks his head, turns the ignition key and quickly pulls away from the kerb.

'We'll talk when we get home.'

Under the noise of the engine, he hears his son say something, doesn't quite catch the words. But he's almost sure he heard, 'It's not home. Not anymore.'

Dear Sandie Shaw,

Charlie's in big trouble. Last week Saul climbed over the gates at our school and broke one of the windows in the headmaster's office. Then he said it was Charlie. And Charlie got into trouble at school again and then with Dad. Saul laughed when he told us what he'd done. I knew it was no good telling Dad, but I tried. But Saul stood behind him and did this thing – like he pulled his finger across his throat and pointed at me. When I told Evie she looked really worried. She just said I must make sure I was never on my own. So I'm scared all the time. And I promised I would look after Charlie when Saul started following him and doing horrible things to him. I don't think I can look after my brother when I'm so frightened.

Chapter 42

'Don't do it again, Charlie. Please?' Chloe catches hold of his arm as children push past them towards the school gates. Her worry takes her breath away. 'Come in today? It's Friday, your favourite day. We have a nature film this afternoon. You know how much you like them.' She's trying to persuade him even though he has that firm set to his mouth. She keeps hold of his sleeve. 'Come on, please? You haven't been in all week and you can't keep doing this, you'll get into awful trouble.'

Two magpies are on the roof of the school, their chattering translating into scornful laughter.

'Miss Lampton keeps asking me where you are, and I have to lie, I have to say you're poorly. I don't think she believes me anymore, because she says I have to bring in a note from Dad if you're not in school next week.'

'I hate school, Chloe. I hate the teachers. I can't do anything right.' Charlie hunches his shoulders. 'I'm scared all the time.'

'I'm here, Charlie. I'll be with you. Please.'

'Try to understand, sis, I can't...'

'I don't ... I can't.' Chloe hiccups a huge sob. 'I'll help. Tell me how.'

'Look, you'll be okay.'

'I won't be okay without you. I won't.'

'Just stay in school until I come back this afternoon. Remember Evie won't be here, she's got that netball thing. But Saul won't touch you if you stay in school.'

'He's not after me, you know that, Charlie. You'll be safer in school.' *Why won't he believe that? Safer than at home.*

She tries to grab hold of him, cries out, when he spins on his heel and runs towards the park.

'I'll come back for you,' he shouts over his shoulder. 'I'll be here when you come out this afternoon.'

When Saul and his friends might be here. Chloe gazes around. The playground is empty, inside the school, the bell is being rung for registration. She wants to run after her brother. Be with him rather than face more questions from Miss Lampton.

'Charlie!'

He doesn't look back. There's a low rumble above, the sky has darkened, a blend of muddy greys. Heavy splats of rain hit the ground around her. 'You'll get wet,' she murmurs.

Charlie keeps his promise – he's waiting on the corner of the road. And Chloe wishes he hadn't, because so are Saul and his friends. He knows Evie isn't home.

They won't give up. Even in the rain, they're here, hunched under anorak hoods, hands shoved in pockets, eyes skimming over the parents and children huddled under umbrellas, running to cars out of the wet. Charlie and Chloe try to mingle, hoping they won't be noticed. Further along the street, past the school railings, just as they think they're safe, they are seen.

'Where do you think you are going, little shit. Nowhere to hide.' Saul jogs behind them, treading on the back of Charlie's shoes, until one of them comes off, and he hobbles to a halt.

Charlie gives Chloe a push. 'Run. Go on, go. Go home.'

'No.' She turns to face Saul, her face screwed up against the rain. 'You're a nasty bully, Saul Wilson.'

Sneering, he leans down until he's so close she can smell cigarettes on his breath. 'Go home, little girl. Run away, while you still can.'

'You don't scare me.' She's angry, keeps her voice loud. She's hoping one of the parents will notice. But no one is looking this way. Chloe spends a lot of time wondering why her and Charlie's lives have changed so much. Looking at the thick black eyebrows, the pale grey eyes, the pimple-scarred chin of her stepbrother she knows this is one of the people who has altered their family forever. The flood of rage makes her put her hands on her hips, straighten her shoulders. 'I'm not leaving you, Charlie.'

Even as she speaks Saul and two of the other boys pick Charlie up and hold him aloft, arms and legs dangling.

'Just go. I'll be all right,' he shouts. 'Run, Chloe, run.'

Chapter 43

They carry him, bouncing him up and down for the next five minutes. When they get to the park, they head for the duck pond. With a loud cheer they throw him in. He lands, face first, arms splayed, in the dirty water and flounders around, his feet struggling for foothold in the slimy mud. They don't wait to see him crawl to the edge of the pond, coughing, spitting out the algae-ridden water. High-fiving one another they run away.

Limping home, leaving a trail of water behind him, and carrying one shoe, he forces back the fear, makes himself angry. By the time he stands at the back door, he's ready for Lynne's fury.

'What the hell...'

As soon as she begins shouting, he yells back, his heart racing.

'It's not my fault, it was Saul. I told you before, and you wouldn't let me tell Dad.'

'Because you were lying then and you're lying now.'

'I'm not. He and his stupid friends threw me in the pond in the park. He's done this. Ask him! Ask him!'

'Lies. Nothing but trouble. You—'

'He's right. You should have believed him the first time. Your precious son has done this sort of thing before.' Evie's standing by the kitchen door. She grabs a towel from the hook by the sink, walks over to Charlie, begins to wipe the mess from his hair and face. 'Sorry, Charlie, I only got back ten minutes ago. Our team got knocked out of the competition, but I was home too late to pick you up from school.' She turns to glare at her mother. 'Last time it was the canal. He could have drowned. Luckily, then, I saw what was happening and got him out.'

'What the hell are you talking about? Five minutes home and already causing trouble.' Lynne snatches the towel out of Evie's hands. 'Get him outside.' She pushes Charlie. 'Get outside. Take your clothes off out there.'

'No.' He pushes at her arms. 'Get off me.' He tries to pass her.

She grabs him. 'Don't you dare answer back. Don't you dare raise your hand to me.'

'He didn't. Just leave him alone, Mum. Let me get him to the bathroom, get him cleaned up.'

'I will not. He comes home filthy, telling a load of lies about your brother and you take his side.'

'Because it's true. If Charlie says Saul chucked him in the pond in the park, it's because it's true. He's been bullying him for months. Like I said, if he weren't your blue-eyed boy, you would have seen that. But, oh no, he can't do any wrong can he? He's nasty, sly and he's a bully.'

Lynne slaps her across her face.

There's a quivering pause where they stare at one another, Evie holding her face. She shakes her head. 'Come on, Charlie. Come with me.' She takes his hand.

'Stop right there.' Lynne grabs her.

'Fuck off!' Evie bends her mother's fingers back until she lets go. 'Just fuck off.'

Chloe is waiting in the hall, her fingers over her mouth, her eyes wide.

The three of them walk upstairs. On the landing Saul watches them, a grin on his face. They ignore him, go into the bathroom, and close the door.

Dear Sandie,

Charlie says we should run away. He says we don't belong here anymore. But where would we go? How can we? I want Dad to help us, but he's not the same dad we've always had. Evie looks after us but she can't make things right. And she said a bad word twice. I wish I could say bad words to Lynne. Home isn't home anymore. Someone broke into the school last weekend and broke chairs and stuff in our classroom and sprayed paint all over. Charlies tie was found under the teacher's desk. A policeman came to the house and talked to Lynne. I listened and they are going to blame Charlie. I am really frightened.

Chapter 44

Graham hears the sobbing as soon as he closes the front door. He drops his keys in the bowl on the hall table and listens.

'Lynne? Is that you?' He puts his foot on the first tread and waits. 'Lynne?'

'Graham?'

He hears rustling, and she appears at the top of the stairs, her uniform wrinkled, her hair dishevelled. She flops down on the top step, a crumpled tissue in her hands.

'Everything's such a mess, Graham.' She's gasping for breath. He can barely make out what she's saying.

'What is it? What's happened?'

'Nothing. Everything. It's all...' She waves her arms, taking in the upstairs, the downstairs, the whole house. 'We shouldn't have got married. It's. All. Wrong.' She drops her head onto her arms, crossed over her knees, and rocks.

'Hey, hey. Now, stop that. Tell me what's wrong and I'll sort it.'

He takes the stairs two at a time until he's holding her, rocking her, shushing her. This is his opportunity to step up.

'Come into our bedroom so we can talk without being overheard,' he says.

She lets him lead her there.

'I can't cope anymore, Graham. I've been trying for the last two years. It's not fair. He hates me...' She flaps her arm towards Charlie's bedroom door. 'He'll always hate me...'

'What's happened?' Graham's confidence falters. He closes their bedroom door, the familiar sick unease curdling in his stomach.

When they sit on the bed she leans into him, her head under his chin. 'This morning the school rang – again. They said they couldn't get hold of you.'

'Phil and I have been out all day. We were at the accountants and then the solicitors. What's happened now?'

'He's been truanting.'

'Charlie? Why?'

'I don't know. Do you think he'd tell me?' Her voice rises. 'And the science classroom was trashed on Saturday and Charlie was seen doing it. Someone reported him. Of course he denies it. The police came here because of the damage, Graham. They talked to me as though I was something they'd stepped in. I told them he's my stepson – that I have no control over him, and that they need to talk to you...' She makes a heaving sob. 'They want you to go to the police station with him.'

Graham's body stills even as his brain seems to be going into overdrive, picturing Charlie's defiant face. The nausea increases. 'I don't ... it's all so hard to take in...' He shakes his head slightly. 'The police?'

'Tomorrow. They said you have to take him in tomorrow.' Her cheeks are scarlet, her eyelids swollen.

First the school, now the police. Why is Charlie like this? He doesn't know what's happening with his son.

He feels her shaking his arm. 'And then, tonight, when he came home, he was filthy and he blamed Saul.' She pushes herself away from him. 'But Saul couldn't have done anything to him because he was home. He came home straight from school. He was upstairs doing his homework when Charlie got here.'

'Did you ask Saul?' Graham is careful to keep his voice calm.

'Of course I did. I'm always fair with all of them, you know that.' She rubs the tissue over her face. 'But it's all too much. The school, the police. You have to do something. Please. If this carries on, I won't be able to do my job. They've already asked at the surgery what's wrong. They know I'm struggling.'

116

'I'll find out what's going on before I take him to see the police in the morning.' Graham is striving to accept this is happening. He can't help feeling that Saul is somehow behind everything. Evie has hinted as much, but he daren't say that just now. Sorting out this business with the police is what's most important. 'And I'll ring Harrison tonight. As Head he should know how to deal with these things.'

As soon as he says that Graham knows it's not enough.

'You're not listening. I'm struggling to cope with them.'

'Them? Chloe as well?'

'Yes. The way she looks at me – yes. And ... and she follows whatever he does a lot of the time. And sulks.'

His stomach clenches again. 'Most kids sulk sometime, love. But you've not said that before...'

'I didn't want you to think it's just because they're your children. I love them like my own, but they resent me.'

'We've talked about this before, Lynne. I thought you understood. Their lives have changed so radically. It must still feel strange sometimes.'

'I do. Oh, I do understand, Graham. But they are so...' She shakes her head. 'It's making me ill.'

'What do you want to do about it?'

'We need help, Graham.'

'What sort of help?'

'Professional help. Someone who specialises in difficult children.'

He winces. 'Are they that bad?'

'Haven't you been listening? Yes, they are. A social worker will be able to give us some advice.'

117

'A social worker?' This is really getting out of hand. 'Really?' She's not going to back down on this. He can tell by the way she's staring at him, vigorously nodding. 'Okay, love. But just advice...'

'I have a friend who's a social worker. I've been talking to her. She's said she will help us – advise us which way we should go.'

He hesitates. This is all going too quickly. He's not in control. 'They're my kids, Lynne.'

'I know.' Her tone softened into the voice he'd learned to love as she nursed Anna at the end, when she first met Charlie and Chloe at the funeral. He'd heard the kind way she spoke to them, even though they'd refused to look at her, hidden behind him. She'd smiled, said she understood that they were grieving.

'It's difficult, Lynne.'

'I know. We could just ask what's best, you know. For – for them and us. Shall I give her a call?'

He doesn't want this. 'No. I'm really not sure the situation warrants that, Lynne.'

'It's that or I can't stay here.'

'Oh, come on.'

'I mean it, Graham. For the twins' sake as much as anything. We can't carry on like this. It's impossible.'

He gives in. 'Fine. But just for advice. Nothing else.'

The floorboards on the landing creak. Someone is listening.

Chapter 45

Charlie scrambles to his bedroom, digging his nails into the carpet on the stairs, the tears hot on his cheeks. He sits, his back against the wall, his head on his knees. He hears the footsteps, refuses to lift his head even though he knows it's his dad standing in front of him.

'Charlie?'

The fury takes him by surprise. It courses through him, makes him jump to his feet, push his father away. He's hot, there's lots of spit in his mouth. He's going to be sick. He leans forward, sees her watching him from the bedroom door.

'You!' He shouts. 'You.'

'Now, Charlie.'

'It's her. She's lying. I hate her.'

Lynne covers her face with her hands. 'See? This is what he does. I can't...'

'Charlie.' His dad sounds frustrated but he still puts his arms around him.

'I don't want to be here anymore. Send us to Granny's. Let us live with Granny.'

'I can't, love. Granny's too old and tired. She couldn't look after you. She can't really look after herself.'

'Just ask her. Please, Dad. And I didn't go into the school. I didn't do anything to the science classroom. Honest.'

'I want to believe you, love. But we have to sort this out – you not going to school, the damage... We have to talk to the police.'

'I told you. I didn't do anything 'cept not go to school.' He's

119

crying. 'Don't make me go to the police, Dad. I know I should have gone to school—'

'That's not why you have to go to the police station, Charlie. It's about the damage...'

'But I didn't do it. And I couldn't go to school 'cos of him.' He's breathless. 'It's not my fault. It's Saul.' He points at Lynne. 'And her.'

'Now, Charlie...' Graham's voice is barely a whisper.

'You just don't want us anymore.' Charlie pushes him away with his fist.

'Don't say that son, it's not true.' Graham tries to hold Charlie's hands, but Charlie manages to wriggle away.

'It is. You're going to send me away, aren't you?'

'No! No, I'm not.' But Charlie pushes past Lynne and runs down the stairs. 'I wouldn't do that, Charlie. Honest.' He hears his father shout. 'Honest.'

Sandie Shaw, I hate Lynne.

Chapter 46

It's happened so fast.

At least that's how it seems to Charlie and Chloe. It's two days later. They've only been home from school an hour and are sitting together on the floor watching *Crackerjack* when their father comes into the lounge.

'There's a lady here to talk to you both.' Their dad is half smiling, half frowning.

'Why? What does she want?'

Graham shakes his head. 'Now, Charlie, I think you know.' His voice wavers. 'We have talked about this.' He crosses to the television and turns it off. 'I think it will help us all as a family. You know – sort out what the problems are.'

Charlie and Chloe exchange glances. Both know what, or who, the problem is. Chloe moves closer to her brother.

'The lady is called Heather and she'll talk to you on your own, and then with us all. Okay?' He's changed his tone of voice to the 'let's not be silly' one. The one he used when they were little, when either of them was having a tantrum.

'Alright,' Chloe says, despite the sudden overwhelming fear inside her. Somehow she knows things are never going to be the same after this.

'Now, get off the floor and sit on the settee,' he says, before leaving the room.

They perch on the edge of the new slippery black leather sofa. It's cold against their legs.

'I hate this settee,' Chloe whispers, not knowing what else to say. Charlie doesn't answer. She can feel him trembling. He slowly moves his head. 'I hate everything in this room since Lynne altered everything.' She wants him to know whatever happens she's on his side.

Charlie frowns at the sideboard and television cabinet on the spindly legs. Even though, unlike Chloe, he'd never touched any of those old books in the big bookshelves, they'd made it feel like home to him. The swirly carpet has gone, replaced with a cream one that they can't walk on in shoes. 'S'all stupid,' he mutters.

The door opens.

Chloe grabs hold of Charlie's hand.

The lady smiles and pulls up the small leather foot stool to sit in front of them. She smells of outside, fresh air. Chloe watches her from under her eyelids: Brown sandals, brown leggings, oversized yellow blouse, yellow-looking bracelets jangling on both arms, yellow hair spread out over her shoulders.

'Hi, my name's Heather. I'm here to help everyone if I can.' They watch her, cautiously. 'How about we start with how things are at school?' Her voice is soft, like the woman on *Blue Peter*; musical. She smiles at Graham and Lynne. The bangles clunk together when she moves her hand, an obvious hint for them to leave the room. As soon as they close the door, she says, 'So, who's first?' Neither of them says anything. 'Or both together?' Chloe puts both hands between her knees, leans on Charlie. 'How about I ask a question, and then, if you feel like telling me anything...?'

Charlie stands, goes over to the door, and opens it. There's no sign of their dad, but Lynne is sitting at the bottom of the stairs.

He waits, outstaring her, until, glaring, she gets up and walks along the hall to the kitchen. He closes the door.

'Is there a problem, Charlie?'

'Not now.'

'Good. Right. In your own time, tell me a little about school, what lessons you like, what you like to do when you're not in school, how you get on with...' She looks at the notes, smooths the paper with the flat of her hand. 'Evie and Saul?'

Charlie gives Chloe a pleading sideways glance. She closes her eyes to let him know she understands.

'We like Evie.' She nods, emphatic.

'And Saul?'

They shrug. What's the point? She's an adult, she won't believe anything they say about Saul. Her pen makes soft scratchy noises as she writes. She looks questioningly at them.

They shrug again. Chloe looks at Charlie. He shakes his head. Chloe understands: if they say how nasty Saul is, the lady will tell Dad and Lynne and they'll say it's lies, so why bother.

'Okay.' She puts the top back on her pen, rests her arms on the file on her knee, threads her fingers together. 'So tell me how you feel about Lynne.'

Chloe rocks. She looks down at her lap.

'We hate her,' Charlie says. He glances at Chloe. She moves her head, makes a small acquiescing sound. Encouraged he carries on. 'She's mean to us. She has a no eyes smile when – if she talks to us. Because lots of times she won't talk to us, even if we ask her something. She's mean.'

'Okay.' She drags the word out. 'Your daddy tells me you lost — your mummy went to heaven when you were very small?'

'She died,' Charlie says. 'She died when we were nearly six. And I don't believe in a heaven. We don't,' he adds.

Chloe wishes he hadn't included her. She's not sure if there's a heaven or not. She wants to think their mummy is somewhere nice.

'That's all right,' the lady says. 'I understand. You loved your mummy, didn't you?'

'Course.'

'And you feel Lynne has taken her place? And taken your daddy away from you as well?'

'Dad. We call him Dad now.' Charlie wants the lady to know they're not little kids anymore.

'Sorry. Thank you for telling me. So, like I said, you think Lynne has taken your dad away from you?'

She understands. Charlie squeezes Chloe's hand. 'She has – Miss...'

'Heather. Call me Heather.' She smiles, moves her head to one side, studying them both in turn, takes in a deep breath, as though thinking what to say, but then asks, 'Do you know any fairy tales?'

What has that to do with anything?

'Chloe does,' Charlie says. Fairy tales aren't something boys read.

'Which do you know, Chloe?' Her voice is still soft.

'I know Cinderella, and Snow White and Hansel and Gretel.' Chloe blinks, not understanding. She chews the corner of her bottom lip, feels awkward. Waits.

'And do you know who is in every one of those you've just named?' She looks from Chloe to Charlie.

They shake their heads.

'It's a wicked stepmother.' Heather moves her head up and down. 'And like in fairy stories a stepmother can't replace a mummy. So, like in fairy stories, a stepmother could be seen as a bad person – a wicked woman who is taking away someone's dad...'

Just like *Her*. Charlie's relieved. Heather's seen what they see – Lynne's wicked. She's going to save them. Save them and Dad.

'But that's not what is really happening in real life, is it?' She's keeping her eyes on Chloe, and Charlie suddenly knows just what she is doing. She's shutting him out, just talking to his sister – persuading her she's right. She's on their stepmother's side.

Everything becomes silent. Chloe glances at Charlie, not sure what's happening.

'A stepmother wants to love their daddy's – dad's children as much as she loves him...'

'That's not true, she hates us.' Charlie jumps up off the settee where he and Chloe have been sitting for the last half hour. 'She's a ... she's a ... bitch,' he blurts out. 'We hate her.' He looks around, sees the wedding photo of his dad and *her* on the sideboard, the one that's replaced the photo of their mummy and dad. He charges across the room, picks it up and throws it on the floor. With one swipe of his arm, he sweeps Lynne's collection of small ceramic animals off the sideboard and grabs the vase of roses and holds it above his head.

'What the...?'

The lounge door opens and their dad comes into the room, closely followed by Lynne. When Charlie sees her, he throws the vase at her. The water is a long, pale arc in the air, the roses dropping one by one. Graham holds out his arm to protect Lynne, but it hits her on her shoulder.

She screams.

The stillness lasts no longer than a few seconds before the room erupts into chaos: Graham crosses to Charlie, pulls him around to face Lynne. 'Apologize. Now!' She's standing, her hands over her face. Charlie knows she's pretending; he just knows it. He laughs, even as his father is shaking him.

Heather, struggling to get up from the footstool, has dropped the file. 'Mr Collins, please.'

Chloe curls up on the settee, her arms over her head. She doesn't want to be here.

'No!' Charlie is shouting. 'No. No. No.'

Clutching tight hold of his son, Graham slaps him on the legs. Again and again, he slaps, the crack of skin on skin loud in the shocked silence.

Chloe puts her hands over her ears but can't shut out the sound. She hears the social worker call out to their dad and looks up to see her grabbing hold of his wrist, pulling him, shouting at him

'Mr Collins. Stop it. Stop it this minute.'

Except for Graham's gasping breaths, it's silent. Heather examines Charlie's legs. She makes a tutting sound.

'Are you all right?'

'Yeah.' He bites his lip.

She straightens up. 'I actually came here today on an unofficial basis, as a favour to a colleague. But there are obviously huge problems here.' She gathers her file and her coat into her arms. 'Lynne, Mr Collins, may I have a word? In the hall?'

Chloe holds out her hand to her brother. When he's next to her, she holds him. 'Don't cry.'

'I'm not.' But he is, the tears trickling down his cheeks.

'It'll be okay.'

'It won't They'll send me away now. It's what *she* wants anyway.'

'I won't let them.' Chloe holds him tighter. 'I'll tell them I won't stay here without you. I'm not being here without you.'

126

Chapter 47

'Over the last week I've been in touch with the policeman who talked to Charlie about the damage at the school, and I've had two meetings with his headteacher...' Heather flicks through some pages of her folder. 'Mr Harrison... It appears that Charlie is a very troubled little boy. And, after what I witnessed last week, together with my chats with him and Chloe, I think it would benefit Charlie best to be taken into care for a short while.'

'No! Absolutely not. It's out of the question. Sending him away would do more harm than good. He's not a delinquent for God's sake.' Graham rubs his hands over his mouth, trying to forget the awful interview with the police sergeant, the feeling of failure as a parent. The relief when no charges were made. Graham guesses there was no real proof.

But the young woman is talking again. 'It's obvious that you have a problem with Charlie as well.'

'I don't!'

'Your actions suggested otherwise, Mr Collins.' Her face shows no expression but her voice is uncompromising.

Graham's numbed by a sudden fear. *What the hell is happening?* 'I told you before you talked to the twins. We only wanted some advice, some help. My children...' He swallows. 'My children watched their mother die.' He ignores the almost smothered sigh from Lynne. 'They were barely five and it had been a long illness. It was hard for them – for me, not knowing if I was doing the right thing. Saying the right things...'

'And I took that into consideration. But the situation has

moved on. Charlie refusing to go to school, the damage to school property...'

'No charges were made. I believe Charlie when he says he didn't do it.'

'That may be so, Mr Collins. But there are deeper problems here than I first thought. And I'm concerned that you're not coping with the situation. I think this is the best solution.'

'No!'

She disregards his interruption, looks down at her folder. 'And Lynne has already told me how bad Charlie's behaviour is.'

'What! No, she's wrong. I'm sorry, Miss Butterworth, I'm afraid you've been given the wrong information by my wife.' He stands. 'Charlie's only ten.'

'Best it's sorted now, Mr Collins. While he is still young.'

'This is all a total overreaction.'

'Graham, be honest with yourself, sweetheart.' Lynne takes hold of his sleeve, her eyes wide with sympathy. 'The boy's out of control; he's violent, he's destructive, he lies. I had to tell Heather; you know I did. Because you wouldn't. And like she's said, all this has been corroborated by his school.'

'It's not – he's not as bad as that. This is a complete overreaction,' he repeats. He's angry, recognises he's been backed into a corner. 'He's not. And I won't allow him to be taken away from his home.'

'I'm afraid it's out of your hands, Mr Collins. It's not an action we've taken lightly. The situation was discussed at length in my department's weekly meeting. There are no other options. There is, of course the other, er, unresolved problem ... with the police.'

'That's over and done with.'

'Until the next time,' Lynne says softly.

'I'm afraid I agree with your wife, Mr Collins. There are some deep-seated problems both at home and socially with Charlie. We think a stay in care, where he'll be counselled and able to talk freely, is the best answer. And the sooner the better.'

Charlie's gone. And I can't pretend Sandie Shaw will read this anymore There's no point.

Chapter 48

'Can't sleep, sweetheart?'

'No.' Graham sits up, dragging the pillow behind his head. 'I can't stop thinking about Charlie's face when he realised what was happening, when I left him in that place.' The guilt lies as a lump in his chest. Anna would never forgive him for what he's done; what he's allowed to be done to his children. 'Mind if I put the light on?'

'If you must, I suppose. I do have a full list for tomorrow, though, so not for long, eh?' She tuts and pulls at the covers he's dislodged.

'I think I'll go downstairs, then.'

'Whatever, but please make up your mind what you're doing. And try to be quiet, won't you? Saul has his maths test tomorrow.'

'I will.' Graham can't help the twinge of resentment. He doesn't give a damn about Saul, to be honest. Something he keeps hidden from Lynne.

'You do know you've done the right thing don't you, Graham?' There's an edge to her voice.

He keeps quiet, clenches his fingers together. If he says what he thinks, there will be another row. What's the point anyway? And, after a day of trying to calm Chloe, he's exhausted. He's never known her get so hysterical, even when Anna died. Then she'd retreated into herself. She wouldn't even let him near her.

He stops at the bedroom door.

'I'll need to ring Mum tomorrow, tell her what's happened. She'll be really upset.' He's dreading it. If he doesn't understand how this situation happened, she certainly won't.

Rustling tells him Lynne has flung the bedclothes back.

'No,' she says. 'There's no need to let her know yet. No point in getting her involved. No rush.' In the dimmed yellow glow of the streetlight through the curtains he sees her hold out her arms. 'Come here. Come on, come here to me.'

Chapter 49

Charlie stays very still. The woman crouches in front of him, holding out her hand. He knows she's smiling because her voice tells him. It's soothing. But he doesn't look at her face. He keeps his eyes on her bright pink dress bunched around her knees, and her white sandals. Her toenails are coloured with matching pink varnish. There are bits chipped off on some of them that show the white of her nails.

He doesn't speak. He hasn't said a word since the social worker and his father left him in the hallway of the care home.

'It'll be fine,' the woman says. 'You'll be fine.'

He doesn't answer.

Then she says, 'Oh…' Just that. Nothing else. But he knows why. He looks down at his front. There's a patch of wet spreading across the front of his trousers. He feels the warmth of his pee. Ten years old and he's peed himself. Shame makes him hot all over. He hears the sniggers behind him.

'Never mind.' The woman takes hold of his hand, turns swiftly, so he's swung around to face wide stairs. 'Shouldn't you two be getting ready for dinner? Go on. Now!'

Charlie doesn't look up, but out of the corner of his eye he sees the black shoes, the thick grey socks crumpled down around the boys' ankles. When they stamp up the stairs, he can tell from the sound they are older, bigger, than him. He squeezes his eyelids together. He won't let the woman see him cry.

'Come on then,' she says. 'Let's get you to the bathroom, get you cleaned up before I take you to see Mrs Prior – she's the lady who looks after everything here.' She makes a chuckling noise. 'She makes sure we all behave.'

Charlie grimaces. He doesn't like this Mrs Prior already.

'Come along, Charlie.'

She must have seen his face because her voice has changed. The tone is the same as the teachers used in school when he'd done something they didn't like.

He doesn't talk. He's been in the care home for two weeks and he's yet to say a word. Every night he wets the bed.

Every day clean clothes are left on the end of the bed. He

131

washes and dresses in silence, paying no attention to the three boys he shares the room with, shutting out their chatter, their attempts to get him to answer their questions. He sits at the table with them in the dining room, eating the cornflakes, the toast, ignoring the clatter and voices that surround him. On the small bus to the local primary school, he sits alone. The other boys refuse to sit with him. To them he's odd. He knows that. And he doesn't care.

Sometimes he hears the women in the home talking about him. It's as though they think he can't hear.

'Not one word. Not a peep. From getting up in the morning to going to bed. Every morning having to change the sheets. He won't even talk to Heather Butterworth from social services. She told Mrs Prior he won't tell her why he's behaved as he has, but she won't give up the weekly sessions with him. Mrs Prior says he's just looking for attention and Miss Butterworth should concentrate on the kids who want help. Apparently, he's the same in school. If he wants to be so difficult, I say we concentrate on those who are grateful for our help. It's a shame, but sometimes these kids are a lost cause.'

Charlie doesn't know why he doesn't talk. There are no words to say what he feels. He holds the frustration of being powerless inside him. The pain of his anger, his grief chokes him.

All he knows, all he wants, is his sister. He wonders if Chloe thinks of him, wherever she is.

Chapter 50

Chloe wants to put her hands over her ears but she knows it will make Dad even more angry, so she tries to block out his voice.

He's walking about in front of her shouting. She drops her head so her chin is on her chest. She won't look at him. Yesterday teatime she'd heard him, singing *Happy Birthday* with *her*, celebrating Saul's birthday. Chloe hated hearing her dad joining in. Resented it.

'So, young lady, you will come downstairs and you will sit at the table and you will eat lunch with us. Right?'

He stops pacing, stands in front of her. He heaves a huge breath out. 'Please, sweetheart.'

'No.' Chloe traps her fingers between her knees to stop them shaking. She can see his hands, his fingers are flexing, open, shut, open, shut. But there is no way she will sit at that table ever, ever again: hearing Saul gobbling his food, sloshing it around in his open mouth, Evie giving her sympathetic glances, which she appreciates but doesn't want to acknowledge. Dad pretending nothing's wrong and saying silly things to fill the silence. Lynne saying nothing at all.

With Charlie's empty chair next to her.

Chloe had got into the habit of cutting up her food and then eating only with her fork, so she could rest her palm on the seat of Charlie's chair. Until the day Lynne asked her why she was doing that and made fun of her. That was the day Chloe decided she wouldn't eat with any of them again.

Now her dad is crouching down in front of her.

'You have to eat, Chloe. You'll make yourself ill. It's been days since you had tea with everyone. Everyone's missing you.'

Not everyone, Chloe thinks. 'Not everyone. And I eat other times ... sometimes.'

'I know this is about your brother, and I know how hard it is for you to understand what's happened. But sometimes you just must accept that grown-ups know best.'

Chloe sucks on the corner of her lower lip, shakes her head slightly.

Another long sigh.

'Well, I'm telling you, you have to accept it. There are some things, decisions that can only be made by adults. You'll come to understand that one day. So, come on...' He stands up, holds out his hand.

'No.'

'What can I say to make you see sense, Chloe? You can't carry on like this. What else can I do?'

'Bring Charlie home.'

Chapter 51

'Well, what are we supposed to do, Graham?' Lynne's pacing the floor of their bedroom. 'She can't just stay in there, can she? This has been going on for weeks now. She's not eating properly and you don't need me to tell you she's making herself ill. We need help.'

'Don't even think about that, Lynne. You persuaded me to let that woman into my house last time. I won't let you get round me again.' *Not after what happened with Charlie. He can't lose his other child.*

'Graham! I did no such thing. You agreed.'

Her throat colours in patchy red. He knows she's furious, but when she speaks her voice sounds too tiny, as though she's bottling up her anger. 'Do you think it's right, how she's behaving, Graham? Healthy? In her room all the time? Back home from school and then in her bedroom on her own all evening?'

'She's not always on her own. Evie's with her a lot.'

'Oh yes, Evie.' She narrows her eyes, unable to hide her quick irritation. 'She's encouraging Chloe in this ... this strange behaviour. We can't let it go on. We have to get some guidance.' She stands, as though impatient, to do something about it now.

He puts his hand on her arm, stops her moving. 'No. We had advice and look what happened. Is happening.' His body is taut with tension, his insides hollow. 'I thought ... I hoped, after all that was said by social services.' *By you.* 'That he would have help and then be able to come back home. But it's over six weeks—'

'Because he's gone from bad to worse.' Her tone becomes softer. 'You heard what Heather told us last month, sweetheart. He's refusing to talk to anybody. It's sad, and I do understand how you must feel, but honestly, until he decides to communicate, they'll be unable to get to the bottom of why he behaved as he did.'

'I still think he would talk if I went to see him.' Graham sits down on the settee. *Bloody cold, slippery settee.* He presses the heels of his hands against his eyes.

Lynne sighs. 'We've discussed this before, Graham, I told you what the care home said when I rang there.'

'I shouldn't have slapped him. I've never hit either of my children before.' Graham can't help remembering the time Lynne said he should have smacked Charlie. *Well, now he has and look where they are.*

She's talking again. On and on. He can't shut her out.

'We should leave him alone, it would only make things worse, set him back even more. He needs to learn how to behave. There was nothing *we* could do. We weren't helping him, Graham, you know that.' She's speaking so rapidly now, he can't get a word in even if he wanted to. When she's like this it's better to shut up until she runs out of steam.

But her next words shock him. 'And it's starting now with your daughter. And we mustn't let it get as bad as that. We need to nip it in the bud, do something right now. I've talked all this over with Heather...'

'You met with Heather?' Fury and resentment make his voice abrasive. 'You had no right.'

'And some others,' she says calmly. 'We had a meeting in work.'

'A meeting? Without me? No, you've gone too far this time, Lynne, you had no right,' he repeats.

She fires back as fast as he expected. With words he expected. '*I* have no right?'

'No, you haven't. Not on your own. Not without me.' When he sees the flare of rage in her eyes, he knows this is going to be one of the nasty quarrels, but he doesn't care. 'It's not up to you to decide what to do with my – with Chloe.

'After Charlie you agreed we would talk things over before doing anything. And this … whatever is happening with Chloe, is too important for just one of us to decide. Even for just one conversation between *us*. Perhaps, yes, with discussions with experts, even with a child psychologist, if necessary, but not like this … deciding without telling me. Without me even knowing.'

'You really don't have a clue, do you, Graham,' she says incredulously. 'I have talked with a child psychologist, and the experts within social services because I couldn't talk to you about it. Because you refused to see what's happening right under your nose. I've even discussed it with Dr Hume, my boss. And everyone agrees. Everybody agrees that a break away from here, a short stay with a foster family would break the cycle of behaviour that Chloe has got herself into.' Her voice softens. She touches his arm, moves closer to him. 'We could even call it a little holiday. Suggest to her, it's a holiday.'

'I'm doing nothing, Lynne. Nothing. Not until I've talked to these people myself?'

'Okay. I'll have a word in work tomorrow and see if I can get everyone together for a meeting.'

'And I want Chloe to be there as well.'

'So, just for a while, it's been decided that you might be happier living somewhere else.'

'No!' For the first time since Heather came into her bedroom, Chloe looks at her. She's kneeling by the side of the bed. Today, instead of the brown sandals, brown leggings and the awful yellow blouse, she's wearing blue sandals, blue baggy jeans, and a black polo-neck jumper. She still has loads of clattering bracelets on her arms though. Her yellow hair is scrunched up on top of her head. 'No.'

'From what your dad and stepmother say, I know you've found it hard being here without your brother, and that's understandable. But care is best for him just now. And I think – and please trust me on this – I think you'll like where we've decided to place you.' She reaches up to take her hand. The metal bangles rattle up to her elbow, then down to her wrist when she pulls back as Chloe snatches her hand away.

'Placed' — as though she is just something to put somewhere. She glares at her father at the end of her bed, who looks down at his clasped hands. Chloe wonders if he is nervous, if he wishes this wasn't happening. Just like she's wishing they would all get out of her bedroom.

When she turns her gaze to Lynne, she's sitting with her elbows on Chloe's desk, her head resting in her hands, studying her. A slight smile hovers on her mouth but it's the smile with the hard eyes. *She* doesn't look nervous.

'Where are you putting me?' Chloe asks Heather but stares at Graham.

Graham hears the fear threaded through the defiant question. The meeting last week, that Lynne arranged, went just the way he'd dreaded it would. Everyone seemed to be of the same mind. His insistence that he wanted to leave things as they were, was seen as indifference to his daughter's pain. That he had no idea how to deal with her, or the situation. Once or twice in those ghastly two hours he spent listening to first one, then the other of those child behaviour experts, he suspected that Lynne had exaggerated Chloe's behaviour. But there was nothing he could put his finger on. In the end he'd conceded, agreed that a short stay in a foster home might help her.

But now, seeing Chloe's distress he begins to doubt. 'Perhaps...'

'Let Heather tell Chloe about the foster family, sweetheart,' Lynne interrupts.

'Thank you, Lynne. They're a lovely family called Mr and Mrs Brice, and they have two girls called Andrea and Annette. I think they're eleven as well, but a bit older than you.'

'Twins?'

'Yes.'

'Twins like me and Charlie. I bet their father isn't going to send them away.'

'Now, Chloe.' Heather reaches out again, seems to think better of it, lets her hand drop to her side. The bracelets rattle, loud in the silence following the remonstration.

'Where do they live?' Chloe asks eventually.

'In a village around forty miles from here called Kettleham.'

'Nice and far away then.'

For someone who is just eleven his daughter can be quite sarcastic. Graham forces himself to stay in the room. This situation is one of his own making. If he feels terrible it's his own fault. He looks towards the window. It's open a fraction and the curtains shivers in the draft sliding through the crack. The sky is seamed with different shades of grey driven by a fierce wind. He wishes he was outside, away from this mix of guilt and doubt. He – they – he and Lynne have set something in motion. Again. And he doesn't know how it will end.

Chapter 52

Chloe listens to the chatter and laughter coming from the kitchen. It's strange. Anyone, in any room in this house, can be heard by everyone else. In a way it's comforting, different from Moorcroft, with the large high-ceilinged rooms and long landing where any sound is dulled. When her dad had brought Lynne to live with them, and life became so different, being able to close doors and be alone was something that she and Charlie had treasured.

But after they'd taken her brother away, the muffled silence frightened her. She felt like she'd spent every waking moment holding her breath, or taking little sips of air, listening. Waiting for something awful to happen.

And she's still doing that. Listening. Waiting. She holds the continental quilt up under her chin. She doesn't want to get up. She doesn't belong here.

She'd not known what a foster family was. No one had told her. The only thing the social worker had said was that they would look after her until Dad and Lynne had sorted things out. Chloe wasn't sure what 'things' Heather meant. She suspected it was because she wouldn't stop screaming the day they took Charlie away. And then she'd refused to eat with them. Just with Evie in her bedroom. So she was here because of what she'd done. It was her own fault.

She's been here for three months.

At first, she didn't talk. But it wasn't like at home where Daddy had asked, then pleaded, and finally shouted at her for not speaking. Here, it was as though no one had noticed; they just included her in the things they said, until one day she'd answered and that was that.

They're a nice family – Mr and Mrs Brice – they've told her to call them Jack and Eileen, but that makes her feel uncomfortable. Lynne always said it was rude to call her, or any adult, by their first name. Charlie says — used to say — Lynne was cross because they refused to call her Mum. Chloe's not sure; she doesn't think Lynne wanted to be their mum any more than they wanted it.

She looks around the room. There's only three bedrooms in this house, and hers is the smallest, but it's cosy, all pale blue and white and it looks out onto the back garden with a swing and a slide. Not a double swing like she and Charlie have. Had. But she doesn't care; she hasn't played out there yet.

Sometimes she sees Mr and Mrs Brice's daughters, Andrea, and Annette, playing in the garden. They belong here. She doesn't. They wave to her when they see her watching them, gesture for her to join them, but she doesn't. Even so, they let her share their books. She loves reading. Sometimes she wishes they would leave her alone to read, but she doesn't like to say that. It would be rude.

She misses Charlie so much it hurts her stomach.

Some days it's getting easier to be here. Then she remembers Charlie and feels bad because she hasn't thought about him for a few hours. She doesn't sleep at night; she can't stop thinking about her brother. Where he is. What he's doing.

Chloe hears a whine and smiles. When the sound is followed by a scratching on the bedroom door she gets out of bed and lets the dog in.

'Hello, Jess.' She closes the door and kneels to ruffle the spaniel's ears. 'Have you had a good sleep?' When she gets back in bed, the dog follows, wagging her tail and licking her in excitement. 'I'm not sure you're supposed to be in here, but I'm glad you are.' It stops her missing Oscar a little.

'Breakfast, Chloe,' Mrs Brice calls from downstairs.

'Coming.' She gives the dog a last squeeze and thrusts her arms into her dressing gown.

'Come on, Jess,' she says. It's Friday, the last school day of the week, and she's glad. Kettleham High School is big, bigger than Mossleigh High and she's not made any friends yet. All the girls were already in little friendship groups no one will let her in. Most of the time they just stare or nudge one another and snigger. She thinks they know she's only a foster girl. Doesn't belong anywhere. Andrea and Annette look out for her at break and dinner times, but they have their own friends who make it obvious they don't want her with them.

Every morning she gets a little shiver of fear in her stomach, and it stays with her all day. Because she's alone. Without Charlie she's on her own.

She daren't ask how long she'll be here. She's frightened they will say forever.

Chapter 53

Graham's tired and a little drunk. He forces open his eyes and flattens his pillow under his head. His wife is still asleep. Smudges of mascara and stiffened spikey hair show that she fell into bed without her usual hair-brushing and meticulous regime of expensive creams.

He holds back a deep sigh and stares at the ceiling. How has it got like this? Only four years ago he was a respected part-owner of a successful business, a pivotal member on so many committees and, most importantly, proud father to two wonderful children. He closes his eyes when he thinks of Charlie and Chloe. Most of the time he tries not to – the despair is almost more than he can bear. The last few years are a long line of crushed dreams and bitter regret.

Lynne had seemed to offer a fresh start, but he sometimes wonders if he was still in mourning for Anna when he'd remarried. He still is in mourning. Like a split screen in his head, he sees the images of the two women: Anna, with her quiet ways, unexpected thoughtful gestures and their shared humour, Lynne, confrontational a lot of the time, determined to get her own way, her easy ability to make him feel stupid with just one look, one gesture, one word.

Anna, who'd loved their children, Lynne who found them so difficult he'd lost them.

Lynne mumbles in her sleep, reaches out to put her hand on his chest. He shifts away. His kaleidoscope of resentful thoughts fades as he remembers how proud he'd felt watching her last night at the Inner Wheel Annual Dinner.

She'd been in her element, looking gorgeous in the cringingly expensive purple evening gown she'd set her heart on. He'd been unable to resist her cajoling him in front of the shop assistant.

Being the chairwoman was important to Lynne. She'd

planned the evening down to the last detail: the seating plan at the top table, the string chamber orchestra and, most importantly, her speech. Graham knew it off by heart having listened to her almost every evening for the last fortnight.

Convinced that everyone knew what a disaster his life had become he hadn't wanted to go to the dinner but knew he didn't have a choice.

So he'd got drunk and now, with a pounding headache and blocked sinuses from all the cigarette smoke in the hall, he's regretting it.

Somewhere a dog barks. He thinks it's Oscar, then remembers. Oscar has gone. Graham is ashamed that he gave in and allowed the dog to be rehomed; he was a link between him, Anna, and the twins. But he knows Oscar was pining for Charlie and Chloe, that Lynne was right, they couldn't carry on with him barking day and night. That it's better for Oscar to have a new start with a new family.

So, as with all his misgivings about his life now, he's careful not to say too much about the dog. Not even when Evie asks. He just hopes Charlie and Chloe don't find out. Not until they come home again. Perhaps being away for a little while will help after all, let them come to terms with all the changes since his marriage to Lynne. And yet...

'You all right, Graham?'

'Sort of.'

She snuggles up to him strokes his chest. He stays still. She kisses his shoulder. 'I love being in bed with you, sweetheart. Just the two of us in our own little peaceful world.'

The loud and distorted guitar playing of some heavy metal

group has been coming through the wall from Saul's room for half an hour.

'Hardly peaceful, love.'

'Ah, it's just teenagers, Graham. It's his home as much as ours.'

'I guess.'

'You don't think I'm right?'

Graham hears the warning.

'Yes. Yes, you're right. Our kids *all* need a bit of understanding.'

She stills her hand on his chest, her fingers press into his skin. 'What do you mean?' As if she's waiting for him to say the wrong thing.

'Nothing.' He's ruined the mood. 'Just that all kids are different – like everyone.' He's relieved when she relaxes against him again.

'You're thinking of Charlie, aren't you?'

'I'm thinking of both of them.' He's grateful she seems to understand. 'I want them to know I'm ... we're here if they need us.'

'They do, I'm sure of that. But Charlie wasn't happy, love. You wanted what was best for him.' She kisses him on the jawline, pressing her lips against the corner of his mouth. 'And it was best that he went into care. You know that. And best for Chloe in foster care.'

'Only for now though.'

'You need to give the professionals the chance to find out what the problem is. And, if they say it wouldn't help if you went to see either of the twins at the moment, we have to accept that. They are two troubled children.'

'They're only just eleven, and they've been through so much, Lynne.'

'Exactly. And we couldn't help them. So, let's leave it to the experts. And, for now, let me make you happy.' She lifts herself up, sits astride him. 'Just the two of us in our own little world.'

Chapter 54

'You promised. Dad. You said last month we would go to see Charlie today.' Chloe stares stubbornly at the windscreen even though she can't see anything through the streaming rain.

'I know but it's difficult, Chloe. Please try to understand.'

There's a tingle in her arms and legs. It's not going to happen. She's not going to get to see her brother – again. 'Well, I don't. I don't understand.' She twists in her seat to face her father. You know he'll want to see me. If you've seen him, why can't I?'

'Oh, for goodness sake, Chloe. I haven't. I haven't seen him.'

'Why?' The tingle has changed to a pulsing – a warning. 'What's wrong?'

'Miss Butterworth said it's best we don't see Charlie for a while.'

'Why?' Chloe's stomach contracts against the swell of panic. 'What's happened? Has something happened to him?' Now she does look at him, wanting him to understand how frightened she is, how worried that the other boys are being cruel. to him, like Saul.

'No. I'm sure he's fine.' Her father has turned to his side window, rubbing at the back of his head.

'Don't you know? Why don't you know? If you don't tell me right now, Dad, I'm getting out of the car.'

'Nothing's wrong.' His voice sounds strange, like he has a cold. 'He's safe, Chloe. He's with other boys. Like in a big family—'

'We're his family, Dad. You and me.' She chews hard on her thumb nail. 'How long does he have to stay wherever it is?'

'Not long, I'm sure.' He's blinking rapidly. She knows he's upset. 'Listen, try to accept we can't go to see Charlie. Not at the moment. We can go anywhere else you like.'

'I wanted to see Charlie. That's all I want to do.'

'I know.' He turns off the windscreen wipers. The abrupt ending of the monotonous low squeal brings a thick tension into the car. She listens to the steady beat of the rain on the roof, the wet swish as other cars pass. 'We can go anywhere else you like,' he says again.

'If we're not going to see Charlie, I don't want to go anywhere else.' She waits a moment, sucking on her lower lip. She's frightened of what he'll say if she asks, but still blurts it out. 'How long do I have to stay with Mr and Mrs Brice?' She looks towards the house she's just left and sees Mrs Brice watching from the window tilting her head as if to question why they haven't driven off.

'Don't you like them?'

'No. Yes. They're all right. But I don't understand why we can't be with you. Not with *her*. Just us. You, me, and Charlie? Like it used to be after Mummy…'

'Please, Chloe. Just try to accept that things are as they are. It's difficult.'

'It's not. It is like Charlie told me. You don't love us anymore.' She pulls at the handle of the car door, pushes against it. 'Well, then, we don't love you, either.'

She shrugs his hand off her shoulder and jumps onto the pavement. Running up the path she bangs on the front door. When Mrs Brice opens it Chloe pushes past her and runs upstairs. Flinging herself on her bed she pulls the pillow over her head, trying to muffle her loud sobs. She wants to be with Charlie so much it hurts all over. Is it the same for him, wherever he is. Does he miss her?

Chapter 55

'You told her then?' Lynne's on the settee watching the midday news on television. She's in her uniform, ready to go to work. 'I thought I'd wait until you got back. I rang the surgery and explained; they understood completely that I needed to be here for you.'

'Thank you, that's lovely of you, sweetheart.' He knows she expects some acknowledgement, some gratitude for her gesture. And it's a small price to pay if it keeps the peace, even though, deep down, he feels he's being manipulated. 'It was as I expected. She was really upset.'

'You knew she would be.' Lynne holds out her hand. 'Come here. You're upset as well, I can tell. It's understandable.' He sits next to her. She pulls him close. 'You tried to make things work for us all. There were things you could have done better at the time. I tried to tell you but you wouldn't listen.'

Had she? He doesn't remember. So it's his fault. He should have listened to her. He'd tried to be understanding, he was sure. He'd done what she said were the right things to do to get his children to accept the change. Hadn't he? Sometimes he can't think straight. His throat constricts. 'I just don't know...'

'It will all be all right, Graham.' She presses her forehead against his shoulder. 'I'm sure everything will settle down. It is for the best, you know that. This is what the twins need. This is what we need.'

There's a hollowness inside him. And inside the house — where Charlie and Chloe should be.

He's tired. All he wants to do is sleep, forget everything — just for a few minutes. Forget what a mess it all is.

Lynne gives him a quick hug and stands. 'Come on, let's get you to your precious showrooms. We can go in my car. I'll drop you off. Then I can pick you up later, seeing as we now finish work at the same time. Evie and Saul are big enough to look after themselves. And we've got your dinner tonight with the school governors. I think I'll wear that new black trouser suit I bought last week; it gives an air of expertise, I think. Like I know what I'm talking about. What do you think, Graham?'

'Expertise about what, Lynne? It's only the usual dinner, you know.' That he doesn't want to go to.

She tuts. He's noticed lately that she makes that noise quite a lot. About a lot of things.

'Good grief, Graham, weren't you listening to me yesterday? The idea that the new R.E. teacher wants to teach all those different faiths? It's totally inappropriate in a school like ours, for heaven's sake. Mossleigh Primary is a C. of E. school and it's the only religion the children need.'

'I'm not sure that's anything to do with...' Graham almost says 'you', but stops himself. 'With us, sweetheart. And I don't think the committee dinner is the right place for a debate on the school curriculum.'

'Nonsense. As the wife of the longest standing school governor – which you are, Graham – I have every right. Now we really must go. I have to catch up on the calls I should have done this morning.'

She opens a new packet of cigarettes. 'Oh, by the way I've made an appointment at that new hairdressers that's opened up on the High Street. My usual one made a mess of my hair last time. It's a bit expensive but I heard the mayor's wife goes there, so I thought if it's good enough for her, it's good enough for me. Lend me your credit card will you, sweetheart?' She holds out her hand, opening and closing her fingers, narrowing her eyes against her cigarette smoke.

'I transferred your allowance into your account last week, Lynne.' He doesn't miss the raised eyebrows. But can't deal with the inevitable row. 'Here you are then. Anything to make you beautiful – more beautiful,' he adds hastily.

Lynne takes the card without a word, picks up her nurse's bag and stubs out her cigarette in the already overflowing ashtray.

'I want to run something past you in the car, Lynne. I'm not sure I want to carry on being a governor anymore.' She's frowning. 'Seems a bit pointless since the twins aren't there now.' He's uncomfortable when anyone on the board asks him about Charlie and Chloe. 'And I know the others are questioning my right to be a governor.'

'Nonsense. You still have a standing in the community, Graham. You are valued on so many other committees, especially the Rotary, and I'm right behind you, you know that. Please don't jeopardise our standing in the community.'

'It wouldn't.'

'It would. So, please don't resign. Let's see what happens. Now...' She hustles him to the front door. 'Let's go. I'm still thinking we actually don't need two cars you know.'

Chapter 56

Every night, lying awake, staring into the thick blackness of the small room he shares with three other boys his age, Charlie shuts out the noise of their breathing and restless tossing and turning, and pretends he's alone. He tries hard to send messages to his sister with his mind.

He'd been promised that he would be able to see Chloe, that Dad would bring her. But it hasn't happened. He pinches his top lip between his forefinger and thumb, wonders if Oscar misses him.

He knows he's been in the home for months. And still he refuses to talk.

'You're making it very difficult for yourself, you know,' Miss Isaacs says, rubbing carbolic soap over his hair, while he sits with his knees clutched to his chest in the narrow bath. The white tiled bathroom is cold. The November wind whistles through the badly fitted sash windows and it's pitch-black outside, even though it's only five o'clock in the afternoon. He shivers, goose bumps on his arms, and he rests his forehead on his knees.

'Sit up. I can't wash your hair if you're all crouched over. Here, cover your eyes, I'm going to rinse. Then we'll get you dried and into your pyjamas. Then it'll be supper time.'

He wants to say he can dry himself, put on his own pyjamas, but doesn't. He's decided that he'll be ready to talk when they are ready to tell him how long he'll be staying at the care home.

He's never alone. There's no time to think, except when he's in bed, when he sends messages to Chloe. He's convinced himself that, if he tries hard enough, one day she will reply.

He stands rigid while the woman vigorously rubs his body dry with the scratchy towel, wincing when she's just as rough drying his important bits. That was something his mum used to say to him, 'Don't forget to dry your important bits.' Even when he was four he was trusted to do that, to be grown up enough to dry and dress himself. In this place he has no choices.

'I'm telling you now, my lad, if you don't buck your ideas up and stop sulking, Mrs Prior will have no choice but to send you somewhere where they won't put up with such nonsense.' She taps him on the shoulder with her bony finger. 'Think on.'

A week later, when he comes out of his classroom, Mrs John, the headmistress, and another woman are waiting for him in the corridor.

'This is Ms Hall, Charlie,' The quiet calm in her voice reminds him of his mum and he swallows.

Something's happening – he can tell from the way Mrs John tilts her head, and smiles but looks worried at the same time.

'She's your new social worker. She's going to take you to a different care home. I'm afraid that also means you won't be coming here anymore, you'll be going to a different school. I know you haven't been here long, but we'll miss you. I'll miss you.' She turns to the social worker, speaks to her as though Charlie isn't here. 'You are sure this is for the best? It's just that I feel we were getting somewhere with him. I've been sensing this week that he was going to speak. Something's made him like this. I feel we've failed him.'

'The home doesn't want him anymore. He's going to another home, where they can deal better with him.'

Charlie keeps his head lowered. His insides feel cold and swimmy. What's happening? Where are they sending him?

'There's nothing we can do. He may fit in better in a different home.' The social worker's tone is brisk, just like his dad's was when he left him. 'Come along, Charlie. No need to worry. It'll all be fine.'

And like all the others, he knows she's lying.

Chapter 57

'I don't understand.' Chloe stares from one to the other of her foster parents. 'Why isn't Dad coming?' Mr and Mrs Brice exchange edgy glances. She watches the way he pushes his glasses up the bridge of his nose. Coughs. 'Tell me. Please.'

'It's your stepmother, she's not very well. So your dad can't leave her, I'm afraid.' His voice is sympathetic, quiet. Chloe has never heard him shout. She's never heard anyone shout in this house; they talk when one of them is cross, or upset, or sad.

Like now. She's sad. She wants them to talk to her, tell her why everything's gone wrong. 'He didn't come last month either. And that was because he had to take her somewhere.' She fights back the tears, but they win.

'Come and sit down, pet,' Mrs Brice says.

'It's not fair.'

'I know. We know, don't we, Jack?'

'We do that.' They sit on either side of her on her bed. 'It's hard,' he says.

Chloe tucks her hands between her knees. 'I want to see Charlie. I've never been without him before all this happened. I need him.' Not having him with her has been the biggest thing she's struggled with over the last year.

The blood swooshes in her ears.

'You could take me to see Charlie? Couldn't you?'

The prolonged quiet in the room feels like something physical to Chloe, a gate slowly closing on the hope that had risen up in her. Shutting her out.

Mr Brice takes off his glasses and rubs his eyes.

'I'm sorry, we can't, pet.' Mrs Brice laces her fingers together on her lap. 'Charlie's been moved to another home.' She clears her throat. 'Apparently he was moved last week. Your Dad only told us this morning. And I'm afraid it's further away. Too far for us to take you – we'd need to stay overnight and with Jack's work... I'm sorry, Chloe.' She waits a while. When Chloe stays silent, she says, 'Anyway, your dad wanted us to say he promises to ring you as soon as your stepmother's better. He promises, if he can, he'll take you to see your brother then.'

If he can? Chloe shrugs. 'I think he's just hoping I'll forget about Charlie.'

'Oh, I'm sure that's not true, Chloe.' Mrs Brice shakes her head. 'Your dad loves you both. It must be difficult for him as well, you know.'

'Well, he's done this. He let *her … Lynne,* get the social lady, Heather, to come and see us; to make this happen. Charlie didn't do that many bad things. And if he did,' she says, defiantly, 'it was because of *her.* And *she* made sure he was sent away to some horrible home. And persuaded everyone it was best for me to be here.'

There's that look between them again. Like they know something she doesn't.

'Don't you like it here with us, pet?'

'Yes, I'm sorry. I didn't mean to be rude. I just wish everything hadn't changed.'

'It's all right. Don't worry about that. We just want you to be happy while you're with us. And school's good, isn't it? Last week, when we saw your form teacher, she said you're doing well with your lessons.'

'It's okay. And Andrea and Annette look after me at break and lunch times.'

'Good.'

'What's wrong with *her*, anyway? Lynne? She's ill?' Chloe can't help sounding hopeful when she looks at her foster mother.

'We didn't ask; we didn't like to.'

'Probably one of her migraines.' Chloe pulls a face. 'She gets those. When Charlie and me were home we always had to be quiet.' She sucks her bottom lip, thinking. 'But it can't last forever, can it? Couldn't you ask Dad to come when her migraine's gone. I wouldn't mind waiting if it was only for another week.'

'Well...' Mrs Brice looks at her husband. 'We can ask.'

'It's not as though he can only come to see me once a month, is it? I mean, you wouldn't mind me going out with him more than that. Would you?'

'Gosh, no! No, of course not. We'd love for you to see him, whenever you can, pet.'

'Thank you.' Chloe locks the hope away for something to treasure later. 'You'll ask then?'

'We'll ask.' Mrs Brice pats Chloe's hand. 'We'll do our best. We can't promise what will happen, but we'll do our best.'

Later, lying in bed, gazing out of the window at the pale crescent moon floating through the hazy clouds, Chloe remembers what Evie always said: Lynne pretends a bad headache when something isn't how she wants it to be. What if that's what she's always going to do? What if she and Charlie never see one another ever again?

Chapter 58

Graham treads carefully up the stair. It's two hours since Lynne went to lie down. He hopes she's had a good sleep and the

156

migraine has eased. He holds the envelope the postman has just delivered.

'You awake, love?' He opens the door a fraction. Hears the resigned sigh. 'Sorry, I just need to have a talk.' The room is in darkness except for the light he's letting in from the landing.

'What is it, Graham?'

I've had a letter from one of Mum's friends.' Graham holds the letter up so he can read it in the light from the landing. He can't help the tremor in his voice. He clears his throat. 'Mum's had a stroke. They think it's what happened before when she fell. It was a slight stroke that time. This one's worse.' He says what he needs to say next in a rush. 'I need to see her, Lynne. I thought I'd go as soon as I can get hold of Phil and tell him what's happened, that I won't be able to be at the garage this week…'

He opens the door wider, sees his wife flinch as she sits up, shielding her eyes. 'And you're more bothered about Phil Baxter and the garage? Before me?'

'No! No, of course not. Sorry, love. But I need to see Mum.'

'I don't want you to go, Graham. I need you.' She falls back onto the bed, her voice weaker.

'But, love, Mum's in hospital.'

'So she's being looked after. There's nothing you can do. Please, Graham. Leave it for a few days – see how she is, how things are.'

'But she says they've been trying to get hold of me.'

'Who's they?'

'I don't know. I suppose she means Mum's friends or neighbours—'

157

'So why not say that?'

'Sorry, love. It's just that Betty, Mum's friend, says she's been trying to phone but thinks there's something wrong with the line.' He reads, '"Because it sounds as if someone's answered but then I get the dialling tone." That's why she's written.' He waits to see if Lynne says anything. Should he come further into the bedroom and close the door so the brightness won't hurt her eyes? He decides to stay in the doorway, so he can read the rest to her when – if – she asks him to.

'Actually, I can't remember the last time I used the phone, can you?' Silence. 'Lynne?'

'What? Oh for God's sake, Graham do get to the point.'

He wishes she could understand how upset he is about his mother. 'It's just that I do really need to go. I want to.'

'And leave me like this? Please, Graham. In the morning I'll need you to tell the surgery I won't be able to work tomorrow. This migraine is the worst I've had for a long time; I'm almost afraid to move.' She pulls the covers over her head. 'And Saul will need taking and picking up from his judo class after school. It's important; he can't miss it with him training for his next Dan grading.' She groans. 'I can't take him, feeling like this.'

'But, Lynne, Mum is...'

'Please, Graham. I can't...'

'Oh.' He hesitates. 'I'll try the phone, see if it's working first.'

'You'll stay?'

'I'll try ringing Betty. See what's happening. Okay?'

'You'll stay then?'

'If it sounds as if Mum's stable.'

'She's in the best place. In hospital.' Lynne lifts her head, peers over the covers at him. 'Thanks, love, you're the best husband I could wish for.'

In the hall, he picks up the phone, listens to the dialling tone. He rocks on his heels. It means trouble, but he knows it's the right thing to do.

'Sorry, love, I've thought about it and I've decided I will go to see how Mum is. I can be there and back in a day.'

Lynne doesn't answer. She doesn't move.

'Unless I'm needed to stay longer.' He hesitates. 'Lynne? I'll ask Evie to ring the surgery for you. And, when I ring Phil, I'll see if he can sort something out for Saul.

'Don't bother. I wouldn't want to put you – or either of them – out. I'll do it myself.'

'Oh, well, if you're sure. I'll get off then. I'll keep in touch, probably ring you tonight. The phone seems to be working.' He doesn't chance going to kiss her.

Closing the door he waits a moment. Hears the thud of something hitting it on the other side.

Chapter 59

Lynne isn't talking to Graham. She hasn't since he came back from seeing his mum. He doesn't care, because it means she isn't pecking his head. 'Pecking his head' is a phrase one of the young apprentices in the garage says a lot about his mum, and Graham thinks it's really apt for the way Lynne picks on him for almost everything he does wrong. At least what she says he's done wrong.

He knows why she's not speaking to him. But his mum was in hospital, she'd had a stroke that took away her speech. And he'd known he was right to go against Lynne the moment he saw his mum. Saw the way her eyes lit up, the pathetic crooked smile she gave him, felt the heat of her hand when he took it between his.

So he's put up with Lynne's sulking for the last five days, spending longer days at the garage. Even going for a pint once at the end of the day with Phil.

And he's going to ring social services to find out if they have any news about Charlie. If there's any sign that his son is improving, he'll ask if it's possible to visit him. He wants his family reunited. If it can be, he'll be able to tell Chloe, and it might make things right between the two of them.

But when he arrives home from work, he finds Lynne waiting for him in the hall.

'I've had a phone call from Chloe's foster parents. They said she doesn't want to see you and she said to tell you not to try to contact her.'

'Did they say why?' Graham's voice cracks.

'No. But probably best for all of us. Gives us a break from the drama. Look, let's put the last few days behind us, eh?' She kisses him fleetingly, her lips firm on his. 'I'll make a brew and then get on with the dinner.'

'Right,' he says. There's a sour taste on his tongue. 'Right.' It isn't what he wants to say; he wants to rage, to tell her how bitter he feels, having lost both his children. To shout and swear until his agony gets through to his wife. Underneath, he blames Lynne. Even though he tells himself she tried to get on with the

160

twins, he has an uneasy feeling that he missed something he should have known as a father. The instinct that something was wrong, that Anna would have picked up on.

He's betrayed their children. How, he doesn't know but he recognises in his bones that he can't go back and make everything right. 'Right,' he says again, following his wife into the kitchen.

Wherever you are, Anna, please forgive me. I didn't mean this to happen.

Chapter 60

'It seems your father is unable to visit anymore.' The social worker shifts uneasily in her chair.

'What do you mean? Why can't he?' Chloe can't keep her hands still. She fidgets, pushes her hair behind her ears, blows her fringe away from her eyes. Waits. 'What's wrong? Is it Granny? Has something happened to Granny?'

'No. Well, you know your grandmother is ill, don't you?' Heather waits until Chloe nods. 'She's an old lady. But it's not about your grandmother.'

'So what is it then? What did he say?'

'Well, I haven't actually been able to speak to him personally. But I have spoken to your stepmother.' Heather purses her lips. 'She says he needs a complete break from everything...'

'Even me?'

'I'm sorry, Chloe. He is, she says, totally run down and unable to cope.'

A chill runs through Chloe. 'What does "cope" mean? How is he "run down"?'

'It means he needs to rest. Perhaps he's been working too hard.'

Chloe nods slowly; she understands that. 'He does, he's always busy. He owns a garage and has lots of men working for him. But he could come here? I wouldn't ask him to do anything. We could just sit and talk?'

'No, I don't think that would work. Your stepmother said he mustn't do anything.'

'I think she's said it to keep him from seeing me. She's done everything she can do to stop him coming here, with her pretend migraines.'

'I don't know anything about that, Chloe. But I'm not sure that's true.'

Chloe juts her jaw forward, anger overriding her fear. 'How would you know? I haven't seen you in ages. You never come here.' She's being rude, she knows that, but she can't help it. 'She stopped Dad seeing Charlie as well.'

'No, it's a decision made by my superiors. Best that Charlie is given a chance to settle into the new care home. Anyway, I can't talk to you about your brother.'

'But he's my brother. I should know about him. No one will ever tell me what's happened to him – where he is. I've been asking to see him. Dad wouldn't take me before, and now he won't be coming here, I won't get a chance to see Charlie. Maybe never. Will I? Will I?' She's yelling. It's wrong to yell at an adult but she doesn't care. 'Mr and Mrs Brice have asked you if I could see him. They told me they have and I believe them.

Now you're not here to tell me I can go to see my brother, you're here to tell me I won't be seeing my dad either. And Granny's poorly in hospital, and I can't get to see her.'

'I'm sorry.' Heather flushes. 'I've been—'

'Busy. That's what all grown-ups say when they don't keep their promises.'

'No, I didn't mean that … I haven't … I didn't … I'm sorry, Chloe.'

'What about Charlie then? When can I see him?'

'I'm sorry. As I said, it's better he's left to settle in. He's not in my area anymore but I will try to find out how he is.'

'You'll try?' Chloe jumps up from her chair. 'Well, you can also tell Dad I don't care. And I don't believe he's "run down" … whatever that means. I think he's let *her* tell him what to do because he doesn't love either me or Charlie anymore.'

'Oh, I don't think that's—'

'I don't care what you think. I know he doesn't. She's told him he can't see us anymore and he's agreed. Because he's frightened of her. She's wicked. Wicked and horrible.'

Chloe's voice breaks. She runs out of the room.

Chapter 61

'I'm sorry, Chloe. If there was any way we could keep you here, we would. But it will take me a long time to get over this illness, I think.'

Chloe breathes in and out slowly, trying to calm her panic. She can hear the dull ticks of the grandfather clock in the hall.

It used to keep her awake in the night when she first came here. Now it sometimes soothes her to sleep.

'I'm sorry you're poorly, Mrs Brice.'

'Eileen. I've kept saying, pet, it's Eileen.'

Chloe thinks it's too late to change what she calls her foster mother now, but still says, 'I could stay and look after you with Mr Brice and Andrea and Annette.'

'That's a lovely thing for you to say, pet, but I can't ... we can't foster anymore. Not until we know how things go.'

'So I could come back?' Her world is spinning.

'No, I shouldn't have said that. What I meant to say is that we won't be able to be foster parents anymore. I'm sorry.' Mrs Brice is knotting her fingers together. For the first time Chloe sees how pale she is, the dark shadows under her eyes.

Heather touches her hand to divert Chloe's intense stare. 'We've asked if it's possible for you to go home but...'

'No. I don't want to go back there.' Chloe notices the social worker is wearing glasses. Glasses with round frames. Like one of the Beatles. That John Lennon. She hasn't seen her wearing glasses before. They don't suit her.

Does the social worker look relieved because she's said she won't go back to Mossleigh?

'I thought not, from what Eileen has told me. So we need to find you another placement.'

Placement. Another family to live with, to try to fit into. 'What about Charlie? Could he come with me?'

She hears a door bang, a draught whistles softly under the living room door, someone runs upstairs. One of the girls laughs: Annette, she thinks. *How can she laugh when her mum's ill?*

When she turns her gaze back to the social worker, she's looking at Chloe with concern. 'No. That's not possible, I'm afraid.'

'Well, can I see him then?'

'That's not up to me. Charlie has a different care worker. In another area.'

'I don't understand. Where is he? I don't understand why we can't be placed together.'

'It's just not possible.'

Is that a hint of impatience? Chloe persists, the panic rearing up again. 'How do I know he's all right?'

'Tell you what, Chloe, how about I try and find out for you? But for now I want to talk to you about a new foster home.' Heather adjusts her glasses, riffles through her files and produces a sheet of paper. 'Look, this is the family. I think you'll like them.'

Chloe wants to stay here, but, looking from one woman to the other, she knows not to say that. The decision has obviously been made. She shrugs. 'Whatever.'

'Don't be like that, pet.' Mrs Brice tugs at the front of her cardigan.

Chloe looks at the gas fire on the hearth. The blue and yellow flames are high. The room's hot but her foster mother is shivering.

'Are you all right?'

'I am, just a bit cold. I'm sorry, Chloe, there's nothing we can do about this, I can't change things. And I'm sure you'll soon get to like the new family. Why don't you go with Heather to meet them?'

It's a suggestion that isn't a suggestion. There's no choice. Chloe's frightened, so she stays silent.

'Chloe?'

The moment stretches out.

'What do you think?'

'Will you try to find out where Charlie is? Please. And will you ask if I can see my granny?'

'I'll see what I can do about both things. I promise.' Heather gathers the papers together. 'Right. The sooner we go to meet your new family, the better, I think.' She glances at Mrs Brice, who dips her head.

She can't wait to get rid of me. Chloe glares, even when she sees the hurt in the woman's eyes.

The grandfather clock chimes once.

'Fine. Let's go then.'

Chapter 62

'Who was that? Who were you talking to?' Lynne lets the back door crash behind her when she comes into the kitchen. 'Bloody rain. And I've only just put this lot out.' She bangs the basket of wet clothes onto the table and comes into the hall, drying her hair with a small towel. 'I heard it ring. If you'd given me a chance, I would have answered it. I told you I'll answer the phone. Stop that lot from the garage bothering you at home every time you have a day off. Which isn't often enough.'

Graham's standing still, his back to her, his hand resting on the wall phone.

The kitchen tap is dripping into the sink, soft splashes on the water in the bowl.

She stops rubbing at her hair. 'Why are you always in such a rush to get to the phone? Anyone would think you had a secret lover.' She laughs, but it sounds forced. 'Graham? Hello? Are you listening? Who. Was. On. The. Phone?'

'Sorry, Lynne. It just rang and rang and I didn't know where you were. I thought I should answer...'

'I told you I was bringing the washing in. Didn't you hear the rain battering on the window? No, I guess not. Always in your own world. Well? Don't tell me you have to go to work? You promised to clear out the rest of that rubbish from the loft.'

Not rubbish, Charlie's things from his bedroom. Now all packed away, just like his son. But Graham knows better than to share his anguish with Lynne. He knows how angry she gets, and that's the last thing he can cope with now. 'I know.'

'Well?'

'My mother has died. That was Betty, her friend.' He goes to the sink, turns the tap harder. Looks at the cups he was washing when the phone rang 'I should have gone to see her again.'

Lynne changes immediately. Her voice is soft. 'Well, you didn't, Graham, you decided not to. You mustn't blame yourself.'

He remembers getting into the car, ready to go back to see his mother in hospital, when Saul rushed out of the house to say Lynne had fallen down the stairs. He'd hurried into the hall to see her crying, holding her ankle. Instead of going to see his mother he had taken his wife to the A&E department in the local hospital. Nothing was broken but Lynne had spent the next few days resting on the settee. Still, he can't say that now. Lynne is right, it had been his decision.

'I'll need to go. I need to see her. And there'll be things to sort out ... the funeral...'

'And her house. All her things.' She looks into his eyes. Shakes her head. 'You're in no state to do all that. Leave it to me, love. Let me sort everything out.'

'No.' It's something he must do. 'I can't think about the house, Lynne. There's time enough for that. I just need to see her.'

'I know.' She hugs him again. 'Look, I'll tell Sue next door to keep an eye on things here, and I'll come with you. And while you go to see your mother I'll start to sort things out.'

'I should organise her funeral. It's the least I can do.'

'You're still in shock, Graham, I've seen this so many times as a nurse, and I promise I will do all I can to help you.'

'Thank you, love. Thank you so much.' *This is the Lynne, the real Lynne I fell in love with*. 'I don't deserve you.'

'Don't be silly. I'm your wife, sweetheart. Of course I'll look after you. It's what I'm here for. You just leave everything to me.'

'So that's it, the date is sorted with the funeral director in Lowermill. I can start to arrange everything else tomorrow. It'll just be a small funeral, Graham, at your mother's age, I'm sure she outlived a lot of her friends.' Lynne comes into the lounge where he's sitting with Phil and Margaret.

Graham winces. He sees Margaret raise her eyebrows at Phil. 'Mum did have a lot of friends, love.'

'We'll see. I'll get a notice put in the local newspaper...?' She waits.

'That'll be the *Lowermill Chronicle*.'

'Right. I can do that this afternoon.' Lynne claps her hands together. 'Well, it was lovely of you both to come to see Graham, but I think he's tired now.' She smiles brightly.

'No, honestly, love, I'm fine.'

'And I know you better than you know yourself, my dear. You look exhausted. You need to have a lie down; it's been a difficult couple of days. And as I said, it was lovely of you to call, Phil and … umm, but for now…?' She makes a sweeping gesture towards the door.

'Perhaps you're right, Lynne. I am tired. I've not been sleeping well.' Graham says it as an apology to his friends.

'No problem, mate.' Phil gets up from his chair to shake Graham's hand. Margaret gives him a hug, pats his back. 'Let us know if you need anything, love?'

'He will.' Lynne opens the front door. 'Call anytime. Though of course it's the funeral in only three week's time and we've a lot to sort out before then. I'm presuming you'll manage at the garage without Graham for the next month, Phil? We'll be leaving first thing in the morning to clear out the house and get it up for sale.'

Chapter 63

'I don't know what I would have done without you, Lynne. I'm so grateful.' How many times has he said that over the last week? 'And for sorting out the arrangements for the funeral.'

'Nonsense. I'm always glad to help. And I've sorted out so

many funerals for the relatives of my clients who lived alone, and helped with those who've died in many of the care homes I go to, I know how to give loved ones a final farewell. I hope to do the same for your mother, my love.'

It's been a week Graham will never forget. So many years of memories were in that house. But it has only taken days to clear them away into what they will only ever be now … memories.

Lynne took all his mother's clothes, ornaments and the knick-knacks to the hospital charity shop, the furniture to a charity that she found. For that he's glad.

Everyone has said how wonderful Lynne has been. She's been a whirlwind, making decisions for him, taking the pressure off him. She's been in her element. Sometimes he thinks she's enjoying herself. There's a hint of resentment creeping up inside him.

When he saw his mother's body, she looked younger than she had the last time he'd seen her, the last time he hugged her. He'd known she hadn't forgiven him for the wedding, the children, the infrequent phone calls. He has to live with that now.

When he gets home, he will have time to process everything before they return to Lowermill for the funeral.

'It's good to be going home.'

She smiles briefly at him with a quick sideways glance. 'You all right?'

'I will be.'

'You loved your mother, and she loved you. You're bound to miss her – even though you didn't see much of her.'

Her last words stung. He'd always been so close to both his parents until these last three or four years. When Anna was alive and the twins tiny, his parents spent a lot of time with his family. But he didn't say that. He didn't want Lynne's expansive mood deflated. It's easier when she's like this.

'We've got all the photo albums and Mum's jewellery box in the boot, haven't we, Lynne?'

'Yes, all safely packed away, with the other bits and pieces you wanted to keep.'

His mother had kept all his Air-fix models and the wooden boxes he'd made in school woodwork classes in his old bedroom. For sentimental reasons, he supposes.

'Have you got Mum's wedding and engagement ring. I thought I would give them to Chloe?'

'Of course you must. I'll keep them safe for you, Graham. Now, let's get you home.' She checks the mirror and, changing into third gear, overtakes a coach. 'You know, Graham, I've said it before loads of times and the more I think about it, we don't need two cars. I mean, I need mine obviously for my job. But with you, once you're at the showrooms, your car sits there doing nothing all day. Yolanda says you haven't been anywhere for weeks in it. It seems such an expensive waste of money, the tax and insurance, don't you think?'

Yolanda? Why would Lynne be talking to the receptionist? 'Well, the expenses go through the garage, Lynne. When were you talking to Yolanda?' He doesn't trust the girl. Phil said money is still missing, unaccounted for, from the petty cash.

She wafted away his question. 'Oh, I saw her in the supermarket.' She glanced at him, frowning. 'On the few days I couldn't pick you up, you could always use one of the cars on the forecourt, couldn't you?'

'I'm not sure, love, I do like my Cresta.'

'Yes, but when it costs so much to run, seems stupid.'

'I told you, the business pays for my car—'

'Huh? Well, think about what I said. You'll see it makes sense just to have one car on the road. And I need mine.'

Graham rests his head on the side window of the passenger seat. He's so tired. The tablets Lynne got for him to help him sleep since his mum died do the trick, but they also make him feel useless during the day.

'I can't think straight at the moment, Lynne. Too much going on in my head.'

'Of course, love.' She casts a sideways glance at him. 'You just rest.'

Chapter 64

Charlie's been living in Madeley House for the past month. He's sitting on the stone wall under the shade of oak tree, the large weed-covered lawn is spread out in front of him. He comes here every day, whatever the weather. It's as far away from the large stone building as he can be.

If he turns his head to look over his shoulder, there are uninterrupted views of undulating fields, blotches of dark green, dense trees on the hills. An uneven quilt of green fields disappear into blue mist, blending with the sky. He's watching, scanning the grounds. Vigilant.

The other boys leave him alone; he's the odd one out. He's been the odd one out at the last three places he's been at. He's still refusing to speak. It's not even for a reason now – he just doesn't want to speak, to be part of their world. And if anyone objects to that he's got his fists; he's learned the hard way how to look after himself. With each placement it becomes more difficult to blend into the background. His reputation goes before him. He's seen as a challenge; someone who's told he will be 'knocked into shape'. Until they give up.

This home is the worst. He hasn't a clue where it is but he does know it's isolated and, unlike all the other places, the boys aren't sent out to local schools but continue their education, such as it is, within the home. Listening at doors, on the stairs, he's discovered this is the sort of place where boys are sent who have been in trouble with the police. Or have a reputation for running away from care homes. Like himself. He heard the main man, who seems to be over all the others, Mr Lumley, complain yesterday that he preferred the way the old place was run — 'a proper approved school', he'd called it. He'd spat out, 'Not this namby-pamby *community home with education.*'

Charlie had heard the murmur of agreement from the other men in the staff room before he'd had to hide in the laundry cupboard on the landing. Hold his breath so tightly his chest hurt, when the soft tread of footsteps passed the door.

There's movement across the large square of grass. In the opposite corner, where the stone walls meet, under the overhanging branches of another oak tree, Charlie can see a man. He's standing still, with his back to him, his legs straddled. Perhaps he's just having a piss. Charlie waits. But then the man stiffens, throws back his head, makes a weird noise.

And then he knows; he knows what he's seeing. He's seen this happen before, since he's been living here. Only that was

173

in the corridors in the middle of the night, when he'd got up to go to the bathroom.

The blackbird singing in the tree above him, the low rustle of the breeze through the leaves, seem to disappear. All Charlie can hear is the ragged drawing in of air into his chest.

The man moves to one side. A small figure is hunched on the wall. Charlie recognises him as the kid who had been locked in the wardrobe in their dormitory last night. Who'd shrank back when Charlie had opened the door and tried to persuade him to come out.

Now the boy bends forward, retching. A stream of vomit hits the ground in front of him. When he straightens up, he wipes his mouth with the sleeve of his jumper. He's crying. Charlie sees the child's crumpled face, the shake of his shoulders. Should he do something? Tell someone about what just happened? But he'd have to speak. And tell who? No one from social services has come near since he arrived. Lumley can do what he wants. Charlie shivers. Keep out of it, he thinks. There's nothing he can do to stop it

The man laughs. He turns, fastening his trousers, and stops still. He's looking over at Charlie.

He's in the shade, isn't he? Mr Lumley won't ... can't see him? Charlie feels a rush of saliva in his mouth. He shrinks back until the solid trunk of the oak presses against his spine. A branch sways down in front of him, as though protecting him under the cover of its leaves

But the man is walking towards him. He's grinning. Charlie wants to run but he can't move. And anyway there's nowhere to go. To escape.

Out of the corner of his eye, Charlie sees the flash of a small figure running away, crouched over. Go out of sight.

'Right, lad, let's 'ave a look at you.' The hand on Charlie's shoulder is heavy, forcing him off the wall. His legs want to give way, but he clenches his fists; he will fight, if he needs to.

In his head he hears Chloe saying, 'It'll be all right, Charlie, it'll be all right.' But he's heard her say that a million times over the last few years, and it never is.

The fingers are rough under his jaw as his chin is lifted. 'Ah Collins. I thought it was you, always creeping around. Spying. Seeing nothing. That right, isn't it, lad? You see nothing.' He jerks Charlie's head back so swiftly he's not prepared and a bone cracks. A pain shoots through the back of his neck and he closes his eyes. 'I said, you saw nothing. Nothing. That's right, isn't it?'

Charlie doesn't move under his grasp. Doesn't speak.

'Ah, right, yeah. You're the bastard who won't talk, aren't you?' The man grins. 'Well, that works in my favour, at least. And don't worry, there'll soon be plenty for you to see.' He pauses, looks around, digs his fingers hard into Charlie's shoulder, jerks his chin up again. 'Look at me.' His eyes are narrowed, lips stretched in a grin when he says, 'I've got something special lined up for you, m'lad. We've got our monthly party coming up; friends coming over from...' He nods towards the tall iron gates, closed at the end of the long driveway. 'From away. Something to look forward to, eh? Something my friends are looking forward to an' all.' He leers. 'But I'm thinking, with you 'aving seen young Thatcher enjoying himself just then, that it might do you good to have a day or two in the cellar. Just in case you're thinking of grassing, like.'

A prickle of hot sweat sears Charlie's scalp, a shrill whirring filling his ears. He's heard other boys talk of being locked in the small windowless room in the dark. Men coming in the night to give beatings. Or worse. He knows he wouldn't last just one day. He'd go mad.

He clenches his jaw. Watches the man's face. Sees the satisfied grin.

'That scares you, don't it? Being in the dark, is it? Summat for me to remember.' Lumley's thumb gently strokes Charlie's chin. 'So I know you'll stay stum. Which is good ... for you.'

Charlie curses himself; he's let his guard down. Never look straight at them, never let them see what you're thinking. How you feel. He concentrates, lets his gaze glance past the man's head, exactly as he's learned to do over the past few years.

'Right, can't stand here chatting to you all day, Collins, I've got too much to do keeping an eye on the rest of you lazy buggers.' He pushes him. 'We don't like silent insolence 'ere. But in your case, I welcome it. We can both look forward to next Saturday, eh?' Charlie closes his eyes. 'Go on then, fuck off ... for now.'

Inside, Charlie runs, taking the steps two, then three at a time, running along each landing, pumping his legs as fast as he can, his head reeling. He knows what has just happened. What will happen.

His room is empty. Slamming the door closed, he leans against it, breathing heavily, his imagination relentlessly hearing the scared whispers he's heard from other boys, quiet footsteps in the night, muffled sobs.

Anger floods through him. He's ashamed he hadn't hit the man. And he knows what's going to happen.

He'll leave. Run. Get right away. Charlie hasn't anticipated the sense of relief that engulfs him.

Chapter 65

Despite the February chill, Charlie is uncomfortably hot. The thin cotton sheets have wound themselves around his legs. His bladder presses, but he doesn't want to move until he's ready to leave. Until he knows it's safe to escape.

For some reason, the image of his mother floats back and forth in his mind as he waits. The touch of her hand on his cheek, the smell of her scent, of Youth Dew. He knows what it was called because Chloe kept the half empty bottle of it after his mother was gone. The perfume evaporated eventually, but sometimes, she held the bottle to his nose, ordering him to sniff hard. It always made him sad but he didn't tell her because she always said it meant their mother was still close – still watching over them, even at the worst of times. With that woman their father had brought into their lives.

He remembers once telling Chloe he didn't believe that their mum *was* watching over them, that he didn't believe in Heaven. Or God. He's often felt bad about that since. When he gets out, he'll find Chloe; tell her that he was wrong, he's sorry. And that he's missed her, has thought about her every day. He sighs, the loss sharp.

He sits up. With no idea of the time, he listens to the boys around him: the snores, the farts, the restless tiny cries. He has to move.

The night is as dark as it's going to get.

He reaches under his mattress for the pillowcase holding his few possessions, slips his legs over the edge of the bed, an inch at a time. His heart is pumping so hard it's as though it's moving his ribs. He's never felt so terrified.

The floorboards move under his bare feet, creaking in protest at his weight and he stops mid-stride, balancing on one leg. Wobbling. Through one of the curtainless windows the waning moon shines a pale lemony light across the dormitory, lighting up the lumpy shapes of each boy under his covers.

'What's happening?' One boy sits up. 'What are you doing?'

Charlie doesn't answer.

'Oh, it's you, weirdo.' He slumps down. 'Well, stop making such a fuckin' racket. Idiot.'

Charlie presses down the door handle. He warily swings it back and peers out along the narrow uncarpeted corridor. No sign of anyone, every door closed. The dark windows and the glow of the small wall lights make scary shadows.

He steps out. There is no going back.

Creeping towards the fire door, he forces himself not to run, to be careful of each step. He grips the bar that opens the fire door. But it won't move. He kneels down, gripping the metal and drags the bar down with all his weight, then pushes with his shoulder. Nothing.

His hand touches something square, and a chain rattles. The fire door is locked and bolted.

Charlie slides to the floor. When he'd checked it earlier, it wasn't like this. They must only do this at night. Did they suspect him? Are they waiting for him back in the dorm?

He isn't going back. Scrabbling on hands and knees he crawls as fast as he can into the bathroom, sliding onto the cold linoleum and closing the door behind him.

He remembers there's a drainpipe outside the window. Gripping the pillowcase between his teeth, he stands on the rim of the lavatory, clambers onto the sill, and unlatches the catch. It's difficult, but he forces himself backwards through the small frame, feeling around with his bare feet, holding on to the window frame until he's able to wrap his legs around the pipe.

He lets go, half-falls, half-shimmies down the pipe, each jolt of the fastenings shocking and hurting his thighs. Biting his lips to try to stop himself yelping at the pain, he tries to grip the pipe to slow down.

There's a crack above him, a sudden swaying away from the wall. He holds on as best he can. The drainpipe snaps and Charlie falls.

The ground is hard. Winded, he lies still. Has he been heard? The pipe coming away from the wall was so loud someone is bound to have heard, will come rushing out. He waits to be discovered, looks up at the windows. There's a dim light in one. It's the room where the smallest, newest boys sleep (or lie awake, terrified on their narrow beds). There is nothing he can do about that. Nobody has looked out for him. They are all on their own in these places.

As he watches the light goes out. He sees a silhouette, but it could be his imagination. He keeps still and waits – but nothing happens: no angry shouts, no hands grabbing him, no blows.

Eventually he rolls onto his stomach and winces against the pain in his right ankle. Easing himself upright, he picks up his pillowcase, and limps away.

Chapter 66

Lynne's talking to Sue Fitz in the garden. Her voice travels across to Graham who's sitting at the kitchen table nursing his third coffee of the day.

He's exhausted. His insomnia has been worse than usual over the past two nights. The tablets she gave him don't seem to be working anymore. He has good reason not to sleep; it's been four days since he was informed by social services that Charlie is missing.

Graham can't remember why he can't see his son; his memory is patchy. The social services have told Lynne the care home doesn't think it advisable, yet they never say why. They're not telling him something, but he can't put his finger on what that is.

His son has become more and more remote from him. Lynne always argues that, as professionals, they know best and it's less disruptive for Charlie if he leaves things alone.

She says the same about Chloe.

Sometimes, when he's on his own, the floor above, in Chloe's room, creaks and he glances upwards. Smiles. Until he remembers. The pain of his daughter's rejection is too much to bear, so he tries not to think about it. Or tries to stitch the happy memories of the past together to cover the truth of the present. Once, he wrote to social services asking them to mediate for him, but he didn't receive a reply. Lynne says she spoke to Heather Butterworth on his behalf but she wasn't Chloe's caseworker anymore and couldn't help. Now he accepts Chloe's silence.

He hears the neighbour asking if Lynne will contact Charlie and Chloe to tell them about their grandmother.

'Oh no. We don't actually know where the boy is. He's run away again.' Graham listens to the sympathetic clucks from Sue Fitz when his wife adds, 'Besides, who knows how much trouble he would cause. And the girl says she doesn't want anything to do with us.'

'That's shameful. After all you did for them.'

A flood of anger runs through Graham. It's nothing to do with Sue Fitz. He cups his hands over his eyes, wishing he could stop them talking, but he's too tired to face them.

'I know, but that's life, isn't it, Sue? Who knows how our kids will turn out, however much you try to be a good parent? So it's my job now to take as much of a load off Graham as I can.'

'Well, I think you're wonderful, Lynne, I really do. But it's only what I would expect. You've got a heart of gold.'

Graham hears Lynne laugh. It's a dismissive sound. 'Oh, I wouldn't say that, Sue, I only do the best I can.'

'Well, I would. And so would everyone else who knows you.'

There's a pause in the conversation. Graham imagines them smiling at one another. But a small voice inside him insists there should have been a better way to deal with Charlie and Chloe.

'Are you all right, Graham?'

He jumps. He hadn't heard Evie come downstairs.

'Mum blowing her own trumpet I hear.'

He won't admit it, but it's what he's been thinking.

'Now, now, Evie, she's doing her best for me.'

'If you say so.' She comes around to kneel in front to him. 'Do you want me to get in touch with Chloe? Tell her that her grandmother has passed?'

'Thank you, love, but she's said she doesn't want us to contact her. I think it best she's left to come round on her own. Perhaps one day...'

Evie takes hold of his hand. 'You're such a nice, decent man Graham.' She flicks her head backwards, to indicate the two women. 'You need to stand up to her sometimes, you know.'

'And you're a good girl, Evie. But you don't understand.'

'No. I don't. I truly don't.' Her voice is sympathetic. 'I wish I could help.'

'There's nothing for you to do, Evie. I'm fine. Your mother's sorting everything out. She's only letting Mrs Fitz know we'll be off to Lowermill in a minute.'

'You don't mind me not coming with you?'

'No, your mother's right, you never really knew the twins' grandmother.'

'Never got the chance, did I?'

It's said lightly but it's another thing to bring back the remorse, the grief.

'No, you're right. I'm sorry.'

'Not your fault.' She hesitates. 'I think I should tell you something.' She smiles. 'I do hear from Chloe every now and then. I've always written to her, you know.'

Graham's heart thumps. 'I didn't know.'

'No, I'm sorry. She doesn't write back to me here. She sends her letters to a friend of mine. She thinks my mother would recognise her handwriting and hide them from me.'

'Surely not?'

Evie moves her head. 'I think probably she would, Graham.'

'I think you're being a little harsh on your mum, love.'

'Maybe we'll have to agree to disagree on that. Anyway, that doesn't matter. I thought you should know she's okay.'

'Thank you. Does she ever mention me.'

'No, I'm sorry. It's only stuff about school, what's she's doing, you know, stuff like that. Nothing heavy.' She stands up. 'She's apparently going to a new foster home. She seems okay about it. Try not to worry about her.'

'It's hard. The not knowing. I miss her. I miss both of them.' He doesn't know why he's said that. What is it about this girl that makes it easy for him to confide in her?

'I do as well.'

'Do you?'

He's surprised. Charlie and Chloe are rarely mentioned.

'Yes. Look, if I ever get the chance, I'll try to persuade Chloe to write to you or something.'

'Thank you.'

'Anyway…' she hesitates. 'I would have told you before but I think I should tell you now – I'm moving out.'

'Oh, your mother hasn't told me.'

'She doesn't know. Yet. I'm going to live with a friend. I'm almost eighteen, I've taken my A- levels and I think I've done fairly well. Anyway, I'm going to apply to the civil service for a job. It's decent money and my friend…' She looks into his eyes

183

as though assessing what to say next. 'My friend is my girlfriend, if you understand?'

'Yes?'

'I'd rather Mum doesn't know about that; she's a bit ... you know.'

Graham squeezes Evie's hand. 'As long as you're happy, love.'

'I am. And Beth, that's my friend's name, is wonderful. So we're renting a flat together.'

Graham hears Lynne's footsteps on the path. Evie looks over her shoulder. 'I'll see you when you come home. I'll still be here for another few weeks. I hope the funeral goes ... well, you know what I mean...' She touches Graham's arm. 'Look after yourself.'

Before she can leave the kitchen Lynne calls to her.

'Evie, Graham, and I will be off in a few minutes. There's nothing for you to do here until I get back. Just make sure Saul eats proper food, not that junk he's so fond of.'

'I'm sure he'll do as I say, Mother. Not!'

'No need to be so sarcastic, young lady. Just do as I ask. Graham, are you ready? Rinse your cup out, will you? Have you got everything? I want to be there before dark.'

He sees Evie roll her eyes. She takes his cup from him and goes to the sink.

'Thanks, Evie.' He smiles 'I'm about ready. I'll get my coat.'

'The cases are in? And you've hung your suit up on the hanger over the back seat, haven't you? You don't want it crumpled. And it's not over my things? That dress and coat cost me a fortune.'

'Cost Graham a fortune, you mean.' Evie whispers the words just loud enough for her mother to hear.

Graham sees Lynne's quick scowl, knows there's potential for a few harsh words, and puts his arms around his wife, turning her away from her daughter.

'I've done everything you told me to do, love. And thank you, for everything, Lynne. I don't know what I would have done without you lately. I'll always be grateful.'

Out of the corner of his eye he sees Evie shaking her head.

Chapter 67

As soon as Chloe hears the crunch of car tyres on the drive she slips into her coat, stuffs Evie's last letter into her pocket and drags her suitcase from the bed.

At the top of the stairs she looks down to the hall. They're waiting for her. The tight-knit group of four. A family.

Something she'll never have again.

Everything's moved quickly over the last month, her past life disintegrating piece by piece. Heather telling her that she's moving to another foster home, that her granny has died. That Charlie has run away from his last care home. That he's missing.

When he comes looking for her, she won't be here. The thought terrifies her. But later, she remembers Evie will always know where she is. When he comes, Evie will tell him. And then they will both run away. Escape where no one will ever find them. She mustn't say anything – they mustn't know how sure she is Charlie will find her. Because they'd be watching, waiting to catch him, to take him away from her again.

Heather stands, car keys dangling from her fingers, a smile fixed on her face. Just like everyone else. Chloe is the only one not smiling. Why should she? Why should she pretend, just to make them feel better. She's scared, she doesn't smile when she's scared.

'Ready?' she says to the social worker.

'Got everything?'

'Yes.' Chloe stands, the case heavy in her hand. Faces the family. 'Thank you, Mrs Brice. Mr Brice.'

'What have I always said?' Mrs Brice laughs. 'Come here.' There's a slight tremor in her body when she hugs Chloe. 'It's Eileen and Jack. Yes?'

Chloe nods. *Too late now.*

'Keep in touch,' Mrs Brice says.

'I will.' *What's the point?* She will never come back here.

Mr Brice pushes his glasses up the bridge of his nose. 'Here, let me carry that to the car.'

'No, it's okay, it's not heavy.'

'Be good.'

'I'll try.' She has no choice. Otherwise, she'll be like Charlie, moved from one place to another.

'See you,' Andrea and Annette say in tandem.

'See you,' Chloe says. She won't.

The house is tiny. It's in a row of houses that all look the same; all red brick, a front door, two windows downstairs, two upstairs. No garden at the front – it's straight out onto the pavement. You could fit this house into Moorcroft four times. Chloe shuts down the memories.

When Heather scrapes the tyres along the edge of the kerb as she stops the car Mr and Mrs Grantly are standing on the

186

doorstep already. As if they expected us to arrive right at this minute, Chloe thinks.

'Come in, come in.' They flatten themselves against the door so Chloe and Heather can pass. 'Go through into the living room. Yes, that door...'

They've set out a tray of tea and biscuits on the largest of a nest of tables. Two smaller tables are placed in front of the floral settee and matching two armchairs.

'Take your coats off. Do sit.' Mrs Grantly straightens the pale blue cushions, runs her palms along the edge of one. Her smile quivers at the corners of her mouth.

She's as nervous as me.

'I'm sorry, I need to get on,' Heather says. 'I have a meeting.' She pushes up her sleeve, taps her watch face. 'In half an hour at the other side of town.'

'Oh. Shame.' Mrs Grantly fastens the buttons on her navy cardigan, unfastens two, pulls at the cuffs. mouth. Her husband smiles at Chloe, his pipe clenched between his teeth. 'Don't fuss, Mother, I'm sure us and Chloe will get on fine. Sit down, lass. Have a biscuit.'

Once Heather's gone, all Chloe wants to do is go to her bedroom but Mr and Mrs Grantly want to talk. She feels awkward, worried she's chewing too loudly the biscuit they insisted she have. She sips her tea and tries to make the biscuit soft enough not to make a crunching sound.

They watch her, smiling.

'You're our first,' Mr Grantly says. 'We've only just become foster parents, and we're glad you're with us.'

Chloe is surprised; they look older than Mr and Mrs Brice,

perhaps they're not as old as they seem. She doesn't know what to say, and still has a mouthful of biscuit. She gives one of her best smiles through closed lips.

'Now, there's no need to be shy. If there's anything you need, anything at all, you must say. All right?'

Chloe takes another sip of tea. It's strong, bitter. 'Thank you. You're very kind.'

'Not at all, this is your home now, isn't that right, Mother?'

'That's right. Your home,' Mrs Grantly repeats, nodding vigorously.

'And we've put you down at the local school. We'll take you to look at it tomorrow, so you know where it is. On Monday, we'll come with you to see you settled in.' He puts his empty pipe in the ashtray on the hearth.

'Settled in,' Mrs Grantly repeats.

'So no need to be frightened of anything.'

'Anything.'

Just everything. 'Is it okay if I go to my room now, please?'

'Of course, I'll take you up.'

Chloe follows Mrs Grantly up the narrow stairs. The walls are covered in wallpaper, large red roses, and vines. Claustrophobic. She's glad to get onto the landing.

'Bathroom.' Mrs Grantly points to one door and then the one opposite. 'Here's your room.' She opens the door. 'I hope you like it, but if there's anything you want changing you will let us know?'

'It's lovely. Thank you.' It's pink. Very pink: the walls, all the furniture, even the bedpost, are painted pink. Then she sees a small table under the windowsill. 'Oh, a record player!'

'We thought you'd like one? And if you tell us what songs you like we can buy the records. Or you could choose yourself?'

Chloe thinks about Sandie Shaw. She could buy another of her mother's favourite record, *Always Something There to Remind Me*, but she thinks it might make her cry. She doesn't want to think about her make-believe letters to the singer; the security they gave her when she was scared or confused. Until Charlie was sent away. Tears burn the back of her eyes.

'I'm sorry, have I upset you?' Mrs Grantly stares at her, eyes full of worry.

'No. Honest.'

Chapter 68

'It's like you're rooted to the spot.' Lynne stands by the door of the lounge sifting through a pile of mail. She still has her raincoat on over her uniform and drips are falling onto the carpet around her stockinged feet. She's smiling. 'You all right?' She's in a good mood – it's going to be a good day.

'Sorry, Lynne, I can't seem to get going.' Graham calls to her retreating back as she goes into the kitchen. He turns to stare out of the window. It's been raining on and off all day, the garden drenched, topped by a sky swirling with dark clouds. 'I keep thinking about Mum...'

'Oh Graham, give yourself a break. You can't carry on like this.' Her voice is raised above the sound of the kettle boiling. 'It's a fortnight since the funeral. She had a good send-off, even though there weren't many there.'

189

It had felt rushed to him – the short service at the crematorium with only a handful of people there. The few words spoken by the local lay preacher, who Graham didn't know and who didn't know his mother, gave no comfort to him. It turned out later that many of his mother's friends had known nothing of the funeral.

When he'd mentioned that to Lynne she'd fixed him with a hard stare and asked him what he had done towards the arrangements. So he knew better than to raise it again.

He says instead, 'I should have gone to see her again.' *I should have brought her here, where I could have looked after her.*

'Well, you didn't. We've been over and over this. You decided not to. So it really is your own fault if you're brooding, isn't it?' When Lynne comes into the lounge again, she's taken off her raincoat and is rubbing her thick hair with a towel. In her other hand she's carrying a cup of coffee. The nutty aroma reminds Graham he hasn't eaten or drunk anything since morning. 'It's no use fretting about it all the time.'

'I know. And there's also the...'

'Yes?' She stops rubbing at her hair.

'I've been thinking about Mum's wedding and engagement rings. I think I should take them to the bank to be stored. Until Chloe gets in touch?'

'Why are you worrying about that?'

'It's just that Mum idolised Chloe. She'd want her to have them. They're hers.'

'Do you really think she deserves them?'

The chill in her voice increases the dread he's felt since he realised the rings were missing.

'It's what Mum would have wanted.'

She sits and takes a sip of her coffee, leaning against the back of the settee. 'Yes, well, I've got them safe.' She smiles. 'Don't worry. When I get around to it, I'll take them to the bank.'

'I was going to take them this morning on my way out, but I couldn't find them in your jewellery box.'

There, he's said it. He knows it sounds confrontational. When she straightens up, he thinks she's going to explode. His insides churn. But all she says is, 'I'm not sure I like you going through my things, Graham.'

'Yes, sorry. I just thought ... that's where you said you'd put them.'

'I still don't want you rooting through my things. I'd thank you not to do it again. And what do you mean, on your way out?'

'I was going to the garage. There are things to do and I haven't shown my face there much lately.'

'I'm sure they are managing fine without you for a week or so. You did say you were going to get on with the decorating in the spare room.'

Evie's room. Another spare room now.

'There's no rush, is there?'

'I'd like it doing as soon as possible. The colours on the walls are vile – I hate that purple and orange paint. Typical of my daughter. I want you to wallpaper in there with that paper I bought last week, please.' She drains the cup of the coffee. 'As soon as you can.'

He pushes himself out of the armchair and stands. 'It's a bit late to start now,' he says apologetically. 'And there are still a few things left that Evie needs to collect.'

'She'll have a job, I chucked it all out with the rubbish last week. Anyway, she wouldn't dare come back here since she moved in with that girl.'

'There's nothing wrong with Evie living with Beth, Lynne. Not if they love one another.'

'Love?' She makes a scoffing sound through her teeth. 'Rubbish! And disgusting.'

'You shouldn't think like that. Lynne. And you really shouldn't have thrown Evie's things away.'

'I'll think and do what I like in my own house.' Her voice is cold. 'If you were so set on going to your precious garage, why are you still here?'

'I couldn't find my keys.'

'To your car? The car we agreed would be sold? They're there in the bowl, where they always are.'

'No, they aren't.' He walks past her to the table at the end of the hall. Sees the keys. 'Well they weren't there ... before...'

He sees her gaze harden.

'Before what?'

'Nothing.'

Lynne looks at him, head to one side. 'If you were older I'd say you were having a senior moment, Graham. or you need new glasses. When did you last have an eye test?'

'I'm sure the keys weren't...'

Lynne waits.

What's the use of arguing? 'Perhaps I didn't look hard enough.'

'Maybe you just thought you looked, Graham.' Her tone of voice has changed completely, it's soft, concerned. 'You have been a bit forgetful lately. I do think we should get you an appointment with the doctor. I'm sure I can get you in tomorrow at the surgery with Doctor Hume. He's a lovely man.' She puts one arm around his waist. 'And at the opticians while we're at it. Better not to drive until we know what's wrong, do you think?'

He's tired all the time, his brain persistently muddled. 'I don't want to give up driving. I need to.'

It's as though she doesn't hear him. 'Maybe even think again about whether to sell your car?'

'I said before, I'd rather not, Lynne.'

'You said yourself you haven't been to the garage for over a fortnight. Yolanda says they're managing fine without you, so perhaps you need to think about cutting down on your time there.'

Yolanda again. What's going on between her and Lynne? He'll have to ask Phil to have a word with her. She has no right to be telling Lynne what's going on at the garage behind his back. And he still needs to talk about the money that's constantly going missing from the petty cash. Someone's taking it, they have to find out who.

'I should get back to work full-time.'

'And then, when you do decide to have a day in there, I can take you in and bring you home. It'd be a total waste of money having a car sitting on the drive all day.'

'I've told you, the business pays—'

She pats his arm. 'Leave it all to me. You sit back down, sweetheart. I'll make you a coffee and then get on with making something for us to eat. Fish pie all right?'

193

'Yes, but, Lynne...'

'I'll be back in a moment.'

Graham sits in his armchair, not sure what, if anything, he's agreed to. He can't think straight, but he thinks she's trying to control what he does. Or is she simply looking after him? Is he being paranoid?

Chapter 69

'I'm off to the allotment, if you fancy coming along?' Sid Grantly knocks on Chloe's bedroom door, peers around at her.

'I'd like to.' She glances outside. The sky above the rooftops across the street is a clear blue and the sun flashes on the glass in the upstairs windows. 'It's just that I've got a really good book to read today, Mr Grantley.' She waves it in the air. Library visits every Saturday morning with Mrs Grantley have become a routine and Chloe looks forward to walking into the large stone building. It always feels like going through the doors into a new world; as if the stories are bouncing around in the air, saying, 'Pick me, pick me.'

She said this once to Mrs Grantly, whose eyes sparkled, the wrinkles around them deepening in delight. She'd said she'd always thought that as well.

'What will you be doing?' Chloe asks now.

'Just watering today. You know, the tomatoes, the cucumber plants. That type of thing. Bit of weeding on the lettuce patch. See how them lettuce you put in are doing.' He taps the doorframe with his empty pipe, studies the bowl before reaching inside his pocket for his packet of tobacco. 'Up to you, love.' He smiles at her. 'As I've said before, no need to stand on ceremony. You've been here long enough to feel at home with us; just call me Sid. And call Mother, Edith.'

Chloe grins. She thinks it's funny that he calls his wife 'Mother' when they've never had children of their own. 'Yes, sorry, I keep forgetting – Sid.'

'No need to say sorry. You never need to say sorry for barmy things like that.' He lights his pipe. Chloe quite likes the smell of the fresh tobacco. 'Well, lass, fancy coming or not? It is a grand day out there...'

'I do.' She closes the book. Thanks. Give me a minute to get my wellies from the outhouse.'

'I'll be out at the front door.'

Chloe hops around, shoving her feet into the wellington boots and trying to put her jumper over her head at the same time.

'No need to panic, love, Sid'll wait for you.' Edith Grantley is baking, her face bright red in the heat. The kitchen's full of the sweet smell of cooking apples. Steam from the hot water in the sink is escaping through the open window. 'He looks forward to spending time with you at his allotment, you know. You're good company.'

Chloe stops still, her heel stuck half-in her squashed boot. She suddenly realises how happy she is since coming to this little house a few months ago. It reminds her of her grandmother's home, the same cosy feeling. She hobbles over to Edith and hugs her from behind, resting her head on her back.

'You okay, lass?' Edith leans back to look into her face.

195

'I am, Edith, I am.' It's all she needs to say. The school she's going to is all right, she's made a couple of good friends there who live nearby, and she's living with two of the nicest people she's ever known. Even nicer than Mr and Mrs Brice. And last week she'd had a surprise letter from Andrea and Annette, saying they'd like to come to see her sometime in the summer holidays. 'I'm lovely.'

'That you are, love.' Edith laughs and hugs her.

'No, I mean everything's lovely.'

'I know.' She lets Chloe hold onto her arm while she gets her foot into the boot. 'Now, off with you while I get this lot sorted, or it'll be time for you both to come back home for your tea.'

'Will you teach me how to grow vegetables and flowers, please, Sid?'

'I will, if that's what you want, lass.'

'Thank you. Because Mrs – Edith and me cook and bake together. And lately we've been sewing and I'm getting quite good at that,' she says. 'And growing things is something you and me do, isn't it? So I'd like to know more.'

'If that's what you want, Chloe, that's what we'll do.' He puffs harder on his pipe. His face has gone a funny colour.

Chloe is a bit concerned. 'Are you okay?'

'I am.' The whites of his eyes are slightly pink. But then he says, 'I am. I am that!'

'Right!' She laughs. 'Good.' She wants to skip sideways instead of walking when they turn the corner of the street towards the allotments. But she knows she's far too old to be skipping in public.

She gazes up at the sky. The blue is the bluest she's ever seen. Then she sees it, one cloud floating towards the sun, causing a hazy shadow on the hills above the allotments.

For a little while she'd forgotten about Charlie.

Chapter 70

'Come on, Graham, love, just take the tablets. I haven't got all day. One of us needs to go to work.'

'I thought I'd already had two this morning?' Graham stares at the pills Lynne has dropped into his palm. 'After I had my toast earlier.'

'No. You had two last night.' She hands him the glass of water. 'You dozed off before I could give them to you this morning. These are your first lot for today.' She studies him. 'You've only been on them a week and I think you might be looking a little better. You've more colour in your face.'

He doesn't feel better. The sleeping tablets Lynne gave him after his mother died made him disoriented, but these pills make him feel as though he's floating around on the ceiling, looking down at himself.

'I wonder if I should go down to one tablet a day, Lynne? Or just two at night? I don't feel at all right.'

'Two tablets twice a day, Doctor Hume said, remember. He totally agrees with me. You've got yourself in a complete state. Anxiety and depression. We'll soon have you on your feet again, sweetheart, and outside in the fresh air.

'Right, I have to go, I need to get Saul to school. Don't move.

I want to see you still sitting in this chair when I get back home at lunchtime. Understand?'

She's a complete mystery to Graham. First she's angry with him because he hasn't started on the list of jobs she's given him, now she's insisting he does nothing.

'I've locked the back door and the Yale will be on the front door. I'm not expecting any one to call, or any deliveries, so no need to answer if the bell rings. I'll just get my bag and I'll be off.' She goes into the kitchen.

He jumps when Saul crashes his bedroom door and thunders down the stairs. He skids to a halt outside the lounge door, grins at Graham. 'Still rough?' Doesn't wait for an answer before slinging his school bag over his shoulder and yelling. 'I'll get in the car, Ma.'

The front door slams. He's gone.

Graham breathes a sigh of relief and closes his eyes again.

'Graham, I've just found this on the bookcase in the hall. What's it doing there?' Lynne has a large, dilapidated album in her hands.

'Oh, it's my old album from when ... from years ago.' He feels awkward and uncomfortable under her direct gaze. 'It was in the airing cupboard. I needed a clean towel when I was going to have a shower yesterday. It was at the back of the shelf where the bath towels are kept.'

He thought he'd tucked it down the side of his armchair. Even though he knows she's holding it he still fumbles for it. 'I thought...' Stops. 'Where did you say you found it?'

'Never mind that, what did you want it for?'

Graham's stomach lurches. For some reason guilt swirls

inside him. 'I just found it and wanted to look at it.' It had been missing for a long time. He'd been puzzled but excited when he found it.

'Why?'

'Memories, I suppose.' Tiredness washes over him again.

She tuts. 'We have memories. I can get you our wedding album if you like?'

'I do look at our album sometimes, Lynne.' He's eager not to upset her. 'It's just that these are different...'

'You mean, these are from before you and me?' She tilts her head. 'Pity you don't get that sentimental about our memories, Graham.'

'I do.'

'I don't know why you keep living in the past, I honestly don't.'

He waits until she bangs the front door behind her before he says quietly, 'It's because I'm not happy.'

Chapter 71

'What are you thinking about, love?' Edith stops pinning the paper pattern onto the material spread out on the carpet and looks up at Chloe.

'I was just hoping that Charlie is as happy at me right now. Sometimes I try really hard to send him happy thoughts. Let him know I'm thinking of him.' Chloe's fingers tremble as she sews large tacking stitches along the seam of the skirt she's making. 'I just wish I knew where he is, where he's been all these years.'

'Doesn't anybody know?'

'No. My sister, Evie, says she always asks whenever she goes anywhere different with her job, but there's never any news.'

'And you still haven't had any contact with your father?'

'Not for years. Once he married again, everything went wrong for me and Charlie.'

'When you say, "everything went wrong", what do you mean, love?'

'I don't know how to say it.' Chloe tries to put how she feels into words. 'It was like ... too big. Before, when Mum was alive, even after she'd gone, Charlie and me would talk to Dad. We could say what we felt. He would understand and try to make things better for us.' She shakes her head, not knowing if she can get this kind-hearted woman to understand. 'But his wife didn't like us. Charlie knew that straight away. It took me a while to sort of see that, you know?'

Edith nods.

'We didn't know how to say that to Dad. At first I tried...' Chloe sits back in her chair; lets the skirt material fall into her lap. 'I tried to tell him what was happening, what she was doing to us. How angry Charlie was. My father wouldn't listen. I think he just wanted a peaceful life.' She shrugs, not wanting to re-live those feelings. 'In the end he chose her.'

'But you were only — how old when he went into care? When you were first fostered?'

'Charlie was just ten when he was sent away. Then, a few months later, I went to stay with Mr and Mrs Brice. I was almost eleven.' Chloe bends over the sewing machine, pushes her foot on the pressure pad and guides the material through.

'Unbelievable,' Edith mutters. 'No age. No age for children to be sent away.' She starts marking out the dress pattern on the material with white chalk.

There's a strange feeling in the room now. Unspoken words. There's no need to talk. Only the quiet whirr of the sewing machine and the snip of Edith's scissors fill the air.

'You enjoy dressmaking, don't you, Chloe?'

Chloe stops the machine, taken by surprise and blinks at Edith. She smiles. 'I do. I like the feel of the cloth when I'm working with it.'

'You'll be leaving school next year. Have you thought what you'd like to do? I've noticed how good you are at this.' She points with her scissors at the sewing machine. 'You took to it like a duck to water, as Sid would say.'

Chloe laughs, then lets Edith's words sink in.

'Can it be a job? A career?'

'It certainly can. Sid has a friend who's a tailor. He works from home but he told Sid he's always made a good living for himself. We could see about getting you into college to learn?'

'I think I'd like that.'

'And even find a shop that would give you an apprenticeship. On the job training. You're fifteen so no harm in making enquiries.' She gives a small groan as she shuffles on her knees to cut a different part of the pattern.

'Are you okay, Edith?'

Edith laughs. 'Old bones, love, just old bones.'

Chloe doesn't like her saying that. It makes her sad. 'You're not old. I could finish that off for you if you like?'

'No, no, it's fine. Not that I don't trust you to do it right,' she adds hastily. You made a good job of cutting out that waistcoat for Sid's birthday last month.

'I loved the feel of that material. It was so warm and soft. And I loved the colours and the pattern.'

'It's tweed, a herringbone pattern. And he loves it too. It's hard-wearing, so it'll keep him warm against the wind on the allotment through a lot of winters.'

'I like that thought. Wherever I am, it'll be nice to think of him keeping warm in something I helped to make. I'll be able to picture him on the allotment.'

'Good grief, child! You're talking as though you're already leaving us. I didn't mean that when I said about a career.'

'I'm not, Edith. I was just thinking about what you said, about college and an apprenticeship somewhere. Doing sewing for a living.' The more Chloe thinks about it, the more she likes the idea. But then the thought of being grown up enough to have a job, to be with people she doesn't know, scares her.

'You'll still live here with us, you know.'

'But I will have to leave one day. Another child might need you to foster them.'

The woman stops cutting the material, sits back on her knees. 'Yes, I know. One day. And you'd always come back to see us, wouldn't you, love?

'I would. I will. But it won't be the same, will it?'

'No, it won't. Things change. But we won't, me and Sid won't. Not when it comes to you – you'll always be welcome in our house. So just you remember that.' She waggles her scissors at Chloe. 'Think on, eh?'

Chloe laughs. She leans over the sewing machine and

straightens the seam. 'I'll remember.' She squeezes her eyes tight to stop the melancholy. 'I'll remember,' she says, softly.

Chapter 72

They wait until the front door closes and they hear the clicks of high heels on the pavement and the thwack of the car door shutting before any of them speaks.

The first is Sid. He twists so he can look at Edith next to him on the settee.

'Well, Mother, what do you think?'

'I think it'll be all right.'

'I think you'll both be wonderful.' Chloe sits back, smiles at them. 'Look how brilliant you were with me, with my sullenness, my nightmares.'

'You were different, lass.' Sid studies his new pipe, admiring the patina of the wood on the bowl. 'Eh, Mother?' He glances at Edith who nods. 'You were angry about your dad, his wife. Losing your brother…'

Chloe likes that Sid never calls Lynne her stepmother, always her dad's wife.

She shakes her head. 'I still am angry about Charlie. And even though we didn't find him, I'll always be grateful you helped me to try. I know that you did it without social services knowing.'

'Yes, well, Mother has always been a bit of a rebel, haven't you, pet?'

Edith laughs. 'I just don't like being told what to do.'

'Who would dare!' Sid takes her hand and kisses her palm. 'So? Do we take this new child on? She's only nine, younger than our Chloe was, but it sounds as if she needs some stability and love.'

'*Our Chloe.*' Chloe swallows. She'll be sorry to leave the comfort of her life here. But she's doing the right thing.

'You'll love it here, Tracey, I promise.' Chloe smiles at the little girl crunched up next to her on the backdoor step. She leans forward, trying to see her face hidden behind her long brown hair but the child shrinks lower, resting her forehead on her knees. 'Sorry, I didn't mean to frighten you. There is nothing in this house that will ever hurt you. I promise.'

Tracey moves her head slightly.

Chloe's not sure Tracey understands properly.

'Believe me, Mr and Mrs Grantley are the nicest people I know. I've been here for over two years and I've been very happy. And I bet I was as nervous as you feel now.' Chloe keeps talking. Tracey isn't looking at her but she can tell she's listening because her breathing is light, as though she doesn't want any sound to stop her from hearing what Chloe is saying.

The stone step is warm, the yard a sun-trap on days like this. And what used to be an outside lavatory, now filled with brushes, mops and buckets, has a thriving climbing rose covering the walls. Chloe can just about make out the faint perfume from the pink flowers.

Someone rides a bicycle down the alleyway. A bell rings, shrill and loud. Tracey gives out a small cry, moves quickly to curl her body between the back door and Chloe, her fingers hot and sweaty on Chloe's arm.

It's as though she is cowering from the world.

'It's only someone on a bike, nothing to worry about.'

But perhaps the little girls can't stop worrying. Edith has confided in Chloe that Tracey's father beat her almost every day. Her school had informed social services about the bruises on her arms and legs.

'It's gone.' Chloe waits until Tracey is sitting alongside her again. 'And you're safe here. You'll be safe here until you can be with your mum again.'

'And Mark? My little brother?'

Chloe barely hears the whisper but her heart leaps. 'You have a brother?'

'He's just a baby. He's with Mummy. It's nearly his birthday. I'll miss his first birthday.'

Something Edith hasn't told Chloe. She knows why. Two brothers, neither with their sisters now. Birthdays missed.

Above them the sash window of the bedroom that has been Chloe's and is now Tracey's, is opened. She hears the scraping noise of the cupboard drawer which always sticks when it's closed.

Brass band music starts up in the living room. Sid's favourite, *The Floral Dance.* He'll be sitting in his chair, foot tapping, reading his newspaper, pipe empty between his teeth because Edith frowns on him smoking inside.

The three of them had agreed that Chloe would talk to Tracey on her own. She remembered how alone she'd felt when she first set foot in this house. Sid and Edith thought it would make Tracey feel welcome, having her there, and she knows they want her to still feel that she belongs here, even if her life is changing direction.

Tracey stares up at her, her eyes large with anxiety.

'If it's possible, Mr and Mrs Grantley will make sure you get to see him.' Chloe smiles. 'They will, you know, they'll do their best.

'Mummy is in a big building with other mummies and children. I couldn't stay, they said there was no room for me.' The tiny flecks of yellow in her brown eyes glisten with tears. 'I don't belong anywhere.'

'You do,' Chloe says firmly. 'You belong here ... like me.'

Chapter 73

'Are you sure you'll be okay, Chloe?'

'I'll be fine, honestly.' Chloe hugs Edith. She grins at Sid and then turns her smile to her new boss, the tall, skinny owner of the room that's going to be hers for the next three years. 'It's a nice room, Mr Nudel, thank you. And there's a kitchen, Edith. You taught me to cook so there's no way I'll starve.'

'It is a shared kitchen,' Ezra Nudel says. 'And, I'm afraid, a shared bathroom.'

Edith frowns. He adds, 'I'm sure there will be no problem. Our two senior tailors, Herbie and Albie, are very respectable.' He points at two doors at the end of the landing. 'Their rooms are across there. I have two more apprentices, Gareth and Scott, but they live on the next floor up. They only share the kitchen with you. I'm told they are very rarely in there.' He looks at Edith, presumably waiting for her to laugh. She manages a smile.

'Edith, it will all be fine.' Chloe links arms with her.

'Chloe is our first female tailor.' His face lights up. 'Some of our women customers will be pleased, I'm sure. We've been moving into ball gowns and dresses for special occasions these last six months. They'll be much more comfortable dealing with Chloe.'

'As long as Chloe is comfortable with the living arrangements, Mr Nudel,' says Sid, 'That's all that matters to me.'

'And she will be. I, too, am sure.'

In the pause, Chloe can hear a bird singing. Not the birdsong outside, this is a melodious bubbling tune. She looks at Mr Nudel.

'Herbie, one of our tailors, has a canary in his room. I pretend I don't know,' he says. 'To be truthful, I don't approve of birds in cages. But I know it's company for him.' He nods, smiling. 'Who am I to deny that to any man?'

Ezra Nudel pulls at the cuffs of his shirt sleeves until their appearance below his jacket sleeves seem to suit him. 'Now, if we could all go downstairs, there are a few forms for Chloe to sign, including her contract to me. Because she has six GCE O-levels, we agreed she will enrol for an OND...'

'An Ordinary National Diploma,' Sid reminds Edith.

'I know.' She nudges him, smiling.

'Right.' Ezra Nudel coughs. 'She will have day release, one day a week at the Manchester Polytechnic.' He stretches out his arm, indicating the stairs. 'So, shall we get the formalities over with?'

Sid and Edith hesitate at the shop door. 'You're sure?'

'I am. This is what I want.'

'We know, but...'

'But nothing, you two. You've done so much for me, you really don't know how much, so please believe me, I will be fine. Now you have someone else to help. Tracey is a little girl who really needs you.'

Chloe waves when the bus passes. Framed in the window, Edith looks as though she's crying, despite her broad smile. Sid is peering around his wife to give Chloe the thumbs-up. She does the same and waits until the bus is lost amongst the other traffic, before going back to the shop. To her new home.

Visualising the career and a life she's chosen for herself, Chloe's excited. At least that's what she's telling herself. Sid and Edith would be devastated if they knew the fear inside her. This place, this room, this idea of a career, is her choice. But sitting on the edge of the bed, staring at the two suitcases they've lent her, crammed with clothes they've bought her, Chloe can't help feeling alone again. She's felt like this deep down since she was nine, when Charlie was taken from her.

But it's a familiar emotion and she's lived with it for long enough to know what to do. She'll bury it in the same way she's always done, by living each day at a time.

Part Two

Chapter 74

May 1978

Charlie can't remember all the places he's been, when or how he arrived in Wales. He just knows that he's been here, on the outskirts of Cardiff, for over two years.

He wakes slowly, stretches, flexing his fingers in his woollen gloves, his toes in the heavy worn boots. He squints up at the stones of the tunnel above him. They glisten in the morning light, drop water on the surface of the canal that softly laps four feet away from him; a safe distance.

He fingers the lump under his eye. He'd given as good as he got last night, the two blokes who'd tried to rob him got nothing. Not the first time while he's been dossing here, maybe he needs to be thinking of moving on. In his years on the streets, he's been beaten up more times than he can remember, robbed, left with nothing. But he'd taken any job he could, and he's survived.

Sitting up, he looks around the tunnel for any signs of movement nearby, checks inside the large duffle bag he uses as a pillow, feeling for each of his few belongings: tracksuit bottoms, tee-shirts, old towel, his washbag with his razor, soap and flannel. And right at the bottom, wrapped in a pair of socks, his childhood watch.

Aching with the cold, he moves slowly: standing, rolling up

his blankets and pushing them into the bag. At five in the morning there is no one else awake, but he can see the shapes of figures huddled under layers of clothes, sleeping bags and newspaper. Hear the hollow coughs, grunts and snores. Staggering a little, last night's beer still filtering through his system, he makes it to the entrance of the canal tunnel before relieving himself.

Slinging the bag over his shoulder he stumbles along the rutted path until he comes to the part when the stones have fallen from the wall. He climbs over and, clinging onto the straggly dead shrubs between the sparse grass, he clambers up the slope to the road and pushes through the hole in the wire fence.

He takes a shortcut, stumbling over the rubble of demolished terraced houses. The silence is only broken by the flutter of the birds he disturbs, and the noise of the bricks that slide as he treads on them. He stops when he sees movement, afraid it's rats, the one thing he hates. He's seen too many of them.

But it's not rats. A large, ginger cat sits looking at him. It's gaunt, and when it gives a loud yowl, he sees it has missing teeth.

'Hello, you.' Charlie's voice croaks through lack of use.

The cat delicately manoeuvres itself around his legs, mewing constantly. He bends down to stroke it, stops when it flinches. 'It's okay, Cat.' He keeps his fingers still until he feels its nose subtly touch them. 'You hungry? Well, I'm sorry, so am I. And it'll be a while before I get anything. I need to move.'

His footsteps echo down the empty streets. The public lavatories are closed and locked, he knows that, so he doesn't even try the handle. The small broken window at the back has been his way of getting in for weeks now.

The water is cold, the soap a thin sliver, his towel so threadbare it's barely dries him, but peering at the cracked mirror over the hand basin Charlie thinks he's as presentable as he can make himself.

Wriggling back out, he's greeted with a small cry. The cat is waiting for him.

'You can't follow me, Cat, I'm off to work. I doubt *Bwyty Un* will welcome you.'

But the cat follows him anyway.

When he pushes open the back door to the small restaurant, the aroma of toast makes him swallow. He stows his bag in his locker, walks though to the kitchen. It's empty apart from a man with his back to him. A slight tremor runs through Charlie's shoulders. A stranger: someone else to deal with.

But when the man turns at the door swinging close, he beams. His grin reaches his eyes, his thick eyebrows rising high on his forehead.

'Ah, you must be Charlie, the washer-upper?' He's smaller than Charlie, but stocky, and with a mass of black curls that make him seem taller. 'Tomas said to expect you first. Toast?'

Charlie smiles to show his appreciation.

'Butter and marmalade?' The man crosses the kitchen with a plate in his hand. Charlie takes it. He's not used to looking at anyone full in the face, but there's something about this man's steady gaze that makes Charlie relax.

'I'm Simon Cadwallader. First day here. I'm the new assistant manager.' He holds out his hand. 'Good to meet you.'

'And you.' Charlie grasps Simon's hand. It's a firm strong handshake. Friendly.

213

Chapter 75

'So, I can tell you're not from around here.' Simon grins. 'I'd go so far as to say yer not even from Wales with yon accent.'

Charlie smiles at Simon's attempt at a northern accent. He stays at the large sink, scrubbing at the line of grease in the roasting pan.

'You do, do you?' To soften the curt reply he glances sideways and gives the man a quick smile.

In care, silent, the only thing anyone knew about him was what was in his files. He's left all that behind. Who he was then isn't who he is now. Whoever that is.

'Sorry, mate, not being nosy.' Simon pats him on the shoulder.

'Don't. I don't like being touched.'

Simon backs away, raises his hands. 'Sorry.'

'No, I'm sorry.' Charlie rests against the sink. 'Bit tired this morning.'

'Ah.' Simon looks around the kitchen, so Charlie does too. The lunchtime rush is over. Alun, the chef, sits on a chair at the far end of the kitchen with the prep cook, working through his menu for the week. Two of the staff are cleaning the workspaces. The low hum of voices comes from the small restaurant on the other side of the swing doors.

'Look, when you've finished up here, grab something to take with you to eat and get off to your digs, I'll empty the glass and dishwasher.'

The idea of him having 'digs', being able to afford anywhere that could conceivably be called that, makes Charlie's lips twitch.

'No, you're all right, I'm in no rush.'

'Well, in that case, when you've done that,' Simon points to the pan, 'call it a day and have something to eat here. There's a bit of the chicken chasseur left over, and some pizza. Take what you want for later. It'll only get wasted.'

'Thanks.' Now and then, when he could, Charlie has been leaving the kitchen to give bits of the leftover chicken and fish to the cat sitting patiently outside the back door. The thought of being able to save it from starvation gives him a good feeling.

'And, if it's all right with you, after I've made sure everything's done, I'll join you?'

'Everything all right?' Charlie hopes he's not going to be laid off, he's become used to the routine of the job over the last few months. 'I think I've done everything I'm s'posed to do.'

'I'm sure. I didn't mean just you.' The man raises his eyebrows. 'I meant check all round. You know, first day and all that.'

'Oh, yeah, 'course.'

'Look, I don't know anyone here yet. I know we had the staff meeting before we opened it'll be a while before the servers are finished in the restaurant, and I'm hungry now. I just thought … a bit of company, you know…'

Charlie hesitates. The idea that anyone would like to spend time with him isn't something he's used to. His shoulders give an involuntary jolt. Simon waits, looking friendly but cautious.

'I'd like that,' Charlie says. 'Yeah, that'll be good.'

Chapter 76

When the shop bell rings, the door opens, letting in fine drizzle on a gust of wind, Chloe presses the button on the vacuum with her foot, and it whirrs to a stop.

'I'm sorry, we're closed.'

The man pauses, hesitating, his coat dripping on the carpet. 'I was hoping to see Ezra?'

'Mr Nudel has gone home.' Chloe glances at the large wooden clock above the shop counter. It's almost seven o'clock, but the man makes no attempt to leave. 'Could you close the door, please, you're letting in the rain.'

'Sorry, yes. It's cold and wet for September, isn't it.' He clicks it closed. 'And blowing a gale. Earlier a customer told me it's the tail end of that hurricane passing us. Flossie?'

'My name's Chloe.'

'I meant they've called the hurricane Flossie.'

'Oh, I see.' She bursts out laughing. 'I feel a bit stupid now.'

'I should have explained better.' He smiles.

It's a nice smile, Chloe thinks, nice eyes, look almost green in this light. Not surprising, he has copper-red hair. 'Anyway, like I said Mr Nudel's left.'

'I'm the rep from Alberhey Woollen Mill in Huddersfield. Ezra said he'd look at some samples of cloth?'

'I'm sorry.' She looks first at the clock and then to the door, hoping the man takes the hint. It's almost time for *Coronation Street*.

He puts the briefcase on the floor. 'It's taken me ages to find you.' He flushes scarlet. 'I mean the shop, of course.'

216

'Of course.'

'Ian Turnbull.' He holds out his hand.

He seems harmless enough, not much older than her, not much taller than her. She shakes his hand. His fingers are long and slender. And cold. She feels a little sorry for him.

'I'm Chloe Collins. He'll be here around eight in the morning, if you'd like to come back?'

'Right.' He looks past the mannequins in the shop window at the rain lashing on the glass. 'There's not much point in going home. Do you know if there's somewhere to stay overnight around here?'

'I don't. Sorry.' Chloe shakes her head. 'I suppose you could try the Prince of Orange. I think they sometimes do B&B. But if not they should be able to tell you who will.'

'The Prince of Orange?'

'Yes, just back along the street, turn left and you'll see it on the far end of Mountbatten Street. You can't miss it.' She waits for him to leave.

'Have you much to do?'

Chloe makes her voice firm. 'Why?'

He looks taken aback.

'Sorry, I didn't mean to be forward.' He shifts his case from hand to hand. 'I don't suppose you'd care to have a drink in the pub with me? All above board, of course. I just wondered...'

'I'm not ... I don't...' Chloe sucks in her bottom lip. 'It's raining.' She's annoyed with herself for saying the obvious.

'It is,' he agrees. 'We could run? Just a drink?'

'I'm not sure...' When was the last time she went out with anyone. Evie, months ago, but never a man. Never a boyfriend.

217

'I don't...' *Stop being so pathetic.* She looks down at her blouse and skirt. 'I'm still in my work clothes.'

'So am I,' he says. And, if you don't mind my saying, you look nice.'

He looks harmless enough.

He waits through the next long awkward moment. 'Sorry, I shouldn't have asked.'

'No, it's fine, I was just...'

'Taken by surprise?'

Chloe laughs. 'Yes.'

He rubs his cheek. 'Me too. It's not normally the sort of thing I do.'

'Well, in that case,' she says on impulse, 'yes. I've not celebrated passing my exams at the tech yet.' She's surprised. She hasn't even told anyone in the shop. 'My Ordinary National Diploma,' she adds, feeling even more mortified. She laughs, self-conscious.

'Oh, brilliant. Congratulations.' He smiles. 'That certainly means a celebration then?'

'Okay.' She looks around. 'Let me get my coat and umbrella.'

Chapter 77

Chloe waits until Ezra Nudel has settled into his office before knocking on his door.

'I've brought you a cup of tea, Mr Nudel.'

'Well, that's very kind of you, my dear, but it's not your job to do that. I'm perfectly capable of getting my own tea.' He points at the kettle and cups in the far corner of the small, cluttered room.

'I know. I just wanted a word with you if you have the time, please?'

'Of course, of course.'

'I haven't said anything to the others yet about gaining my certificate. I should have come to see you before now, but I thought the college would let you know.'

'Indeed, my dear, they have. And you have completed your time working here. How do you feel about that?'

'Well...' Chloe tries to find the right words. 'I've loved it. Thank you. I've learned a lot about fabrics – designing, especially designing and making the gowns over the last two years. I prefer that to making men's suits. Although,' she adds hastily, 'I enjoy that as well.'

'Don't you worry about telling me your preferences, my dear. You have been an asset to the business with your expertise. You have exceptional sewing skills, and your tact in dealing with some of our — what should I say? — more demanding lady customers is beyond valued.'

'Thank you.' Chloe hopes her surprise doesn't show on her face. Her employer isn't known for giving praise. 'There is something else...'

He sips his tea. 'Oh? I do hope you're not going to ask me for a rise, my dear. I think Herbie and Albie might have something to say about that.' He chuckles, but Chloe can see the wariness in his eyes.

'Not at all. It's nothing like that. I think you knew when you took me on Mr Nudel...'

'Ezra,' he says.

'I realized some months after I came here that my foster mother must have had a word with you – told you that I would also have to move from my foster home. I know it could have been awkward letting me live here as well. I know how surprised the others were that you even took me on ... being a girl.' She smiles even as she remembers the sideways glances, the mumbles, the awkwardness whenever she met any of them upstairs.

A chuckle rumbles low in Ezra's chest before bursting out into a loud guffaw. 'Herbie and Albie aren't the most accommodating of men, I must admit, my dear.'

'Oh, they were always courteous – and kind. But it must have been difficult for them. And I always wondered if the other, younger apprentices left because I came to work here?'

'No, they were not suitable.' He straightens his shirt cuffs. 'You have been, as I said, exceptional. As for Herbie and Albie, you soon won them round with your diligence and willingness to learn.' He grins. 'Don't think I didn't see the way you singled each of them out equally when you needed to learn a particular process. You appealed to their pride. Their seniority.' He looked at her over his half-rimmed glasses. 'Very clever, my dear, very clever. And I'm sure they – we – will all want to celebrate your qualification. I was only saying the same thing to Mrs Nudel a few days ago. She suggested you all come for a meal at our home.'

'Really?' Chloe doesn't try to hide her surprise. She has always been a little cautious when Mrs Nudel comes into the shop; she is a tall, elegant woman who rarely smiles.

He nods. 'I shall tell her that you would like that?'

'It would be wonderful. Thank you.'

220

'Good. Now, I must get on if that's all?'

'No, actually.' She smooths down her skirt and makes her voice as neutral as she can. 'I came in to tell you there was a rep from Alberhey Woollen Mill, an Ian Turnbull? He came here last evening, after we'd closed. He's coming back this morning. He stayed at the Prince of Orange overnight, so said he'd be early.'

She won't mention she'd joined him for a drink. She isn't sure Mr Nudel would approve. But it was one of the best evenings she'd had in a long time. After his initial shyness, Ian had been good company. They'd talked so much they were both surprised when time was called. He'd walked with her to the shop, watched while she locked up, and waved through the door window before leaving. She is a bit disappointed he didn't attempt to kiss her.

She's put a tray of silver buttons on the counter searching for the right ones for the latest gown she's working on, when the doorbell rings and Ian comes in. He grins. Chloe looks around to see if anyone has noticed but, to her relief, there is no one else in the shop.

'Hi.' She smiles. 'Let me call Mr Nudel.' She leaves the counter and walks to the back of the shop.

'Just a minute.'

Chloe stops. 'Yes.' Looking at him, she sees redness rising from his neck to his cheeks.

'I just wondered...'

'Yes?' She lowers her voice and waits for him to speak, hoping he might be going to ask to see her again.

He doesn't. His words come out in a rush. 'I was hoping I could write to you?'

'Write?'

'If that's okay?'

She quells the disappointment. 'If you'd like.'

'And perhaps next time I'm this way again, we could go somewhere nice? The pictures, or a meal? Like, a proper date?'

Chloe pretends to consider his suggestion, knowing already what she will say, when the bell rings, the door opens and a couple walk into the shop.

'Yes. That would be fine,' she says in a loud voice. 'I'll get Mr Nudel now. Just wait there, please.'

She's smiling when she climbs the stairs.

A date. And an invitation to the Nudel house for a celebration meal. Chloe feels something flutter deep inside her. Anticipation? Excitement? Apprehension? She isn't sure: it's unfamiliar but not unpleasant.

Chapter 78

'What happened to you?'

Charlie pushes past Simon. 'Nothing. Bit of a scrap, that's all.' He's attempted to sluice the blood off his face and knuckles in the staff washroom but it has revealed the cuts and bruises. His t-shirt is ripped at the neckline and his jeans covered in wet patches where he's tried to sponge off the mud. He's hidden the torn anorak in his locker.

'Looks as if it was more than that.' Simon circles around

Charlie, looking him up and down. 'Bloody hell, mate, you're in a right mess.' His hand is warm on Charlie's arm.

He shakes him off. 'My business. I'm fine.'

'Not when you come into work looking like this. It's not right, you must know that.' Simon shakes his head.

'Right. I got fucking mugged.' The rage inside Charlie threatens to burst out. He takes in great gulps of air to push it down. It's simmered inside him all night while he shivered in the cold air, hugging his arms around himself, in the doorway of the newsagents, three shops down from the restaurant.

'Where?'

'Does it matter?'

'Well, yes it does. For when you tell the police.'

'I won't be telling the bloody cops anything. All right? And I don't want to talk about it.' But he does. He wants to tell Simon about his life, his existence. The way he's always had to be on his guard; how, over the last two months, for the first time in years, he's let his guard down. Let himself be vulnerable. He's let his imagination run riot with the realisation that he likes Simon, and not just as a friend. And that's scares him. It's made him careless. He scowls at Simon.

'Right. Well, you need to get cleaned up. You don't want the others seeing you like this.

'I can't. All my stuff got sodding nicked.'

'What do you mean, all your stuff? Was it a burglary? Did they get into your digs?'

The rest of the staff are drifting in now, staring with concern when they see Charlie. The low murmur tells him they are talking about it. After years of trying to stay invisible, he's now the centre of attention, and he hates it. He turns back on them, leans over the large sink, and talks to Simon.

'Look, I don't have any bloody digs, all right? I'm sleeping rough. Have done for over the last five years. What I had was in my bag. Now it's gone. Everything.'

Even his childhood watch that his father gave him for his birthday. His and Chloe's. Chloe was given a watch too, a Sleeping Beauty one, he always remembers. It's the loss of the watch, that link to his past, which hurts most.

Simon flicks his hand at those still watching. 'Come on you lot, show's over. Get the breakfast.' He turns back towards Charlie. ' Do you mind my asking where you've been sleeping?'

'Down by the canal,' Charlie mutters. He won't be able to go back there. Not with that new lot of bastards who arrived yesterday.

'How long for?'

Charlie shrugged. 'Few months.' He pulls a length of towel from the cabinet on the wall and makes a great show of drying his hands.

'Right.' Simon pulls a set of keys from his trouser pocket. 'Number seven, Argyll Street. That's where I live. It's my house, there's no one else there. Go and get cleaned up, take a bath. Find yourself something decent to wear. My trousers won't fit you, but I'm guessing you'll get into my t-shirts, jumpers and boxers.' His face flushes. 'Course your own might be okay, so ignore the last.'

Charlie rubs the back of his neck, feeling the heat of embarrassment. 'I can't...'

'You can. And, if you want to carry on working here, you

will. I'll see you when you're sorted.' He waits until Charlie's facing him.

'Number seven, Argyll Street. You can't miss it. There's a black Mini Clubman parked right outside.'

'Right.' Charlie goes to the kitchen door and turns slightly to look at Simon, who has a concerned crease between his eyebrows. 'Thanks.'

The cat is waiting on the step.

'Sorry, Cat, I've nothing for you.'

As he walks he pushes his arms into the sleeves of the tattered anorak. The cat follows him. And when he finds the house on Argyll Street, it waits.

'I'll be back in a jiffy,' he says. 'Hopefully – if I can find some milk for you. Just wait there.'

'That's better. You look a bit more human now. Shame about the jeans. You can have an advance on your wages later, to buy new ones.'

'I owe you. I made a cup of tea and I gave the cat some milk and some tuna.'

'You have a cat?'

'No. Yes. He sort of adopted me a bit back.' Charlie laughs, sheepishly. 'Cupboard love. Well, it would be cupboard love if I had a cupboard. I get proper cat food from the shop next door, but I think he prefers what I give him during the day, er, bits and pieces of food, you know.' It dawns on him that Simon will guess where the 'bits and pieces' came from.

Simon nods. 'I like cats myself – not much of a dog person.'

'I like both. I had a dog when I was a kid. A big soft lump of a thing. A red setter we called Oscar.'

'We?'

'Yeah, my sister and me.'

'What is she called?'

'Chloe. As far as I know she's still called Chloe. I was told she went into a foster home when we were kids. I still don't know where she is.' When he sees Simon open his mouth to ask a question, Charlie adds, 'Not a clue.'

That's more than he's told anyone ever before. He clamps his lips tight.

'Have you ever looked for her?'

Charlie shakes his head, turns to the sink, and runs steaming water over the pans that have accumulated in his absence.

'Let me get that advance. Then you can buy a new pair of jeans.'

'I'll nip to the Red Cross charity shop on Newport Road. It's as good as anywhere. I'll look for a couple of tee shirts and a jumper as well.'

'I'll round it up so you might be able to get a different anorak. I saw the state of it when you came back.' Simon hesitates. 'Though I am pretty good with a sewing needle.' He waits, as though expecting Charlie to laugh.

He doesn't. In his stolen bag he'd had a reel of black thread and a needle he'd stolen from a shop a long time ago. His stitching might not be that good, but it had kept his clothes intact.

'I can try to mend it this evening, after the last shift? And if you like, only if you want, of course, you can kip at my place.

There's no bed in the other bedroom but we can sort something out for you to sleep on.'

'I don't know.' Since he's admitted to himself that he's attracted to Simon, that could prove a problem. The man might run a mile if he ever guessed. 'Could be a bit awkward,' he blurts out.

'Why?'

'Both of us working here?'

'Alun and Derek over there?' Simon gestures to the chef and one of the servers. 'They share a flat. And you've seen the house – it's big enough for us not to get under one another's feet. Anyway, please yourself. The offer's there. No strings. Except I'll want a bit towards the rent, once you're back on your feet.'

'Who says I'll stay?'

He smiles. 'Nobody. But you'd be welcome. It's a big place for just me to rattle around in.'

Chapter 79

'I'm worried about money, Graham.' Lynne sits at the side of the bed, takes his limp hand in hers, squeezes it.

'Why are you worried?' He winces against the pressure of her fingers. 'I want to get up.'

She pinches the skin on his arm.

'Lynne, that hurt.'

'Sorry, I'm sure.' She tuts. 'Just a playful touch. Don't be such a mardarse.'

Graham rubs his skin.

Another red mark. He has asked her to stop. But she gets offended so quickly. He studies the line of purple, blue and pale-yellow bruises along his forearm.

'Are you listening?'

'What?' He sees her glaring at him. 'Sorry, I didn't hear, love.' He makes his tone pacifying.

'You never do. I said I'm worried about money.'

'I don't understand. Your allowance...'

'I told you last week. It's not just my account. It's all of them: the joint, mine, yours.'

'Mine?' He can't remember the last time he saw a statement. 'Where are the statements, sweetheart?'

'Oh, for God's sake, I told you. Last week. I showed you.'

'I don't remember.'

'You don't remember the things you don't want to remember, Graham. We're not managing. I've had to up my hours in work.'

'Why? There's always money coming in from the garage.' His head's fuzzy. He shakes it, struggling to order his thoughts. 'When I went into the garage last week—'

'When your friend Phil took you to the garage, against my advice.'

'He was doing you a favour, saving you time. Anyway, Margaret showed me the books and the business is thriving.' *Even though I'm not pulling my weight.* 'But, if you're worried, while I'm still not on top form, we could cut back on all the dinners and social stuff we go to. Besides the expense, it's exhausting.'

'Typical. You want me to give up on everything that gives us the bit of social standing, just because you're tired?'

'I'm not saying that.' He sighs. 'I'm only saying we don't need to go to so many. I want to get better, and I want to stop taking so many tablets.' She starts pacing, moving so rapidly it's making him dizzy. 'Can you stand still a moment, love? I think I'm going to make an appointment with my doctor. See what he thinks.'

'So what I do for you is not enough? Even though I'm going on Doctor Hume's advice?'

'I didn't say that, Lynne.' Graham needs to close his eyes, to sleep again.

'I gave up being the Chairwoman to look after you. You chose to resign from the school governors board. Do you want me to give up everything?'

'No, no, of course not. You said you were worried about money.' *Has he just said that?* 'I thought—'

'That's the trouble, Graham, you don't think.'

His eyes are so heavy. 'This is about Saul, isn't it? Is he gambling again?'

He hadn't meant to say that out loud. He is awake immediately. His hands shake. His whole body shakes. He can't stop it.

'What do you mean?'

He can smell her breath, sour from last night's wine.

'I heard you last night.' Graham can't get his breath, he's wheezing. 'I heard the two of you shouting.' He coughs. 'He's in debt again. He's in trouble again, isn't—?'

The slap across his face stops his words.

Chapter 80

Simon switches off the television and sits back down in his armchair. He clicks his lighter, cups his hand around the cigarette and lights it. The lines deepening between his thick eyebrows worry Charlie.

'What'll happen to the restaurant, d'you think?' His forehead is throbbing with tiredness. He's not been able to sleep over the last week, reading in the newspapers of the strikes spreading all over the country makes him uneasy.

'With Callaghan and his bloody lot sticking to their guns?' Simon settles into his armchair and stretches out his legs. He takes a long pull on his cigarette.

'Yeah.'

Cat, who's been lying in front of the fire, jumps up onto Charlie's lap and begins to purr. Stroking his fur soothes Charlie.

Simon thinks for a moment. 'To be honest, I don't know. Tomas is a good employer and he'd see us right as far as the wages go. I'm meeting with him tomorrow. We're none of us on bad pay, and I think Chef and his crew will just take the five per cent the government has set and get on with it.' He stubs out his cigarette in the ashtray on the arm of the chair. 'But with drivers being on strike, I'm not sure about getting the everyday supplies. I'm guessing we'll have to take things on the chin and work with what we can get.' He shakes his head. 'I'm just hoping Tomas sees we've been making a good profit over the last few months. I don't know how his other restaurant is doing. He could, I suppose, cut his losses, and close one down.'

Fucking hell. If it's *Bwyty Un* and he's out of a job, Charlie won't be able to pay Simon any rent. His pride wouldn't let him stay. This small stone terraced house, the tiny box-room that just about takes in his single bed, a set of drawers and a windowsill piled high with the charity shop books, is somewhere he feels comfortable. And his friendship with Simon is precious to him. He hasn't said that. He's not that sure of Simon's feelings. He's been content to play the long game, see what happens. But if he loses his job, he'll be on the streets again. In this bloody weather. He listens to the hailstones pounding on the window.

'You cold?' Simon reaches to turn the gas fire higher.

'Nah. I'm okay. Just thinking.'

'It'll be fine. Don't worry. Though I'm guessing we'll need to watch the gas.' Simon gestures towards the fire. 'Extra jumpers time.'

Charlie lifts his cigarette. 'And I've been wanting to give these up for ages.'

'After Christmas, eh?' Simon half-laughs 'Christ, just listen to the two of us miserable buggers.' He stands. 'Fancy a beer?'

'Aye, go on then.'

Simon comes back from the kitchen with a bottle of *Double Diamond* for Charlie but doesn't sit down again. He runs his fingers through his hair so the curls almost stand on end. His cheeks redden.

'All being well at *Bwyty Un,* do you think you'll stick around for Christmas?'

'Bloody hell, I don't know, it's weeks off yet.'

Why can't he admit he wants to? Why can't he say he'd like

231

nothing better, that this house is the closest to a home that he's had in years. Over the years he's learned not to trust anyone. Until now.

'About five.' Simon crosses to the window. 'Hell's Bells, it's blowing a gale out there. Looks as if it's turning to snow.' He pulls the curtains closer. 'I'm just saying if you wanted to stay it's fine by me. Especially since I tasted your so-called speciality.'

'The chicken and veg effort?' Charlie grins.

'Yep. Bloody luverly as my kid brother would say.' Simon sits back in the chair.

'I didn't know you had a brother.'

'Two actually, Steven and Scott, and a sister, Sarah. All younger than me. All still living with my mum and dad. Which is why I asked about Christmas. I got the usual, "You will be coming home, won't you" message from Mum. I'm usually working in restaurants that open on Christmas and Boxing days. But Tomas says as there are no definite bookings, he's decided the place will close this year. So, if you would like to come home with me, you'd be very welcome. It's only for three days, of course. Tomas is opening on the thirtieth for the New Year, so we'll need to be back to get ready.'

Charlie is suddenly apprehensive. He stops stroking the cat and looks at Simon, taking in every detail of his face, his brown eyes, his hair, already speckled with silver at the age of twenty-six, the dark pinpricks of stubble on his jaw.

'As mates, nothing else, you barmy sod.' Simon shuffles in his seat, looking uncomfortable.

'No,' Charlie says, quickly. 'I didn't think...'

'You're totally not my type!'

232

'Oh. No, sorry.'

They were talking in quick succession.

'Of course, if you just wanted to be on your own, you're equally welcome to stay here.' Simon runs his knuckle across his chin. 'And be a miserable, unsociable bugger.'

'Hmm, put like that...' Charlie chuckles, raises his beer in acknowledgement. 'What about Cat?'

'He could come too. We could take his food and litter tray. We wouldn't lose him, now he doesn't like going out.'

'Think he's scared we wouldn't let him back in.' The cat squirms, tucks his head under Charlie's arm.

They laugh. 'It's as though he can speak English,' Simon whispers. 'So? Christmas with the parents? What do you think?'

'If you think they wouldn't mind?'

'They don't. I've already asked them.' Simon finishes his beer.

Charlie's stomach flips. It'll be a big step for him, being in a family home after all this time. He can't remember the last time Christmas meant anything to him. Not since he was a kid. Stop being such a coward he tells himself. He smiles. 'In that case, I'd love it. Thanks.'

'No problem. And now I'm going to turn in. Early start tomorrow. Meeting with Tomas, try to make him see *Bwyty Un* is worth its weight in gold, whatever *Bwyty Dwy* is doing. And I want to get the rotas up to Christmas sorted, hopefully give the staff something they can rely on. And have a talk with Chef to see what his ideas are for the menu and try to get as much stock in as possible.'

'You'd better turn the fire off; I'll be going up myself in a bit.'

'Sure?'

'Yeah.'

Simon pats Charlie's shoulder as he passes. Listening to his footsteps on the stairs, Charlie touches his jumper where his friend's fingers had rested.

Chapter 81

Chloe hasn't slept. The fluttering in her abdomen settles into an uneasy excitement. For the last few years getting her qualification as a tailor has been all consuming. Now she's starting as an equal in the shop with Herbie and Albie. More importantly, with Mr Nudel. *Ezra.*

The others went downstairs to the shop ten minutes ago. Standing on the landing she hears Herbie's canary singing in his room. Thinking about the bird in its cage makes her sad but it's company for Herbie. She can understand that. She often wishes she had someone with her when she's alone in her bedroom. Chloe stops, stunned by her next thought, by the name that comes instantly to mind. Ian Turnbull. She doesn't know anything about him. But he looks at her as if he wants to know her better. It scares her. This hasn't happened before; she's been careful not to let it happen. Careful not to let anyone near enough to hurt her. Yet the picture in her mind now, of the warmth of Ian's body as they sat together on the seat in the pub makes her feel maybe he might be the someone she needs.

She only just reaches her workstation before Ezra Nudel comes into the shop. Albie winks at her. He's switched on her sewing machine and brought the current gown on its mannequin into the workshop.

'Thank you,' she whispers.

'Good morning.' Ezra takes his coat off, hangs it on a hook in the staff room. 'Bit cold out there this morning. Now...' He riffles through the order book. 'Three fittings, and stocktaking today. How are you getting on with Mrs Stanley's gown, Chloe?

'She's coming in today to choose the buttons for the back, Mr Nudel. I sorted some out for her to look at. She was happy last week with the fit and the sleeves, but we had a discussion about the neckline; she wasn't happy...' Chloe points at the mannequin. 'I'd be grateful if you would have a look at it when she tries it on, please?'

'Hmm. The problem?'

'I think ... it's too low for...'

'For the mayor's Christmas dinner?' He pulls at the cuffs of his shirt until they show just an inch below his jacket sleeve. 'You must remember she and Mr Stanley are valued customers.'

And very difficult, and patronising. 'Of course.'

'Let me know when she comes into the shop. I'll pop into the fitting room.'

'And the silk for her stole hasn't arrived yet. Some delay along the line. I've chased it up three times now but there's still no definite delivery date.'

'Hmm. I wondered if these strikes on the railways and the docks would affect us. Leave it with me, Chloe, I'll contact my associates in London, see what is happening. In the meantime, perhaps we should ask Mrs Stanley if a stole in the same material as the gown. would be acceptable.'

'She really does want silk.'

'Well, let's see. We can only do what we can do.'

The workshop is quiet for a few minutes after Ezra leaves, before Herbie voices what the three of them are thinking.

'I wonder if these strikes will mean we will be short of all material before long.'

'Who knows. Who knows what is going to happen in this mad world we live in, Herbie?' Albie picks up the trousers he is working on and peers at the waistband. 'Ezra might think about closing the business. Like us, he is not a young man anymore. For now, we can only do what we can do.'

Chloe bites the inside of her cheek. The future, her future might once more be unsure.

Chapter 82

'Mind if I say something?' Simon's shoulders are hunched against the icy sleet slanting down from a black sky. 'God, I'm cold!' He pulls the hood of his duffle coat further down over his forehead. 'Charlie?'

'What?' Charlie has to raise his voice above the wind and the hiss of cars passing, headlights on, windscreen wipers racing back and forth, clearing away the slush.

He knows what his friend is going to say. Simon had talked about his family last night. Charlie had been focussed, listening carefully, picking up cues when he could, bouncing them back so the conversation stayed on Simon's brothers and sister. It had been difficult. Hearing that his friend has a sister had made his heart leap. Charlie clenches his fist. He's spent the night trying not to think about Chloe.

A bus passes, the lit windows holding condensation-blurred passengers inside.

'Simon...' *Please don't.* 'Let's just get to work, eh? This cold – it's freezing me bollocks off.' He tries a short laugh. 'Let's run.'

He jogs a couple of steps and looks back when he realises his friend hasn't followed. He resists the urge to hold out his hand. 'Come on. We'll run together.'

'I haven't run since I was twelve, I'm not starting now. I'm not built for it.'

'Aw, come on.' Charlie's walking backwards, the sleet behind him. The streetlights are still on even though it's almost six in the morning. He shudders, he's always hated this time in the morning. But today he's not alone and an unexpected spark of joy makes him smile.

So when Simon says an emphatic no, he says 'Okay.' He stops, conceding that Simon's short bulky figure is more suited to a casual stroll. And the pavement is slippery. He waits, chances holding his hand out. 'Come on then,' he says. When Simon catches up with him, Charlie slings his arm around his shoulders and, heads down, they walk to the restaurant.

Charlie knows he hasn't heard the last of it though. Sitting by the serving counter, drinking coffee in the empty kitchen after the lunchtime rush, Simon clears his throat.

Charlie watches him over the rim of his cup. *Here we go, like a dog worrying a bone.* 'I don't want to talk about this, Simon.'

'How do you know what I'm going to say?'

'Yer going to ask...' Charlie holds the cup between both hands, his knuckles white. 'You want me to talk about...' His shoulders jerk.

'Last night.' Simon says. 'I want us to talk about last night.' He lowers his voice, even though the rest of the staff are in the restaurant. The laughter and chatter in there contrasts with the tension between them. 'I saw your eyes when I was talking about my family. About Christmas.' His next words come out in a rush. 'I might be speaking out of turn...'

Charlie huffs agreement.

'But is there nothing you can do to find your sister?'

And there it is. Charlie shrugs. 'She's never tried to find me. Not from the minute I went into care. Not once.' He knows his voice is harsh. He doesn't want to upset his friend, but he needs him to stop. 'Leave it eh?'

The relief is almost overpowering when Simon says, 'No problem.' He stretches his arms over his head, yawns. 'Right, I'm going to ring my mother, tell her we'll be with her on Christmas Eve. We'll drive over after we've cleaned up.'

But Chloe isn't finished business, Charlie knows that. She is waiting in the wings. And Simon will be the one to introduce her again.

Chapter 83

'What do you want to do? How about getting something to eat, I'm starving.' Ian pulls into the car park and turns in his seat to look at Chloe. He checks his watch. 'It's gone twelve.'

'I did say on the phone to give today a miss, with the weather like it is.'

'What — and miss seeing you? However dicey it was driving over the moors on Standedge, no gritting on the road, it's worth it.'

He makes it sound as if she hadn't meant it when she'd said it would be dangerous. 'It was a bit daft driving over the tops from Huddersfield, you know. I didn't want you caught on the moors.'

'And I'm not. I'm here.' He leans over, kisses her, his tongue probing her lips. Chloe doesn't like that; she hadn't the first time he'd tried it. But perhaps it's normal, perhaps that what couples who've been seeing one another for a few months normally do. With a short gasping laugh, she pulls away and peers out of the side window. 'There might be more to come, looking at that sky.'

'Naw, it'll be fine.'

'Ian, you've got work tomorrow.'

'It'll be fine,' he says. 'I bet it'll hold off for a bit. Let's go to the Prince of Orange, they do a good Sunday lunch there, if I remember rightly.'

'They do,' Chloe says. 'Sorry, I hadn't realised you'd not eaten.'

'I bet you had breakfast.' He smiles. 'I was so excited to see you, I forgot.'

He's so intense sometimes. Chloe stifles the thought; she should be flattered. 'That's so lovely, Ian.' She gave him a light kiss, not missing his quick glance around the car park to see if there was anyone around. She moves back when he tries to pull her tighter. 'It's too cold to sit here. Let's get to the pub before

239

it gets too full. We'll get something to eat and then you must set off home.'

He raises his eyebrows. 'Trying to get rid of me already?'

Has she upset him? A second later, he smiles. 'As long as I set off before three o'clock it'll be fine.' He taps his hands on the steering wheel. 'Still, if I get stuck this side of the Pennines I could always kip at yours?'

'And you could always think again, Ian Turnbull.' She softens the words with a playful poke on his arm, hoping he's joking. Her stomach tenses.

He grins. 'Worth a shot.'

She grabs the car door handle. 'Come on, let's get in the warm.'

'There's something I want to ask you,' he says, 'and I want to see your face when I do.'

'Intriguing!'

'Wait there while I come round.'

It's one thing she likes about him: his manners. She waits for him to open her door and, hand under her elbow, helps her out of the car.

'Are you going to tell me what it is?'

'Let's get a drink inside us first. I think you'll like it.'

Chloe lies in bed listening to the wind howling outside, rattling the roof tiles. A flying dustbin lid clatters along the ginnel at the back of the shop. She pulls her duvet up around her neck. There's no chance she will be able to sleep, even if it wasn't so noisy outside. All she can think about is what excuse she can give Ian.

She wonders how he's managing on the tiny bed-settee in Albie's room. They'd arrived back at the shop at the same time as Albie. A drift of snow followed them as they rushed in, Ian with his arm around her waist. It felt territorial of him, but she tried to ignore that.

As soon as the old man understood that Ian was trapped on this side of the Pennines because of the snow, he'd insisted Ian stay in his room.

She smiled at the memory. Liking Ian doesn't mean she wants to sleep with him. Yet.

Perhaps Ian likes to make all the decisions when they go out because he's lived alone for four years. His parents dying in an accident must have had an effect on him.

Chloe turns over onto her back, watching the curtains move in the draft, throwing shadows on the ceiling.

She doesn't mind him choosing what they do on dates. It makes her feel safe. Years of being the odd one out, the 'foster girl', has left her uncertain where she fits in. With Ian she doesn't feel that; she's part of a couple.

But does she want to have Christmas with him and his sister?

She takes in a long breath and blows it out slowly, a ploy she's learned to calm herself.

It's a kind thought. He only means well. He's talked a lot about his sister and her children, they seem very close. She pulls the duvet over her head and groans. Celebrating Christmas with his family makes their relationship appear to be more serious that she feels it is. She's not ready.

But how to say no without offending him?

Chapter 84

'You okay? There's nothing to worry about, you know.' Simon is concentrating on driving and doesn't take his eyes off the road ahead but it's the third time he's asked Charlie since they set off from Cardiff. So he's clearly aware Charlie is shuffling around in the passenger seat.

'Sorry, I didn't mean to distract you.' Charlie tries to stretch out his legs, but there's no room.

Simon grins. 'When I bought the Mini I didn't reckon on having a six-foot-something friend as a passenger.'

'Ignore me. I can't remember the last time I was in a car. I'm not used to them.'

He can, but he won't tell Simon. The only times he's been in a car since he was ten were when he was being taken from one care home to another. Whenever he hitched a ride after he'd run away for the last time, it was always in lorries or commercial vans.

'We can stop for a break in one of the service stations if you like. It's only another hour before we get there but if you need a leg stretch?' Checking his mirror, Simon carefully overtakes an oil tanker. 'We've just passed a sign saying there's one in a mile.'

'D'you mind?'

'Not at all. Once we're over the Severn Bridge, we've only got another thirty miles to home.'

Home, he says the word so easily. Charlie always envies Simon's comfortable acceptance that he has somewhere he calls home. He doesn't resent it but he does envy it.

Simon parks well away from any other vehicles. Charlie eases himself out. The drone of traffic on the motorway carries on the strong wind that blows his hair around and make his eyes water. But it's good to feel the cold air on his face.

'Smashing view of the bridge and the river,' Simon shouts, pointing to the grey towers rising high in the sky and the steel cables hanging in elegant curves. The wide Severn is moving swiftly.

Charlie zips up his leather jacket. 'Yeah. But I'm dying for a pee...'

'Come on then.' Simon locks the Mini.

'Cat'll be safe?' Charlie says. 'With both of us gone?'

Simon cups his hand around his eyes to look through the window at the cat on the back seat in his box. 'I think he's asleep. We'll only be five minutes.'

They cross the car park side by side, heads down against the wind.

Inside the square wooden building; the sound changes to the buzz of people talking and the jangling of crockery and trays.

'Did you want something to eat? I told Mum we'd be with them around teatime. But if you're hungry now...?'

'No.' The smell of so many people crowded together, with greasy food and the faint whiff of the public lavatories, decides Charlie. 'No. Anyway, we can't leave Cat on his own for too long. Let's just use the loos and get on our way.'

'Great. And I'll get a newspaper as well, see what's happening about the strikes.'

Simon drives along the slip road and filters into the traffic. 'It's a good job we haven't that far to go, the weather's closing in again. I'll be glad when we're there.'

'Yeah.' Charlie hears the relief in his friend's voice and ignores his own flicker of nerves.

'It'll be okay, you know. We always have a good time at Christmas.'

'I know.' Charlie peers at the cat box. *Wish it were you and me on our own back in Cardiff, Cat.*

Chapter 85

'You must be Chloe. I'm Helen.' The woman holding the door wide open is small, but unmistakably Ian's sister: same copper red hair, same green eyes, same long straight nose. Her smile so wide she's showing the gum above her top teeth. 'Welcome. Ian said to expect you.' She pulls a wry face. 'He also says he's sorry, he'll be a bit late. Something to do with work.'

'Oh. Right.' This is so far out of Chloe's comfort zone. *Why had she given in to Ian.* She's regretted it the moment she stepped into the train in Manchester.

'Have you been to Huddersfield before?'

Chloe remembers when she came with Edith and Sid once to look for Charlie. 'No.'

'Well, come in. Excuse the chaos.'

This is an understatement. The hall holds four bicycles and several roller skates, A huge pile of coats hang over the newel post and toys and clothes are on almost every stair up to the landing. With thuds and screams of laughter three children and a dog charge down the stairs into the living room and fling themselves onto the settee. The tallest one turns on the television. Music blasts. Chloe stifles the urge to put her hands over her ears and run straight out of the front door.

'I know.' Helen raises her eyebrows in a sympathetic gesture. 'Horrendous, isn't it? Kids, quieten down.' Gripping Chloe's arm, she pulls her along the hall. 'Put your bag down and come into the kitchen, so we can have a chat in peace.'

The words sound innocent enough but Chloe has spent years learning how to read people's tone of voice. A chat? Or an interrogation? However friendly Ian's sister is being, she must be suspicious of an unknown woman he's unloaded onto her.

Would it be like this with Charlie and me if we'd grown up together?

The sense of loss, though familiar, takes her by surprise. *I don't want to be here.* The relationship between her and Ian has grown mostly through letters. The prospect of spending so much time with him, with his sister and her family is making her uneasy already.

Helen sits on a high, black stool by the stainless-steel island in the middle of the kitchen and points to the other. Chloe attempts a casual stance, crossing her legs and resting her elbows on the worktop, chin upped in her palms.

'Lovely kitchen.' The window looks onto a garden hemmed by a beech hedge and filled with outdoor toys, a slide and swing. A swing – so many memories here of her childhood.

'Thanks. Coffee?' Helen had started spooning instant coffee

245

into mugs before she asked. 'Good journey? Ian says you're a tailor. In Manchester. Bit of a strange job for a girl?' She's still smiling.

'Not really. It's what I wanted to do. It's also meant I can make my own clothes.'

'I can tell. I love your dress. Perhaps, sometime, when you and Ian ... perhaps you'll make something for me?' Helen puts the coffee on the worktop, touches Chloe's shoulder briefly before sitting herself. 'I'm glad Ian found you. The trail of girls he's had. I thought he'd never settle down.'

Her words startle Chloe. How to answer that? So he'd brought other girlfriends here? To be vetted by his sister?

To change the subject, she waves towards the children's laughter. 'How old are they?'

'Andy's six, Janice is seven, Billy's eight.'

There's a rapid rhythmic knock on the front door, followed by excited screams.

'Uncle Ian, Uncle Ian!'

'His knock,' Helen exclaims, unnecessarily.

'I guessed.' Chloe laughs. The pleasure of seeing him fuses with a niggle of nervousness.

The train carriage is cold. Chloe huddles, her hands pushed inside the sleeves of her coat. She can see her breath, small white puffs of air. Watching the snow-covered moorland as the train rattles slowly past, she wishes she was already back in her flat.

She's unsure how she feels after her time at Ian's sister's. It added another layer of doubt about him. There's no question he likes his own way; everything they've done over the last few days was his choice.

The only time she'd asked to do something was the cinema visit. She wanted to see the new Clint Eastwood film. He'd agreed but when they were queuing she saw it was a film called the *Invasion of the Body Snatchers.* Ian couldn't apologise enough. He said he'd made a mistake but still wanted to see it. 'Might as well,' he'd said, 'now we're here.'

Chloe hated the film.

If the trains had been running the following day, she would have insisted on returning home. Then with Helen looking on, Ian had produced a red rose and declared he'd booked a table at the local high-end restaurant.

Chloe felt she had no choice but to go, but she was left uneasy in a way she didn't understand.

Chapter 86

'Bloody hell, I'm glad we're home.' Charlie stamps the ice off his boots on the doormat. The houses across the street are almost obliterated by a thick sheet of snowflakes.

'Come on in, let's get warm.' Simon takes the cat box from him and sets it down on the floor. 'I'm sorry the heating packed up in the car. I'll need to get that fixed.'

'It's okay. Perhaps that's what Minis are for — to have to cuddle up to keep warm...' Charlie's voice trails away. *What a bloody stupid thing to say*.

Simon blinks, but otherwise appears not to have heard.

Cat yowls.

'Okay, okay. Here we are.' Charlie unfastens the cat box.

Cat slowly emerges, elongating his long body. He shakes himself and stalks over to the fire, sitting pointedly on the mat. They laugh, the awkward moment passed.

'Well, that's telling us. Right, your majesty.' Simon strokes Cat before switching on the fire. 'I'd better turn on the central heating as well. I think, just for tonight, we deserve everywhere in the house to be warm.'

'That was one hell of a journey.'

'The Mini isn't meant for weather like this. I can't remember when we last had snow like this in Cardiff. I was a bit bothered by that last skid coming down Green Street.'

'No snowploughs on the motorway with the strikes, so I should have expected the side roads to be worse. I thought I'd lost it then.'

'You handled it brilliantly.' Charlie unwinds his scarf from his neck. *What the hell is wrong with me? Embarrassing.*

Simon gives a a smile that comes and goes in a second. All he says is, 'Nice to know you weren't frightened to death.'

'Well, as someone who hasn't a clue about driving who am I to criticise?' Charlie tries a chuckle. It sounds odd. He clears his throat. 'Want something warm to drink? Or a beer?'

'Both. Coffee first. Give me your coat, I'll hang it up above the radiator in the kitchen.'

'I'll feed Cat. I bet he's hungry.'

'That cat is always hungry, with or without teeth.'

Charlie edges past Simon to put the kettle on. He rubs his palms together as though warming them, to cover his sudden self-consciousness. 'I had a great time, Si. Thanks for asking me to be part of your family celebrations.'

'No problem.' Simon is still arranging the coats on the clothes maiden. As if he senses something changing in the air, he turns, his face guarded. 'Thanks for being there. It wouldn't have been the same without you.' Cat appears, snaking his way around their legs. 'And you, Cat.'

They smile.

'Glad to be home,' Charlie repeats.

'And me.'

Chapter 87

Chloe picks up the post at the front door and goes through the envelopes until she finds what she's looking for: a letter from Ian. The wave of railway strikes since Christmas has made it difficult for them to meet and the post has been just as erratic.

But it's given her time to think about their relationship. Over the months, in person and through his letters, she's become aware of his inflexibility, his refusal to listen to anyone else's opinion. Including hers. But he's her first boyfriend – maybe that's normal? She's still surprised he wants to see her at all. But he's rapidly changed from cautious affection to an intensity that she's finding stifling. So far they'd done little more than kiss, but she knows he wants more. She's not ready to go any further yet, but he could finish with her if he gets bored. She remembers his sister saying he's had a trail of girlfriends before her. If he takes her hesitation as rejection, he could reject her first.

At lunchtime she goes up to her room. Sitting on the bed, she opens Ian's letter. It's brief, almost formal. She reads the first paragraph twice. This only tells her how little she knows him.

He's left Huddersfield, accepted a job as a sales rep for a company a friend has set up. He's in Cardiff, in Wales.

Chloe lets the letter fall onto her lap. The casual way he writes about such a life-changing decision is difficult to take in, especially when the strikes have the country in such a turmoil.

So this is how he's ending things with me?

Automatically, she folds the paper in half and sees more writing on the back.

Fancy coming to Cardiff?

Chapter 88

Still not sure she was right to come to Cardiff, Chloe watches the train squeal its way out of the station, trailing fumes of diesel and hot metal. She hoists her bag onto her shoulder and looks around. The flagstones are wet: snowy sludge drips from the awning onto the railway line. A cold, fine drizzle glistens on her coat.

'Chloe! Here! I'm here.'

She scans over the heads of the passengers hurrying to the exit. Ian is waving his arm and grinning. He pushes through the crowd and grabs her hands. 'You're here.'

'Only for the day.'

'I know.' He looks hard at her, as if he thinks she's going to change her mind. 'But let's just see, shall we?'

'I have to get back tonight.'

'We'll see.' Before she can say any more he turns, pulling her with him. 'Let's get you in the warm. Come and see the flat, it's not that far away.'

'Well, what do you think?' Ian swings his arm around to take in the living room. 'It's not in the best part of Cardiff but it's a nice enough area, it's fully furnished and there's quite a nice view from the bedroom window...' He stops, disappointment turning his mouth down. 'I was hoping you'd feel the same as me.'

'It's really nice. But Ian, I think you've got the wrong...'

'Don't say any more.' He holds up his hand. 'Once I've explained you'll know I'm right. Can't you believe in me?' He lifts his eyebrows, makes a comic pleading expression.

'I like my job. I like living in Manchester. Please understand, Ian, I need to feel secure. I have to. I need to be able to look after myself.'

'You've got me to look after you now.'

'It's not enough ... not what I'm used to. We've only known one another for a few months...'

He pushes out his lower lip.

She reaches out, touches his shoulder. 'Ian?' He shrugs her hand away. *He's sulking, he's actually sulking.* 'I'm going to go now, Ian. I shouldn't have come.'

To her surprise he laughs, grabs hold of her waist and spins them both round.

'Don't be silly, it was a joke.' He throws his head back, laughs again.

Chloe knows the laugh isn't genuine. 'Stop it, Ian. Please. Put me down.'

He backs off, his hands held up in mock apology. 'Sorry, sorry, Miss. I won't do it again.'

'It's not funny.'

'No, you're right, it's not. And I'm not taking anything for granted, Chloe. But I thought you felt the same. I've made plans.'

His voice is getting more and more aggrieved.

'Well, maybe you should have told me your plans before you moved here. I didn't even know you were thinking about it until I received your letter.'

'It was too good an offer. And I was sick to death of the last place. Boss treating me like a general dogsbody. I don't put up with that from anyone.' He dips his head a few times to emphasise his words. He sits on the nearest armchair and pulls at his tie. 'Life's too short.' He takes such a deep breath his shoulders rise up to his ears. 'So, what do you think, Chloe. Join me on my adventure?'

She might as well have said nothing. Instead, she says, 'How about we go out, get something to eat? I'm starving.'

Chloe wipes her lips with the napkin and pushes the plate to the middle of the table. 'Thank you, Ian.'

Things have been a little stilted between them throughout lunch.

For the first time in six months she's acknowledging the feeling lurking in her subconscious; that it's easier to go along with anything he says. She remembered a saying her Granny

252

had often quoted, 'Don't rock the boat until you know you can swim.' Chloe had never understood it as a child, but once Lynne moved in, she'd seen what it meant by watching her father. He hadn't rocked the boat. In the end he'd thrown her and Charlie overboard. The bitterness startles her. She hasn't thought about her father for a long time.

Get today over and done with, she thinks.

'There's still one sandwich left.' Ian lifts the top slice of bread. 'Egg and cress?'

'You have it. I couldn't eat another thing. It was lovely.' Chloe hesitates. 'I would have liked to have tried that other place, mind. That one with the Welsh name?' She has an uncomfortable feeling she knows what he will say.

'Naw, you'd hate it.'

'Why?' Walking around earlier, she'd suggested this other small restaurant and his instant refusal surprised her. Now she wants to test her instinct about Ian. 'It did look lovely from outside with all the plants on the windowsill. Why didn't you want to go in there?'

'I ate there the first day I came here.' He sniffs, pushing his lips up to his nose. *Almost a sneer?* 'And I swear a couple of the waiters bat for the other side. You know – queers.

She's right. 'And you didn't like the restaurant because of that?'

'Made me uncomfortable – the way they flaunt it.'

The casual way he says it shocks Chloe. *I thought the world had moved on from these ideas.*

'I don't think you should...'

'Wouldn't touch the place with a bargepole,' he interrupts her, sniggering. 'Excuse the pun.'

'That's not funny, Ian.' Her whole body goes cold.

'Oh, come on. Just a joke.'

'It's not though, it's nasty.' She's becoming angrier and angrier.

'Hey, careful. Are you calling me nasty?'

'I'm saying it's nasty to think like that in this day and age.' *Thank goodness you've not met Evie and Beth. Would you think the same about them? Been as obnoxious?*

He shrugs. 'Up to you.'

'Yes. Chloe reaches for her coat from the back of her chair. 'It is.'

'And you'll tell me soon about...?'

Unbelievable. Just get out of here.

'I have a lot to think about.' She casts around for something to say, to shut him up. 'Work for a start.'

'There must be something around here. Another tailors? Or something in one of the stores?'

'I'm not a shop girl, Ian. I'm fully qualified as a tailor.'

'No, I know. It's just...'

'I really do need to be going.' She looks at the sky through the café window. 'Those clouds don't look so promising. I bet by the time I get into Manchester it'll be snowing again. I have to catch that train. This was my only day off, and with another one-day rail strike tomorrow, I can't afford to miss it, or I'll be in trouble with Mr Nudel.'

'Of course. I'll walk with you to the station. See you off, if you're really sure you have to go?' The aggrieved tone again.

'I need to.' *I need to get away from you.*

'You can go now, Ian. Please don't wait on the platform until the train leaves. It's freezing.' Chloe steps up and waits in the train door while a woman with a small child moves down the carriage.

'I wanted...' Ian's last words are drowned out by the train's hooter.

Walking through the carriages, looking for somewhere to sit, she glances through the windows and notices him dodging around people on the platform. He's keeping in step with her. Watching her. She finds an empty seat by the window. Ian points upwards.

'What?' Chloe is very aware of the curious stares of the other passengers. She reaches up to the small top window, slides it open.

'Chloe, I've been meaning to say all day...'

'What?'

He rubs his hand over his mouth. 'I should have said...'

There's a whoosh of brakes and the carriage creaks into movement.

He begins to run to keep up with the train, cupping his hands around his mouth. Above all the noise she hears him.

'Marry me, Chloe. I want you to marry me.'

The last she sees of him, he's standing at the end of the platform, snow swirling around him, his arms outstretched.

Not on your life, she thinks.

Chapter 89

Graham stops outside his stepson's bedroom door and listens. There have been at least five young men in there over the past two days. When they'd arrived they'd stomped up the stairs led by Saul who gazed blankly at Graham before raising two fingers. He'd not seen them again but they'd made their presence known with raucous laughter, and loud music

When the door handle turns, he hurries down the stairs, clutching the pile of white envelopes that he's just found under the bed.

Misery sits heavily inside him. This isn't home anymore.

'I didn't hear you come downstairs.' Lynne comes out of the kitchen, drying a plate.

'They're still here, I see,' he said. 'Or should I say, *hear*.' Despite his weak legs and fuzzy head he sometimes tries to reach out to her.

Her challenging glare makes Graham's scalp tingle.

'So my son isn't entitled to have his friends in his home?'

He can't deal with another quarrel. 'Sorry, Lynne. It's just the noise. And I'm tired. I think it might be those new tablets you said the doctor prescribed.'

'I didn't *say* he prescribed them, he did. Dr Hume is as worried as I am about you.' She stops, seeing the envelopes. 'What have you got there?'

He backs away.

'It's my post. Bank statements.' He sees her anger. It makes him flustered and he's babbling. 'I don't understand.' He reads out the letter. 'It says here I've reached the limit of my overdraft.

Six thousand pounds. I don't remember asking for an overdraft on that account. I wouldn't, not for that amount.'

'Of course you did,' she answers, overriding his words. 'You told me you had.'

He's shaking, not taking in what she's saying. He thinks he's going to vomit. 'And my credit card is at the maximum as well. How can that be? I haven't spent all that.'

She rolls her eyes. 'You were at the garage last summer, even though I said you weren't fit to work. Yolanda said you and Phil went out a couple of times. You must have used your cards then. For cars? Supplies?'

'Impossible.' He drops onto his armchair. 'Margaret deals with all the supplies. And we don't just go out and buy cars, not like that.' He shakes his head, trying to get his brain to work. As far as he can remember he'd mostly sat in the office, chatting to Margaret, the relief of being away from the house almost overwhelming. He'd pretended to go through the books she'd shown him but to be honest it had all gone over his head. It didn't matter – he trusted his friends.

'I wouldn't use these cards, anyway. Not my personal cards.' He's reluctant to ask her if she's been buying yet more clothes with his card.

'What are you trying to say, Graham?' Her throat mottles red.

He lets the sheets fall from his fingers to the floor. His childhood fear of poverty ripples through him; when his father had lost his job, his mother crying. Being in debt terrifies him.

'These.' His fingers quiver towards the statements. 'These

were hidden.' He's going to cry. 'You'd hidden them. It's him again, isn't it?' He lifts his chin up towards the ceiling. 'You've either given him the money, or he's in some sort of trouble and you've had to bail him out.'

He sees her coming at him and folds his arms over his head. Feels the pain when the edge of the plate cuts into his scalp.

Chapter 90

Ezra Nudel stands straight-backed in front of Chloe. Despite this he looks distinctly uneasy.

'You wanted to see me, Mr Nudel?' Has a customer complained about her work? Or is this just to tell her Mrs Nudel has invited her to a meal at their house? But why the frown?

'Ezra, please,' he says.

His tone gives Chloe a prickle of alarm.

'I'm afraid I have some news that might make life a little difficult for you, Miss Collins … Chloe.'

'Are you sacking me?'

'No! Not at all. Well, not as such. You've done nothing wrong; in fact, your work is always exemplary. But I regret to say I've decided to close the shop.'

The shock winds Chloe. She clenches her hands tight over her stomach. *Breathe. Breathe.* 'I'm sorry. Could I sit down, please?'

'Of course, of course. Oh dear, this must be such a shock for you.'

She collapses into the chair. 'I can't...' She lowers her head to her knees. *What will I do? Where will I live?*

'That's right, just sit a moment. I am so sorry to spring this on you. But with the lorry drivers striking, and the potential fuel crisis, I can only see problems ahead. We will be unable to take any more orders when the stock we have is gone. With no stock and no orders, I will have no business.

What will I do?

He's still talking. 'As I am well over seventy, I think, under the circumstances, this is the time to – as my father would say, "shut up the shop".'

'I understand Mr Nudel, I really do. It's just...'

'I checked the books last week and, if we can fulfil the orders we have in the next month, I will be able to give you all a generous redundancy package, together with your last pay packet. If I try to carry on after that, I won't.'

There's nothing to say. Pull yourself together, Chloe.

His shoulders rise and fall with a huge sigh. 'Of course, I'll give you excellent references for your next post.'

Wherever that will be.

Ezra Nudel leans against his desk, studying the pages of his order book as though waiting for Chloe's reaction. She wonders how the others took the news.

'Thank you. I appreciate you telling me Mr ... Ezra. Thank you. I'd better get on with the sleeves of Mr Hopkinson's jacket.' She glances at her watch. 'He'll be here in an hour for his fitting.'

She stops between his office and the workshop, to take deep, shuddering breaths. So many decisions to make now.

There's a murmur of voices from the workshop. Over the years since being cut from her family Chloe's become attuned to the tone of people's voices, to the vibe in a room. Being sensitive to atmospheres has helped her to keep safe. Avoid getting too close to people. But she's fond of these two elderly men she's been working with for three years and hearing Herbie and Albie in the workshop, she recognises the anxiety in their whispered words. She empathises with them.

Each man looks up from their sewing machines when she walks through the curtain.

'Bit of a shock, eh?' Albie purses his mouth.

'It is, Albie.' Chloe hesitates. 'What will you do?'

'Something I've been thinking of for a while, I suppose. Go and live with my shvester, my sister, Adara. She's been mithering me for years, so I guess the time's right. She lives in Cornwall, lovely place by the sea. A bit of a change, eh?'

'Sounds wonderful.' Chloe smiles. 'You, Herbie?' He's way past retiring. A single man who's lived in the same room for over forty years.

He shrugs, positioning the lapel of the jacket he's sewing on his machine. 'Not a clue. I have no family. But I do have some money saved, so I can look for somewhere to rent while I make up my mind.' Despite his words, he looks near to tears. Before she can answer he adds, 'There is a letter for you, Chloe. The post was late this morning. They're on strike again on Thursday, so lucky it came at all.' He presses his foot on the pedal of his sewing machine and squints down at the needle on the material.

'Thanks, Herbie.' She picks up the letter from the counter, recognises Evie's handwriting. Strange, her stepsister has been so much on her mind and now a letter from her. She only writes occasionally but it's always chatty, full of her life with Beth, and her work in the civil service.

She puts the letter by her sewing machine, and glances around.

'Where are Tommy and Julian?'

'Packed it in, *schlemiel*.' Albie shakes his head. 'As soon as they found out, they went. I told them they'd regret it. Who else will take them on, half-apprenticed? I told them they should wait to see what Ezra could offer when the shop finally closes but they said they were off to get new jobs.'

'Where will they live?'

Albie gives an exaggerated shrug. 'That's what we said. But they thought they knew better. Who are we to give advice? Two old men.'

'Two wise men,' Chloe said. She saw them exchange looks, as though gratified and trying not to show it. 'I think you're right. Better to wait.'

Though now she's made up her mind about Ian — and she has — she shouldn't wait to tell him. Better done sooner rather than later.

At lunchtime she opens Evie's letter. It's really just a note, asking her if they can meet up, and leaving a telephone number to arrange it. Nothing else.

For the second time today, Chloe has a sense of foreboding. The strange, almost curt words from her stepsister frighten her. Something's wrong. Some memories transform with time: some alter, some shrivel and are lost. But the worst, the most frightening never go away.

For some reason this short note brings back sitting in the car outside her first foster home. Her dad refusing to take her to see Charlie but saying he would soon. She hadn't known she would never see her brother again.

She rereads the message a number of times but can't find any clues to why Evie needs to see her.

Chapter 91

Chloe sits in her bedroom determined to get the letter to Ian out of the way.

Or perhaps she could have a bath first, lie in lavender and camomile scented bubbles to calm herself and think what to say. It might be more relaxing. The weight of last night's lost sleep tightens the muscles in her shoulders.

Ian's reaction to someone who has a different way of life to his has sickened her. Now, looking through his letters, she can see that he's only written about what he's doing, his life. It hadn't occurred to her before.

By the time Chloe steps, shivering, out of the bath, she knows what she will write. She's recognises that the old shame – always seeing herself as less than other girls because she was fostered – had made her grateful that Ian had chosen her.

She's stronger knowing that. And there's no point in challenging the way he thinks because he won't change. She doesn't want to be unkind; she just doesn't want to see him again.

Dear Ian,

I've thought for a long time before writing this. And I know you'll be hurt, but please try to understand. I'm not ready to be with anyone all the time at the moment. I don't want to live with anyone, and I certainly don't want to be married. We've only known each other for a few months. It's too soon to make any commitment. When I do I want to be completely sure, and I'm sorry, I'm not.

I would like for us to stay friends but if that's not what you want, I will understand.

Chloe

She doesn't intend to keep in touch with him, and she's sure he'll be so angry he won't either. But it seems better to end the letter in that way.

Chapter 92

'So, I...' Evie glances at Beth who nods. '*We* thought you should know something we found out last week. That's why I wrote to you.' She looks around the lounge of the pub, rubbing her hands together. 'I'm frozen. Let's find somewhere to sit, shall we?'

'By the fire?' It's a cosy old-fashioned pub, full of dark oak beams and brass hangings. Chloe leads the way.

'That's better,' Evie unwinds her scarf, pulls off her duffle coat and piles them on the wide windowsill behind them. 'I'll get them in, shall I? And get the menus? We might as well have something to eat while we're here.'

'Half a shandy for me, please.' Beth puts her coat on the back of the chair. 'Chloe?'

'I'd like a glass of Lambrusco, please.' She thinks she might just need a bit of a lift from the alcohol. Both women appear anxious.

'Right.' When Evie returns, she slides the tray onto the table. 'They serve lunch until two o'clock so we've plenty of time to order.' She shares out the drinks and menus and sits. 'Cheers.'

They lift their glasses.

'How's things with you and your new man?'

'New man? You make it sound as if I've had a string of men. His name's Ian and I won't be seeing him again.' *I can't tell you why.* Chloe notices how close Evie and her partner are sitting. They were holding hands when they came into the pub.

'Oh, that's a shame. Why?'

'Just not worked out.' She attempts a smile. 'Right. Put me out of my misery. What's up?'

The two women exchange glances. Beth sits back. She clearly thinks this is a family issue.

'We met Phil and Margaret in town when we were having a mooch around the January sales.' Evie looks concerned. 'They told us a few things.'

'What about?'

'Your dad. They're worried about him.'

'Why?'

'Well, your dad has written to Phil to say he wants him to buy his share of the garage or he'll be putting it up for sale.'

'Dad wouldn't do that.' The shock flashes through Chloe. 'That was Grandad Burn's business. He built that up from nothing. Dad knows how important the garage was to Mum.

He'd never sell. He wouldn't do that to Phil. And why write? Have they fallen out or something?'

'On the contrary, Phil said he hasn't even seen him since last June.' Evie tugs her short hair, a nervous habit Chloe remembers from her childhood.

'Hasn't he been to the house to find out what's wrong? If Dad's ill?'

'He's tried. The furthest he got was the front doorstep. He couldn't get past my mother. She said your dad wasn't well enough to see him. She told Phil to put in an offer for Graham's share of the garage, or it would be on the open market.'

'He didn't see Dad?'

'There was no way Lynne was letting him in the house. And she said Graham had told her to ask Phil to give all the books to the accountants, so he could work out what the business is worth.'

'I bet she did. God, she's a devious cow. Is the business all right, though?'

'Phil says the pay limits the government's imposing on companies caused a few rumbles among the men at first, but he's found a way around it to give more than the five percent.' Evie drops the volume of her voice. Nobody at the nearby tables knows who they're talking about but Chloe understands. What Phil is doing to get around the three-day week is illegal; it's best to be careful. 'Some way of giving them cash instead of through their wages. He really wanted to talk it over with your dad, but it's not been possible. The business is doing okay, the work is there, but Phil says they've all missed your dad for a long time. You know how hands-on he always was.'

'He was,' Chloe says.

'And there has been paperwork, accounts, bank stuff, where he needs Graham to countersign. Phil said he fell right into Lynne's trap when he said that: gave her a good excuse to get her mitts on the books.'

A blast of cold air sweeps into the room as a large group of people rush into the pub, laughing, chattering, brushing snow off.

Evie reaches for Chloe's hands.

'I'm sorry, love, but I think she's up to her old tricks again.' She leans forward to make herself heard. 'I'm guessing she's controlling him, like she did with my father. He managed to leave her but it nearly broke him. He was a wreck, but at least he got out. I think things have gone beyond that with Graham, Chloe. You need to see him.'

'He wouldn't want me to. He told me years ago he didn't want anything to do with me.'

'He did? Or was it her?'

'The message was that he couldn't cope with me. He'd already got rid of Charlie before that.'

'Or she had.'

'You keep saying that, Evie, but he could have left her. He could have stopped her. Kept us.'

'Graham's a man who will do anything for a bit of peace, Chloe. And I think Lynne recognised that from the very beginning. I think she's manipulated him all along.'

'He's not weak, Evie.' Chloe fumbles with the sleeve of her jumper, finds a tissue and blows her nose. The memories come back with sickening clarity.

'He wasn't. But as far as I can see, she's done everything she can to isolate him. She manipulated your school, social services, everyone, to get him away from you. She tried that with my father, but he left her.'

'Dad could have done the same.'

'Could he? Lynne has learned from her mistakes with my father. My father tried to take me with him but she told lies, made it impossible for him to even see me.'

'But you see him now?'

'Actually, I have, since I was fourteen. I found out where he lived. He's in Bath. He told me why he left. According to everyone else she was a saint. Some saint, eh?'

'Does Saul see your father?'

'I'm not sure we have the same dad. Perhaps that's why he was always the favourite. I'm the product of the man who got away. Maybe Saul's father was different. I don't know.' She shrugs. 'What do you think you'll do?'

'I don't know. I could go to see Phil and Margaret. I'll have to ask for a couple of days off work next week, though I won't be needing to ask much longer.'

'Why?'

'Mr Nudel is closing the shop. With everything that's going on, the strikes, shortage of everything, I can understand it.

'What will you do? Where will you live?'

'I don't know.' Chloe grimaces. 'But you know me Evie, I'll land on my feet as usual.'

Why do I always put up a front whenever I'm with Evie? Not that she's fooled.

You can come and doss down with us until you sort yourself out. Can't she, Beth?'

'Of course.' Beth smiles. 'There's plenty of room.'

'Thanks, that's generous.'

'Nonsense. You'd do the same for us.'

A gust of wind makes the window next to Chloe rattle. She glances at it. 'Actually, I think we should miss having a meal here; have you seen outside?'

Beth follows Chloe's gaze. 'Good grief, more snow! We should make a move, Evie, the roads are going to be really bad if we stay any longer.' She looks around. 'And it seems everyone else has got the same idea.'

Customers are leaving, filing out of the door; the publican has started to cash up at the till.

Evie lets Beth help her into her coat. 'Thanks, love.'

Chloe slides along the bench. She fastens the buttons of her coat, follows Evie and Beth out.

They stand just inside the door, gazing out at the flurries of snow.

'Did Phil and Margaret mention anyone else who has seen Dad lately?'

'Phil said nobody has seen Graham in months.'

'I suppose that settles it then. I need to see Dad, find out what's going on.'

Even if it opens up old wounds.

Chapter 93

'Yes? Can I help you?'

There it is: the smile that doesn't reach the eyes. What did Charlie used to call it? The 'no eyes' smile. Bringing Charlie to mind makes Chloe waver. If she ever needed him, it's now. She pretends he's right beside her.

'Hello, Lynne. I don't think I've changed that much.' She's not playing one of the woman's stupid games.

The mouth compresses. 'What the hell do you want?'

'To see my father.'

'Well, you can't, he's not well. *And* he wouldn't want to see you.'

'Let's just ask him, shall we?' Chloe steps up to the door within inches of her stepmother. Lynne's aged, with deep grooves either side of her mouth, and Chloe can smell wine on her breath. 'Are you going to let me in?'

'No.' Lynne tries to block her, but Chloe's taller. She stands her ground until Lynne gives way.

'Thank you.'

She didn't know what to expect, but it wasn't this: a slight figure almost swamped by the settee he's slumped in. He looks over his shoulder and his mouth is moving but all Chloe can hear is her heart hammering.

'Dad.' He looks terrified. 'Dad, it's me, Chloe.'

He looks past her. Instinctively she knows what he's asking. 'Charlie's not with me.' She won't tell him she doesn't know where her brother is. She can't be that cruel, even if she's blamed her father for taking Charlie away from her all these years.

He lets his eyes drift over her face until he suddenly smiles and attempts to stand.

'No, don't get up.' Chloe sits on the settee next to her father, ignores the gasp from Lynne. She puts her hand on his trembling fingers. 'It's been a long time. I thought I should come to see you.'

He doesn't take his eyes off her.

'It's freezing in here,' she says. The wind is whistling down the chimney behind gas fire. 'You're shaking, Dad. Are you cold? Why have you only got a shirt on? It's blowing a gale out there and snow's forecast again.'

'He's fine, aren't you, Graham.'

'Yes. I'm fine, love.' His voice isn't the one Chloe remembers. It's thin, hoarse.

'Why isn't the fire on?' She leans sideways to reach for the switch.

'Leave it! We're warm enough.' Lynne sits in the armchair opposite. She undoes the top button of her thick cardigan as if making a point, her head tilted, her narrowed eyes challenging.

'Dad?'

He straightens, his lips straining into a smile.

'I'm fine, Chloe. It's good to see you. I thought I would never...'

'So, tell us, why are you here?' Lynne interrupts, crossing her arms.

'I've come to see Dad.' Chloe looks up as the clock on the mantelpiece chimes. 'Oh, where's that oil painting that was above the clock, Dad? Your favourite? That artist's work is fetching a fortune these days.'

'Huh?' Her father stares vacantly towards the wall, then back at her.

'He went off it. He gave it to someone, didn't you Graham?' Lynne scowls, 'You should have let us know you were coming; we might have been busy. Or out.'

'But you weren't. And if you've something you want to get on with, Lynne, feel free.'

Her stepmother flushes. Chloe remembers how she always blotches red when losing her temper and can't resist adding, 'It is only Dad I want to talk to, so you don't have to stay here.'

'You don't get to tell me what to do.' Lynne pulls out a packet of cigarettes and a lighter from her cardigan pocket.

'Okay, if you want me to be straight. I'd like to talk to my father on his own. Please.'

'Anything you have to say to him,' she says and sucks deeply on the cigarette, 'you can say with me here.'

'Dad?'

'Graham.'

Chloe hears the warning, blown out on a long stream of smoke.

He coughs. 'Lynne's right, love. Just say what it is you want to say.'

'I came to see how you are.'

'After all these years?' Lynne challenges.

'Not my choice, if you remember.' Chloe won't give the woman the courtesy of looking at her. She points at the bottles of tablets lined up on the small table by the settee. 'You're not well, Dad?'

'Bits and pieces, love, bits and pieces. That's all.' Graham peers sideways at his wife.

Chloe remembers Evie's words. 'She's controlling him, like she did with my own father', and now Chloe sees the reality of his life: this house is his entire world. '"Bits and pieces"? What's exactly wrong? What has the doctor said?'

'He has me.' Lynne cuts in. 'If you bothered to remember, you'd know I'm a nurse – I'm all he needs, aren't I Graham?'

'Yes, dear.'

A nurse stinking of wine and cigarette smoke.

'Why are you here?'

Chloe swallows, her throat dry.

'I saw Evie,' she says, and hears Lynne's hiss of indrawn breath. 'I don't know what's going on here, Dad, but I'm worried about you.' She waits for a reaction from him, but there is none.

Lynne stands up. 'Your father's tired. He usually has a nap at this time. So...'

Chloe leans towards Graham. 'Tell me what's wrong, Dad. Tell me why you want to sell your share of the garage.'

He frowns. 'What?'

'Stop confusing him. It's fine, Graham, she's going. I won't have you upset.'

'I can see something's wrong, Dad. What's happened?' He tightens his hold on her fingers. When she looks into his eyes, they are rimmed with tears. 'Dad?' What is it?'

'That's quite enough.'

Chloe feels a pincer-like grip on her arm. She's dragged to her feet.

'Get your hands off me.' She struggles against Lynne's hold.

'I think you should tell your daughter to leave now, don't you, Graham?'

'Dad?' Chloe looks back at him as she's pulled towards the hall.

'I don't know. Perhaps...' His hands cup the top of his knees.

'See. He doesn't want you here.'

'What's wrong with him?'

'All I've ever done is care for him.' Lynne drags open the front door. 'I'm worn out looking after your father, and neither you nor that lout of a brother of yours have ever bothered to help.'

Chloe's skin prickles. There are so many accusations she wants to throw at this woman, but she allows herself to be pushed out onto the steps.

'I'll come again, Dad,' she calls, 'I'll be back soon.'

Lynne follows Chloe, pushing her down the path with short stabs. 'Oh no you won't, madam. This is the last time. He has dementia—'

'Dementia?' The word stops Chloe's breath. 'He's been diagnosed? You've had a doctor diagnose that?'

'I don't need a doctor to tell me what's wrong with him. I should know I've seen this many times before.' She speaks quickly. It sounds practised. 'He needs to go into a geriatric ward where he can be cared for. I'm exhausted. There are beds in Withington Hospital in Manchester...' She falters, as though realising she shouldn't have told Chloe. 'I've spent years in NHS care homes and I know dementia when I see it.

'And I'll tell you something else, madam, I'm going to sell this mausoleum and I'll finally live the life I deserve.'

'You can't do that.'

'I can and I will. Now, bugger off. And don't bother coming back.'

Chloe shivers, unsure what to do. She doesn't know how long she's been standing at the end of the drive. The sky is now a murky brown. A cold wind hurts her face as it whips up swirls of snow, amber in the streetlamps.

A light goes on in what was Charlie's bedroom. A bulky outline of a figure is lit up. Intuitively she knows it's Saul. He must have been upstairs all the time, listening to them. She can't help feeling a long-forgotten fear.

But she has to help her father. The man she's seen today is not the man she knew when she was little. He's a man she has to rescue.

Chapter 94

It's the only place she can think to go. The pavement has been swept clear the snow piled up in dirty heaps in the gutter. Above the doorway, are the names: Priest, Mitchell & Green, Solicitors. She's sure this is the family firm her father and Phil used for the business.

'My name is Chloe Collins. I need to see someone. It's quite urgent.'

In the taxi she'd tried to think what to say, how to explain her worries. Her anger. And she is angry, she acknowledges that. *How can one person do that to another?*

'Urgent,' she says again.

The woman at reception desk looks at her impatiently over the top of her ornately framed glasses. Chloe realises it's four thirty on a Friday afternoon, and totally the wrong time to hope she can see someone.

'Next month's fully booked. The week beginning the nineteenth of February?' The receptionist taps each page with a perfectly manicured red nail. 'Or the week after?'

'I've come to see you because of my father.' She's crying.

The woman blinks nervously. She jumps up, comes around the oval desk and holds Chloe. Her plump arms, her soft bosom are an instant comfort. With each gulping sob, Chloe remembers her first foster mother, Eileen Brice, and she's back to that shocking day she was told her dad wasn't going see her ever again. The memory overwhelms her and her knees buckle.

'Here, sit down here.' She's led to a chair. A door opens and a man, wearing a trilby and holding a raincoat over his arm, peers out.

'Mrs Martin? What's happening?'

'It's this young lady.' Her arm rests across Chloe's shoulders. 'She needs to see someone urgently. I know it's late, Mr Green, and you said you needed to get off on time tonight, but if you could just...' She moves away, returns with a box of tissues.

Self-conscious, Chloe wipes her eyes.

'I suppose.' The solicitor hesitates 'It's nothing pressing, I was only thinking to miss the traffic. But later is as good as now. Come on then, Miss...?

'Collins. Chloe Collins.' She gives Mrs Martin a grateful smile, and follows him into his office, the flood of relief stronger than the mortification of breaking down in front of strangers.

Chapter 95

'Right, Miss Collins.' Mr Green closes the thick beige file on his desk. 'First, the matter of the garage. It can't be sold to a third party unless your father signs an agreement.'

'Which she might make him do,' Chloe interrupts.

'You or your father's partner, Mr Baxter, would have to prove coercion. Although as your father's solicitor, I could deal with the paperwork personally and make sure I'm present. And if I had any suspicion that someone was forcing him...' He opens and closes his fingers. 'I've known your father for many years. I would ensure that everything was above board, Miss Collins. However, so far I have not been approached to draw up any document to end the partnership between him and Mr Baxter, or for the sale of business.

'As for Moorcroft,' Mr Green sighs. 'Mrs Collins, your stepmother could have a claim to stay in the house as your father's wife, even if she does try...' He clears his throat. 'Even if your father does need...'

'He doesn't. She says he's got dementia but I don't believe her. She's isolated him from his friends, and – a long time ago – she got rid of my brother and me.' Chloe tries to block the pain of losing Charlie. 'And I still don't know where my brother is.'

He nods, slowly. 'I understand your distress, Miss Collins. I'm only mentioning the possible legality of your stepmother's position.' He shuffles his papers. 'As I've told you, the house is not legally your father's; it's held in trust for both you and your brother, Charlie. Your father is well aware of that, though, from what you have told me, his wife is not.'

'So she can't sell the house?'

'She has no rights to the house whatsoever. As I said, your grandfather, Mr Charles Burns, left the house to his daughter, Anna – your mother, in trust for the two of you. When she sadly passed, her will stated the same, the house became your father's for as long as he lives.' He smiles. 'It's quite simple.'

Chloe shrugs. 'I don't understand why Dad never told us.'

'Perhaps he thought it unnecessary?' Mr Green removes his reading glasses. 'The issue now is, will you tell your stepmother?'

'I don't know.' *How will Lynne react? What will she do to Dad once she knows? How much worse can it get?*

Chapter 96

'You all right?' Simon studies Charlie. 'It's been a good evening, thirty-two covers, and twenty at lunchtime, which is amazing when people are strapped for cash. Tomas might think twice about closing *Bwyty Un* if we carry on like this. But you look shattered?'

'I am. I think I've seen enough mucky pans for today.' Charlie pulls his apron over his head and throws it into the basket by the kitchen door, 'I'll see you back at the house.'

'I won't be long; I'll just check with Chef what we've got in the cupboards for the menu tomorrow. It's more difficult than ever to get supplies.'

'We could always go to the market first thing in the mornings ourselves.'

Simon grimaces. 'We *could*. But we'll be burning both ends of the candle even more then. And who's to say the markets are faring any better with the lorry drivers' strike in full flow.'

'I suppose.'

'You go now. Get that kettle on, we'll have a brew. And maybe a chat?'

'Do you want to talk?' Simon sits opposite him at their dining table. Both plates of fish pie, brought back from the restaurant, sit uneaten in front of them. 'I could tell you've had something on your mind all day.'

Charlie rubs grains of salt off his fingers. 'Yeah?'

'Yep.'

Charlie sits back, unsure how honest to be. 'I've been thinking. Seeing you with your family at Christmas, it made me think about my sister. I'm always thinking about her, wondering where she is. We're twins. But now I'm thinking, maybe, of finding her again.'

Simon waits.

'But I can't, I won't go to my father's house. Even if Chloe is livin' there.'

'Do you think she might be? She'll be twenty by now, like you. Won't she have moved out?'

'She is. And yes. I'd guess she'd have left as soon as she could, if that woman carried on being a bitch. But even if he is the only person who knows where Chloe is, I don't want to ask him. The only other thing I can think of is to write to someone else who might know. Maybe Mr and Mrs Baxter. He was my father's friend and his partner at the garage. She worked there as well. I was friends with their son, Mark.'

'Okay,' Simon says again.

'I'll ask them not to tell my father.'

'Why?'

'I don't want him to know, that's all. I just don't.'

'Won't that put them in a difficult position, if they're friends?'

Charlie pauses. 'I hadn't thought of that.'

'It's up to you, Charlie. Why not just write to them about Chloe, not say anything about your dad. What's the worst that could happen if they do tell him?'

'He might ask them not to tell me.'

'Why would he do that? After all these years? Maybe he'd be glad to know you're alright? Things change. Now might be the time to get your family back, Charlie. What can that woman do to you now?' Simon lifted his hand. 'Sorry, none of my business. You do what you want.'

He's right, that woman can't harm me now.

'I'll write to them. I won't mention my father and I'll cross that bridge when – if I have to.'

'Only if that's what you want.'

'It's a long shot anyway. I don't know their proper address, just the road.' Charlie shrugs. 'The family might not even be there anymore.'

Simon reaches over, covers Charlie's fingers with his. 'You won't know unless you try,' he says gently.

They both look at their hands, then each raise their eyes to one another. Simon nods. Charlie brings his thumb over Simon's. They fall silent. Charlie knows this is the most significant moment in his life for a long, long time. His pulse throbs in his throat.

'You're right,' he says.

'Good.'

'But after I've written I don't want to talk about it again, Si. Unless...'

'You get a reply.'

'Is that alright?'

'Of course.' Simon half-stands, leans forward across the table and kisses Charlie lightly on the lips before sitting down again

They don't speak. Neither wants to rush what is happening between them. It's okay.

Chapter 97

'The issue now is will you tell your stepmother?' The solicitor's words have gone round and round in Chloe's head since Friday.

Chloe waits a few moments after knocking on the Baxters' door. At least she can put Phil and Margaret's minds at rest about the business. Best to do that before she goes to Moorcroft.

She can hear footsteps before the door opens.

Chloe's wide smile falters. She remembers a tall, muscular man with a shock of brown hair. This man is thin, almost bald. He puts the glasses perched on top of his head back on his nose. 'Hello?'

'It's Chloe Collins, Mr Baxter.'

'Chloe...? Chloe Collins? Good God!' He holds out his hand. 'Good God,' he says again, pulling her into the hallway. 'It's been years. Where have you been? Come in, out of the cold. Let me take your coat. I can't believe it. Chloe Collins! Margaret! Margaret, look who's here.'

She hears chair legs grate on tiles, looks past Phil to the kitchen and sees Margaret standing, a vegetable peeler in her hand. She's easier to recognise, still plump, still wearing the same page-boy haircut, but it's dark, not the blonde she used to be.

'I'm interrupting.' Chloe apologises. She lets Phil help her out of her coat and pushes off her wet boots to place them on the doormat. 'It's almost lunch time.' She's chosen Sunday morning, thinking it would be the only day Phil wouldn't be at the garage. But she must be disrupting their day.

The sound of her voice galvanises Margaret who gives a small scream, rushes from the kitchen, and flings her arms around Chloe's waist, her head slotting beneath Chloe's chin.

'Oh, it's you, my lovely.' The same rich Cornish accent. 'We haven't seen nor heard anything about you for years. Years! We stopped asking your dad about either you or Charlie; he'd get so upset.'

Chloe doesn't know what to say.

'We never really understood what happened to you and Charlie. Do you keep in touch with your brother?'

'No.' Chloe's heart thumps under her ribs. She can't think about him, not just now. 'I looked for him for years but I didn't find him.'

'That's awful.' Margaret looks up at her. 'A shame. Come through to the kitchen and tell us what you're doing here after all this time. I'll make a brew. Our Mark will be home in an hour or so. He'll be so pleased to see you.'

Mark had been Charlie's friend much more than hers. Chloe remembers how they would reluctantly let her join in with their football games, as long as she agreed to be in goal. How long ago? It has to be more than ten years since she's seen him. Since she's seen Phil and Margaret.

It's like stepping back in time for Chloe: the same warm pine kitchen units, the mosaic tiled floor, the view of the garden: the small greenhouse, the tidy vegetable patch, bare at this time of the year. The shed, that Margaret used to say was Phil's escape to avoid helping with the housework, is still standing. That memory makes Chloe smile as she sips her tea.

But it's not reminiscences that have brought her here today, and she knows the two people sitting on either side of her on the settee are waiting.

Chloe puts her cup carefully on the saucer.

'Evie told me about the garage.'

'Evie? We saw her, didn't we, Phil?'

'Aye. In Manchester. Shopping.'

'We didn't know she was in touch with you...'

'I made her promise a long time ago not to tell anyone. And I asked her never to tell me anything about Mossleigh. It hurt too much. But this is different. She thought I should know and I'm glad.'

'It's not your fault, love, but we've really had the dirty done on us.'

'I know, Phil, that's why I'm here. Evie suspects her mother is somehow behind it, so I went to see Dad to find out for myself.'

'That must have been difficult for you, lovely. How is he?'

'He looks ill. A bit bewildered to be honest. Evie's right: Lynne is trying to get Dad to sell his half of the garage. She's also planning to sell the house. She intends to put him into Withington Hospital in Manchester.'

'Why in God's name does she think she can put Graham into a place like that?' Phil demands.

'She says he has dementia.' Disbelief floods through Chloe again.

'Has she had him diagnosed?' Margaret looks sceptical.

'She was adamant her diagnosis was enough. She said, as a nurse, she could easily get him into the hospital.'

'Surely that can't be right?' Phil's face is tight with anger.

'She also says she will sell Moorcroft and leave. Presumably with what she thought she would get from the sale of the house...'

'And the business,' Phil butted in. 'She's a bitch and a half!'

'Phil!'

'I'm sorry, Margaret, but that's what she is. A malicious and greedy bitch.'

'But she won't get away with it. She doesn't own even half of the house.' Chloe can't help the small smile that thought brings. 'When I left there, I went straight to the solicitor at Priest, Mitchell & Green. Mr Green told me Moorcroft was left to Mum, in trust for me and Charlie by Grandad Burns. So I'm going to tell Lynne she has no rights as far as the house is concerned.'

'What did the solicitor say about the garage?'

'Mr Green told me he hasn't received any instructions about the garage from you or Dad.'

Phil presses his knuckles to his forehead. 'I've been such a stupid beggar. I should have gone to see the man myself as soon as we found out what she was trying to do. I've been fretting about this for over a month.'

'He also told me she doesn't have power of attorney, which was something I hadn't thought of. So her hands are tied. Mr Green said he would only deal with business matters with you and my father together. Go and see him, Phil, he'll tell you the same thing. It'll put your mind at rest.

'For now, though...' She grimaces, 'I need to go to tell Lynne about the house.' She stops when she hears a key in the front door, then footsteps in the hall.

'It's our Mark,' Margaret says, glancing past Chloe. 'Mark, come and see who's here.'

Chloe's first thoughts are that she wouldn't have recognised Mark if she passed him in the street. He is, she admits to herself, there is no other word for it, extremely good-looking.

'Hi.' He smiles from the doorway.

'You don't know who this is, do you lad?' Phil gives a low laugh.

'It's Chloe, Mark!' Margaret joins in with her husband's laughter. 'Chloe Collins.'

'Bloody hell! Chloe Collins.' Mark crosses his arms across his chest, leans back surveying her, his smile even wider. 'And all grown up. Here, give us a hug, eh?'

She half stands. The next thing she knows, she's lifted from the chair, folded into his arms, and is clasped in a brief bear hug before he holds her at arm's length.

'Well, I would never have known you.' He laughs.

'Me neither.' She feels self-conscious under his gaze.

'What are you doing here?' He holds up his hands. 'Sorry, I

284

didn't mean it to come out like that. I meant to say, it's brilliant to see you, but why now, why here? Charlie?'

'No. Not Charlie.'

'Aw, shame.'

'Chloe's been to see one of the solicitors at Priest, Mitchell & Green about the garage—'

'I told you to go and talk to them, Dad.'

'You didn't.'

'I did. Weeks ago. When we first heard that Graham was wanting to sell his share of the business.'

'I don't remember.'

'Getting forgetful in your old age.' Mark is the only one who chuckles.

Chloe looks down. Margaret draws a quick breath. Phil clicks his tongue behind his teeth. Frowns

'Sorry, only joking. Bad taste?'

'Bad taste,' his mother agrees. 'Chloe's stepmother says Graham has dementia.'

'No!' Mark looks from his parents to Chloe, eyebrows raised. 'Has he?'

'No. I don't think so.' Chloe remembers the bottles of tablets, next to her father. 'Though I am wondering if I should try to see his doctor? He seems to be on all sorts of tablets. I need to ask if they could be affecting him, making him drowsy or something.'

'Not a bad idea,' Margaret nods.

Chloe grimaces. 'Or she's drugging him on purpose to make him look as if he has dementia. Is that a bit far-fetched?'

'I wouldn't put anything past her.' Phil scowls. 'Geriatric ward – unbelievable!'

'What?'

'She wants to put him into Withington, Mark.'

'Hang on. If you are right and she is giving him drugs, once he's out of her clutches, he'll get better.' He shrugs. 'Won't he?'

'Mark's right, love.' Margaret nodded.

The relief that washes over Chloe is short lived. 'But she'll know the drugs will wear off. What if she's just saying that? What if she really means to do something worse?' She won't put it into words but she can see from their faces they understand.

'No? Surely not?'

'Like I said, Margaret, I wouldn't put anything past her. I need to go now.' Panic churns in Chloe's stomach.

'To see her?' Phil frowns.

'Yes.'

'Is that safe, lass? We could get the solicitor to write to her?'

'I'll be all right. Is it still snowing?' She looks towards the kitchen window. 'It seems to have stopped, thank goodness. I'll get my coat and boots.'

'It's lethal underfoot.' Mark follows her gaze out of the window. He stands. 'I'm betting there are no buses running. I could take you in my van? If I come in with you, we could perhaps persuade your dad to leave? Between the two of us?'

'No, I think that might make things worse. Especially if Saul's there.'

'If Saul's there, it would be better if I was as well. You don't know him these days. He's up to his eyes in the drugs game.'

'No, honestly, I'll be okay on my own.' *Am I being stupid?*

'Well, at least let me give you a lift there. And stick around.'

286

'Yes, let Mark do that, my lovely.' Margaret says. 'That'd make me feel better about all this, anyhow.'

'Okay. Thanks, Mark. I'd appreciate it.'

'That's settled then.' Phil helps Chloe into her coat. 'And, Mark, make sure she gets home safe afterwards.'

Chapter 98

Mark pulls the van up at the kerb at the end of Ingram Avenue. 'I can go closer to the house?'

'No, it's fine. I'll get out here.'

'Look, let me come in with you. I won't say anything, but I'll feel better if I'm there.'

'It'll only cause problems. She'll want to know who you are and it'll be difficult enough me getting in, let alone a bodyguard.'

He grins at that. 'Quite fancy myself as a bodyguard.'

'Yes, well, I don't need one.'

He's serious right away. 'Let's hope not, Chlo.'

No one other than Charlie ever called me Chlo. She tries not to think about that. 'I'll just tell her she can't sell Moorcroft, and then I'll come out.'

'Right.' He sighs. 'But be careful. And remember I'm here.'

'I will. Thanks.'

Walking up the drive she wonders if she's being watched. She forces herself not to look up at the windows. Her uneasiness grows stronger the nearer she gets to the house. It's as though she's absorbing something dark within its walls. She halts, forces her legs to work again, the image of the cowed way her father sat in his chair bolsters her resolve.

She raps loud on the knocker and fixes a determined expression on her face when she hears footsteps.

'What are you doing here again?' Lynne steps outside, pulls the door to behind her. She's inches away from Chloe. There's a waft of alcohol on her breath again. 'Your father doesn't want to see you.'

'It's you I've come to talk to.'

Lynne's body language changes. Her eyes flicker. 'I've nothing to say to you.'

'No, it's more the other way around.' Chloe sidesteps her and pushing open the door, strides into the hall. 'I've plenty to say to you.'

'What the hell?' Lynne tries to grab her but Chloe shrugs her off and goes into the lounge.

Her father twists in his chair, his eyes wide with apprehension. 'What...?'

'Hello, Dad.' She speaks softly. 'Nothing to worry about.'

'I'll be the judge of that.' Lynne's voice crackles with anger.

Chloe turns to face her, her heart hammering. 'I came to tell you that you won't be selling the house.'

She waits, watching the mottling rising on the woman's throat to her face.

'Lynne? Selling our house?'

'Shut up!'

Graham looks confused. 'But you can't.' He glances from her to Chloe, his face clearing. 'You know?'

'I do, Dad.'

'Know what?' Lynne moves closer to Graham. He flinches. Chloe puts herself between them.

Lynne snaps at him. 'What's the big secret, eh?'

Chloe takes Graham's hand. 'It'll be all right, Dad.'

'I said...' Lynne glares.

'If you'd just let me speak, I'll tell you.'

Chloe thinks she hears a sound – a movement – from the kitchen. Chloe takes a quick look at the door. If it's Saul and he comes into the lounge, she doesn't know what she will do. *Stay calm.*

'You can't sell Moorcroft because it doesn't belong to you.'

'I'm his wife. It's as much mine as his.' The sneer twists Lynne's mouth.

'That's the point, you see. The house doesn't belong to Dad.'

'What're you talking about?' Lynne picks up a packet of cigarettes and slowly taps one out. She uses a lighter from the coffee table, but her hands are shaking and it clicks uselessly. She flings it back on the table. It skids across the surface and drops to the floor. 'Huh?'

'Moorcroft is held in trust for Charlie and me.'

Another noise from the kitchen? Chloe takes in a quick breath. If it's Saul, how will she get past him?

She tries to listen but Lynne gives a derisive laugh. 'As if...'

'It's true.' Chloe momentarily wishes she'd let Mark come with her. But there's nothing she can do about that now. She straightens and squeezes her father's fingers, pushing away her fear, determined to make the woman understand. 'I've been to see Dad's solicitor and he told me. It was part of our grandfather's will. The house was left to my mother...'

She sees the unease in the loosening of Lynne's mouth and carries on. 'In trust for us. The house is ours. Not Dad's. Not yours.'

If Saul is in the house, this is when he will appear. Chloe's scalp tingles in anticipation. But instead there are a few seconds of silence in the room before Lynne shouts, 'Fuck off!' She spins around, stabbing her forefinger at Graham. 'You knew about this?'

'Yes, but...' Graham cringes. 'I didn't know—'

'Just shut the fuck up.'

'Don't talk to him like that.' Chloe's anger rises as rapidly as Lynne's. She doesn't care now if Saul is around — one way or another she'll deal with him. Helping her father is what matters. She gives his hand a gentle shake. 'Dad, do you want to get out of here? To come with me?'

'I don't know. I can't...' He takes his hand from hers, twists his fingers together. He won't meet her eyes.

'Okay, love. Don't worry.' She won't put any pressure on him.

Lynne points at the door. 'Out.'

'I'm going.' Chloe stops in the hallway. 'I've said what I came to say and I'm going.' She glances towards the kitchen but it's in darkness, then upwards to the gloom of the landing, but can't see anything. Or anyone. She shivers, dark memories of her childhood flooding back.

'Out! Get out. Now.'

Chloe allows herself to be ushered to the front door. She drops her voice. 'Anything happens to my father and I'm warning you...'

'I don't know what you're talking about.' Lynne looks up the stairs and then back at Chloe. 'Just get out.'

When the front door slams behind her, Chloe holds on to the porch wall, takes in a long breath. Light snow settles on top of the undisturbed layer already covering the lawn. The whiteness contrasts with the dark shadows of the hedges. The streetlights are a hazy halo of amber. She shivers and hurries down the steps and towards the end of the drive to the safety of Mark's car.

Chapter 99

'You think you're so bloody clever, don't you?' Saul steps out of the shadows at the end of the drive.

Chloe gives a short scream and stumbles backwards against the stone post. Pain shoots through her shoulder. When she steps to one side, Saul does the same.

'Let me pass.'

'Not until you get it in your thick head you can't win.'

With his back to the streetlights, she can't see his face but his voice betrays his malice. His fingers press into her shoulders. She twists from side to side to free herself but he's taller and stronger than her.

'What do you want?'

'What. Do. I. Want?' Saul questions himself in a thoughtful tone. He grabs Chloe, pulls her close, slowly pressing her backwards into the dense line of beech hedges. Snow cascades over her. She stares up at him, tries to free her hands to hold him off, but they're trapped between his body and hers.

'What do you want?' she says again. She won't let him see how frightened she is.

'What d'you think I want, bitch?'

'I don't know. Let me go. Leave me alone.'

'Ah, well, you see, that's one thing I can't do. You're threatening my cash cow, aren't you.'

'I don't know what you mean.' *I was right, he was there all the time. Listening.*

'No? No, I guess you don't. And I'm not going to spell it out for you, because I remember what a little snitch you always were, and I'm guessing you haven't changed. So all I'll say is leave my mother alone.'

'You were in the kitchen? You heard?'

He's leaning even closer to her, his mouth against her ear. 'I heard,' he whispers.

He stinks of stale sweat and a sharp, slightly vinegary smell. She remembers Mark saying Saul is on drugs. The fear swirling inside her is making her light-headed. She jerks her head away from his and takes in a deep, trembling breath.

'Get off me! Leave me alone.' She lets herself relax for a second, then tenses and tries to wrench away from him.

He makes a low grunting noise. 'No, you don't.' He shifts, one arm holding her like a vice, his other hand on her neck. He clenches his fingers, one slight squeeze. 'I'll leave you alone when you leave us alone, you stupid bitch. You don't know what you're interfering with.'

He's going to kill me. 'Stop it.' She forces the words out.

He tightens his hold on her throat a little. 'Don't *you* tell me what to do. I'll do the telling. And I'm telling you to keep your fucking nose out of our business. Back off from my mother. She plays her own game, and it suits me. It suits me right down to the fucking ground.'

He's moving her backwards until sharp branches dig into her spine. She forces herself to say, 'I'm not scared of you.'

But she's crying silently, only realising when the warmth of tears touches her cheeks. She's glad it's dark. That he can't see.

'You should be, believe me, you should be.'

His voice brings back the past; the times he crept up behind her, pulled her hair, whispered threats in her ear.

'So, like I said, stop shoving your snout where it doesn't belong. Ma's going to sell the fucking house.'

'She can't. It's not hers, And Dad knows that as well. He'll stop her...'

'That old fool doesn't know whether it's day or night. You do realise your precious father will be getting a right slapping now, don't you?'

'No. She wouldn't.'

'She would. She does. And now I'm going to give you a little something...' He sniggers. 'Just a little something for you to remember when you next think you might try to stop her.'

He's pressing against her, rhythmically moving, the hot hardness of him touching her stomach.

'No! Get off me!'

His movements quicken, even as he laughs. He doesn't answer, his breath hot against her neck. But then he yelps and his weight is off her. Her knees give way.

She hears Mark's voice. 'Ever think of touching Chloe again ... of going anywhere near her ... and I'll kill you.' She hears a thud, another yelp. 'Got that?' Another thud. 'I said, got that?'

Saul's voice is no longer threatening. 'Yeah,' he whispers. 'Yeah.'

'Good.'

Chloe is lifted up.

'I can walk,' she says, putting her arms around Mark's neck.

'I know,' he says, carrying her towards the car.

Chapter 100

'Are you sure they don't know where you live?' Mark grips the steering wheel and peers through the windscreen at the window of her room above the shop. The tall stone building is in darkness. There are no streetlights at this end of the street.

'Manchester is twenty-five miles away and a whole life from Mossleigh, Mark. Until this month I haven't been near the village for over ten years. So yes, I'm sure I'm as sure as I can be.'

He switches on the car's inside light, turns to face her. 'But now you've become a threat to them.'

'I needed her to know I will tell the police if anything happens to Dad.'

'Exactly. They know you're keeping an eye on them. What's worse, she now knows she's no chance of getting her hands on the house. They may come looking for you.'

'They don't know what I do, have no idea I've been living and working here for three years. I've not left the area and, except for the pub, it's not a place where people come to, unless they want a tailor.'

'I don't want to frighten you but Saul is mixed up with a really nasty bunch. I might have scared that nasty bugger for now, but I don't trust him. Or his mates. And I bet he has contacts in Manchester.'

A cold shiver runs down Chloe's back. But she forces a smile. 'I'm not worried. And this isn't the centre of the city, it's the backstreets. Please don't worry.'

'I don't like to think of you on your own here, Chlo. Especially after what's just happened.'

'Herbie and Albie live here as well.'

'Two old chaps?' There's doubt in Mark's eyes. 'What can they do?'

'We have the shop phone. We'd call the police. Another month at the most and Mr Nudel will be telling us he's closing down.' *I should be looking for somewhere else to live, and another job. Not something to discuss here.* 'Right, I'd better get in, I need a bath after tonight.'

'Make sure you lock up properly.'

'I'm a big girl, Mark. I've been responsible for myself for a long time now.'

'But you're back in Lynne's sights now. I want you to promise you'll ring our house if there's any sign of trouble? I'll come and get you.'

'I will. But I'll be fine.'

Still, it's quite a nice feeling to know that someone from her childhood, someone who knew her then, cares about her. Almost like having roots. Belonging somewhere.

Chapter 101

Despite her confident assurance to Mark last night, Chloe has slept badly and by six o'clock she's in the kitchen, moving around as quietly as she can, making a coffee.

Back in her room she clicks on the electric fire and jumps back into bed. Cradling the warm cup between her palms she mulls over everything that's happened. Seeing her father as he is feels unbearable. She shakes her head, trying to dispel the overwhelming misery. *Come on, think of something else.*

Leaning back against the headboard, sipping her coffee she gazes around her room. It's different from when she first moved in. She's put her own stamp on it: the blue curtains and the covering on the small armchair were the first things she'd made, the five seascape photos are in frames Sid made. The bookshelf he'd put up for her is crammed with books she'd bought from charity events at the local Salvation Army centre. The sheepskin rug at the side of her bed was a moving in present from Edith and Sid, as was the enormous spider plant hanging in its holder from the hook in the ceiling.

She's neglected the Grantleys, she knows that. But as well as Tracey, the little girl who came after her, they'd gone on to foster two sisters and last time she'd visited she'd felt in the way. It wasn't Sid and Edith's fault; it was her own insecurities, Chloe knows that. But she can't help it.

Knowing her job is ending makes her anxiety worse. But an idea is forming in her mind. She's fully qualified, so she could try setting up a small business of her own. She has all the tools but she'll need a good sewing machine. Perhaps she could buy one from Mr Nudel – Ezra – and she's sure he'll be able to give her some business advice.

The thought lifts her spirits. Now warmer, she gets up to start work. When she crosses the landing she hears Herbie's canary singing. She stands listening. When she catches sight of herself in the long mirror on the far wall, she's smiling.

The postman arrives as Chloe is coming back to the shop with the lunchtime sandwiches.

Herbie takes his sandwich off Chloe. 'Thank you, my dear.' He piles the envelopes onto the counter. 'First post in almost a week.'

'Think yourself lucky,' the postman says. 'I shouldn't be working, but what choice have I got with three kids to feed? It'll get worse before it gets better with this bloody government. Sitting up there in their high tower while we poor buggers slog away for a pittance.'

They wait until he slams the door. 'Maybe one thing we should be grateful for, Herbie,' Albie says. 'We, at least, will have our pensions.'

'But Chloe won't. Have you thought what you will do, my dear?'

'I have a few ideas.' She takes a bite of her cheese sandwich, spreading the post along the counter.

'Any idea where you will live?' Herbie stands at her side, opening an envelope.

'I do need to start looking,' she admits. 'It will be strange not having you two for my neighbours.'

She's taken Herbie and Albie's presence for granted since she moved here. Where will she go? How to even start looking?

'Perhaps your young man will have some ideas about that.' Albie's stretched out on his chair, his ankles crossed.

He has a slight smirk on his face that vanishes when Chloe says, 'I'm not seeing him anymore.'

'Oh, I am so sorry...'

'Every time you put your great clogs in it, Albie.' Herbie waves a large envelope at him. 'Every time!'

'No, it's not Albie's fault, I haven't said anything, so how would you know? And it's alright. It's my choice.'

Both men look relieved.

'There is one letter here for you, my dear.' Herbie passes a white envelope to her.

Ian's writing. She doesn't know how she feels.

'Would you mind if I read this upstairs?'

'Not at all.'

'Go. Go.'

Chloe sits in her armchair. She has an overwhelming sense that she doesn't want to read Ian's letter. Perhaps she should wait until after closing? *He's probably furious. Or he'll be pleading for a second chance.* She thinks about the last time she saw him. Hears his words in her head. 'Marry me.'

Oh damn.

But she'd better get it over with.

Chloe,

Receiving you letter was quite a relief, I can tell you, because I was just going to write to you. Last time I was at Helen's I met an old girlfriend. Well, I was with her when I first met you. Anyway, we've

been seeing a lot of each and I've realised I still love her. I'm moving
back to Huddersfield. My job in Cardiff didn't work out. I knew that
within a month. I've given up the flat and by the time you read this
I'll be back home and will have moved into Karen's house.

Obviously, we will not be able to see one another again. But it
was nice knowing you,

Ian. x

'Nice knowing you.' And a kiss. Chloe can't stop the giggle
bubbling up in her throat.

She doesn't know why she wants to laugh but it's a relief.
Because she wanted to end it, she doesn't feel rejection niggling
away at her. Ian has saved face by dumping her. And it's not
because she's worthless, unwanted, but because he's clearly a
man who always sees the grass being greener in the next field.
What was it his sister said? 'The trail of girls he's had. I thought
he'd never settle down.' Perhaps, like her, the 'trail of girls' found
out what a narrow-minded man he is and escaped.

She sits back in the chair, flicking the corner of the letter
back and forth against her fingertips, before carefully folding
it away. 'Ah, well.'

She's pleased she's not hurt or upset; perhaps she just needed
to meet Ian to get out of the rut she'd settled into. And to show
herself the true picture of her life: she isn't always going to be
discarded because of who she is. Sometimes people who leave
her can't decide what they want for themselves. Or, they have
no choice, like Mrs Brice getting ill.

Or like her father, thinking he was doing the right thing for her.
Perhaps in a way, he was. The thought of growing up in Moorcroft

with Lynne and Saul makes her shudder. Did he know then how things were going to turn out? She doubts it. But even so...

The idea comforts Chloe.

Chapter 102

'Come in, shut the cold out. Let me take your coat. No, no, don't bother taking off your shoes, the floor tiles in the kitchen are freezing. You'll get chilblains.' Margaret frets over Chloe, holding her hands and rubbing warmth into her fingers. 'You're frozen, it's gone bitter again out there; I thought it was too good to be true, all that sudden mild weather.' She hangs Chloe's coat over the banister. 'Actually, I'm surprised to see you here; I didn't think the trains were running.'

'They're not. I managed to catch a couple of buses.' She doesn't say she's walked the last couple of miles. 'I needed to come to Mossleigh. I'm looking at a flat on The Ridgeway.'

'Oh?'

'Mr Nudel stops taking orders next week, so by the end of January the shop will be closed.' Chloe speaks calmly despite the anxiety she's held in her stomach for days. She gives a tiny lift of her shoulders. 'Mr Nudel has said I can stay on in my room for a short while afterwards, but I'll still need to find somewhere soon. And find another job.'

Margaret is listening intently, a look of sympathy or consternation, Chloe can't decide which, in her eyes.

'It'll be alright,' she hears herself telling Margaret.

'What will you do?'

Chloe clears her throat. 'It'll all work out.' She manages a smile. 'Providing this flat I'm going to look at is habitable. I've also had an idea. I thought of advertising in the local paper to do clothes alterations, making dresses, that sort of thing. Even upholstery – I've done a bit of that for my own furniture. I can turn my hand to most things,' she adds.

'I'm sure you can, my lovely, and you're always welcome to stay here until things sort themselves out.' She's speaking in the motherly way that Chloe remembers from her childhood.

'Thank you, that's so generous of you...' She almost says Auntie Margaret, only stopping herself in time.

There's a sudden crash as the back door opens and closes.

'Bloody hell, Mum, it's cold enough to freeze the...'

'Chloe's here, Mark.'

Chloe grins, knowing what Mark was just about to say.

'Oh, sorry.' He gives an exaggerated shiver. 'Cold enough to freeze your toes off.' He grins back at her. 'I thought the train drivers were on strike?'

'Buses are running, just about.'

'Chloe's going to look at a flat on The Ridgeway.'

'In Mossleigh? Not somewhere in Manchester? You sure?'

'Yes.' Chloe knows what he's thinking. 'I want to be near Dad.'

'Even after...?'

'Even after what?' Margaret has opened the oven door but now she closes it and straightens up, looking at them, concerned. 'What's happened?'

'Nothing,' Chloe says. 'Just Lynne being her usual self, remember? Nasty.'

Margaret frowns. She doesn't look convinced. 'You know the offer of the spare room here still stands?'

'I know, Margaret. And thank you. But this place sounds ideal; it's got two bedrooms. And I'm still thinking I could set up on my own, gradually build up a business.'

'You could do that here, lovely. It'd be no problem.'

'It would be too much of an imposition. I'll see what this place is like. But thank you anyway.'

'It wouldn't be any trouble, would it, Mum?'

'No. But let Chloe do as she wants. The offer's there.'

'I'll check out this flat.'

'I'll take you, if you like. I've got the day off,' Mark says. 'Just give me chance to get washed and changed.'

'You both need something warm inside you before you go anywhere,' Margaret calls after him as he bounds up the stairs. 'No arguing. I've made a chicken hotpot.'

Chloe's more than happy not to argue.

Chapter 103

'What will you do? You can't possibly think that place is any good?'

Chloe sighs, feeling her face flush. 'It wasn't that bad,' she protests, even though her heart plummeted when she entered the grimy, littered hallway. Two paint-peeled doors on the ground floor. From one boomed hypnotic music, from the other the screaming and shouting of a domestic dispute. The flat Chloe was supposed to look at was up the bare, stained stairs.

'It was a fleapit.' Mark steers the van out of a small skid when the traffic lights turn green and the wheels don't grip on the packed snow. 'Was that the only available place?'

'Yes, that had two bedrooms, and in my price range.' Chloe glances upwards at the heavy iron-grey clouds. 'I'd better get back to the shop, I have a couple of things I want to finish.'

'You're determined to be in Mossleigh?'

'I am. I need to be close to Dad. I intend to see him as often as I can, despite Lynne and Saul.'

She noticed he didn't warn her about Saul this time. But his lips are pressed together and he sniffs before he says, 'Well, you surely can't even consider that place? Remember what Mum said — you could stay with us until you find somewhere that's half-way decent. Not like back there.'

'I know. And it's good of her...' Chloe waits while Mark manoeuvres around a car left abandoned at an angle in the road. 'I'll think about it.' *But would it be fair, when they're dealing with all the worry about the garage?* 'I've been meaning to say something to you, Mark. I've already told your mum and dad I'm sorry about the garage, but I know it affects you as well. You work there, and, I suppose, one day you'll be taking it on...'

'Don't you be worrying about that, Chlo.' He glances quickly at her. 'What's made you think of that?'

'Well, I've been thinking a lot about the future. The way Dad is now, I really can't see him going back to work.'

'No, not if he's that bad. Unless, as you said before, it's what she's been giving him? Drugging him? And with that bastard of a son of hers up to his neck in that scene, I wouldn't be surprised.'

'How will we know unless I get him away from her? Which

303

is why I'm looking for a two-bedroomed place. She'll only leave – divorce him – if she thinks she'll get her share of the assets. And now she knows she can't legally sell Moorcroft, whatever Saul says, there's only the garage...'

'Don't mither about that, you've enough to worry about. Ah, this is better.' The road they've turned onto has two lines down the middle where the tarmac glistens wet between heaped snow. Mark guides the van through them.

She knows he's changing the subject to stop her worrying. 'Have you and Phil thought what you might do about the business though?'

'Like I said, don't worry. Who's to say what will happen?'

She's surprised by his cheerful tone. 'I think we should all be prepared?'

'It'll get sorted.' He glances at her, smiles. 'If we can carry on like this until we get to the motorway, I think we'll be okay.' He gestures upwards with his head. Grimaces. 'As long as that lot stays up there.'

Mark's casual answers about the garage reassure her. Maybe he has a plan?

Chapter 104

It's starting to snow again and it's almost dark by the time they get back to the shop.

'Are you sure you'll be alright driving back home in this?'

'We've had these winters before, Chlo.' Mark pats the steering wheel. 'And this van hasn't let me down yet.'

'Well, let me know. Ring the shop when you're home, will you, please?'

'I will.. Just don't worry.' He leans over, gives her a light kiss on her cheek.

It might have started out being a rubbish day, between the train strike, having to walk two miles to get to Mossleigh, and then the waste of time flat, but Chloe feels remarkably upbeat when she opens the shop door.

She sees the faces of her two workmates putting the covers on their sewing machines and tidying scraps of thread and material from their tables.

'Has something happened?'

'Ezra came in this afternoon. He says this time next week the shop will be closed. We knew it would be but still...' Albie pulls a face. 'Everything is finished, except for those.' He dips his head towards a small bundle of cloth on one shelf. 'Last three suits and the alterations to the hunting jacket of Colonel Kemp. If he puts any more weight on he'll need to find another tailor.'

They laugh. But there's dejection behind the shared humour.

Chloe finds herself saying, 'Thank you both for looking after me these last three years. For accepting and helping me with learning the trade. I'll always appreciate it, you know.'

The two men look startled before they cross the shop to hug her.

'Like a daughter to me you've been, Chloe.' There are tears in Albie's eyes.

Herbie stands back, nodding and blowing his nose loudly. 'End of an era, it surely is. Ezra has said you can stay until you find somewhere else to live, hasn't he?' he asks, flicking his fingers in an exaggerated wave at Albie, as though it's his friend's fault he too now has tears rolling down his face.

'Well, as long as it doesn't take ten years, yes.' Chloe grins.

'No luck today, then?' Albie hangs a tweed jacket on a hanger, smooths the sleeve with the flat of his hand.

'No.'

'Something will turn up.' Herbie nods. '*Mirtzeshem*. God willing.'

'I know.'

'And work?'

'Well, I've had a few ideas and I'll be fine. Don't you worry. We must keep in touch.'

'We will,' they chorus. '*Mirtzeshem*. God willing.'

Yet she knows they probably won't. They'll go their separate ways, in their different lives.

Chapter 105

'Thanks for inviting me.' Chloe stamps the snow off her boots, takes off her gloves and pushes them into her coat pocket.

'I don't like thinking about you in that shop on your own.'

'I'm upstairs in my room, as always, Margaret. I'm safe enough.' Chloe sniffs the air. 'Something smells good.' The aroma brings a memory she can't quite place. She follows Margaret into the kitchen, sees the large plate of fruit scones. 'You've been baking,' she says unnecessarily, trying to hold on to whatever it reminds her of.

'I have. It's one of your mother's recipes. Before she told me her secret ingredient my scones were always flat as a pancake.' Margaret pauses as she looks in the wall cupboard for cups. 'She was a wonderful baker, you mum,' she says softly. 'I'll butter one for you.'

'Oh, lovely, thank you.' Chloe sits at the table; watches Margaret cut a scone in half and butter it. 'I don't remember Mum baking. Or I didn't think I did.'

'Well, you were only a bairn. You and Charlie were so small when she...' She smiles. 'Here. It'll keep you going until we have tea later.'

Chloe takes the plate holding the buttered scone. 'Thanks.'

'Mark still outside?'

'He's shovelling the path clear.'

'Again! I'll be glad when this weather changes.' She hangs her apron on the hook behind the door, looks in the small mirror, and comes around the table to sit next to Chloe.

'Is everything okay, Margaret?'

'Yes, love.' She makes a moue with her mouth. 'It's just that I have something to tell you.' She stops. 'Well, to show you, really.'

'What is it? Is it something to do with Dad? Or the garage?'

'No, nothing like that.' She reaches inside her cardigan pocket, her face unreadable. 'It's your Charlie.'

Chloe stops a gasp in her throat. 'Charlie?'

'He's written to Phil and me. We got the letter this morning. From the date stamp it's taken nearly a fortnight to get here. It was just addressed to us, with "Penny Oak Street, Mossleigh" underneath. No house number. So it's lucky it got here.' She passes the envelope to Chloe. 'Here.'

Shock ripples along Chloe's skin in goosebumps. Her hand trembles when she takes the envelope. She doesn't open it.

'Read it, my lovely. He's asking us to find you. It's incredible;

307

first you come to us after all this time and now we get a letter from Charlie.'

'Does Mark know?' *All the way here he didn't say a word about this.* Chloe can't decide if she's resentful or glad.

'Yes, he was here when the post came. I asked him not to tell you. I thought it best coming from me. Was I wrong?'

'No. I don't know...' Chloe tells herself that she's calm, that this is the moment she's waited for so long. But she can't speak.

'It's good news, isn't it?'

Chloe's nodding, she can't stop nodding. And smiling, even while tears slip silently down her face.

'Do you want me to go while you read it?'

'No. It's...'

'It's the shock. I'll make a brew.'

The envelope is wrinkled, waves of lines run across it; somewhere, since it was posted, it's got wet and then dried out. Chloe smooths her fingers across it. Charlie has touched this envelope. She brings it to her face and breathes in the smell. *I'll open it in a minute. I'll wait, and I'll open it in a minute.* Even as she thinks this she's sliding the letter out and unfolding it. At first she can't focus. She forces herself to concentrate. Her eyes take in how his handwriting slants across the page. *Did he always write with such large letters?* It feels wrong that she can't remember. Somehow, though, she knows he's written it in a hurry, as if, if he didn't do it quickly, he wouldn't write it at all.

'Here, drink this.' Margaret puts a cup in front of her.

Chloe picks it up, does as she's told. She sips the strong tea and grimaces; it's so sweet it sets her teeth on edge, but she's grateful. Margaret has given her time to get her thoughts together.

'It's the shock,' Margaret says again, smoothing Chloe's her hair from her face.

'Yes.' Chloe keeps her eyes on the paper. 'I never thought this would happen.' Her heart starts to race. 'He's living in Cardiff. I can't believe it; I was in Cardiff only weeks ago. So close...'

She stands so quickly her head swims and she needs to hold on to the table. 'I have to go. Would you mind if I don't stay, Margaret? If I take his letter with me? I have to write back and I think I need to be on my own. I have to let him know I want to see him, that I looked for him for years.'

Chapter 106

It's quiet on the narrow snow-covered street outside, emphasising the silence in the house. It doesn't bother her being alone in the building. Everywhere is locked up, her room warmed by the electric fire, the television on with the sound turned low.

The paper is shaking in her hands as she reads what she's written to her brother, trying to see the words through his eyes. Through the eyes of a young man she no longer knows.

Charlie, you don't know how much I have hoped this day would come. I can't tell you how I felt when Margaret gave me your letter – joy, yes, but also fear – fear you won't forgive me for not finding you first. There is so much I want to say, so much to tell you, but it can all wait until you are actually standing in front of me. Until I can see you and give you the biggest hug I always dreamt I would give you on the day we were together again. But mostly I want you to know I never stopped looking for you. When you were first sent away, I wasn't able to. We were children, we had no power, no control over our lives. One person had that and we both know who that was. And it wasn't Dad, you must believe that. When we can talk I'll tell you everything that has happened and why it really wasn't his fault.

Soon after you were taken away, I was as well. But I went into foster care. I think I was glad – frightened, but glad, I didn't want to live at Moorcroft without you. And please believe me when I say I always asked about you. And I was always told they'd moved you to different places. But not where you were. I left foster care at sixteen and I've lived where I am now ever since. And I have searched for you. I never gave up hope. And now my hope has been answered.

I have missed you so much, Charlie. I can't believe you live in Cardiff. I was there only weeks ago. Please let me know where you want us to meet. Your sister, Chloe. X

Chloe wipes her eyes, blows her nose, sighs, a long, ragged rush of breath, before folding the letter and sliding it into the envelope.

It isn't enough. It doesn't come close to what she really wants to say. All Chloe can hope is that her brother believes her when she says she looked for him. Never forgot him. And that it wasn't their dad's fault.

Now she has to wait.

Chapter 107

'Something on your mind?' Simon pockets the key to the restaurant, pulls up the hood of his cagoule and peers left and

310

right through the rain to check for traffic on the main road before stepping off the kerb. He nudges Charlie with his shoulder. 'Or do I need to ask?'

'That obvious?'

'I'm not making light of it, honestly, Charlie. Waiting for that reply must be driving you mad, but you can't carry on like this. You tossed and turned in bed last night, and you've hardly said a word in work today.' He slips his hand through Charlie's arm, pulls him close. 'Come on, let's get home out of this freezing sleet and then we can talk.'

'I'm sorry.' Charlie is used to keeping his worries to himself. He hadn't thought Simon had noticed.

'Ah, *gwirion*, don't be so daft.'

They walk in silence along the wet pavements lit by the streetlights. Every now and then they dodge the spray of water thrown up from a passing car.

When they turn into the side streets shadows loom between the dimmer streetlights. Charlie quickens his step. The years of being on the streets make him cautious of the dark places: the unlit doorways, the alleyways running between houses, the trunks of the trees on the edge of the pavement.

'Hang on.' Simon's breath becomes a gasp. 'You forget I'm older than you. What's all the rush?'

'Just want to get home.' Charlie moves his hood so he can see Simon. His face is strained but he briefly grins. 'Give over. Older? By six years? Yer nowt but a youngster.'

Simon catches hold of his arm. 'Slow down. Calm down. I can always tell when you're worrying; you go more Northern.'

Charlie shoves his hands deep into his raincoat pockets.

'Sorry. I'm wondering if I've done the right thing, writing to the Baxters, dragging everything up again. It's thrown up so many memories. I can't think about owt else. For all I know Chloe's just got on with her life, wants to forget what happened when we were kids. That's if they know where she is. She might have done what I did and disappeared. Though God knows I hope she hasn't done what I did.'

'You mean go on the streets? I doubt that, Charlie.'

Why?' What if she had no choice? I shouldn't have written, that's all I'm saying, Si. I should have left well alone.'

Chapter 108

'It's good of you to bring me into the city, Mark, just to post my letter.'

'It's better posting it from the main post office. There's a good chance of it going today from there. Especially now the postal workers are slowly coming off strike.'

'Still, you took time off work and I'm grateful.'

'You're joking, Chlo. This is *the* most important letter to be posted today. If it weren't for the weather, I'd have driven you all the way to Cardiff for you to put it into Charlie's hands.'

'You are such a nice man, Mark Baxter. But I wouldn't have had to write if I was going to see him, would I?'

He laughs. 'Guess not.' His face suddenly serious. 'But I would have, you know. I'd have done it for you.'

'Thank you.' His words bring a lovely warmth inside her.

They drive in silence. He's so easy to be with, Chloe thinks.

312

But she's not going to let herself like him too much. She needs to get to know Mark as the man first, not only as Charlie's old friend.

Charlie. Chloe's stomach clenches. What if he's changed his mind? His letter took so long to be delivered. What if he thinks Margaret and Phil don't know where she is? Or worse, they do and he thinks she doesn't want to see him?

She has to believe her letter will get to him soon, otherwise she'll drive herself mad.

'What a winter it's been,' she says, trying to get away from worrying about her brother. 'Between the weather and the strikes, it seems to have been one thing after another.'

'I've felt sorry for all the poor buggers on strike. They must be at rock bottom. And hard on their families.'

'At least we've been lucky with our men, they've kept working. I don't know where we'd be without them.' Mark slows down at the traffic lights. 'Nothing's shifted in the showrooms for months but at least we've kept our heads above water with the workshop.'

'But it'll pick up slowly, I'm sure.'

'Hopefully. Especially since we got rid of Yolanda in reception. Did Mum tell you? Dad caught her stealing from the petty cash.'

'No!'

'Yeah.' Mark gives a shrug. 'Dad suspected it was her for a while. And then Mum checked the storeroom safe and accounts and there were bigger discrepancies. Dad didn't like her working at the garage, anyway. He never liked the fact it was Lynne who'd persuaded Graham to give her the job. Then last week one of the mechanics – Brian – said he saw her in a café with Lynne. Yolanda was giving Lynne a package. Turned out it was money from the safe and she was getting her cut from Lynne. Obviously both in on it.'

'Has Phil reported it?'

'Can't really prove anything. And Dad was bothered about upsetting Graham. So he didn't let me do anything about it.'

'Wrong though.'

Mark shrugs.

'Like I said, Yolanda's gone now. But it's one more reason to keep an eye on Lynne and her bloody son. You can bet he's at the bottom of it.' He pulls away at the green light. The traffic edges forward.

'I think we'd better stick to the main roads on the way back home. I doubt the snow ploughs and gritters have been out yet. Anyway, there's something I want to tell you. Good news!'

Chloe turns sideways. *Now what?*

But he's smiling. 'I've been looking into my finances over this last month.'

'Oh?'

'Last week I went to see the bank manager.' He takes a quick look at her. She sees excitement in the lift of his eyebrows. 'And I went to talk to Mr Green at Priest, Mitchell & Green. Both the bank manager and the solicitor think I should put in a bid to buy your dad's share of the garage. I've got some savings, and I can get a loan to cover the rest. There's a good chance you're looking at the new partner of Collin's Garage.'

Chapter 109

It's three weeks since the shop closed. The blizzard that has been driving the white sheet of snow horizontal for the last week has finally worn itself out and there's a stillness outside. Deep wells of footsteps are imprinted in the middle of the narrow street. Chloe is relieved to be moving out. Lately she's begun to dislike the absolute stillness throughout the building. Each time she walks through the shop she shivers: with no cash register, shelves empty of cloth and the long mirrors gone, it feels so alien.

She studies the small pile of cardboard boxes on the floor that hold all her possessions. *Not much to show for twenty years. But that's fine.*

A colour catches her eye, a piece of deep green material by the curtain to what was the workshop. Bending, she picks up the fragment of satin and rubs it between finger and thumb, loving the feel of it. Mrs Stanley's ball gown: the first gown she'd made. The woman had been so difficult to please and yet she'd recommended Chloe to her friends and her reputation for making outstanding evening dresses had grown from that one order. Perhaps that is the way she should go, as a dressmaker?

There's a swish of tyres on the street. She looks through the window, sees Mark waving from the van.

The bell rings when she opens the door. It's a sound she will remember for a long time. She smiles: good memories. Once her boxes are out, she locks it from the outside and, following Ezra's request, pushes the key through the letterbox, for him to collect.

'Ready?' Mark waits until she fastens her seatbelt.

'Ready,' Chloe says.

Chapter 110

'I can go out of the room,' Simon says, softly. 'I could start making us something to eat?'

'No, stay. Charlie looks down at the pale blue envelope on the table. 'I don't think I could eat anything anyway.'

'For later?'

'No, but thanks.' Charlie throws Simon a quick smile. 'I could do with a beer though?'

'Okey dokey. Back in a minute.'

Cat winds his way around Charlie's legs. He scoops the cat up and holds him close to his cheek, listening to the low rhythmic rumble of contentment. It calms Charlie.

'Here you are, love.' Simon puts the bottle of beer on the table next to the envelope. 'I can go upstairs or something?' he offers again.

'No, I'd rather you were here. I'll do it now.' Charlie holds Cat away from him. 'I'll put him on the settee.' Cat doesn't open his eyes, allows himself to be carried, draped like an upside-down U-shape in Charlie's hands. When he's put on the chair the only sign that he's noticed the change is the slight twitch of his tail.

'That cat's spoiled.' Simon laughs. He sits at the table.

Charlie smiles. 'Leave him alone. Right...'

He feels oddly released from his body. Like he was watching

himself, seeing his thoughts. *I'm scared. I'm scared in case my sister says it's too late, that we've been apart too long for us to mean anything to one another anymore.*

'Take your time. Drink your beer.'

'What if she doesn't want...?' Charlie can't say the words out loud.

'She'll want to see you.' Simon's voice is calm. 'If she's as you've always described her.' He pulls out the chair next to him, pats the seat.

'Will you open it for me?'

'If you like. But you read it to yourself first. It's your letter. Your sister. I'll be here.' He rips the envelope open, takes out the letter and, without looking at it, hands it to Charlie. Pushes the bottle of beer closer to him. 'Have a drink.'

Charlie takes a huge gulp of the beer, chokes and half-laughs, embarrassed. He reads.

Outside, a car passes and stops a few doors away. Car doors close. Laughter. Goodbyes are called. A front door slams.

Charlie hears but barely registers the meaning of the noises. As always, reading takes all his concentration. Even as he carefully takes in the words he can't help being conscious that the last person to touch this paper, to hold the pen that made these words, was Chloe.

'She wants to see me.' *She wants to see me. She wants to give me a hug.* 'She says she went into foster care. Not a care home like me but with a family. And she was glad. She says she didn't want to stay in our house after I'd gone.'

He holds out his hand to Simon. It's trembling badly. He makes a conscious effort to control his voice. 'But she also says it wasn't my father's choice to get rid of us.' *Not dad … father.* A long time ago, he made the choice never to call the man 'Dad' again.

Simon holds Charlie's hands.

'Does she say why she thinks that?'

Charlies reads the sentence out loud. 'We were children, we had no power, no control over our lives. One person had that and we both know who that was.' He looks at Simon. 'I know what she means. She means it was the woman my father married. That Lynne. I hated her from the minute he brought her into our home. I was always convinced she'd done something to my mum. But even if it was her, my father still allowed it.' His voice cracks. 'I'll never forgive him for that.'

'Even if it sounds like Chloe has?'

'For God's sake, Simon, we were kids.' For a moment he can't speak. He gulps. 'He let her make our lives a misery. We were kids…'

Simon stands. Puts his arms around him and holds him as tight as he can. 'I know. I understand. I love you, Charlie Collins, and I'll never let anyone hurt you so badly ever again.'

'But what can I do?' Charlie turns his face into Simon's chest, his voice almost inaudible. 'I can't go there. I want to see my sister … I want to see her so much. But I don't want to see him.'

'So tell her. Tell her just that. She'll understand. And you'll sort something out between the two of you. I'm sure of that.'

Dear Chloe,

I haven't gone a day without thinking about you either. Where you are. What you're doing. When I wrote to the Baxters I didn't know if you still lived in Mossleigh. Or if, like me, you'd left. You can probably tell I'm not much of a letter writer. But I want you to know I have never blamed you for not finding me. I took loads of trouble so nobody could find me. And yet we could have met because you say you were in Cardiff where I live now.

Charlie stops writing. *Do I say with my boyfriend? Why am I even questioning myself? Why shouldn't I say?* He can't think that his sister is anything but kind. She sounds like she always did when she was a kid.

I live with Simon. He's my partner. I'll tell you one day how we met and I'm sure you'll like him, he's kind and caring.

But, Chloe, I can't come to Mossleigh. Or if I do please don't expect me to meet our father. I can't forgive what he did. What he allowed to happen. I'm sorry if that hurts you, the last thing I want is to hurt you. I have missed you so much. I want to give you a great big hug as well.

Your big brother (by ten minutes) Charlie. Xxxx

Chapter 111

'Chloe? You have a visitor.'

'Oh? Who is it?' *Charlie?* Dragging her thick woollen dressing gown from the end of the bed, Chloe stretches up to pull back the curtains and look outside. An unfamiliar car is on Penny Oak Street. 'Just coming.'

Climbing off the bed she fastens her dressing gown belt and runs down the stairs.

'Evie!' *Not Charlie.* But it's still good to see her stepsister.

'Morning.' They hug. 'Thanks for your message on the answering machine saying you were staying here. I've got a day off work, so I took the chance to call in. Hope you don't mind, Mrs Baxter?'

'Margaret, please. And no, you're very welcome. Would you like a cup of tea?'

'That would be lovely, Margaret, thank you.'

'I'm being spoiled, Evie,' Chloe says. 'Nine in the morning and still not dressed. But I am looking for a flat.'

'Nonsense! It's lovely having her here, Evie. Good to have another woman to moan to. Phil and Mark say I shouldn't worry about things I can't do anything about, but I can't help it, the country seems to be in such a mess. Trains not running, lorry drivers not working.' Margaret waves her hands at the television. 'Even at one point they said gravediggers were on strike, that the army or relatives would have to dig graves. Can you imagine!' She shakes her head. 'Bin bags piled up. Rubbish all over the place. We could have been overrun with rats.' She takes a long, much needed breath.

Chloe and Evie smile at her sympathetically.

'It's been difficult,' Evie agrees.

They sit self-consciously at the kitchen table. Chloe wishes they could talk in private but knows she shouldn't expect to.

'Beth good?' she says, instead.

'She is, thanks. She's working. So...' Evie leans forward, her arms on the table. 'Charlie wrote to find you?'

'He did,' Margaret says cheerfully. 'Isn't it wonderful that Chloe came here just at the right time?'

'I wouldn't have done if Evie hadn't told me about what was happening with the garage. I did go to see Dad, to try to talk to him, Evie.'

'She let you in?'

'And then practically threw me out when she realised what I was asking.'

'Typical. How did he look?'

'Awful.'

'Poor Graham.' Evie pursed her lips. 'Sounds as if she's up to her old tricks again.'

'I need to get him away from her.'

'She really is a nasty piece of work.' Margaret pours the tea 'Sorry, Evie.'

'Don't worry about it, Margaret. Thank you.' Evie takes a cup from her, while still looking at Chloe. 'What's happening?'

'Our Mark says he can raise the funds to buy Graham's share of the business.' Margaret sits with them, her elbows on the table. 'But Chloe thinks her dad doesn't really want to sell.'

'It was like he knew nothing about it,' Chloe says. 'But if it happens and Mark is able to step in, that would be wonderful.'

'Still, you must fight your dad's corner against her,' Evie says.

'I will. Lynne won't get away with it, don't worry.' There's a quick flashback, a sense of Saul pushing against her that she tries to dismiss. But Evie must have seen her expression.

'What is it?'

'Nothing. Everything. Sorry, it's all a mess, Evie.'

'I know. But it's good about Charlie, isn't it? You must be over the moon.'

'I am.' Chloe smiles. 'I can't tell you how much it means to me.'

'I can guess.'

'Have you written back to him?'

'Last week. I told him a bit about what happened to me, what's happening here. There's too much to say really. Not had a reply yet, though.'

'Post is all over the place at the moment.' Evie takes one of the biscuits Margaret has put in front of her, dunks it in her tea, takes a bite. 'I'm sure he'll want to help. He's made the first move, Chloe, he wants to see you. It'll be you and him against the world again, you just watch.'

But what if he's changed his mind. 'I can't hope for that, Evie.'

'Well, I can, and I think that's what will happen, love.'

The telephone rings. Chloe jumps. 'Do you think...? I did put your number on my letter, Margaret.'

'Let me get it. If it is Charlie I'll hand it over. Hello? Oh, hold on a moment Phil.' She mimes to Chloe, 'Sorry.'

'Have patience, he'll answer, one way or another.' Evie says quietly. She pushes back the sleeve of her coat, checks her watch. 'I'd better be going, I said I'd meet Beth for lunch in town and I have a couple of things to do before then.'

'I'll see you to the door.'

'If you do need any help, let me know. I mean it, Chloe, anything.'

'Thanks. I know. I know, if it wasn't for you, I wouldn't be here. I would never have known he was looking...'

She stops, looking at the doormat. There's a white envelope tilted at an angle against the door. 'I didn't hear the post,' she says, to fill in the pause. *It's come.*

322

'Do you think it's...?'

Chloe bends to touch, to take the envelope between her fingers.

'Well, I'll leave you to read it then.' Evie kisses Chloe on the cheek. 'Ring me whenever. I hope it's good news.'

Diplomatic as ever. Chloe returns the hug, grateful to her stepsister.

When she closes the door she goes back up to her bedroom to read Charlie's letter.

Before she goes to bed she's written her reply.

Dear Charlie,

Oh, I am so happy you replied, and that we are back in touch after so long. I cried when your letter came. As I said before, I can't wait to see you. And Simon. If you love him, I'm sure I will as well.

Please don't think I don't understand how you feel about Dad. I felt the same way for many years. But I didn't know what was happening. Lynne has been – well, I don't really know how to say it – except that it looks as if he's frightened of her and has been for a long time. And Saul still lives there.

He's just as horrible as he always was. When I went to Moorcroft a few weeks ago, he tried to frighten me. Luckily Mark Baxter was with me and stopped him. Mark asks to be remembered to you. He says he always hoped he would catch up with you one day. He's turned into a nice man, Charlie. Remember how you and he would only let me play football with you as long as I agreed to be in goal!!

I went to Moorcroft because of something Evie told me. She'd met Phil and Margaret and they'd told her Dad wanted to sell his share of the garage. Lynne is making him do it. I'm not sure that Dad has any say in it. I know that it's really difficult for you but I do wish you could bring yourself to be here, if not for him, for me. I'd feel so much better if I knew you were here. I can't explain everything in a letter but there is so much more to say.

All my love, Chloe xx

Chapter 112

'I should go, shouldn't I?' Charlie watches Simon reading Chloe's letter. He feels he's at a crossroad in his life and, even though he knows what he wants – desperately wants, he's frightened it will be like pulling a scab off to reveal all the past misery.

'I'd ring Chloe, but when I speak to her after all these years, I want to see her face.'

'Why?'

'So I know.'

'Know what, Charlie?' Simon puts the letter back in the envelope. He waits.

'I don't know. Something. Owt. Something that tells me she understands how I feel about my father. That she accepts it.'

'She does say she felt the same way for many years. But that she didn't know what was happening. Perhaps if she explains?'

'Hmm. We'll see. For now I just want to be with her.' Charlie shudders.

He pictures the last time he saw her. They hadn't hugged, it wasn't something he did, he was a boy, though he sometimes had to put up with her hugging him. Besides, he'd thought he'd be back home soon. He remembered whispering to her. 'Don't start skriking.' That's what he'd said. He was cross that she'd cried in front of Lynne. He hadn't believed his father would walk out of that first care home, leaving him with strangers. He'd thought it was a trick to make him behave. Or behave in the way *she* wanted; did as *she* told him. But he'd soon understood *she* wanted rid of him and his father had agreed. His memory of telling Chloe not to cry haunted him for a long time.

'Now you've found her.'

'Yeah. I'm glad you persuaded me to write. I'd always stopped myself before. I can't tell you how many times I thought of trying, then chickened out. Being a coward.'

'You're not a coward, love. Far from it. I can understand how difficult it must have been.'

'I thought she wouldn't want to know, because she'd think I was running away from her; like I was deliberately distancing myself from her. In my mind I didn't just want to escape the care home I wanted to get away from my father as well. If he didn't want me, I didn't want him. And I thought, if ever he changed his mind and wanted to see me, I would make sure he couldn't.'

'Like a revenge?'

'Yeah, I guess so. In a way. By the time I realised what I were doing, I knew I'd left Chloe behind as well.'

'You can say all that to Chloe. You'll put it right when you see her.'

'But not him. I don't want to see him.'

'Are you sure?'

'Yeah, I am. And nothing will change me mind. I'm going to see Chloe, to help her sort stuff out. But I want nothing to do with him.'

Simon was quiet for a few seconds. 'Will you tell her what it was like in the care homes? Especially the last one?'

'No. I wouldn't want to upset her. It's all in the past.'

'Even Madeley House?'

Charlie presses his lips together.

'Abuse like that is abhorrent,' Simon says, gently. 'People should know about it.'

'Why are you bringing all that up, Si?'

He shrugs. 'It's been at the back of my mind since you told me. It makes me so angry.'

'I know. Perhaps I shouldn't have said.'

'No. We mustn't ever have secrets from one another. But you could report it to the police. It's probably still happening.'

'No point. Who'd listen to me?'

'Somebody might. Those men shouldn't get away with it.'

'I know. But they did. And they will. Nobody will do owt about it. I bet it goes on all the time, in a lot of those places. And nobody will do anything to stop it.'

The bedroom is in shadows. It's an hour since Charlie got into bed. Simon has unsettled him, talking about Madeley House. Maybe he will report what he saw, even if he's not believed. Maybe one day. He turns onto his side and looks at the profile of the man he loves, who, he knows, will protect him. Whatever happens.

326

But, for now, it's enough, more than enough, that he will be with his sister again. He settles back on his pillow, relief settling through him.

Then something occurs to him. He nudges Simon.

'What about Cat?'

'What?' Simon sits up, startled. 'What's the matter?'

'Cat? What will we do about him? If we go?'

'Oh.' Simon shuffles under the covers again. 'Don't worry, I'll ask Alun to look after him.'

'Chef wouldn't mind?'

'No. He and Derek don't always work the same shifts. And they both like Cat, so he'll be fine. As long as he's fed, he just sleeps, you know that. They'll look after him until we get back.'

'As long as they do.' Cat's something of a symbol of hope to Charlie, he represents the way life has turned a corner for the two of them. 'As long as they do.'

Chapter 113

'Look, before we go to the solicitor's on Wednesday, there's something I should have told you.' Mark's frowning. 'I didn't want to say anything in front of Mum and Dad.' They watch Phil's car leave. 'Now they've nipped to the shops, I need you to know there's been some rumours.'

'What about?'

'Saul. In the White Horse last weekend I heard something that's going around the pubs about him.' He turns, shoves his hands in the back pockets of his jeans. 'Been going around for a bit apparently. I've told you he's supposed to be into drugs. Some say he deals.'

Chloe shakes her head.

Mark sighs. 'He always was a shifty bugger in school. And got away with stuff any other kid wouldn't've. His mother—'

'Wouldn't have a word said against him.' Resentment and anger simmers inside Chloe. 'She always refused to believe he was bullying Charlie. Refused to believe he'd do anything wrong.'

'And still covers up for him, as far as the rumour mill goes. That's what I wanted to tell you.'

'She knows?'

'And helps him.'

'How?'

'Not sure. But this bloke in the pub said that the local health board is looking into the practice she works at: drugs disappearing, stuff going missing in the care homes, complaints from relatives of the patients Lynne deals with. That sort of thing.' Mark shrugs. 'All up in the air and first enquiries, but if she is stealing – whether it's drugs, money or anything else, you can bet it'll be something to do with Saul.'

Drugs! Chloe's fingernails dig into her palms. 'It's what I said. She could be giving Dad something without him knowing. Not what the doctor's put him on but other drugs. Oh, God, I feel sick. I have to get him out of that house.'

'She's not going to let you do that, even if your dad was capable of making that decision for himself.' They exchange a glance. 'She needs him right where she wants him until he's signed everything over to her.'

'You think?'

'Yes.'

Chloe waits, hoping he can come up with an answer, because she can't.

'What if, when we get into the solicitor's, I say I've changed my mind? I've decided not to buy his share,' Mark suggests. 'Give us time to think of something. Some way to get him out of her clutches.'

'Would you do that?' Chloe feels a spark of hope.

'I could, but we don't know if someone else is interested. Someone who would jump in as soon as I backed out. And once she's got the money, she could put him away in the hospital. Or worse…'

'She wouldn't…?'

'To protect Saul? I think that woman is capable of anything. Once your dad signs, he'll be of no more use to her.'

Chapter 114

Chloe hasn't slept. Leaning on the bedroom windowsill she watches the night drain away. Details emerge of the hills in the distance, the roofs of houses, the church, her old primary school. The sun materialises, every now and then breaking through the wintry sky.

'Chloe? Are you awake?'

'Yes.' She leans back, looks at the closed door. 'Come in, Mark.'

The handle turns. 'I've brought you a cup of tea.'

'Oh, great, thanks. You can come in, you know.'

'I guessed you'd be awake.' He peers around the door.

Conscious of her mussed hair and thinking she must look awful, Chloe runs her fingers through her hair, rubs at her face.

'Not slept?'

'Bit worked up. I keep thinking he might not turn up.'

'He will. Your brother will be feeling just as apprehensive – it's been a long time since you saw one another; you're both bound to be nervous. It's a big day.' He hands her the cup. 'Drink this, it's one of Mum's specials: hot and sweet.'

'Ah. She does know I'm not in shock? Or is she just preparing me for one?'

'It's her "go to" tea.' He grins. 'Mind if I...?' He points to the end of the bed,

'No. Do.' She watches him settle, conscious of his closeness.

'Charlie says they will be staying in a hotel in Manchester. He didn't say which one, but he said they'll be here around eleven o'clock, but not to totally rely on that.' She smiles. 'He said that neither he nor Simon has a sense of direction so they could be coming from Manchester via Southport for all he knows.' Chloe laughs. 'No sense of direction, just like me.'

'Dad and me are going into work. It's Mum's day off from the office but she says she's going to meet a friend for coffee later – and probably lunch. You'll have the house to yourself.'

'That's very kind of her but I can't drive her out of her own home.'

'Her choice. She knows you'll need some space.' His gaze on her softens. 'This is a big day for you,' he says again. 'The biggest – for both of you.'

He stands and without speaking holds out his arms.

Chloe doesn't hesitate. She goes to him, welcoming the closeness of his body against hers. His lips are firm, warm. She returns the kiss, every instinct in her responding.

When they lean away from one another, they smile. Mark holds her face gently between his palms.

'You okay?'

'I will be.'

He kisses her again, a brushing of his lips on hers. 'It will be okay. You'll be okay.'

Chloe smiles. 'I know. I'll see you later.'

The knock on the door is quiet, almost hesitant.

Chloe has been sitting on the stairs for the last hour. She glances at the hall clock. It's exactly eleven. Her legs wobble when she stands. She checks herself in the long mirror, touches her hair, notices how pale she is.

The knock comes again, this time a little louder. Perhaps he can see her through the frosted glass?

Three steps, she tells herself. Take the three steps but the panic is lodged right above her diaphragm, she can hardly breathe.

'Chloe?' His voice, low and deep, isn't what she remembers. His silhouette against the white of the light outside is tall, broad-shouldered. 'It's me.'

'Yes.' She turns the latch. She steps back, pulling the door with her.

And there he is. He looks as stunned as she feels, his mouth slightly open. They stand, eyes fixed on one another. A jolt goes through Chloe, like needles. It's as if the protective numbness she's preserved inside her for so long is melting. All the tears she's felt over the years, all the distress she's pushed down, refused to acknowledge, now tips out. They are both crying. He falls into the hall, into her arms, and she clutches him, her hands high on his back. She presses her face against his chest and breathes him in.

She doesn't know how long they stay like that but eventually she feels the cold sweeping into the house. Taking his hand she closes the door, leads him into the kitchen. The aroma of the vegetable soup Margaret's made for their lunch fills the air.

Not letting go of his fingers she pulls two of the chairs close.

'Tell me everything, Charlie,' she says. 'Tell me where've you been.'

Chapter 115

'Please understand, Chlo. I don't want to see him.'

'Yet?'

'Happen.' Charlie rubs the back of his head.

'He does that.'

'What?'

'Rubs the back of his head when he's not sure about something.'

Charlie shrugs. 'I didn't know that was what I was doing.' He falls silent.

'Don't worry about seeing him for now.'

Even when he was telling her of his time in the care homes, she instinctively knew he'd only given her an outline of the years. And that isolation has haunted him, as it has her. Being completely alone, having no one at all, is unbearable. She can understand why he blames their father.

'I don't expect you to come to the solicitors with us. It wouldn't be the right place for you to see him after all this time...' *Not that I know where the right place would be.* She watches him take out a cigarette and light it.

'D'you mind?'

'No. Though it's not my house and I haven't seen Phil smoke indoors.'

'Perhaps better not then.' He slides the cigarette back into the packet. 'Getting a bit dark already.' He gestures to the living room window.

She looks at her watch. 'Good grief it's almost four. Where did you say Simon was?'

'Well, he went back to the hotel after he'd dropped me off, but he's been sitting in the car outside for the last half an hour.'

'No! Why didn't you tell me?' Chloe jumps up from the settee and goes to look. Sees a man sitting in a black Mini. 'Oh, no. Please, Charlie, go and tell him to come in. I feel awful.'

He laughs. It's a nice laugh. She can hear the echo of the chuckle he had as a boy.

When he opens the front door she walks through to the kitchen, letting them have a few moments to catch up, so Charlie can tell his partner how he feels, what they've talked about, where they've been in the lost years.

After a while she hears a lull in the conversation between them. She carries a tray with the three coffees into the living room.

'Chlo,' Charlie stands. 'This is Simon.' He takes the tray off her. The man is shorter, slightly older than her brother, with a mass of unruly curls. To her surprise he gives her a hug.

'Well, now.' He steps back, grinning. 'There's no denying the link between you two. Same eyes, same smile.'

'Really?' She and Charlie study one another. Even though they've been staring at each other for the last few hours, it hasn't occurred to her that they look alike, only that the more she looks at him, the more she sees the brother she knew when they were children. 'I guess so,' she says, slowly and laughs. She reaches out, grasps the hands of each man and clings on to them. 'Here we are, altogether at last.' And bursts into tears.

For the second night in a row, Chloe can't sleep. But tonight she isn't filled with apprehension. Happiness is keeping her awake, not nerves. Savouring every moment of the day she replays them over and over.

She smiles when she thinks back to earlier. Despite trying to tell Charlie and Simon they were happy tears, they'd still insisted on sitting on either side of her on the settee, their arms around her, while she smiled and sobbed and noisily blew her nose.

In the midst of it all Margaret arrived, exclaiming how happy she was to see Charlie, that they hadn't eaten the soup and insisting she would be making a celebratory meal later and that Charlie and Simon would certainly be staying to eat it.

An hour after that Phil and Mark came home. Mark wrapped both arms around Charlie, held him at arm's length, grinning, saying he would have recognised him anywhere, except for the beard, the hair, and the fact that he'd grown an extra three foot. And Charlie had replied that Mark would have passed him on the street. They'd all laughed.

Chloe is glad that Charlie and Mark quickly settled back into the bantering good humour that had been the basis of their friendship when they were ten years old.

Yet there was an underlying distress at one point when Mark asked Charlie why he hadn't taken refuge with Phil and Margaret when he had run away. There was deep sadness in Charlie's voice when he said it had been too close, that it had taken all his courage to come back to Mossleigh now. That he is only forcing himself to be here because of Chloe.

Sleet begins to hiss on the window. Chloe grabs hold of the hem of the curtain and drags it to one side to watch the sliding patterns in the light of the streetlamps. She lies back against the headboard, noticing the reflected slanting shadows on the walls.

She's thinking about tomorrow. Now she knows about those first days in that first care home, heard him stumble over the years of being bullied, she knows she has no right to ask him to be at the meeting with the solicitor.

It's enough that he's here. Enough that he'll be waiting for me afterwards. Enough that he's back in my life again. And that he's said he will support me in whatever decision I make about Dad.

Chapter 116

'They're here already. That's her car.' Phil gestures with his thumb at a red Ford Cortina parked in front of the solicitors.

'A new car every year. Wonder how she pays for that, as if we don't know.' His voice dark with suppressed anger.

'Let's just get today over with, Phil.'

'It's not right. None of this is right,' he says

'But it's what's going to happen, my lovely,' Margaret says, 'And it will be fine. It will be all over in an hour.'

And then what? What happens to Dad afterwards? The fear that has kept Chloe awake all night is making her queasy. Phil and Margaret don't know about the fears she discussed with Mark last night.

Now she appreciates the small touch of his hand on hers, his whisper. 'It will be all right.'

But she doesn't believe him. Her fear for her father's safety far outweighs her regret that her grandfather's garage is going out of the hands of the family.

'Are we ready then?'

'Yes. I want to see Dad.' Chloe's heart is racing.

'Of course you do,' Mark murmurs. 'Let's just get this done. And then we can see how to help Graham. He raises his voice. 'Okay? Mum? Dad?'

They nod, don't speak. Mark takes her hand in his and holds it close to him as they walk into the building.

The solicitor's office is stiflingly warm.

Chloe steps around her stepmother to hug and kiss her father. He hardly acknowledges her and when she crouches to look up into his face, his mouth is slack and his eyes flicker blankly.

'You okay, Dad?'

He doesn't answer.

'Of course he is.' Lynne glares at her. 'What are you trying to say?'

'Nothing.' Chloe goes back to her chair ignoring the sneer from Saul.

Mr Green keeps his eyes fixed on his papers on his desk, waits until they all settle. Then he removes his glasses, and studies them one by one.

'Good morning,' he says.

Chloe senses Phil's impatience. Sees Margaret's hand move to his knee to stop him jiggling his leg.

'As we all know why we're here...' Mr Green spreads his hands, palms up, over the forms. 'Shall we just get on with it?' He doesn't wait for an answer. His eyes linger on Graham. He frowns. Speaking slowly he says, 'Mr Collins – Graham, before we continue, I just want to say what an honour it's been to have worked as your solicitor over the years...'

'Hah!' Saul snorts.

The solicitor stares hard at him before he continues. 'And I know my father thought it an enormous privilege and pleasure to help your father-in-law, Mr Charles Burns, set up such a successful business.' He smiles at Phil. 'And then a successful partnership between, if I may be so bold as to say, two good and lifelong friends.'

Chloe sees Phil force a smile. Margaret fumbles in her pocket before bringing out a tissue. Chloe sees her father watching the solicitor. She sees Lynne try to take his hand, but he shakes her off to free himself.

'But time moves on, and things change. And – sometimes –

that is good. So today, all I need to do is to clarify the details of the sale of Mr Collin's share of the garage to Mr Mark Baxter.'

'What?' Graham half stands. He's trembling as he attempts to straighten up, ignoring Lynne's grip on his arm.

'Graham! Sit down.'

'What do you mean?' There's a tremor in her dad's gravelly voice.

'I need to clarify the details of the sale of your share of the garage to Mr Mark Baxter, Mr Collins.'

Graham takes a step forward to grip the edge of the solicitor's desk. He moves stiffly, turning to stare at them all. 'Sale?' he says. 'Of my garage? I'm not selling my garage. Phil? You're pushing me out for Mark?'

'No!' Phil leaves his chair and pulls Graham close. 'No. Bloody hell, mate, I wouldn't do that. But I thought you wanted to sell...' He looks at Lynne. 'At least that's what we were told.'

She glares at him. 'It's what *he* wants.'

'No. No, I don't. What's happening? No!'

'Bloody hell,' Phil says again, patting Graham on the back. 'This is the best news I've heard in a long time.'

Graham blinks rapidly. 'I don't understand...'

Lynne stands, her fist clenched. A red flush creeps up her throat. Chloe sees that her eyes are full of panic. 'You haven't a clue. What're you doing? What the hell?' Lynne scowls at Graham.

The stunned silence turns quickly into a confusion of voices.

'Please everyone, calm down. Please calm down.' Mr Green's pleas are ignored.

338

'Graham, come on, we're leaving.' Lynne threads her arm through his and tugs at him.

He looks around, his eyes stopping on Chloe. He lifts his hand. She does the same but he's been pulled away.

Saul moves towards Chloe, blocking her view. No one is looking her way. Phil and Mark are talking to the solicitor; Margaret is sitting in her chair, looking stunned. Chloe feels a cold prickling on her skin.

Saul leans forward, his eyes on hers, and slowly draws his forefinger across his throat. 'Stupid, stupid Graham,' he murmurs.

Chapter 117

'Something's going to happen to Dad, Mark.' Chloe stands shivering by the side of Phil's car. I n*eed to do something. But what? What?* 'Saul's going to do something, Mark.'

'What, love? How do you know?'

'I just do. You saw the state of him when she more or less dragged him out of there?' Her hands are shaking when she gestures towards the solicitor's office. 'I have to do something.'

'What do you want to do?

'I don't know.' Chloe closes her eyes, shakes her head. 'I don't know if I should go to Moorcroft. But then...'

'She might not even let you in.'

'I'd make her. I'll push my way in.' *Oh yeah? With Saul there?*

She can't keep still. Frustrated. 'I don't know...' *I do know.*
'I'll go to see his doctor, see if he will talk to me. Find out what

medication he's on, whether it should be affecting him in the way it is.'

'I'll come with you.'

'No. I'd rather do this myself. And Charlie's waiting at your house. Please tell him what's happened. He's promised to help. He and Simon don't have to go back to work for another week. If there's some way I can get Dad away from that woman, I will. Especially now.' She gives Mark a watery smile. 'I'd rather you told Charlie what's happened. What I'm doing.'

'Are you two getting in the car?' Phil is smiling, but the worry lines between his eyebrows deepen when he sees how upset Chloe is. 'Do you want to go and see how your dad is? We could call in at Moorcroft on our way home?'

'No, it's all right, Phil, I'm going to see his GP. Ask what medication he's on.'

'Well, in that case, we'll drive you there.'

'Thanks, Phil.'

Mark stops her as she's about to get in the car. 'Whatever you find out at the doctor's, don't go to Moorcroft without me.'

'I won't.'

'Ring the house. Tell Charlie and me what's happening.'

'I will.'

Chapter 118

'Well,' Doctor Pollitt looks from his computer to Chloe. 'I last saw your father about a year ago, according to the records.' He frowns, leaning over his desk, peering closer. 'With a bout of

340

tonsillitis. Actually, Nurse Collins, our practice nurse, er...' He looks quickly at Chloe. 'Your stepmother of course, she actually diagnosed the problem and collected the pain relief tablets I'd prescribed.'

He sits back. 'You must know, of course, I really can't talk to you about your father's health. I let you in here because our receptionist told me you were so persistent and rather disruptive in the waiting room.'

Probably an understatement. Refusing to move from the front of the queue for the best part of fifteen minutes, ignoring the mutterings and complaints behind her, had been mortifying. But she was desperate. She'll apologise to the woman on her way out. 'I'm sorry if she thought so.' Chloe made a rueful face. 'I need to know what medication my father is on.'

'Why not ask him? Or your stepmother?'

There's a pause. He clears his throat, glances at his watch. Has he suddenly remembered the investigation into Lynne? Is he regretting agreeing to see her?

Should she tell him about Lynne controlling her dad's life? Would he believe her?

He stands up. 'So, if that's all?' Doctor Pollitt doesn't quite meet Chloe's eyes. He goes to the door, opens it.

'Thank you for seeing me,' she says.

He doesn't answer.

The receptionist walks away from the counter to a back room before Chloe can apologise. *Not that I blame her, really.* Chloe cringes.

A few flakes of snow float down, settle on the steps outside

341

the surgery, glitter momentarily in the light of the doorway, disappear into the dampness made by other flakes. Chloe watches, lost, unsure of her next move. She needs to think but there isn't time. What happened in the solicitor's earlier must have made Lynne desperate. *And now what? What will she do?*

Chloe shuffles to let a couple go past her, then a woman with a crying child. She's in the way, she can't stand here forever.

Ring Mark. Tell him and Charlie she's going to Moorcroft. Ask them to meet her there.

There's a telephone box on the High Street. Hopefully it's working. She walks quickly.

The receiver is cold against her ear. There is no dial tone. Frustrated she replaces the receiver and backs out of the box, trying to remember where she's seen another telephone box in Mossleigh. She knows there is one on the corner of Yorkshire Street and Ingram Avenue. That's where she'll go. She'll wait for Mark and Charlie there.

Chapter 119

'How long did she think she'd be in the doctors?' Charlie is unable to keep still; he's paced the floor of the sitting room for the last twenty minutes.

He should have gone with her to the meeting with the solicitor. Not been so bloody-minded. Listened to her when she said how weak their father – his dad was. Forget being bitter. Forget what's gone.

'She didn't know. Couldn't be that long, though.' Mark's leaning against the wall, his arms crossed over his chest.

Charlie paces again. 'What time did she go in?'

'Around two-thirty, three.' Mark rubs his thumb nail across his lower lip. 'I asked her to give us a ring when she came out and not to go near Moorcroft. I'm not sure she'll take any notice.'

'We can't hang around doing nothing.'

'Try to stay calm, Charlie.' Simon hugs him. 'I'm sure she'll contact us as soon as she can.'

'It's this hanging around, Si. It's doing my head in. If I'd not been so selfish, if I'd agreed to be at the meeting I'd be with her now. It'll be my fault if...'

The phone rings.

Chapter 120

It's taken Chloe nearly half an hour to walk to Ingram Avenue. She stands uncertain in the telephone box before picking up the receiver. When Mark answers, Chloe wastes no time. 'Mark I'm at the end of Ingram Avenue.'

'What? What are you doing, Chlo? Why didn't you ring earlier. We've been waiting to hear from you for almost two hours.'

'I know, I'm sorry. The telephone box near the solicitor's was broken and I couldn't find another.' *Why lie?* 'I needed to be here, Mark. It's Dad...'

'What's happened?'

'Nothing. Well, not as far as I know. But it will.'

'Don't do anything. Don't go near the house.'

'Put Charlie on. I need to talk to him.'

'Chlo?' Her brother's voce is rushed. 'Mark say's you're near the house?'

'Did Mark tell you what happened in the solicitor's?'

'Yes, but—'

'Please, please come, Charlie. Whatever you think of Dad please do this for me. I'll never forgive myself if anything happens to him. You were right. You were always right, Lynne is evil. She's corrupt, her son is corrupt. And they are both dangerous.'

'Which is why you shouldn't be there on your own.'

'So come. Please Charlie, come and help me. Please.'

She listens to muffled conversation before Charlie is back.

'Chlo, we're on our way. The three of us will be with you in twenty minutes at the most. Stay there. Don't do anything. Love you.'

And then he's gone. Chloe holds the receiver tightly in her hand. It's a connection to her brother.

He's coming. He'll help.

Chapter 121

Chloe jogs on the spot, her breath small jets of white haze in front of her face. It's half an hour since they said they would be here. Twenty to six. They'll be stuck in traffic at this time of the evening. She looks around. Frost makes the tarmac glisten. Soon there'll be a lethal covering of ice. *Calm down, they'll be here. Nothing will have happened to them.* But the cold is deep

344

inside her now and she can't stop shuddering despite her thick coat and fur-lined boots.

The same dog walker has walked past her twice, shuffling, cautious on the slippery pavement. The second time he studies her. *Probably thinks I'm casing the joint.* Despite her growing panic, Chloe smiles.

But when the man hesitates as though he's decided to challenge her, Chloe knows she has to move. It must look suspicious, her standing for so long on such a quiet avenue in this weather. It's a relief to have the decision made for her. She looks at her watch, gives an exaggerated sigh, peers theatrically up and down the avenue, throws up her arms and stomps away from the dog walker.

When she gets to the end of the drive, she checks behind her. The man has gone. With relief, Chloe moves quickly past the gate posts and into the shadow of the beech hedge.

Lynne's red Ford Cortina isn't in front of the house. Four parallel lines of tyre tracks divide the thin layer of snow. *Coming or going?*

Moorcroft is in darkness, no light in any of the windows, no dim glow anywhere inside the house, nothing through the glass conservatory.

This isn't what she expected. If there's no one here, where are they? A niggle of anxiety won't leave her: monsters in the dark. Her father hasn't been allowed to go out on his own for months. It's a fifteen minute drive from the solicitor's. *What's happened?*

Her nose hurts as she breaths in the cold air. *Don't be stupid. Wait for Charlie and Mark.*

She stares at the dark windows. Is her father in there? Watching her? Wondering what she's doing? Wanting her to come to him? Or frightened that she might? There will be repercussions if she does.

Chloe treads in the lines of the tyre tracks, hesitates at the first step to the porch. Is Lynne, or worse, Saul, waiting in the shadows? All she can see is a dim, blurred reflection of herself in the glass of the front door.

Creeping closer, she cups her hands around her eyes and rests her forehead against the pane. Nothing. She crouches and cautiously lifts the letterbox, stares into the house. Listens. Nothing.

She can't leave it like this. She shouts, 'Hello?' Rings the bell. Hammers on the door. *Nothing.*

A car slides on ice on the road. The clunk of gears changing, engine revving. Headlights. *Charlie and Mark. Or is it Lynne?*

Chloe turns, her stomach knotted. But the car goes past the end of the drive. She feels a flood of relief, then frustration. *Where are they?*

Chapter 122

'Bloody traffic.' Charlie pushes his black woollen hat further up his forehead with the heel of his hand. 'Isn't there a shortcut to Moorcroft along here?'

'There is, but I thought this way would be quicker. We passed the turn off before we hit this lot. Must be the tail end of the rush hour – folk coming home from work off the motorway.' Mark taps his fingers on the steering wheel. 'Or there's been an accident.'

'I can't stand this. How long have we been waiting here?'

'About fifteen minutes.'

Charlie's insides are doing somersaults. He can't stop his leg jiggling with nervous impatience. 'How long once we get going before we're there?' Too many memories are going through his head, the stuff of his childhood nightmares.

'If we get a clear road, only about five minutes.'

'I could get out and run?'

'You could. But who's to say we won't get there before you?'

'I'll go back and take the shortcut.'

'Charlie, better we stick together.' Simon touches Charlie's shoulder from the back seat. 'Better three of us, if there is trouble.'

'It's like Mark said earlier, Si. Knowing our Chlo of old, she won't wait. I wouldn't be capped if she's at the house now and then God knows what's happening. She could be there on her own with them two nasty buggers. You heard what Mark said that bastard Saul did to her before – or would have done if he hadn't been there. I'm sorry but I can't sit here and hope this bloody lot in front of us shifts. We could be too late.' He's already getting out of the car.

'Okay but be careful,' Simon calls.

'Go then.' Mark ducks his head to be able to see Charlie as he stands on the pavement. 'We'll be with you as soon as we can.'

'I'll see you there.' Charlie says, slamming the car door closed. *And hope I'm not too late.*

347

Chapter 123

Chloe's convinced Lynne and Saul have done something to her father. The way they dragged him away from the solicitors, she's certain of it. She has to get into the house. *But I should wait. I did say I would wait.* She stares past the snow-covered lawn to the shadow of the beech hedge but there are no vehicles on the avenue.

Just a quick look at the back of the house.

The snow is deeper around the side and untouched. It crunches quietly underfoot. At the back of the house, she walks backwards on the path, staring at the upstairs windows. All in darkness.

Except for one. There's a faint light. *Which room?* The small spare room – *Dad's old office.*

She rattles the handle of the back door. Locked.

She bangs on the door. 'Dad? Are you there? It's Chloe.'

She thinks there's an answer but it's inaudible.

'Dad, the door's locked. Are you on your own?'

This time she hears nothing. Did she imagine a voice? What if they're stopping him from answering? Saul's words come back to her from before, his voice gleeful: 'a good slapping.'

She looks around for something to break the panel of glass in the door. There's a covering of frozen snow over everything. *The dustbins.* She grabs the lid handle of one, carries it to the door, and turning her face away, she bashes it against the glass. It cracks but holds. On her next effort it breaks, the noise loud in the silence.

Still no one shouts or appears in the kitchen. Shards of glass stick up like stalagmites. Impatiently she picks out the last few spikes, throws them into the kitchen and stretches her arm though to feel for a key in the lock. The door grates over the broken glass when she pushes it open. Ignoring her fear of Lynne or Saul, she sprints along the hall, takes the stairs two at a time, flicks light switches as she passes. No more darkness, no evil waiting in the dark; she'll confront it face to face.

On the landing she stops. Only one door is closed: her dad's office. The handle doesn't move. It's locked.

'Dad? Are you in there?'

No answer but she can hear shallow breaths from the other side of the door.

'Dad? It's me, Chloe.' She rattles the handle. 'Why is the door locked? Have you locked yourself in?'

'You shouldn't be here.' His voice is hoarse.

'It's all right.'

'No. It's not. Please...'

'Is the key on your side?'

'No.'

She's locked him in. Chloe puts the flat of her hand against the wood where she imagines his is, and whispers, 'I'm not leaving you here like this.'

'She'll be angry to find you here. You don't know what she can do.'

'I know exactly what she's capable off, Dad. Where's the key?'

'I don't know.'

She runs her fingers over the ledge above the door, feels around the skirting board. 'I'm going to look...'

'Don't go into her room.' There's a movement, a noise like

someone sliding down the door, a bump on the floor. A whisper. 'Please.'

Anger urges her on. 'Please don't be frightened, Dad. It'll be okay. I won't be a minute.' She crosses the landing, stands at the threshold of the door to what was her parents' room, and gazes around, sucking in her bottom lip. *Where?*

The key has to be hidden. Or does it? Is Lynne so confident she's in control, so arrogant she thinks there's no need to hide the key to the room she's locked her husband in. But there aren't any keys in sight. Chloe riffles through the shelves in the wardrobe, throwing handbags, scarves, jumpers on the floor. Tips out the drawers of the dressing table, the drawers of the bedside tables. With each failure her panic grows.

'Chloe?'

'Still here, Dad.'

In desperation she runs her hands under the mattress. Her fingers catch on a key ring.

'Found it,' she shouts. The moment of triumph makes her turn too quickly. She stumbles against the foot of the bed, dislodging the corner of the mattress. Two small canvas bags fall out, landing on the carpet with a thud.

Chloe steadies herself, looks at the bags. She hasn't time to waste. But why were they hidden?

Kneeling she pulls at the ties of one, shakes it. A glitter of jewellery falls out: gold chains, rings, earrings. Opening the other bag she shakes out dozens of credit cards. All in different names. *So it's true, Lynne has been stealing from her patients.*

'Chloe?'

'It's all right. I'm coming, Dad.' Looking around, she sees a shoulder bag she'd tossed to the floor. Shoving the canvas bags into it she runs across the landing and kneels at the door. 'I'm here, Dad.' Her hand trembles, trying each key until she finds the right one. 'Are you behind the door? You have to stand up.'

'I can't.' But there's a shuffling and when Chloe gently opens the door, he's standing in the middle of the room. In his pyjamas. It's freezing. She crosses to hold him. 'Oh, Dad.' He's so thin she can feel his ribs, his spine, the bones in his arms. 'I'm here. It's all right.'

His arms fall to his side. 'I think I've done something wrong.'

'Don't worry. Let's get you dressed. Where are your clothes?'

'I don't know.' He looks helplessly at Chloe. 'I think I did something wrong. Lynne was angry. I'd forgotten to write something ... or something. I made it right, though. She wasn't angry anymore. She didn't let Saul come in again.'

Chloe's anger flares again. 'Don't worry about that for now.'

'It's a muddle.' He slumps down onto the bed. The light from the landing makes his shadow waver on the wall. 'Feel ... feel odd.'

'It's okay. It's because you're cold.' At least she hopes it is. 'Let's get some warm clothes on you. We've got to get out of here.' *Now!*

'She doesn't let me...'

'I won't let her stop us. Please.' She goes back into the other bedroom, finds a dressing gown and a pair of socks. 'Let's put these on you.' She fumbles helping him into the dressing gown, pulling on the socks, tension making her hands clumsy. 'Slippers?' No slippers. *How long has she been here? An hour, half an hour? Where are Charlie and Mark?* 'Good. Can you stand? That's it. Right, we're getting out of here.'

He stops. 'I can't.'

'You can, Dad.' Her arms around his waist, Chloe gradually urges him forward, step by step. 'You're doing great.' *Hurry. Please. Hurry.* They'll need to get out by the back door. She hasn't thought this through. He's only in his socks and there's broken glass on the floor. Will there be shoes in the cupboard under the stairs? Will she have to carry him? *Can she?*

They're halfway down to the hall, when they have to stop for him to catch his breath. Chloe waits, hiding her anxiety. Looks around. The walls are bare, all the paintings are gone. She can guess where.

She hears the sound of a car on the drive. Footsteps.

Graham freezes. 'Back. Go back.' He half turns, pushes at Chloe.

The door opens slowly, is pushed wide. Saul's staring at them. He grins.

Chloe feels a sliver of fear.

'Well, well. Ma, look here. We have a visitor.'

Chapter 124

'And look who's behind you.' Charlie says from the drive. The years on the streets have helped him to understand danger. Not to rush headlong into a situation. But it takes all his willpower to stay still and wait for Saul's reaction.

Chloe catches her breath. Relief changes to sudden panic when Saul roars and leaps at Charlie. She screams. Behind her Graham cries out.

The light from the hall streams over the two men. She sees

blood burst from Saul's lips, and the hatred on Charlie's face. This is a brother she doesn't know. Has never known. Charlie has found the boy who so many years ago bullied him day after day and he can't – he won't stop until he sees his tormentor on the ground. This isn't just her brother saving her and their father, this is him saving the little boy he once was.

A figure flies at her from nowhere. Chloe doubles over, winded by Lynne's punch to the stomach. She falls backwards against Graham, hits out at Lynne, trying to protect her father. But it's not her husband Lynne wants. She grabs at the shoulder bag.

'That's mine. And what's in it is mine.'

Chloe is hauled down the stairs, the bag strap burning her fingers as it's wrenched through them. She holds on, the edges of the treads digging into her spine as she is jerked downstairs.

Behind Lynne, she sees a flash. 'Charlie! He's got a knife.'

A blow to her face jolts her head back, the pain sudden and stinging. She hits out and feels a satisfying crack under her fist. Lynne's weight drags Chloe downwards. Chloe grabs hold of the banister. The bag is twisted from her hand. The contents clatter onto the wooden floor. Lynne crouches down, one bloodied hand over her nose, trying to gather up the cards and jewellery with the other.

A yell. Simon and Mark run in. Holding Charlie to him, Simon grabs the hall phone. Chloe catches a glimpse of Mark dragging Saul back outside, his forearm wrapped tight around his neck. Thick, viscous blood pours from Saul's nose and lips. A flash of the knife again. Mark falls back into the darkness.

Saul comes at her. *He's killed Mark, he's hurt Charlie. He'll kill me.*

She sees his hands balled into fists. *No knife.*

'Get upstairs, Dad. Go!' She stands up to urge him away.

Saul grabs her neck, his fingers gripping hard. Pressure pulses in her head. She stares into his eyes, they're bloodshot, full of hatred. Rage shoots through her, replacing the fear. She thrusts one knee up as hard as she can. He collapses against her. She pushes him off and he rolls onto the floor, holding his groin. Retching.

Chloe slides down the stairs, coughing, breath rasping in her throat.

Saul, still heaving, reaches out to grab her. She sees Charlie kick him. Saul curls up, rolls away.

'Chlo?' Her brother leans over her.

'Bastard!' Saul is on his feet. He thumps Charlie in the back. Charlie falls down by Chloe. Saul staggers towards the door.

Afterwards Chloe can only remember images of the fight. She remembers seeing Charlie holding onto Saul. Or pushing him? Mark crawling up the steps. She remembers the flood of relief — *He's not dead.* Seeing him roll onto his side, the knife sticking out of his thigh. Blood smeared on the steps. Seeing him reach out and grasp hold of Saul's ankle. Saul kicking out at Mark, losing his balance, falling forwards, arms flailing. For a long time she can't get the loud sickening crack of bone against the stone pillar of the porch out of her head.

Nor Lynne's horrendous shriek.

Then cars screech to a halt on the drive, blue lights flashing. Shouts. Running.

The day shift is coming on. Chloe watches the two nurses, heads huddled together, discussing the patient's notes. They don't bother to keep their voices low and the men hunched under covers in the five other beds in the ward, move restlessly.

Another nurse, a short, dark, plump woman about her own age, marches across the ward – regulation black shoes squeaking on the tiled floor – to the three large windows and drags the heavy curtains back to let in the weak dawn light.

Somewhere a telephone rings, trollies rattle, a car horn beeps outside.

Graham moans and Chloe tightens her hold on her father's thin fingers, studies him. He shifts his head on the pillow but doesn't wake, his eyes stay closed, yet flicker under his eyelids, the filmy skin criss-crossed with thin blue veins.

'It's okay, Dad, I'm here,' she murmurs.

He quietens, lies still. His pale lips puff slightly with each breath, chest quietly rises and falls under the covers. Covers that are almost flat, he's so thin.

Chloe deliberately and with determination, quells the anger that bubbles inside her. There's no point to it. The woman who has controlled him for so many years has been arrested, her son is dead. Lynne and Saul are no longer a threat.

She straightens her back, stretches her neck upwards, twisting her head from side to side, trying to release the tightness in her muscles. It's been a long night and she's exhausted. The questions by the police seemed interminable but, in the end, the two detectives appeared to be satisfied they had the information they needed. For now.

Sometime earlier, while the doctors were examining Graham, she'd sat alongside Mark's bed in A&E waiting with him until his knife wound could be cleaned, stitched and bandaged.

Although, afterwards, he'd argued he wanted to stay with Chloe, Margaret was equally adamant she and Phil took him home as soon as he was discharged.

Chloe is grateful. The terror that consumed her twenty-four hours ago still lurks, threatening to take over. She's struggling to contain it.

And her worry about Charlie and Simon makes it worse. She hasn't seen them since she watched them being taken away in the police car.

She is holding her father's hand. She lets her head droop and she rests her forehead on top of their hands.

'Chloe?'

'Dad.' She sits up, leans closer to him and smiles reassurance.

'What happened?'

'Don't worry about that for now.'

There's movement behind her. Graham looks past her shoulders. His face crumples. She sees tears trickle down his face. But he's smiling.

'Charlie?' His voice cracks. 'Is it you?'

Chloe looks round. Sees her brother.

Charlie's grinning.

'Hello, Dad,' he says.

Chapter 125

Chloe walks out of the county hall courtroom between Charlie and her father. They stand at the top of the steps waiting for the others to join them. The sun casts flickering leafy shadows under the tall sycamore trees that edge the wide drive. Chloe narrows her eyes against the brightness. It's a warm July day but she shivers.

'It was cold in there.'

'It's all the stones and high ceilings.' Graham's voice wavers a little.

She glances at him. 'Okay, Dad?'

'Yes.' Graham's face is pale. But the wary, haunted expression in his eyes that was constant in those early days has long gone. 'Glad it's over, though.'

'Well, I for one am bloody glad she got what was coming to her.' Charlie takes a deep breath.

'It's done, now,' she says, seeing her father wince. She turns, smiles at Mark as he emerges from the large wooden doors with Margaret and Phil. Evie and Beth follow. Evie looks a little subdued. It must be hard seeing your mother sent to prison for seven years, whatever sort of parent she's been. Chloe gives her stepsister a sympathetic smile. 'You okay?'

Evie gives a small shrug but smiles back. 'Just about. I thought at one point she was going to get away with it. All that fake remorse. I'm glad the magistrate wasn't taken in.'

'I think the doctors at the practice and that manager of the care home swung it. They'd trusted her for years.'

'Bit like me.' Graham says.

'Phil's booked a table for us all.' Margaret bustles across and herds them off the steps. 'The restaurant's only five minutes away but we should get a move on.'

'Not your fault Graham,' Evie says, following Margaret. She holds out a bent elbow to him. 'Come on, link in.' She goes down the steps, Beth's arm around her.

'I think I'll walk with her.' He looks at Chloe, as if for permission.

'You don't need to ask, Dad. That would be lovely. I think Evie would appreciate that.'

He hurries to catch up.

Mark puts his arm around Chloe's shoulders. 'Is your dad okay?'

'He will be. Today's been hard for him.'

'I think he needed to see it through, though.' Simon joins them, slips his arm around Charlie.

'You're probably right,' she says.

'He looks tons better than twelve months ago.'

'He does. I think the move to Cardiff with you has done him good, Charlie.' Chloe gives her brother a quick hug. 'You didn't need to take him in. Mark and I would have found somewhere for the three of us.'

'Oh. I think I — we did. He's no bother. And we have a lot of catching up to do.' Charlie glances at her. Smiles. 'We're fine.'

'We should think about selling Moorcroft. So you can buy a bigger house.'

'We should. We will. Then we can both move on.'

'Come on, you lot.' Margaret's waving, gesturing for them to hurry up. 'We don't want to lose the table by being late.'

Charlie grins at Simon. 'Race you!' He begins to run, then turns so he's going backwards. He laughs when Simon pulls a face at him, sauntering back to grasp his partner's hand. 'I'll get you running one of these days.'

'Not on your bloody life,' Simon says. He pushes Charlie. 'On the other hand...' He sets off jogging.

'Hey!' Charlie laughs again and chases after him.

'They're happy,' Mark says.

'They are.' Chloe smiles.

'Just a minute, Miss Collins.' He stops and takes hold of her hand. He gently pulls her towards him. 'What do you think of the idea we get married?'

'I think it's an excellent idea.' Chloe wraps her arms around him, nestling her head into his shoulder. 'And as soon as possible.'

ACKNOWLEDGEMENTS

I would like to express my gratitude to those who helped in the publishing of *The Stranger in my House.*

To all the staff at Honno, for the individual expertise, advice and help in getting *The Stranger in my House* (and all my previous books) to publication. Thank you.

To Janet Thomas, my editor, for her professionalism, steadfast support and belief in my writing down the years. More than an editor, a dear friend.

To Lynzie Fitzpatrick, for the brilliantly evocative cover design of *The Stranger in my House.* I love it!

Special thanks to my dear friends and fellow authors, Thorne Moore and Alex Craigie, for their encouragement and enthusiasm for *The Stranger in the House.* Without you, I would have given up writing on many an occasion. Also a grateful mention for my Arran cohorts, Barb Taub, Georgia Rose, Darlene Foster and Terry Tyler, authors in their own right, for their unstinting support, laughter, and, on times, sympathy, during our shared writing retreat – and beyond. Thank you all.

As ever, to my husband, David, always by my side, always believing in me. Always loved.

And my thanks, always remembered, to someone who I have never mentioned in any of my acknowledgments: an English teacher, Leslie Ellenore, who, just before he emigrated to New

Zealand, told me that he looked forward to one day reading a book I had written. He's probably long since passed by now, but I'm hoping he has family who may one day read these words of gratitude.

Last but certainly not least my thanks to you, the reader, for picking up this book and giving my story a chance.

ABOUT HONNO

Honno Welsh Women's Press was set up in 1986 by a group of women who felt strongly that women in Wales needed wider opportunities to see their writing in print and to become involved in the publishing process. Our aim is to develop the writing talents of women in Wales, give them new and exciting opportunities to see their work published and often to give them their first 'break' as a writer.

Honno is registered as a community co-operative. Any profit that Honno makes is invested in the publishing programme. Women from Wales and around the world have expressed their support for Honno. Each supporter has a vote at the Annual General Meeting. For more information and to buy our publications, please visit our website www.honno.co.uk or email us on post@honno.co.uk.

Honno
D41, Hugh Owen Building,
Aberystwyth University,
Aberystwyth,
Ceredigion,
SY23 3DY.

We are very grateful for the support of all
our Honno Friends.